Leaving Everest

Leaving Everest

MEGAN WESTFIELD

Hugs!
Megan Westfield

This book is a work of fiction. Names, characters, places, and incidents are the product of the author's imagination or are used fictitiously. Any resemblance to actual events, locales, or persons, living or dead, is coincidental.

Entangled Publishing, LLC
2614 South Timberline Road
Suite 105, PMB 159
Fort Collins, CO 80525
Visit our website at www.entangledpublishing.com.

Embrace is an imprint of Entangled Publishing, LLC.

Edited by Karen Grove
Cover design by RBA Designs
Cover art from Adobe Stock
Map design by Jessica Riehl

Manufactured in the United States of America

First Edition February 2018

embrace

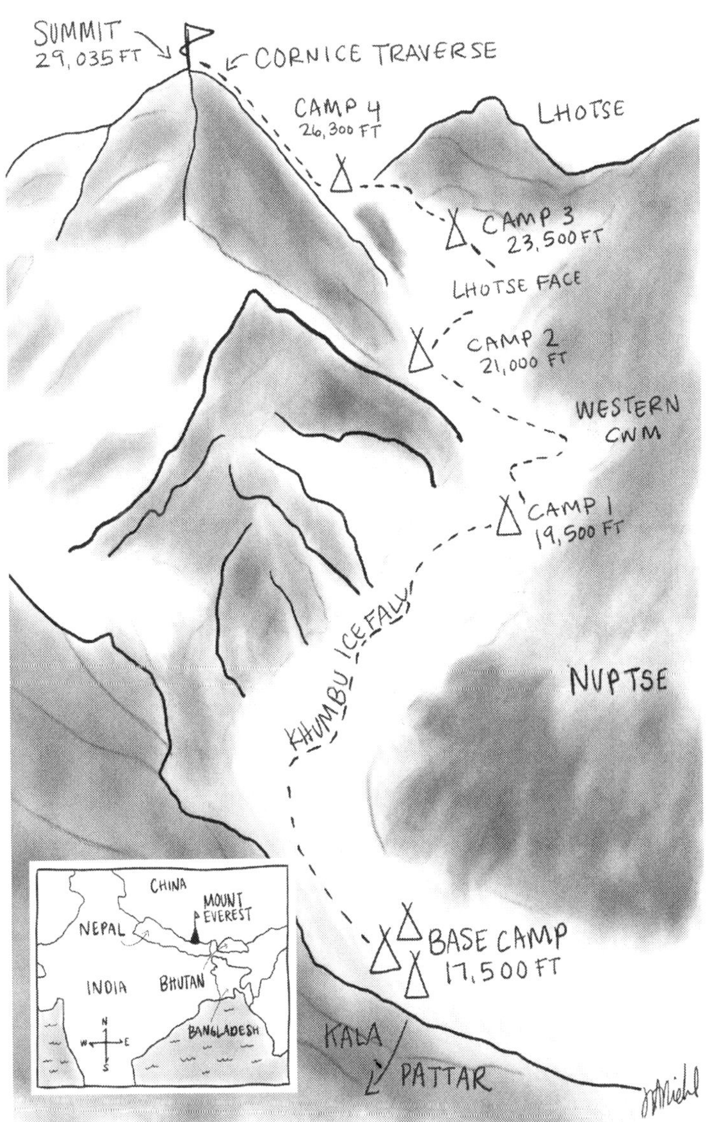
MOUNT EVEREST: SOUTH COL ROUTE
SUMMIT
29,035 FT
CORNICE TRAVERSE
CAMP 4
26,300 FT
LHOTSE
CAMP 3
23,500 FT
LHOTSE FACE
CAMP 2
21,000 FT
WESTERN
CWM
CAMP 1
19,500 FT
KHUMBU ICE FALL
NUPTSE
BASE CAMP
17,500 FT
KALA
PATTAR
CHINA
MOUNT
EVEREST
NEPAL
INDIA
BHUTAN
BANGLADESH
N
W
E
S

Chapter One

I stepped around a sharp bend in the trail, straight into a pair of yak horns.

I leaped to the side. The wrong side. Pebbles shot out from beneath my hiking boots, falling a thousand feet into the gorge where the Imja River ran swollen and milky turquoise. Yak after yak passed by as I held my breath and struggled to balance on the lip of the precarious slope.

As soon as there was a break in the yak train, I dashed across the trail to the uphill side where I had solid footing and a nice, strong pine tree to hold on to as I waited for the rest of the yaks to pass.

The near miss was my fault. I shouldn't have been listening to music with both earbuds in. Especially right now, at the start of the Everest climbing season when the trail was busy with dozens of expeditions hauling two months' worth of supplies up the sixty miles between the Lukla airstrip and Everest Base Camp.

I popped my earbuds out, now hearing the melody of the yaks' neck bells and the *clop* of their hooves on the rocky trail.

"Namaste," I said to herders spaced out among the animals.

The near miss hadn't been only because of the earbuds. My mind had been somewhere else entirely: across the Indian and Pacific oceans to Seattle, where my friend Luke lived. That's because just ahead on the trail was the outcropping where I always recorded a video to post on the Circumference app for him.

The problem was, Luke hadn't posted on Circumference for seven days. I'd posted two Circ videos during that time. To post a third was questionable. Desperate.

In truth, I *was* desperate. This Everest season would mark two years since we'd last seen each other. The only thing connecting us now were the Circ videos flagged with our secret code, #YCCM—*You Can't Catch Me.*

The game had been simple at first: when one of us would summit a mountain, we'd turn the geotag off, take a three-hundred-and-sixty degree video panorama, and flag it with #YCCM. The other person had to use the surrounding peaks to guess the location. But then we started posting more often and had to get creative with our high points, like the one Luke posted from the bunk bed in his dorm room freshman year. Or the one I took while standing atop a sand castle I'd built in Thailand.

We posted so often now that it was practically daily unless one of us was on a trip where we didn't have wifi, so seven days of silence was significant. My consolation was that it wasn't just our #YCCM Circs that had stopped; he hadn't posted anything at all in that time. He could have lost his phone. Or he could be on a climbing trip in the North Cascades or something. After all, it was spring break at his college, University of Washington. I'd looked that up on day three.

Once the yaks were clear, I got back on the trail, and it took me no time at all to reach the outcropping. I ditched my heavy backpack and climbed the short vertical stretch of granite.

Below were the stone houses of Tengboche, the Sherpa village where Luke had grown up. This outcropping was significant to Luke and me because we had spent a lot of time hiding out here as kids, poring over Dad's *Complete Guide to the World's 19,000-Foot Peaks.* Desperate or not, I decided to go ahead with the Circ.

Standing in the center of the outcropping, I faced my phone outward and pivoted in a slow circle, videoing a glimpse of the river to the east and the rhododendron forest to the south. Continuing west, I filmed the giant Himalaya Mountains standing guard over Tengboche, and then finished the Circ by panning north to the distant wall of snowy white snaggleteeth where Mount Everest was hidden. As soon as I reached a full three-hundred-and-sixty degrees, the Circumference app chirped and snapped closed.

What do you want to say? the screen prompted.

I bit my thumbnail.

Where are you?

Why have you not posted?

I miss your Circs.

I miss you.

I closed my eyes and hugged the phone to my chest. I'd known all along we wouldn't keep our Circ game going forever, but I wasn't ready for it to be over. Now that I was officially not going back to the U.S. for college, it was unlikely he and I would ever cross paths again in real life. To lose Circ would be to lose him altogether.

I stared down at my phone. *What do you want to say?*

If we're going to stop playing, please can you give me a sign so I can close my account and stop living for your Circs?

Instead, I typed in #*YCCM* and nothing else, as always. The Circ would release as soon as my phone connected with the wifi at the store in Tengboche, where Dad was probably waiting for me by now.

I down-climbed the outcropping and continued up the trail. Tonight we were staying with Luke's mom, Mingma, so at least I'd be able to make sure his silence wasn't because he'd been in an accident or something.

Soon I was on the final rise before the village. With each step higher, the mountains ahead grew taller, and the panorama widened. Unlike the view from the treed outcropping, this was a fully unobstructed view, and it never failed to fill me with an overwhelming sense of possibility. The extreme altitude, remoteness, and inaccessibility of the Himalayas meant there was still so much unexplored terrain here. And now, I could be among those doing the exploring.

This was the start of a new chapter in my life. A chapter in which I wouldn't have to say good-bye to Dad and where I could work toward my dream of climbing the tallest five mountains in each of the world's mountain ranges with peaks higher than 19,000 feet. The Top Five project. It had been done only eight times before, and never by a woman, and never without the use of supplemental oxygen, as I wanted to.

At the store, I spotted Dad through the window, rubbing his two-week, graying trail beard as he paid for some snacks for tomorrow. While I waited for him to finish, I retied the orange bandana I used as a headband and wiped my dusty, sweaty face with the bottom of my fleece vest.

Once outside, Dad handed me a recent but already dog-eared issue of *Vertical View* magazine. "Apparently our Nanga Parbat climb made the *Ascents Report* section."

"Wow." I flipped to the back of the magazine as we walked through the village and there it was: "Winslowe and Winslowe: Father-Daughter Team Tackles Fabled Gray

Spider Route on Nanga Parbat, Pakistan."

It was a very short write-up, but it included a thumbnail picture of me at the bottom. A several-years-old picture in which my short hair and wind-burned cheeks made me look like a teenage boy with acne. My face heated but, regardless of the terrible picture, the article was a good thing because it mentioned Winslowe Expeditions, and that kind of publicity always helped business. Mentions like this were also extremely valuable in my first—and most improbable—hurdle of climbing the Top Five project: becoming a sponsored athlete with an outdoor equipment company. Because without a sponsorship, there would be no way to fund the climbs.

At the monastery, we turned uphill, weaving through terraced pastures and teahouses with brightly colored metal roofs toward Mingma's house. Smoke curled up from her chimney and a stray black dog I didn't recognize basked in the sun on her doorstep. As we neared, it sat up and barked.

Mingma's head popped outside and, seeing us, she ran out the door and snapped me into a hug. At five-eight, I towered over her, but she was strong, and her grip was tight. When she finally released me, she said hello to Dad and then led me inside to the mouthwatering smells of *dal bhat* and freshly baked chapati bread.

I could speak some Sherpa, and I understood a lot more than I could speak, but when someone was talking a million miles an hour like Mingma, I was a lost cause. Nevertheless, I grinned back at her, nodding along like I could understand perfectly. I was just so happy to be there with her—especially after her thyroid scare this winter, which was the reason she would not be Winslowe Expeditions's head cook at Everest Base Camp this season.

Mingma motioned for Dad and me to take off our packs and sit down on the floor for lunch at the knee-height table in the middle of her one-room house. She yelled out the door, presumably for Luke's little brother, Pasang. I glanced around as I sipped water from my bottle. Everything was the same, with the exception of some more trinkets added to the small Buddhist shrine in the loft and a few pictures tacked to the wall, many of which lined up with Luke's #YCCM Circs. One was of Luke and a large group of friends in front of the Space Needle. Next to him was a girl who looked a lot like ^Olivia200x^, the cute, curly-haired blonde who followed him on Circ and who I'd often wondered if he was dating.

I squinted. It was definitely her, and worse, her arm was around him.

My heart sank. Was that why he stopped Circing?

Pasang slipped into the house. Even though he was a preteen now, he hovered shyly next to the stove like a little kid. I gave him a wave, and only then did a smile break through.

Our lunch conversation was partly in English, partly in Sherpa. *Sherpenglish.* As Dad and I ate Mingma's divine *dal bhat*, she told us all about Luke: how he would be guiding a second summer on Mount Rainier and how he still had his job at the University of Washington outdoor recreation center. "He's been sending money home to help with repairs," she said, pointing up at the ceiling beams, which still had cracks from the earthquake.

Pasang, who was sitting next to me, waited patiently for a break in the conversation. "Luke's—"

Mingma talked right over the top of him, and he shrunk back. She was once again going too fast for me to fully understand, but the message was clear: she was overflowing with pride for Luke's accomplishments at college. He had changed his major from atmospheric science to biology. Which was better for getting into medical school.

Medical school? Wow.

Pasang tugged at my sleeve.

"What?" I whispered.

He spoke too quietly to hear beneath Mingma's continued raving. I shot Pasang a confused look while still trying to pay attention to Mingma so I could figure out Luke's relationship status and if he had indeed gone on a spring break trip in the Cascades.

Pasang was so excited now that he could barely keep seated.

"Luke's here!" he repeated in a voice that, for him, was as loud as a shout. He pointed over his shoulder.

My blood went still. Luke, as in *my* Luke? Mingma had just been telling us all about his spring at UW. How could he be here?

"*Chomolungma,*" Pasang said, using the Sherpa name for Mount Everest.

My phone whistled with a notification for a new #YCCM Circ.

In slow motion, I pulled my phone closer and hit play. The Circ was nearly the same panorama of the mountains and Tengboche that I'd just posted, only a lot closer in. Like from inside the village. My pulse sped up. His Circ swept down to the ground and past a black dog watching the camera intently, and then slowly across an open doorway where a girl with long, coppery brown hair sat at the floor table with... Pasang, Dad, and Mingma.

"What in the—"

Urgently, Pasang grabbed my shoulder and turned me toward the door.

The floor dropped out from under me.

Because right there, leaning against the doorframe, was Luke. Yes, *my* Luke, right there in flesh and blood and a purple University of Washington ball cap.

Chapter Two

Luke's face was serious as his dark brown eyes analyzed me from beneath the shadow of his hat.

My mind struggled to catch up. I couldn't believe it was really Luke standing right there in this doorway as I'd seen him so, so many times before. He'd always been confident, but the way he stood now, even straighter and more self-assured, made him look five years older instead of the two years older he actually was.

His name—Luke for Luke Skywalker—was something his father had called him and everyone kept up after his father's death on Cho Oyu during an expedition with my dad. With his huge dimples and smile, he'd always been hopelessly adorable in the same way as his namesake.

But now, this guy in the door...*cute* and *adorable* were out the window. His thermal pullover jacket molded to his profile, revealing the defined bulk of his upper arms and torso before tapering to a waist that was solid but as narrow as my own. He was all Hemsworth-brothers Hollywood action hero, right down to his piercing eyes, strong jaw, and rich tone of his skin.

Mingma jumped up, scolding Luke for sneaking up on us like that. Without breaking eye contact with me, a teasing, satisfied grin broke out across his face.

I whipped back to center, focusing forcefully on the teapot in the middle of the table. My cheeks burned. That was some stunt he'd just pulled with the Circ.

Why hadn't someone warned me he was in Tengboche?

Or perhaps someone had: Mingma in her rapid-fire Sherpa when we'd first arrived. A good lesson in why you should never fake-understand a foreign language.

Dad went over to Luke, shaking hands and hug-slapping him heartily.

Now it was just me left at the table. Well, me and Pasang, who was watching me with furrowed brows, probably wondering why I wasn't joining everyone at the door. I quickly collected myself, but still, my head spun and my pulse raced as I walked toward Luke.

I stood in front of him, and for several beats of my pounding heart, it was like the two of us were the only people in the world. My eyes were on him, but I couldn't bring him into focus. From this perspective, nothing about him had changed, but at the same time everything about him was completely foreign. It was Luke. Right here in front of me. And he was so incredibly handsome.

"Emily Winslowe," he said finally.

I wrapped my arms around him, and he did the same, with a grip that was tight and strong but not constricting like Mingma's. I was dizzy with too many sensations. There was reprieve from the worry about him not posting on Circ and happiness that we were back in Tengboche together after all this time. But there was also hurt that he hadn't so much as hinted he was coming here.

Most of all, I was shocked. A shock that was quickly

turning to panic.

I wasn't ready for what was happening in my body. It was like my old crush had gone from fifty to a hundred in less than two minutes. The feelings I'd been toying with for almost two years over the safe filter Circ provided were now real-life, directly in front of me.

Random details jumped out, intoxicating my senses and preventing me from releasing him from the hug. Like how firm and warm his body was. How he smelled like sunscreen and cold, fresh Himalayan air. And how there was a trace of stubble on his cheek, which was currently pressed against mine.

This was my friend. The best friend I'd ever had, even though in the latter years we'd been around each other only a few months a year. I didn't want to let go. I wanted this moment to be happening without anyone else in the room because it somehow felt like a direct continuation of those moments right before the earthquake. Like a continuation of what had been on the cusp of happening, something that would have put us squarely out of friends territory.

We let go at the same instant.

"It's good to see you," he said. His teasing smile and crinkly eyes were gone, replaced by the same pensive expression he'd had when I first saw him.

All I managed was a nod as Mingma ushered us back to the table.

Pasang slid his bowl to the right so Luke could take his customary place next to me. Thank goodness I'd already finished my *dal bhat* because there was no way I'd be able to swallow food right now.

Dad had a million questions for Luke: what he was doing here this season, how college was going, and which climbs he'd done in the Cascades. I quickly learned he was in Tengboche because he was going to be guiding for Global

Adventurers, the largest and most expensive commercial outfitter on Everest. They would have forty clients climbing this season. *Forty!*

I was still too overwhelmed by Luke's sudden presence to fully follow the conversation, especially as he and Dad threw around terms like *Bugaboos road trip, drinking age, master's thesis, concert,* and *internships.* It wasn't just that he was suddenly here, it was also that he'd changed so much.

Down-table, Pasang watched me expectantly. He smiled shyly, wanting me to share his excitement over the presence of his accomplished big brother. I gave him a grin, and he turned back, satisfied.

Sensing the exchange, Luke glanced over at me. I was suddenly conscious of how I'd look to him after he'd been in college for two years, surrounded by real American women, like ^Olivia200x^, who were beautiful, refined, and feminine. Now he'd know the truth that his old buddy had never been one of them. Self-consciously, I touched my hair, which was still damp with sweat from the trail. As that picture in *Vertical View* proved, I was a tomboy at best.

In the village common below, children's voices rang out. School was over for the day. Word must have gotten around that Dad and I were in town, because a whole group of children were at Mingma's door within minutes, begging me to come play soccer.

I quickly agreed because I needed the excuse to get away so I could process my thoughts and not act like a total weirdo around Luke.

They clamored for Luke to come, too. I silently groaned. He looked over at me, as if making sure I didn't mind, but he must have seen that I did because he said, "I have *sahib* lungs now. I wouldn't be able to breathe."

The kids found this hilarious. There were taunts all around. I couldn't help laughing, too.

"Okay, fine," he said in Sherpa. "I'll be down when I'm done eating."

Although it was the kids he was talking to, it was me he was looking at, and the fleeting wistfulness in his eyes before he changed his expression made something stir deep inside me.

Chapter Three

So Luke was suddenly back in my life, in real life. For the duration of the two-month Everest climbing season, anyway. This was good. But my Circ-fantasies—and my feelings for him—had to stop.

He and I had a chance once, but the earthquake had taken that away. He'd moved on, and that had to be okay. Officially, we'd never been anything but buddies anyway.

It didn't take long, chasing the red and blue soccer ball back and forth across Tengboche's central terrace with the laughing kids, before I was back to normal again. I was still acclimatized to the altitude from the most recent expedition with Dad, but even so, keeping up with the speedy kids had me short of breath and sweaty in no time.

Some of the younger kids dropped off to the sidelines to watch, and the game got even faster. Luke came down and joined the opposite team.

"So it looks like I caught you," he said as he moved in to guard me.

It was a direct reference to our #YCCM Circs. I practically

tripped over my own feet.

"Well, if you think about it," I stammered, "you were in Tengboche before we got here, so technically I caught you."

Luke snatched the ball away from me with a sly smile, just his left dimple showing. Ugh. He'd said that to throw me off, and it had worked perfectly. His team scored a goal.

When the ball got back to me, I kicked it over to the fastest boy on my team, but Luke intercepted, running the ball out to the left. I sprinted to catch up, planting myself in front of him.

"So why didn't you tell me you were coming?" I asked to distract him.

He attempted to maneuver the ball, but I blocked him.

"If I told you, then it wouldn't have been a surprise," he said.

"What kind of answer is that?" I said, taking a swipe at the ball.

"Oh no you don't," he said, lunging in the opposite direction, passing the ball to one of the girls. We slammed together. I stepped back. My ponytail swung twice, then settled against my head.

Our eyes locked, and I felt the full force of an emotion I didn't have a name for, an emotion that was magnetic, mournful, and uplifting all at once.

Girlfriend, I reminded myself, and then I turned and ran down the field.

We played for a while longer, but this kind of exertion at Tengboche's twelve-thousand-foot elevation is no joke, especially while wearing heavy hiking boots. Besides, there was a group of early-season trekkers in front of the monastery coming our way with their cameras.

Luke and I exchanged a look. It was one thing to let loose and play with the kids when it was just us but quite another to do so with a tourist audience.

"I'm going to get pulmonary edema if I don't take it easy," he said to the kids, moving off to the side and doubling over to catch his breath. "I've got to call it quits."

"Me, too," I said.

The kids protested when we left, but they wouldn't have much time before they were called home for chores anyway. Luke and I headed toward the path that led to his house.

"So, Nanga Parbat," Luke said as we walked. "Congratulations."

"Thanks. It was in a magazine. I just saw the article today. How weird is that?"

"I know. That's how I knew."

My face grew hot. He'd seen that horrible picture.

"You knew before that," I pointed out. "I took a Circ from the top."

"A Circ in which you failed to specify that it had been the Gray Spider route, which has not been repeated in the winter since Rosso Messina's ascent in 1981, and that you did it without oxygen. You and Greg are very deservedly in the magazine for that."

His voice! I'd forgotten how sexy it was with that hint of British accent from his years in boarding school.

"So how long are you guys here?" he asked.

"Just tonight, and then we're getting back on the trail. You?"

"I have a few more days. I'm waiting for the Global Adventurers clients to hike in from Lukla, and then I'm doing the rest of the Base Camp trek with them."

When we reached his house, we didn't go inside, automatically continuing upward to the low wall of a potato field where we used to play cards when we were kids.

"I'm surprised you're missing college to be here this season," I said.

"It was a special circumstance. One of Global's teams is

all University of Washington professors and researchers. I'll get six credits while I'm here, and the rest I can make up with online summer classes in between Rainier trips."

"That's good." I loved walking next to him, hearing him talk. The simple fact of being near him made my insides glow.

"Did you know Doc Teresa's climbing with the UW team?"

I nodded. Dad had mentioned it a few months ago. She was a guest lecturer in high-altitude medicine at UW, and between that and fifteen seasons working in Everest ER, she'd gotten a wild hair and decided to climb the mountain this year.

Luke and I sat on the wall, looking out across the familiar view. He took off his hat and ran his hand through his jet-black hair.

"Are you getting excited?" he asked.

"Yeah, we have a couple of repeat clients this year, and that's always nice."

"No, not for the season. I meant college. You're leaving as soon as the climb's over, right?"

"Actually, I'm not going."

Luke sat up straight, as if stunned. "Are you serious?"

"Completely."

His eyes narrowed. "But Greg said you were flying out June tenth."

"I haven't told him yet. It's only official as of two days ago. And, please, don't mention it. I mean, I know he won't care, but I should be the one to tell him."

The creases from his dimples had completely faded, and there was so much there in his eyes. Too much. I had to look away.

He was silent. We both were, and it wasn't like the comfortable silences of old times. The dozens and dozens of miles on the trails. The cumulative days and weeks and months of killing time together in a tent at Base Camp as we read, listened to music, and watched movies.

That look he'd given me...I realized what it was. Disappointment.

It didn't sit well on a belly full of *dal bhat* churned up by high-altitude soccer. I could understand his point of view, though. Look at all he'd accomplished already and where he was headed in life, yet here I was forgoing a college education to continue tagging along with Dad like a failure to launch.

But it wasn't like that at all. I was deliberately choosing to stay put. Sure, I yearned to have the permanence of a physical place I could call home instead of living out of my backpack year-round in tents or hostels. College could get me the kind of job where I could afford a house, but I'd have to give up my dream of the Top Five. I'd lose the mountains altogether, and in the end, the mountains were my life. My salvation.

Now that my time with Dad didn't have an expiration date, I would be able to help him grow Winslowe Expeditions. I had tons of ideas. Once we got settled in at Base Camp and things were less hectic, I'd tell him about my college decision and my plan to try for a sponsorship, and then I'd ask him to put me on the official guiding staff this year so we could eventually work toward running two expeditions at a time.

I glanced over at Luke, who was looking out at the stunning profile of Ama Dablam, the distinctive, Matterhorn-esque mountain east of Tengboche. Still, he said nothing. As a distraction, I swirled my toe in the dirt at the base of the wall.

For the hour we were with the kids in the village this afternoon, it had been nothing but exertion, fun, and laughter. The story of how we'd always been. But it had taken only a few minutes alone together to reveal that it wasn't *us* anymore.

Pasang was outside now, over in the adjacent pasture,

gathering dried yak dung for tonight's fire.

I hopped off the wall.

"Come on," I said with a bonus shot of enthusiasm to mask my dejectedness. "We should go help him."

By dinnertime, so many people had stopped by Mingma's house that it was as packed as a trekking lodge. After we finished dinner, the group naturally divided by gender, with the exception of Pasang, who stayed with the women. A little girl from soccer earlier claimed my lap, and I was more than happy to oblige, as she was warm and soft and smelled like the fresh-baked pastries her grandma brought.

It was nice to be there with the women, but the pastries and laughter were only a partial antidote to still being unsettled from this afternoon. Even over all the noise in the house, I could pick out the lilt of Luke's flawless English.

I turned a little so I could see him across the room. My eyes automatically went to his mouth: a mouth that rippled like an elongated *W* and gave him a default expression of amusement and contentment unless he was specifically feeling something different. I was convinced this was why people always took such a quick liking to him. His mouth was this way now, as he sipped from a glass of *chang,* the Sherpas' homemade beer.

What would it be like to know him in America? In what would have been my life? And was now *his* life?

It was ironic that I knew every high point he'd been on in the last two years, yet I knew absolutely nothing else about his life at UW. Though our Circs had been frequent, they were completely impersonal.

I sighed. That was a lie. For me anyway.

The Circs hadn't been impersonal at all. Maybe I hadn't

ever written anything other than #YCCM, but because of our game, I'd included him in every one of my summits, even on Nanga Parbat when I shouldn't have spared the time to take a picture let alone record a three-hundred-and-sixty-degree video. Because of our game, I was on the constant lookout for high points wherever Dad and I happened to be, and I had assurance that even as far apart as we might be, he had not forgotten me.

Luke and Dad were deep in conversation about something now, and I wished I could hear them. They had been close long before I came to live with Dad. In one way or another, Dad had been trying to save Mingma's family ever since his CPR had failed to revive her husband. The life insurance for climbing Sherpas back then was worthless, and to help, Dad had given Mingma the job as head cook during Everest seasons. He'd also managed Luke's education, and would have done the same thing for Pasang, had Pasang been at all interested.

I turned my attention back to the women who wanted me to show them my latest Thailand pictures. Dad and I went to Railay Beach every year on a low-budget rock climbing trip, and my pictures were pretty much identical to any other year, but the ocean was a novelty in landlocked Nepal, so I pulled out my phone, and everyone gathered around.

By the time I finished, the men were standing up to leave, and the cute little soccer girl, who had not budged from my lap all evening, was fast asleep on my shoulder.

Pasang set up his bedroll on the floor once everyone was gone. Dad was doing the same; he always liked to sleep by the door where there was a steady draft of fresh air. I popped my sleeping bag out of its stuff sack, quickly claiming the spot between Pasang and the wall to make sure Luke and I didn't end up next to each other.

The more I thought about his disappointment in me, the

more it hurt. If I could just get through tonight, Dad and I would be back on the trail first thing tomorrow, and I'd have plenty of time to recalibrate myself before Luke arrived in Base Camp with his Global Adventurers clients.

I went to the sink to brush my teeth and wash my face. When I turned around, Pasang was sliding his bedroll to the right and waving Luke over to the open spot.

Oh no you don't.

Too late. To Pasang, modus operandi was that Luke and I always slept next to each other, just like we always sat next to each other at the table.

Suddenly the house was too warm and the smoke from the fire too pungent. I stepped over Dad, who was bunching his fleece jacket under his head as a pillow.

"I'm going out for some air," I said.

I walked around the side of the house to the milk-nak corral and settled onto the stone fence, intending to stay out there long enough that Luke would be asleep when I sneaked back in.

The smallest of the naks, a black and white spotted girl, drifted over to me. It was Tinkerbell, who I'd bottle-fed as a calf my third year here and continued spoiling every year after that.

I didn't know if she knew me from anyone else now that Dad and I came to Mingma's house so infrequently, but it seemed like she did. She sniffed my legs and pockets.

"Sorry, lady. No treats tonight," I said.

She rested her chin atop the wall, suggesting I scratch behind her ears as a consolation. I complied.

I hadn't grabbed my hat or gloves on the way out, and it was brutally cold outside. It always was at night in the Khumbu Valley, no matter the time of year. I slid off the other side of the fence so I could snuggle into Tinkerbell's neck. Her fur was not as soft as it looked, but it was warm, like a buffalo coat.

Being out here, under the stars of the endless universe, gave me perspective about Luke. In this itinerant life in the mountains, people were always just passing through. Perhaps he was destined to be one of them instead of a fixture. It wasn't the end of the world. I still had Dad.

Tinkerbell bobbed her head, encouraging me to keep scratching her ears. "Okay, friend," I said. She snorted in reply, and I laughed.

"Still spoiling the work animals?"

Luke.

He leaned against the fence. The stray dog, which had followed him around from the front, sat at his feet. The only sounds were the dog's tail thumping against the wall and an occasional *whiffle* as the naks shifted around in the pen. Luke was so close that I could detect a bit of his sunscreen scent from earlier today. I wanted to move even closer.

The quiet between us once again felt okay. It was the dark that made the difference. It acted like the pinhole of a camera, limiting the focus to one thing at a time and making everything else less intense.

"Why wouldn't you go to college?" he asked.

Never mind about that pinhole.

"It wasn't right for me."

"But Townsend College had always been your plan."

"It had been *the* plan, but it was never *my* plan. It just took me a while to realize it."

He shifted his weight. "That doesn't make sense. It would have been free because of your grandpa working there."

"It wouldn't have been free, just a big discount. And it's private. The part that was left would have still been a lot. Especially considering that college doesn't make sense for me, even if it were free."

"Why not?"

"First of all, I don't even know what I want to major in. Speaking of, Mingma told us you changed your major. You're going to medical school now?"

"That's true, but you're changing the subject. It doesn't matter that you don't know what you want to major in. Lots of people start out undeclared."

There was a twinge of desperation in his voice, like he was trying to convince himself that I hadn't turned into a total dunce.

"Townsend College is a great school," he continued. "Port Townsend is practically in the Olympic Mountains, and you're just a ferry ride from the North Cascades, which you would love. They're not as big as here, obviously, but they're technical and uncrowded. It's gorgeous there with those wet forests..."

Yes, I knew the forests in western Washington with their dense ferns and the huge pine trees jabbing high into the sky. I knew how dark and cold those forests could be, especially when the fog rolled in, further obscuring the impenetrable, razor-wire blackberry thickets. The fog and blackberry thickets blocking my way back to my grandparents' house that terrible night ten years ago. Back to their house in Port Townsend. The house where Amy, my mother, had been living ever since she was released from prison last winter.

My insides clenched. "No," I said, this time aloud.

"What if you—"

"It's not right for me. There's a reason I took a gap year, and now that it's over, I don't feel any differently about going to college."

"I don't see why—"

"Just drop it," I said, my voice sharper than I'd meant. "I already made my choice. I'm not going, okay?"

And drop it he did. The awkward silence from this afternoon returned. My insides clenched even tighter.

I turned toward Tinkerbell, putting my hands on her head. She licked my jacket, her tongue as loud as a shoe dragging on cement.

Luke and I had always occupied completely different lives outside the months we were together in Tengboche or Everest Base Camp, but now we were galaxies apart. Yeah, I'd climbed some new peaks with Dad, finished online high school, and gotten my mountaineering certifications, but other than that, there was nothing different about my life than when I was seventeen. Or fifteen. Or twelve, even.

It was one thing to let go of my Circ fantasy and rein in my feelings for him, but there was still an important friend behind that. What if we'd grown so far apart that this would be lost, too? The sadness of this possibility crushed me.

When I couldn't stand his disappointed silence anymore, I climbed over the fence to go inside. I wished even more than before that Luke's bedroll wasn't right next to mine.

"Good night," I said, and it stung when he didn't try to stop me.

I tiptoed through the house and settled onto the floor, my back to Luke's empty bedroll. Mingma was breathing heavily in her sleep, and Dad was doing his soft but annoying whistle-snore.

My pulse was still on the defense, making me restless. I knew I wouldn't be able to relax until Luke came back inside. My ears strained for the squeak of the door hinges.

It was a long time before he finally returned, nearly silent as he lay down behind me. It was physically painful forcing my body to stay still as if I was sleeping. I yearned to repair the rift between us. I yearned for *him*.

A good fifteen minutes later, he whispered my name. Slowly, I rolled over to face him.

It was too dark to see, but I could sense he was just inches away, close enough to make me conscious of my breathing.

Close enough to kiss.

"Do you ever think about Cerro Torre?" he whispered. "Or Fitz Roy and the rest of the Top Five?"

All the time.

But to admit this, on top of everything else today?

There was nothing I loved to daydream about more as I drifted off to sleep after a hard and satisfying day in the mountains. Or a day when a Circ from Luke had made me smile so deeply I was sure the feeling would never fade.

Cerro Torre was steeped in the grandeur and mystique of the jagged Patagonian Mountains of South America. It had a four-page spread in *World's 19ers,* and we'd long agreed it was the most beautiful mountain in the world and the one we most wanted to climb someday.

For us, Cerro Torre was pure and sacred. Here in the stillness of the night, in the comfort of Luke's childhood home—even despite all that I'd *not* become in the past two years—it seemed okay to say so.

"Yeah. I think about it a lot."

"Me, too," he whispered, and shivers ran down my spine.

Chapter Four

It was back to dimples and teasing for Luke the next morning as Dad and I said our good-byes after breakfast.

Luke had always been a big flirt. With me. With everybody. It was one of the reasons he was such a fun friend, and also why it had taken until that afternoon two years ago for me to believe my feelings for him might actually be returned.

He handed me my pack, pretending to stagger under the weight. "Jeez, what do you have in here?"

My whole life.

I said good-bye to Pasang first, then Mingma, who gave me a pristine, white, silk *kata* scarf to carry with me on the mountain for good luck. I knew she hated that she wouldn't be with us in Base Camp, especially with Luke guiding this season. She was holding back tears, and so was I.

"You'll be back next year," I assured her as we hugged.

"But you won't."

Well—

I'd tell her about that two months from now, on our way back through Tengboche after the Everest season. Or maybe

Luke would, once Dad and I were gone.

I stood in front of Luke. His grin, as always, was contagious.

"See you on the glacier," I said.

"See you on the glacier."

Even as we said this, I doubted I would actually see him very much. The population of Everest Base Camp during climbing season was a thousand people, and the Khumbu Glacier it sat on was a mile-long stretch of jumbled-up ice and rock that didn't make for easy travel between the various expeditions' camps. Besides, Winslowe Expeditions and Global Adventurers would be on completely different acclimatization plans and summit schedules.

I purposely kept our good-bye hug quick and breezy.

"Oh, hey, wait," Luke said, just as Dad and I were ready to step off.

He ran back in the house and came out holding a small box of banana-yellow Loftycakes. My favorite American snack food from when I was a kid and next to impossible to get in Nepal.

The tears I'd been holding back broke loose. Not only because he'd remembered my love of Loftycakes and traveled with them all the way here from Seattle, but because I didn't know how I would ever manage to rein in my feelings for him.

Dad and I hiked the remaining miles of trail through the familiar terrain of the upper Khumbu Valley, pitching our tent each night in the common area of one of the progressively smaller Sherpa villages. We arrived at Everest Base Camp four days later.

Tshering, Winslowe Expeditions's lead Sherpa—or *sirdar*—had been at Base Camp with the other Sherpas for several weeks, and he'd already constructed our tent city, which consisted of a large cabin-style tent, fringed by smaller tents for communications, cooking, and storing gear. The individual tents for clients and guides were in a ring around the outside of the camp.

I looked forward to seeing the familiar faces of our Sherpas and hoped Mingma's temporary replacement cook wouldn't mind how much I liked to help out in the kitchen, especially on baking days. Everest Base Camp was the most permanent home I had all year, and I was excited to have my very own tent for the next few months, where I'd snuggle down for the night on thick foam instead of a thin backpacking air mattress.

We were a hundred and twenty miles from the nearest road, but in the Winslowe Expeditions camp, we'd be offering our clients a carpeted dining tent, free wifi, fresh produce, and hot towels and tea delivered to their tents each morning. Some expeditions did even more, like Go Big Mountaineering with their espresso machine and Global Adventurers's karaoke machine and the gourmet chef Luke told us they'd flown in from San Francisco.

Dad's hard-core alpinist friends hate all these trappings of civilization that require such extreme measures and expense to transport, but Everest has never been pure in this way. You don't come to Everest expecting two months of Spam. On this mountain, you get gourmet. Ever since 1856, when the Great Trigonometrical Survey pronounced it to be the tallest in the world, it was fated to be something different.

Inside the main tent, we found a Sherpa wiping down the dining table. This had to be Pertemba, the new cook. Dad introduced us and asked if there were any lunch leftovers. "Yes, of course," Pertemba said, hurrying to dish us up servings of *dal bhat*.

Tshering came into the tent while we were eating, barking something at Pertemba. Seeing us, he barked something else into the radio and then set down his clipboard to shake Dad's hand.

"Good to see you, Boss," he said.

For all that Dad was quiet and considerate, Tshering was straightforward and assertive. That's why the two of them made such a good team. He'd been with Dad every year since...well, the year after Luke's father died.

Tshering gave me a quick, efficient hug. "Number seven this year, MiniBoss?"

I nodded. He was one of the few who knew my actual number of summits. A long time ago, Dad had made an agreement with Miss Eleanor Hansen, the Kathmandu-based grand dame of Mount Everest recordkeeping, to not report my summits. The less the U.S. Child Protective Services knew about what Dad allowed me to do as a Winslowe Expeditions tagalong, the better.

"Doctor Teresa is in the Global Adventurers camp," Tshering said. "She wants you to go up and say hello."

"She's here already?"

"Been here two days," he replied. "Extra acclimatization."

This was exactly like Doc. When she set her mind to do something, she didn't do it halfway.

"Should we head up after we unpack?" I asked Dad.

"Tshering and I have a lot to go over," he said. "Why don't you go on ahead? I'll catch her another time."

I rinsed off my dishes and went out to my tent. Inside, I spread my sleeping bag on the thick cut of foam the Sherpas had carried to Base Camp and staged in my tent, as they had in all the other tents. I lay back on it, breathing in the familiar scent of a tent that had been baking in the sun all morning.

I folded my clothes neatly into the first of two waxed lettuce boxes I had grabbed from the kitchen. The other box doubled as my night table, and that was where I laid my headlamp, earbuds, sketchpad, *World's 19ers* book, and toiletry kit. Inside it I organized my stash of arts and crafts supplies.

Luke had been right about my pack; carrying around a bunch of extras like craft supplies made it very heavy by backpacker standards. But as Dad had once pointed out, my pack was featherweight compared to the loads Sherpas and porters ferry.

Now, the fun part: decorating. I untangled a length of thin cord to string across the tent ceiling like a clothesline to hang decorations from. The feeling of the cool nylon cord against my fingers made me pause. I gripped a section of it and drew it slowly through my closed palm. I repeated the motion, this time closing my eyes to the sensation. It was déjà vu back to two years ago. I'd done the very same thing that day—the day of the earthquake.

Luke and I had been lying around in my tent, playing cards and drinking hot chocolate. He'd already graduated from his boarding school in Kathmandu and would be leaving for University of Washington when the season was over. He'd been working with our support Sherpas that season, hauling bottles of oxygen to the upper caches on the mountain, but on that particular day he'd stayed down in Base Camp.

The winds were blustery that morning, scraping across the tent and pushing it this way and that. Our game of rummy had ended, and we were arguing whether to go another round of rummy—his stronger game—or switch to cribbage, my stronger game. As we bantered back and forth, he plucked the end of a piece of cord from the bag I hadn't put away after teaching advanced knots to a few of the clients.

He flicked me with the cord. "Remember how mad Greg would get when you used to braid this stuff?"

It was a piece of Dad's vintage, ultra-thin Prusik cord.

"Yeah," I said as I tried to snatch the piece away from him.

Though we were being playful, my crush on Luke was full force, and I was nervous being in the tent with him despite the dozens of hours we'd spent in tents together over the years.

I tried to snatch the cord again, and this time our fingers touched. His skin was hot. He let go of the cord.

I dug through the bag and found two more lengths of cord, which I pulled through my palm a few times before setting them up to macramé into a bracelet.

As I started, Luke grabbed more pieces and followed along with my steps. It was funny. Not in a laugh-aloud way, but in a warms-my-insides way.

What was there not to love about this guy? He was so relaxed and carefree, and being around him made *me* feel that way. He was incredibly smart but never showed it off. His smiles—with teeth that were straighter than mine—were perfection, and when his dimples appeared at the sides of his mouth, I turned into putty.

We worked quietly on our bracelets as the wind roared outside, blocking all the other Base Camp sounds and making it seem like our tent was the only one on the glacier.

"Do you think you'll get homesick when you go to Seattle?" I asked.

"I don't think so. I'm hardly here anymore as it is."

"Mingma will miss you."

"Yes, but she wants me to go."

I wanted to ask if he was scared, but this question was more for myself than him, so I didn't. A year from now, I'd be in his shoes, getting ready to head to Washington for college myself. Would he fit in? Would he feel at home there once he got used to it? Would I?

We still had about six weeks left at Base Camp, but already the thought of saying good-bye made my throat thick.

When I finished braiding my bracelet, I knotted the end and untied it from the anchor point.

"What are you going to do with that?" he asked.

I shrugged. "Probably give it to one of the Tengboche kids or something."

"Well, don't. I want it."

"You want this?" I asked. The cord was light purple, which was kind of girly.

He nodded. I noticed that it was me he was looking at, not the cord. My body tingled.

For once I didn't crack a joke. "Only if you're giving me that one," I said pointing to the one he'd made.

"Deal."

I always tried my best to pretend my crush on him wasn't there, but it was. Its force drew me to him, making me wonder things like what would happen if I followed the pull of his eyes and scooted closer? What would it be like to kiss him? What would it be like to be his girlfriend instead of just a buddy?

I craved him. Sometimes, like at that moment, it made me dizzy trying to resist it.

I pushed up my sleeve and held out my wrist. He wrapped the bracelet around it and then bent close to knot the ends. His warm breath flowed up my forearm as he focused. I shivered.

"What?" he asked, glancing up at me.

"Nothing."

Very carefully, he cut the excess with his knife.

"Do you have matches?" he asked.

I dug around in a bin for the tiny, waterproof container of backup matches for the rapid-boil stove. He flicked one against the flinted lid. Very carefully, he fused the knots with the wavering tip of the flame. I forced my focus onto the smoky, waxy smell of the melted cord instead of how close his face was to my hand.

When he was finished, he held out his wrist. It took me a

lot longer to tie the knots on his bracelet because my hands were shaking, and it kept slipping off. He rested his forearm on my knee to make it easier. Beneath the soft skin of the inside of his wrist, his pulse was beating fast like mine. This should have been reassuring, but instead it made me even more nervous. I prayed he wasn't noticing.

Once I finished the knots, I grabbed the matches. I paused before striking. "Promise you won't sue me if I burn you?"

He didn't laugh. Instead, those heart-melting eyes of his cut directly to mine, ratcheting my pulse up even higher.

I flicked the match, carefully lowering it onto the knots, holding my breath so I wouldn't accidentally push the flame onto his skin. The purple cord grew wet in the yellow flame, and then I pulled the match back and extinguished it with a single puff.

After I was done, his arm lingered on my knee. I dared not move as we watched the thread of smoke at the end of the match twist leisurely toward the ceiling, unaffected by the winds raging outside the tent.

It hit me stronger than it ever had before that he was leaving. I longed to tell him how much I was going to miss him. To throw our entire friendship away on the chance that the quick pulse in his wrist had been a sign that he felt the same as me.

He lifted his arm, looking down at his wrist as he pulled his sleeve back into place.

"*Pound Rescue*?" he asked. It was my favorite reality show.

"We finished all of them."

"Walkabout Media's surfing show?"

"Okay," I said, setting up the portable DVD player one of last season's clients had passed along to me when he went home.

For once, it was warm enough to lie on top of my sleeping bag rather than under it, and that's what we did. This time, though, he twisted into me slightly as I lay next to him. As the show began to play, I put the right-side earbud in and handed him the left. He'd already snagged my pillow, so I rested my chin on my folded arms. Our hands were so close that I hardly noticed when he started twisting my new bracelet around my wrist.

And then I did.

The air turned explosive. Even though I had no idea how he felt about me or what it would mean, it was like I knew with absolute certainty that something was about to happen. We moved closer, one imperceptibly slow movement flowing into another as the endless aqua ocean waves rolled across the screen.

Now we were both on our sides, his chest tight against my back, his hand still holding my wrist around the bracelet. My eyes were closed with the sensations of it all: the heat of his body, the woodsy smell of his deodorant, and his heartbeat against my ribs.

That's why it took me a few seconds to notice the tent was no longer being pushed by the wind but shaking like a dog after a swim.

What was going on?

The foghorn-low rumble grew into a roar all around us. With terror, I realized what it was.

Earthquake.

Rocks were shifting and crunching. People were shouting in panic. There could be climbers in the icefall being buried right now. Where was Dad? Where were our Sherpas?

Luke and I threw on our boots and scrambled to get out of the tent.

Then, the unmistakable blast of an avalanche rattled our eardrums. The entire west face of Lingtren Peak had let loose, and in an instant, there was a monstrously large, roiling cloud of snow and debris careening straight toward Base Camp.

Chapter Five

By the time the aftershocks had settled, the earthquake had taken the lives of nine thousand people in Nepal and injured tens of thousands more. The avalanche at Base Camp killed twenty-two people.

The Everest season had been over as soon as the earthquake hit. It was nothing but chaos and tragedy after that. Luke ended up leaving for college early while Dad and I stayed on in the Khumbu Valley, helping to clear rubble and start rebuilding the upper Sherpa villages.

I reflected on the earthquake as I walked the third of a mile up-glacier to say hi to Doc Teresa. As I got closer, there was no mistaking which of the many camps in that direction belonged to Global Adventurers. Theirs was four times as large as a typical expedition camp, with all tents being the same shade of bright yellow as their Yellow Yeti logo. Furthermore, their main tent was as enormous as a circus big top, and it had eight-foot-tall Yellow Yetis silk-screened on all four pitches of the roof.

One of the Global Adventurers Sherpas told me Doc was

in the medical tent. Yes, the company was so big it had its own medical tent. Indeed, I found her inside, fully in her element, unpacking a box of dexamethasone syringes and rocking out to nineties grunge.

"Whoa, MiniBoss," Doc said. "You look about twenty-five! What's going on with your hair?"

"I'm growing it out."

"It's lovely." She continued to stack syringes on a table.

"What are you doing working? You're a client this year."

"I'm still working a little. I mean, we all know that even if I wasn't on staff, I'd still end up treating people, so Global waived most of my fees."

I helped Doc transfer the dex syringes into the medical safe, and then we unpacked containers of blister tape, lip balm, and cough syrup. When I was younger, I wanted to be Doc. She was fun and outgoing, always at ease and making me laugh when I was least expecting it. And even though she was old—around forty-five, I think—she was pretty, with thick, crimpy hair and a permanent rosiness in her cheeks.

"So, what in the heck possessed you to climb this year?" I asked.

"What in the heck possessed *you* like a million times?"

"Because it's there," I said, using the tired George Mallory quote.

"Oh stop."

"Really, you've always scoffed at all of us. And now *you're* climbing."

"I don't know. I guess I got the itch to see how the world looks from the very top."

"You think you're ready to go to twenty-nine-thousand feet?" I asked.

"Ready as I'll ever be. I've been training nonstop. I climbed Denali last summer with Global, and Luke took me up the Liberty Ridge route on Rainier in October."

"Luke?"

"Yes, Luke. Bless his heart. One of his friends came along, too, and three of the UW professors who will be here in a few days."

"That was nice of him." It was odd to think of Doc and Luke keeping in touch outside of the Everest climbing season. Though, it made sense, because they both lived in Seattle.

"I just adore Luke. I have him and some of his roommates over for dinner every few months. Those guys are sweethearts. And the girl, too. They're a lot of fun."

She probably knew more about Luke's real life than I ever would. I wondered if the girl was a roommate or one of the guys' girlfriends. Further, I hoped this girl wasn't ^Olivia200x^. I didn't want her to be pretty *and* a sweetheart.

An older man with short white hair popped into the tent. It was Jim, Global's expedition leader. "Hi, Teresa, did we get any more gauze in?" he asked. "I'm going to change my bandage."

Doc tossed a roll to him, along with a fresh two-inch sterile bandage. Jim had been on Everest as long as Dad, but they barely knew each other. Jim led mountaineering expeditions for Global Adventurers all over the world on the highly commercialized peaks, while Dad stayed local to Nepal, China, and Pakistan, specializing in Himalayan climbing.

"Hey, Emily," Jim said, finally noticing me. "How are things down at Winslowe Expeditions?"

"Good. We just got in today."

He sat down to tend to his injury, then looked back up. "Wait a minute. Didn't I read somewhere that you and Greg did a winter ascent of Nanga Parbat?"

"Yes, they did," Doc answered for me. "A very stupid ascent of the sketchiest, most avalanche-prone route on the whole damn thing."

"Says the doctor who's decided to climb the world's tallest mountain this year," Jim said.

I laughed.

"Well, I didn't mean to interrupt you two," he said. "Emily, I'm having a meeting here tomorrow at eight for some of the expedition leaders. Things are pretty crowded this season with everyone trying to use up their permit extensions. Have your dad stop by if he can."

"Sure," I said.

Once Jim was gone, Doc started unpacking another bag of supplies. "I'm actually surprised to see you here this season, Em," she said.

"Why?"

"It's the end of your gap year. I thought you'd be headed to Washington to get ready for school."

"Nope. Change of plans. I'm not going."

She stopped unpacking and looked at me. "You deferred your enrollment again?"

"No, I canceled it altogether."

"Because of your mother?"

"What? No."

Port Townsend was a tiny, isolated town at the top of a long peninsula. Amy's move there was what first planted the idea about taking a gap year. It would be lying to deny that she was a factor in my decision this time around, but that's all it was. Just one of many factors.

"No," I repeated. "It's because I want to stay here, in the mountains."

"And do what?"

I wanted to tell her my whole plan—including the part about releasing my summit records after this season and trying for a sponsorship—but I hadn't ever said it aloud before, and it somehow felt like I would jinx it if I did. I'd tell her later, after I discussed it with Dad.

"I'm going to help Dad with Winslowe Expeditions," I said simply.

She arched an eyebrow at me.

"What?"

"I'm surprised Greg is onboard with that."

"He doesn't know yet. I was waiting until we got settled in here."

She groaned. "Why does this not surprise me? Let me ask you something. Have you and Greg ever discussed doing anything other than going back to Washington to attend Townsend College? Even the *possibility* of doing something else?"

"He's not going to care. He didn't even blink when I decided to do the gap year."

She swore under her breath. Why did I suddenly feel like I'd made a grave mistake?

"Sorry," she said, seeing how confused I was. "He wouldn't want to worry you. But here's the thing. You should probably go tell him about Townsend College. And don't drag your feet. I know how you two can be when it comes to talking about things."

I didn't have a chance to protest, because she handed me a bag of medicine to sort through and then changed the subject to her favorite topic: the latest Everest Base Camp gossip.

I sat at the small side table in the Winslowe Expeditions main tent, absentmindedly watching videos on my Circ feed. Two days had passed, and I still hadn't told Dad about Townsend College.

Doc was right about Dad and I not being talkers. And now that she'd implied that there was a big problem with my decision not to go to college, I had all the more reason *not* to bring it up. I also didn't understand the urgency, other than needing to cancel my plane tickets. But there was plenty of time for that.

Still, Doc's words grated on me. As much as she was known for being dramatic, Dad was known for being poker-faced. Even as well as I knew him, if there were something wrong, there was a chance I might not have picked up on it. I mean, what if he was sick or something? My chest tightened.

I'd decided to bring it up after dinner tonight, but then some of the Swedish expedition's guides came by to discuss the drama with Go Big Mountaineering not cooperating with this year's route-fixing plan. I'd moved over to the small table to give them some privacy, where I still sat.

I clicked over to Luke's account on Circ. There had been no #YCCM Circs since the one he sent in Tengboche, but he had been on Circ, making work-related posts tagged with @UWash, @HuskySports, @GlobalAdventurers, #HighAltitudeScience, and the official hashtag for the UW Team, #DawgsOnEverest. I knew he was now in Base Camp because he'd posted a Circ of his clients this morning on the lower reaches of the Khumbu Glacier, posing by the piles of tangled prayer flags and WELCOME TO EVEREST BASE CAMP signs. By now, he had a lot of comments. I scrolled the names, quickly seeing that most were UW students, and most of them women. I tried not to be jealous when I saw ^Olivia200x^ among them.

Over at the main table, Dad and Tshering were still deep in conversation with the Swedish guides. Sometimes, when I observed Dad from a distance like this, I wondered what the average American would think of him. Would they see him as an irresponsible man who refused to grow up, as I knew my grandparents thought and Doc sometimes implied? Or would they see him as I suspected some of the Sherpas did: an off-kilter, hippie weirdo raising a daughter in the Himalayas? Or would they see him like the trekkers and some of the people we met abroad did: an extreme sports kamikaze who completely disregarded his daughter's safety.

As for me, I saw him in the way the guides who worked for Winslowe Expeditions did: a climbing legend who still had unsurpassed wisdom and skill in the mountains. He was someone to respect and someone whom you wanted very much to respect you back. And for me, he was a rescuer of sorts—a personal savior—and I was grateful he had been willing to pluck me from my former life and include me so completely in his world right from the start.

Now, Pertemba was bringing out butter tea, which meant the Swedish guides would be here even longer. Just as I was considering giving up for tonight and going back to my tent to watch *Mean Girls* for the thousandth time, an enormous man in a Yellow Yeti parka stepped into our tent. He was so massive that it took me a second to identify the much smaller, square-shouldered, purple ball-capped man behind him as Luke.

But instead of coming over to hang out with me, Luke sat down next to the Swedish guides. Suddenly, it was like I was a child, sitting all alone at the kiddie table while the grown-ups talked business. For a terrible second, I thought Luke wasn't even going to acknowledge me. But then, as he settled into his chair, he looked over and nodded. His lips were rippled in his trademark *W*. Amused and content.

"Got that karaoke machine up and running yet?" Dad asked the behemoth guide.

Oh, jeez. You don't tease about another team's karaoke machine when you're sitting under thirty tissue-paper flower decorations that your daughter made this afternoon.

"Catching up on the latest *Going on Eighteen*?"

I looked up. Luke was standing across the table from me.

"You know it," I replied. I don't know if it was more embarrassing that he remembered that I used to be obsessed with *Going on Eighteen* magazine, or that he correctly assumed I still read it now, as a twenty-year-old.

More than the embarrassment, I was relieved that he'd come over…until I saw his expression, which was hesitant. I'd put him in a weird position. What if he'd come over out of obligation, begrudgingly leaving the adults to come say hi to Greg's daughter?

He sat across from me, automatically pulling checkers out of the built-in caddy on the side and setting them up on the checkerboard-painted tabletop. He pushed the red checkers across to me.

"Don't you need to be over there?" I asked. *With the grown-ups.*

"They're talking about our permit snafu," he said. "And I do believe I have a reigning checkers title to uphold."

Despite his light words, his face was tense, and he was flipping one of the pieces around his fingers nervously. This was very un-Luke-like. Did he really want to play, or did he want me to excuse him a second time so he could go back to the big table? I had a fifty-fifty chance.

"Okay," I said, setting up my red checkers. "After all, I have a checkers title to unseat."

His face immediately relaxed. I'd guessed right.

Pertemba brought butter tea to the behemoth guide as well as to Luke and me. As to not hurt Pertemba's feelings, I took a sip, trying not to grimace as I swallowed. Nak butter tea was one of the few Sherpa foods I'd never been able to adapt to.

Luke laughed. "Here," he said, reaching for my cup and drinking it down on my behalf. I tried to ignore the swell of my heart in reaction to his gesture. In reaction to him in general.

I thought about Luke's whisper in the dark at Mingma's house.

Do you ever think about Cerro Torre?

He'd said he did, too, but I didn't understand how it could be true. Medical school and all the years of training afterward were not compatible with climbing at the level needed for Top Five mountains, so by default he actually had to have given up the dream. Yet, here he was, a guide on Everest, and Rainier, too. It didn't make sense.

As we started to play checkers, my mind remembered the game, which I hadn't played in ages. I also remembered what it was like to hang out with Luke, just the two of us in our own little world.

"So what's the snafu with your company?" I asked.

He rolled his eyes. "It's a permit mix-up with the film crew."

"What are they filming?"

"Uh. Our Cuban team." He said it like I should know this already.

I gave him a blank look.

"Emily, seriously, do you never read the news?"

"Whose news?"

"Your country's news. It's a big deal."

"Yeah, I'm totally up on the news. They started delivering *USA Today* to the remote villages of the Himalayas, you know."

"And to smartphones." His eyes sparkled mischievously. God it was good to see that.

"No Cuban has ever reached the summit of Everest, let alone a whole team," he said. "And now, they are attempting it, with an *American* company, which is only possible because of the U.S. lifting the embargo—"

"Okay, I get it. So it's a Summit Show."

"A big, international Summit Show, and they've had a

crew from Walkabout Media & Productions with them since Kathmandu."

I was listening to him. I really was, but his voice itself was majorly distracting. There were some Americanisms in his speech now that hadn't been there two years ago. Americanisms in a British accent...sigh.

"Anyway," he continued, "the permit snafu is because Walkabout's testing this new high-altitude drone camera for part of the filming, and now there are more crew that need to go up on the mountain than Global's corporate office realized when they arranged for the permits last year."

"Sounds like a big mess."

"But not as big of a mess as you are in right now," he said, swooping in for the kill that led to his win of the first game.

We automatically put the checkers back on the board and started another round. In so many ways this was just like old times, when Mingma would go to bed early, leaving Luke and me to play games at the small table while Dad and the clients did their own thing over at the big table. Except, in the latter years, Luke and I would be sharing earbuds, listening to our favorite band, Jackal Legs, and my whole body would be abuzz with possibility. Just. Like. Now.

"Your turn," he said. The tent's harsh fluorescent light cast a shadow along his profile, making his cheekbones and jaw even sharper. I reluctantly pried my eyes from him.

Luke's handsome face was not helping me adjust to our new normal—one in which two years had passed since we'd missed our chance and we were relearning to be friends again outside of our Circ game. *Friends* being the key word here, and not a love triangle between Luke, ^Olivia200x^, and me.

We were midway through the third game when the two Swedes left. I used the distraction to double jump my checkers, setting me up to win the game.

"Two to one," I announced.

"*Tashi*," he said, using the name Sherpas had given me once I started getting up in the mountains and grabbing summits with Dad. It meant *lucky*.

We put our pieces back on the board, but before we could start, there was jabbering over the behemoth Global guide's radio, and he waved Luke over. "Jim wants us back for a meeting."

Luke gave me a quick hug good-bye. I didn't dare inhale as my arms squeezed a puff of air from his down jacket.

"You might be up one, right now," he said, "but you won't be for long."

My heart surged. Yes, this was good. Despite our conflicting expedition schedules and living on different parts of the Khumbu Glacier, we would be making an effort to hang out. And hopefully very soon.

Chapter Six

"Dad, can we talk?" I asked the next day after lunch.

"Sure, hon, what's up?" He gestured for me to come along while he grabbed something from the storage tent.

"No. I mean really talk."

"I was just going to double-check the oxygen bottle inventory. Why don't we sit down after that?"

I was afraid I'd lose the nerve if I waited. "No, Dad, now."

His graying eyebrows shot up. "Okay, sure." He said something to Tshering on the radio, and then we ducked inside the communications tent. "What's up?" he asked as we sat down on plastic chairs.

"So, um, I decided to not go to college."

He ran his fingers though his buzz-cut hair. This was not a good sign.

"If you're having some doubts, let's talk through them," he said.

"I've always had doubts. But now I'm sure."

"You've got a good thing set up at Townsend College, especially with Amy kicking in money for your dorm."

My blood chilled. My *mother* had been involved in the Townsend College plan? No one had mentioned *that* part before.

"I'm not going to Townsend College. I want to stay here and guide with Winslowe Expeditions. I've thought a lot about it. Now that I'm staying, I can officially be on staff this season, and then after I get my seventh summit—Chomolungma willing—I'll ask Miss Eleanor to release my records. We'd get some good publicity, and we might have enough clients next year to run two Everest teams. And we can—"

"Emily. Hold on a minute. Our staff roster is full for the season, and I don't have any more budget on this trip for wages."

"I don't have to be paid, but I could still be on staff." I was definitely ready for a title other than MiniBoss or Greg's daughter.

Dad looked down. His face was significantly more weathered and wrinkled than most men his age because of his lifetime in the mountains. At the moment, the wrinkles seemed even deeper.

"You're right," he said. "I should be paying you. You do as much work as a base camp manager or a trip coordinator, and you have been for years now. Had we talked about this last summer, I would have been open to it, but I can't bring you on staff this season."

"I don't care about the money right now. We can figure all that out later."

He ran his hand through his hair again. Was he going to say no?

"There's something I need to tell you, and there's no way to put it gently. I can't have you be a guide this season because you're not going to be on the mountain this year past Camp Three."

What? Was this what Doc had been alluding to? That Dad wasn't going to let me climb this year?

He pressed on his temple. "Winslowe Expeditions is not in good shape financially. The oxygen is too expensive, and I absolutely cannot have you up there without it. If something happened..."

I froze. He couldn't be serious.

My six Everest summits thus far had broken several records—not that anyone knew it yet—but it was the seventh that would smash about ten more. Major ones. It was my chance at sponsorship. My chance at the Top Five. I *had* to be able to climb this year.

"I don't understand," I said. "The oxygen has never been a problem before. I'm using only what we don't need for clients. There's no cost."

Dad winced. "I know I always told you that. But I can sell back unused oxygen to the cache in Gorak Shep, or hold it over for next year," he said. "It doesn't recoup all the cost, but it's substantial, and when I let you use the oxygen, I don't get anything back."

I didn't know which was more shocking: the fact that we were only a week away from our clients arriving and he hadn't even hinted that I wouldn't be climbing, or the fact that he'd been *paying* for my Everest summits. At $2,000 per bottle of oxygen, the cumulative sum of my summits could have easily exceeded $25,000!

"I'm sorry, Emily. I wanted you to get that seventh summit so badly, but it's just not going to happen this year."

Something snapped in me. "But future years don't matter. It's mostly because of my age that I've been breaking records. I can't wait until I'm older. I have to do it *now*. You said it yourself—Winslowe Expeditions isn't doing well financially. We need the publicity now more than ever."

Dad shied back at the anger in my voice. There had

been very few times I'd spoken to him like that. Possibly never. "You're right about your records being one hell of an international news story, but breaking records is not the reason we are in the mountains. It's risky. And a gamble."

I didn't care about records and titles, either, but just this one time I needed the attention they could dredge up.

"I apologize, Emily," Dad said. "I should have told you sooner, but I kept thinking I'd figure out some way to make it work, or that you might want to fly to Washington early to get ready for the school year, and it would have been a moot point."

"And now I'm not going to Washington at all," I reminded him.

Dad stared at me. I could practically see the gears grinding in his head.

"Emily, you *can't* not go. We can talk lots more about your college concerns, and you can always change your mind after a semester or two. But for now, you have to stick with the plan."

"It's too late."

"I don't think you understand." He hesitated. "Our financial situation isn't just bad. It's dire. I have no more money. There's not even money I can borrow anymore. The hard truth of it is that I cannot support you any longer than when you get to the airport in Kathmandu. That's why you have to go back."

Then it hit me: not climbing Everest this year wasn't what Doc had been hinting at. *This* was the Big Thing. I'd sacrificed a college education in part to stay with Dad—the only family I had—yet he was essentially kicking me out of the house. My stomach rolled.

"I *can't* go back," I said, trying to keep the panic from rising into my voice. "I already canceled my admission."

He looked at me sharply. "When?"

"Namche Bazaar."

He relaxed. "Okay, good. If you sent the letter from Namche, there's no way it's reached the U.S. yet. Let's hop on the satellite phone with the admissions office right now."

"No, I did it online. It was instant."

Dad's head drooped in defeat. "It's okay," he murmured. "We'll get this figured out. If it's truly too late to do anything for fall quarter, I'm sure your grandparents would be happy to have you stay at their house for a while."

In the same house where Amy lived? Absolutely not.

"I don't need to stay with them. I have money," I said.

"You have fifteen hundred dollars to your name. That wouldn't last two months in the U.S."

I gripped the armrest to steady myself. In a matter of minutes, my entire future had collapsed. It already seemed laughable that I'd ever dared to dream of the Top Five. Now, without warning and with no time to prepare, I had to find a way to support myself. To *survive.*

"I'll stay here in Nepal. It's way cheaper."

"That's not the answer. You need to hear me and take this very seriously. I'm not proud of the situation I'm in. Ashamed, really. But the truth is, I'm so bad off right now that I had to borrow the money for your plane ticket from Doc."

Just when I thought it couldn't get worse. This was how Doc knew something was amiss. My hands flew over my eyes. I wanted to push it all away. I had to find a job, but what could I do? I had no work experience. Nothing to put on a résumé. Except my guiding certifications.

Bingo.

I let my hands drop into my lap and looked right at Dad. "I'll guide," I blurted. "With a different company. Maybe on Denali. Their season doesn't start until summer. I can apply right now. Today."

He shook his head and rubbed at the stubble on his chin. "You've never climbed Denali. And guiding isn't the answer, either. You don't want this to be your life."

"Actually, I *do* want it to be my life."

"No, you want *climbing* to be your life."

"Guiding is good enough for you, and it's good enough for me."

"I'm a fifty-year-old man who doesn't have a penny in his bank account. And this is never what I set out—"

To do, I finished for him. I knew exactly where he had been going with that and why he'd stopped.

There was no more to say. I was numb. Worse than numb, actually. This was the woozy, apathetic euphoria that comes just before succumbing to hypothermia. When the body is hot like a fire while frostbite climbs up the limbs.

I understood everything clearly now. Dad had been an Esplanade-sponsored athlete, hands-down the premiere alpinist of his generation...until he suddenly had to support his ten-year-old daughter. That's when he started Winslowe Expeditions. I'd always been aware of this correlation, but it had been below the surface, phantomlike. Now this, and the accumulation of all I'd just learned, roared out of the water and knocked me to the ground.

I went right to my tent and lay on my sleeping bag.

I didn't read. I didn't listen to music. I didn't sleep. I just lay there.

It was like having the wind knocked out of my lungs, only it was taking hours instead of a few seconds for them to reinflate. Until I remembered something.

The moon last night.

It had been large and only a few degrees shy of perfectly

round.

I sat up and turned on my phone. The weather app confirmed what I was hoping. The full moon was tonight. In fact, according to the app, it was already out.

Whenever there was a full moon while Luke and I were in Base Camp, we had a tradition of hiking to the top of the neighboring hill, Kala Pattar, to watch the sunset.

I popped outside with my phone open to the Circ app. Indeed, the moon had already risen in the blue sky and was a perfect, ghostly sphere over Pumori. I started the Circ with a view of the moon and then tipped the camera straight up into the sky, arcing over the top of Base Camp. Then I lowered it to the barren black rock of Kala Pattar. After skimming south along its humpbacked ridge, I swung the screen back up into the blue sky and around to the moon. The Circ pinged and closed.

Back inside my tent, I added #YCCM to the Circ. But to actually hit send was risky.

It was one thing for Luke to swing by our camp with a fellow guide but quite another for me to blatantly summon him over the internet in our game of *You Can't Catch Me* that seemed to have already had its end.

Likely, he wouldn't come. He was a guide. He had stuff to do. And he probably wouldn't even see the Circ until hours from now, after he *didn't* come.

But at the moment, with my entire life and future in upheaval, I was reckless. I longed for nothing more than to be near him right now, so I released the Circ.

I would be hiking Kala Pattar tonight, regardless of whether he joined me, so I put on my boots and stuffed some protein bars, a water bottle, a headlamp, and extra layers of clothes into a small backpack. I took off on the trail right away so that I'd be out of Base Camp before Dad's daily meeting with the Sherpas was over.

Once I reached the turnoff for Kala Pattar, I dropped my pace to a crawl. I hadn't heard the *ping* of a Circ come in as of the last point I would have been connected to internet, but I didn't let this bother me. If Luke got the Circ, and if he was free, and if he wanted to, he'd catch up.

I hadn't made it five minutes into the grind of the thick gravel when someone grabbed my shoulders from behind.

It was Luke, in an attempt to scare me. My insides grew warm.

"You know better than to hike alone with both your earbuds in." His tone was scolding, but when I spun around, his eyes were crinkly and his dimples deep.

Chapter Seven

He came, was all I could think for the first few seconds. *He came!*

"How'd you catch up so fast?" I asked.

"Great minds think alike."

I scrunched an eyebrow in confusion.

"I was getting ready to come find you when you sent that Circ." He looked west, where the sky was already lavender with the approaching sunset. "It's going to be an amazing one."

Joy lifted my spirits like helium. Luke and I were back on the same page, back to how it used to be when things were easy and spontaneous and we acted in tandem without even thinking about it.

"Yes, it's going to be an amazing sunset. And it will be even more amazing for whoever gets to the top first," I challenged.

Without waiting for a response, I took off upward. Laughter poured from me as my feet sank into gravel while I pushed to get ahead. It was freeing to extend myself to full exertion in the race against the setting sun and the perception of Luke closing in behind me.

After we'd been at it for a half hour, the switchbacks straightened out, and I got the sense that Luke wasn't close on my heels anymore. I took a quick peek back and found him about fifty feet behind. He wasn't as acclimated as me, so I slowed enough to keep the gap between us from widening.

The summit of Everest, which wasn't visible from Base Camp, was now in front of us as we reached the final section of Kala Pattar. It was just a bitty, asymmetrical triangle dwarfed by the breathtaking side-angled slope of Nuptse across the gorge. With each step gained upward, Everest grew taller. By the time I scrambled through the jagged, crushed boulders at the top of Kala Pattar and reached the stone *stupa* with its spokes of prayer flags, Everest was nearly peak-to-peak with Nuptse. The incredible full moon floated between them, as large and as white as a dinner plate. Despite my lungs straining for more oxygen, the beauty of it all entranced me.

Luke reached the top about a minute later, immediately doubling over to catch his breath.

"Nice job, ol' boy," I said. "I didn't think you were going to make it."

All he could manage was a good-natured head shake.

I put on my hat and jacket and sat on the leeward side of the *stupa*, watching the hard line of the black shadows rise up the glowing, yellow-pink surfaces of the monster peaks around us. My hair, loose as it almost never is on a summit, whipped in time with the prayer flags and snapped against my wind-burned cheeks.

Luke sat next to me, pulling a thermos out of his backpack. "Hot chocolate?"

"Yeah."

"It's just the powdered kind."

"Like I care."

He poured some into the lid and handed it to me. It was nice and warm, moistening my throat, which was dry from the cold, thin air. Silently, we looked across the gorge to Everest's oh-so-familiar, blocky summit pyramid. A plume of snow flowed from it like a pennant, announcing the presence of the 140-mile-per-hour jet stream winds that blow directly across its top every day of the year except for a handful of summit-able days in May, and sometimes a few in September.

My shoulders sagged under the knowledge that I would not be among the people who would stand atop it this year.

I felt Luke's eyes on me, so I glanced over.

"Something's up," he said.

It was tempting to let some of my troubles spill out. Luke was good at listening. But to tell him any part of the mess would be to reveal how badly my world was upended and how little I had going for me at the moment.

"I'm just tired," I replied.

"What are you tired from? Napping all day?"

"Don't you know? Sleep begets sleep."

I looked across the distance to Everest and its neighbor, Lhotse, all but the tiniest sliver of Lhotse's west ridge hidden behind the majestic Nuptse in the foreground. My mind kept spinning around the question of why Dad had hidden his money troubles from me. I could have handled it. I could have *helped*.

I had given up a college education for the mountains and to stay with Dad, yet I would still be losing them both. What would Dad and I do from now on? Email back and forth like pen pals? Meet up at a hostel somewhere in the world once a year? He had no money for plane tickets, and whatever I ended up doing, I probably wouldn't, either.

What had happened today was identical to what had happened with Amy. When she was my mother, I was satellite to her planet, and then I'd been cut loose. Now, I orbited Dad, and he was doing the same thing: cutting me loose. It wasn't fair to compare Dad to Amy in this way, but the end result was the same.

Luke cleared his throat. "I know it's been a long time since we've hung out, but you can talk to me."

I tested him with my eyes, searching for a hint that he was asking because he felt obligated, but his face was pure, and the concern on it lined up accurately with the tone in his voice. It was tempting but, still, I resisted. "It's nothing. Just a lot going on at Winslowe Expeditions right now."

What he said about it having been a long time since we'd hung out was exactly what made it *not* okay to spill my thoughts. Our game on Circ had been a buoy of sorts with that subtle yet constant excitement of planning what I'd send him next, or the zing that went through my body when a new #YCCM arrived. It had amplified everything that happened in my life that was good, while giving a buffer to everything that wasn't. But there'd been absolutely nothing in two years other than that.

I'd given him my email address when he left for Washington, and in the months between that and when my email account was hacked, he hadn't written. After this season, he'd be going back to UW, and I'd go on to who knows what, which would likely be nowhere near Washington. I didn't have any reason to go back there and a lot of reasons not to.

I pulled the protein bars from my backpack, automatically handing Luke the peanut butter chocolate chip one and unwrapping the oatmeal raisin one for myself.

We ate, looking out at the huge white moon. Only the tips of the very tallest peaks were illuminated now, and down to our right, deep in the blackness of the valley, Everest Base Camp was a beautiful array of tents glowing like yellow, green, blue, and orange paper lanterns.

"The wind's picking up," Luke said after we finished our bars. "We should probably head down."

With the sky clear and moon so big, we didn't need our headlamps until after we'd picked our way down the rocks into the shadowy side of Kala Pattar. After the gravelly switchbacks, the slope tapered off, leaving us at the trail junction back to Base Camp.

As soon as we started walking the wide and well-traveled Base Camp trail, I began dreading my arrival. Once Dad knew I was back, he would want assurance that I wasn't mad and that we could call Townsend College in the morning and get this all figured out. My whole body bristled with the thought.

I wanted to remain in this bubble of *now* with my old friend. Just being near him was like having a layer of protection between me and all that I didn't want to face about the new reality looming in front of me.

Luke stopped when we were downslope from the Winslowe Expeditions camp. He looked back at me, blinding me with his headlamp.

"Jeez!"

"Sorry."

We both clicked off our headlamps, neither of us making a move to go. We stood there, listening to the great quiet of the Himalayas, where, for the moment, the Khumbu Glacier wasn't groaning and there were none of the typical booms of avalanches letting loose on distant peaks.

Luke shifted. "I have the new season of *Pound Rescue* on my tablet."

Yes to that and yes to not saying good-bye to him just yet. And yes to avoiding Dad for a little longer. If I stayed long enough, I wouldn't have to talk to him until the morning.

"Sounds good," I said. "Let's go."

Chapter Eight

I waited on the side of Global City's massive big-top tent while Luke stopped inside to check in and make us sandwiches from their 24/7 peanut-butter-and-jelly bar. I shot a text off to Dad, telling him where I was so he wouldn't worry. I gave the text a minute to send, then turned off my phone. I didn't want to read Dad's response. I didn't want to think about any of it yet.

I followed Luke to his tent in the upper quadrant of Global City where the University of Washington's colors of purple and gold blazed in the beam of my headlamp. The quadrant's central gathering tent had a sign clipped to the side, labeling it as the DAWGHOUSE.

Luke and I crawled into his tent, and he looped his headlamp strap through an *X* in the tent poles. He clicked the power down on the bulb so the light wasn't overpowering. We unfolded napkins across our laps, then we pulled our sandwiches apart and put potato chips in the center before taking our first bites.

In previous seasons, Luke had shared a tent with

Mingma, so we had mostly hung out in my tent. His tent—this tent—was quite impersonal and typical for a guy, except for the worn copy of *World's 19ers* on his pillow. I'd gotten him that book as a graduation present, purchased with the birthday money my grandparents had sent that year.

I looked from the book to him, finding a hint of discomfort on his face. Claustrophobia, perhaps? Like a two-person tent wasn't big enough for us now that he had a girlfriend? Or that there were things he should have been doing, but he was stuck with me because he'd been a nice guy who'd noticed something was wrong and invited me to watch *Pound Rescue*?

I tried not to think about this as we rolled our napkins up and washed the sandwiches down with cartons of chocolate milk. Luke slid *World's 19ers* to the side and propped his tablet against his pillow. The tablet was a definite upgrade from the rickety portable DVD player I still used.

Luke sat on the far side of the sleeping pad. He unzipped his sleeping bag and spread it wide like a blanket. Even wearing thick down jackets and long underwear, you couldn't just hang out in a tent in the ten-degree Himalaya night without a sleeping bag.

Next, Luke and I would lie down on his bed to watch the movie. Now it was *me* feeling claustrophobic. In just seconds, we'd be squished together out of necessity because of the narrowness of the foam pad, the smallness of the screen, and needing to share earbuds. It didn't matter that we'd watched a hundred movies this way; the last time we'd watched a movie together, we'd ended up cuddling and on the brink of something more.

A pang of regret hit me that our last season together hadn't been a full one. I had this strange feeling that if it had, my whole world right now might be completely different.

Luke was lying down now, scrolling through his tablet for the *Pound Rescue* episodes. If I delayed joining him on his bed any longer it would be awkward. More awkward than it already was.

I lifted the edge of his sleeping bag and crawled in next to him. He reached up behind my head and clicked off his headlamp. The light from the screen was the only thing illuminating the tent now. He handed me the right-side earbud. To my utter humiliation, my fingers were shaking so much that I dropped it.

The episode started, but I couldn't focus at all. Despite the multiple layers of clothing and jackets between us, every point of his body that touched mine was burning.

And his smell! Being so close to him, beneath the very sleeping bag he slept in every night, was like being inside a cozy, warm air freshener made of the Nepalese soap Mingma used for laundry.

My body longed to nudge closer. To prompt him to put his arm around my shoulders as if there had been a time warp and we were back in that afternoon of the earthquake. My willpower to resist this was melting.

No! I scolded myself silently. I couldn't let him see that I had not moved on like he had. That still, after all this time, I was overpoweringly attracted to him.

Luke paused the movie. "What's up?"

He'd noticed. *Shit.* I sat bolt upright, which dragged the tablet off the pillow until the earbud yanked out of my ear.

Double awkward. What to do? *Say something!*

"You know how I said I hadn't told my dad about Townsend College?"

"Yeah."

"I told him today, and it's bad. That's what's been bothering me."

Luke removed his earbud and sat up. "He wants you to go?"

"Yes, but it's more than that. We're completely out of

money. I have to get a job right away."

"Doing what?"

"Guiding."

He frowned.

"What?"

"I didn't know that's what you wanted to do."

"It's what I know. It's what makes sense. Besides, what's wrong with guiding, Mr. Global Adventurers guide?"

He laughed. "Okay, point taken."

Luke's deep, familiar eyes sparkled along with the smile his dimples were framing. His straight black hair stuck up all over the place from wearing a hat today. My mind found him adorable; my body found him irresistible.

Almost too gradually to detect, the bow of his smile lowered until he wasn't smiling anymore.

My smile slid off as well. In the glare of *Pound Rescue* paused on his tablet, our eyes locked. The intensity burning in his made my stomach flip over and over.

"You said it makes *sense* to be a guide," he said. "And you said back in Tengboche that you didn't think college was right for you. So what is it that you *want*?"

A way to climb Cerro Torre and the Top Five.

I wasn't going to tell him this. Especially now that my only shot at it was gone.

"It's not straightforward like that," I said. "Have you ever dragged your feet on something, but it wasn't until that thing was out of the way that you could start thinking about everything that thing might have been blocking? Well, that's how it was for me about college."

He looked away quickly, like I'd hit a nerve. I waited for him to say something, but he didn't.

"Well, it's getting late. I should probably get back," I said, sliding over to the door and reaching for my hiking boots.

"Hang on, Emily."

He scooted closer so he wouldn't have to yell across the tent. "I know it sounds weird that I was implying you shouldn't be a guide when that's exactly what I'm doing right now, but that's all it is. It's just for now. A college job. It was something I fell into because of my job at the outdoor rec center and this being a UW expedition."

"Luke—"

"Just listen. I have a feeling you're thinking about guiding because it's convenient and safe. But the thing is, there's nothing safe about guiding inexperienced clients on dangerous mountains. And it's not climbing, either. It's neither mountaineering nor a career." He swallowed. "You were right to call me on the guiding thing, because the truth is, I don't really want to be on Everest this season. I only did it because it was a free plane ticket home, and with Mom sick, I wanted to make sure she and Pasang were okay."

The heaviness in his voice tugged on my heartstrings, and I knew how hard it had been for him to admit that. I put my arms around him and squeezed. He did the same.

And then neither of us let go. My heart raced.

Why did you never email? After all that had been building between us, why was there never anything more than Circs?

His grip tightened. "You're like me," he whispered. "You have dreams in the mountains. Think of Cerro Torre. Think of the Top Five project. You're good enough to get a sponsorship, and then it could be completely within reach. I would hate to see you lose your dreams because you're being paid to make other people's dreams come true instead."

His words filled my heart to the brim. I didn't mean to, but I laid my head on his shoulder. It felt good and right. "Dreams can change a lot in two years," I whispered back.

He pulled me in a little tighter. "Yes, but some things never change."

Chapter Nine

I awoke to the beautiful glow of early morning light in my tent. I was glowing inside, too—the glow of happiness and possibility. It took me a few seconds to realize the sensation had been from a dream. A dream where Luke and I had been in a real bed instead of a tent, tangled up in sheets and a pretty quilt. He was kissing my neck. My *bare* neck because, beneath the sheets, I'm pretty sure the rest of my body was also bare.

I didn't want to move because I didn't want to lose the memory of it, the sensations. When I finally had to, the glow faded, leaving my insides hollow in the face of my new reality. One in which Luke was not mine. Dad was not mine, either. Nobody was mine. I was completely alone in this world.

Sadly, it was a feeling I knew well, though not as much in recent years. Until now.

I thought about what Luke had asked last night: what it was that I truly wanted. It was the mountains, yes, but now I thought about the other part, the part I'd deliberately given up when I'd decided not to go to Townsend College. A house to come home to—the kind of little white bungalow with a big front porch I'd always dreamed of. A place of permanence and friends, comfort and welcome. I'd so easily let that go in order to continue my roving life in the mountains with Dad.

But now I'd lost them both—the mountains and the home. Having a physical house of my own was as extravagant of an idea as climbing the Top Five, but there was no reason I couldn't have a *life* of my own. That was the ray of light in this situation. I could learn from the loneliness I felt right now, the lack of belonging. Moving forward, I would build my own life, one where I was the center instead of orbiting someone else. Starting right now, with finding a job.

I sat up, drank some water, and turned on my phone. I began with the jobs pages of U.S.-based mountain guiding companies. It was a relief to see I had the minimum qualifications, but troubling to see that most companies wanted additional certifications. Some even listed experience minimums in number of years rather than number of peaks climbed, which put me at a definite disadvantage. And there was the problem that, though I'd climbed mountains nearly twice as high as America's tallest mountain, I'd never actually summited a mountain in the U.S.

I looked at a few more guiding websites, including Luke's company, Global Adventurers, which was even bigger than I'd expected, with a dozen offices around the world and more than a thousand employees. They did it all, everything from senior citizen European tours to major mountaineering expeditions.

Online, I found some examples of mountain guide resumes and then got out a piece of paper to jot down some notes.

"Emily, you up?" Dad called from outside my tent. "Can I come in?"

"Yeah," I said, slipping the paper under my sleeping bag

and then unzipping the door for him.

He came inside and sat cross-legged next to my lettuce-box shelves. His face was weary to the point that I suspected he'd had trouble sleeping last night.

"Emily, I'm really sorry that I kept you in the dark about my financial situation. I should have brought it up last spring when you were deciding to take a gap year. Or even after that. I just didn't want to worry you. There was a plan in place, and if I just got you through to when you left for college, it would all be okay. My money problems shouldn't be your problem, but now they are, and I feel terrible about it."

"It's okay," I assured him. "I'm fine. Don't feel bad. Please."

"Well, I do feel bad."

In just one day, Dad seemed a decade older. More gray hair, more wrinkles. It wrenched my heart.

"It was a little bit of a shock," I said, "but I'm okay now. I'm sorry if I was rude yesterday."

"You weren't rude at all."

I looked down and fanned the pages of *World's 19ers.*

"I keep thinking about how I haven't been paying you," he said. "I should have been doing that all long. Or at least giving you a formal stipend."

"Seriously, Dad, don't even think about it. I'm the one who should have been more considerate about money when I decided to take a gap year. I never even offered to pay my own expenses."

"Don't try to take the blame. This is my blunder."

"It's going to be okay. I've already been looking at some jobs."

"Guiding?"

I nodded.

"About that," he said, eycing the *World's 19ers* book and rubbing his beard. "I thought about it more last night, and I don't think you should go down that path. Not yet, anyway. I don't think you have a concept of how perfectly suited you are for mountaineering, mentally and physically. You've got this immense capacity for it in your power and drive. You have skill on par with Gerlinde Kaltenbrunner and Lhakpa Sherpa, I would say. I know you want to climb the Top Five, and I believe you have the skill to be the first woman to do it."

I was stunned, in a good way. He always praised me at the top of our climbs, but it was never much more than a simple *good job* or *nice work today.* I had no idea he thought these things.

"The thing is," he continued, "being a career guide, you'd never have money for a major project like that. And besides, your paying clients get the best summit windows in the best locations. You'd never be free at the right times of year for the summits on your own tick list. Life only gets more complicated as you get older. If you don't climb for yourself in the beginning, you might never get the chance."

"Exactly. That's why I cancelled at Townsend College."

"No. It's the opposite. You need college so you can get a really good job so you can pay for the trips."

"And if I had said really good job, then I'd never have enough time off for even one major expedition a year, let alone enough time for the acclimation and all the training. That's why pursuing a sponsorship—not college—is what makes sense."

"Yes, but—"

"*You* didn't finish college," I pointed out.

"No, but the business classes I took have been extremely helpful in running Winslowe Expeditions. And I would never have become an Esplanade Equipment athlete if I had not crossed paths with Barrett Browning when I was guiding on Mount Rainier as my college job."

I sighed and looked up at the laminated photos strung

across my ceiling. The picture right above me was a close-up of a snow-tipped rhododendron. Just out of view, Luke had been holding the stem so the flower wouldn't blow in the breeze and make the picture blurry.

Luke.

Something sparked in my mind. The Global Adventurers permit snafu he'd told me about. From a staffing perspective, the extra cameramen who would be climbing were the same as guided clients. And this meant Global might not be meeting their advertised guide-to-client ratios. If true, this could be a chance to get my foot in the door with Global and get off Dad's threadbare dime immediately.

There might be hope of a seventh summit after all.

I wanted Dad out of the tent so I could consider the Global Adventurers idea further. I gave him a firm good-bye hug and assured him that I wasn't mad about yesterday and would think more about college.

As for my Global Adventurers idea, there were three cons.

One: Going to Global City to ask Jim if he needed another guide would require me to be much braver and more outgoing than I actually was. And it was likely he'd say no.

Two: It wouldn't put Dad or Winslowe Expeditions in a good light to have me up there begging for a job from the competition. Dad would be hurt and embarrassed if he found out.

Three: Luke. It had been wrong that I let myself linger in his arms last night. He had a girlfriend, and we were just getting back to how we used to be as friends. By not respecting that boundary, I'd risked ruining it all. What I needed right now was some time apart from him so I could cool down, not the close quarters that would be inevitable if we were part of the same expedition.

But in the end, neither Dad nor I were in a financial

position to let number one or number two stop me from inquiring. And about Luke, well, I'd have to cross that bridge *if* it turned out Jim had a position to fill.

I hiked up to Global City right after breakfast. Doc's tent was easy to find with her sparkly purple camp boots sitting in front of it.

"I talked to Dad. You were right."

"I know. I didn't want to push you guys into something ugly but, well, we both know your dad. He might not have ever told you."

"I feel stupid that I didn't know. You'd think I would have been able to figure it out. I had no idea he was borrowing money from you. I'm sorry."

"Oh, Emily, it's okay. It was just for the plane ticket, and I am more than happy to help. I told him he didn't need to pay me back, but he's insisting."

"I know, but still, I'm twenty; I should be buying my own plane tickets."

"Yeah, you probably should, but it's not your fault for not knowing things that were being kept from you. Not maliciously, of course. You might have had the world's most adventurous upbringing, but Greg Winslowe somehow found a way to be a helicopter parent."

I frowned.

"It's because he loves you, Em." She offered me a Thin Mint from an open box of Girl Scout cookies, and I presented my theory about Global being understaffed.

"That's some good thinking, MiniBoss. I know Jim's been trying to bring in another guide, but it's impossible to find a fully acclimatized Western guide in the middle of Nepal who happens to have the right qualifications and is not already on a job. I'm sure he never even considered looking here at Base Camp. My only question is if Greg knows you want to do this."

I shook my head.

She clucked her tongue, yet she looked proud of me. "Come on, let's go find Jim before you change your mind. It would be a great opportunity for you, and I'd love to have you here with us this season."

Doc walked me through Global City. I kept my eyes peeled for Luke, as it would be really bad timing to run into him right now. Doc left me inside Global's enormous communications tent, standing in front of Jim in his Yellow Yeti fleece and matching hat, wishing desperately I'd insisted on taking a few minutes to plan what I was going to say.

"Uh, hi," I said.

"Hi, Emily, what's going on?"

I swallowed my urge to run away. *Here goes nothing.* "I heard you have more people up on the mountain this season than you'd planned."

"True."

"I know Global Adventurers advertises the lowest Western guide-to-client ratio of all outfitters here, and I was curious if the additional climbers will affect that?"

"Did Greg send you up here to do some reconnaissance?" He threw his head back and laughed. "Don't tell me he's going to run a smear campaign for us not sticking to our advertised ratios."

"He didn't send me. I'm asking for myself."

"For yourself?"

"Well, I do have my Wilderness First Responder and Avalanche II certifications."

"Don't you work for Greg?"

"It's a long story, but no."

"And so you're here looking for a job?"

I nodded.

"Well, I'll be darned." He pulled on his chin. "Now that I know you're not here as a spy—"

I shook my head earnestly.

"I'm just joking, Emily. But, yes, you guessed right. Our low ratios are one of our major differentiators, and breaking that is not something corporate is interested in doing. But they've yet to find me a suitable extra guide who is already acclimatized. So it's been a bit of a thorn in everyone's side. How old are you, if you don't mind me asking?"

"Twenty."

He frowned. "That's young."

"I may be young, but I bet I have more Himalayan summits than your entire guide staff combined," I said boldly.

He laughed. "I don't know if that's true, but I've seen you here so many years that I don't doubt that you have more Everest summits than any single Global guide. How many, exactly?"

"Six."

He whistled.

"Five of those were here in Nepal, on the South Col Route. One was from the Tibet side, and a total of two were without oxygen."

"Well, we do have Luke on the mountain this year, and he's only twenty-two."

"Exactly."

"I wouldn't necessarily advertise your age to our clients. Not that I'm telling you to lie. Maybe just make a point not to bring it up."

"We do that at Winslowe Expeditions, too."

"Perfect. So when can you start?"

Oh my god! I'd done it! He was offering me a job!

"Right away," I replied.

"Right away as in today? Our first rotation is in a few

days, and I'd like to give you as much time as possible to get to know the clients beforehand."

"Today is fine."

He chuckled and cracked his fingers. "This is almost too serendipitous to be true."

It *was* too serendipitous to be true. *Tashi.*

"Go grab your stuff," he said. "Welcome to Global Adventurers."

Chapter Ten

I stood outside Global's communications tent for a few seconds, stunned and blinking in the bright sunlight. Just like that I had a job—my first job ever—and my chance back of summiting Mount Everest a seventh time, with all the doors that might open along with it.

Dad found me as soon as I returned to our camp. I braced myself, at first thinking the news of my new job had already gotten to him, but then I realized he looked excited, and there's no way he would be excited about what I'd just done.

"So…I just got off the phone with your grandpa," he said. "We've got everything taken care of."

What? "Why did you call Grandpa?"

"I'd been trying to get through to the Townsend College admissions office, but I kept getting booted off the phone because of the holds. So I called your grandpa and asked him to make a few calls from his end."

No.

"The bad news is that you truly cannot start this school year. They don't make exceptions, even for the girl who is the youngest in the world to climb Mount Everest without oxygen and is the only woman to ever repeat Rosso Messina's Gray Spider route. Starting winter term is an option, though you will probably have to resubmit your application."

I turned away. He shouldn't have gone behind my back like that.

"Your grandparents are happy to have you stay with them while we figure out what will happen with your admission. I did mention that you may decide not to attend at all, so they know that's a possibility."

I hadn't been to that house in almost eleven years, but I could still see every detail as if I were standing there right now, my underclothes soaking wet from the rain after being lost in the dark woods. I could feel the suffocating bulk of those two police officers filling up the living room before they led Amy and her shirtless boyfriend out of the guest bedroom in handcuffs.

"Amy lives there now," I said. "No way."

"Emily—"

"I won't do it. You shouldn't have talked to them!"

"We'll get this figured out, but in the meantime you have to go back to the U.S. The time to change the plan is *after* you get there."

"I told you, I'm going to get a job. And I did."

Dad raised a dubious eyebrow.

"I'll be guiding with Global Adventurers. Starting today."

"You're going to work for Jim?"

"Yep. See? It all worked out."

Dad was speechless. The fish-mouth kind of speechless, where he kept trying to form words but nothing came out.

"Jim never said anything about that to me."

"Why would he? It *just* happened."

"You'd be jumping in mid-expedition. And you have no experience working for Global Adventurers."

"They're a legit outfitter despite their size. You've said that yourself."

Dad rubbed his forehead. "This is all my fault. You shouldn't have to do this. Do you mind if I go up and talk to Jim?"

Let him go talk to my new boss like I was a child enrolling in nursery school?

"No, please don't," I said.

From the look on his face, I was willing to bet he'd go up there anyway. If there was ever a time to be assertive, it was right now. "I got lucky with this job," I said. "It's an opportunity to get something real on my résumé and to earn some money. Maybe even get that seventh summit. Even if it's not with Winslowe Expeditions, the previous six summits were, and any publicity that would come from that will be good for the company, too."

"I don't care about the publicity or—"

"We both know I need this job, and it's a done deal."

After a long, seemingly eternal silence, Dad relented. We went to my tent, where he helped me pack my things. He hugged me good-bye, and before I knew it, I was walking up the Base Camp trail, all alone.

With a lump in my throat, I realized I'd just left home.

For good.

Tears pricked my eyes. I twisted around back toward camp.

Dad hadn't moved. From the look on his face, I knew he'd have an even harder time sleeping tonight than he had last night.

Could I do this? Could I really leave?

Whether I wanted to or not, I *had* to.

I lifted my hand to wave good-bye. After a moment, he raised his arm and did the same.

Chapter Eleven

Walking into Global's big-top tent was like walking into a different world. Everything was bigger and fancier. The tent was light and bright, with a ceiling that was six feet higher than Winslowe Expeditions's and had sections of clear plastic that served as skylights. There were two central dining tables with a whole row of small tables along one wall and a line of yellow plastic Adirondack chairs with footrests along the other.

Unlike Winslowe Expeditions, where our kitchen tent was separate from the main tent, Global's kitchen was open-concept inside the main tent. On the enormous counter that separated it from the rest of the tent was an astonishing display of steam trays heaped with lunch entrees and side dishes. Off to the side was the PB&J bar and a self-serve toaster with bagels, butter, jam, and squeeze packets of cream cheese. For drinks, there was flavored water, three kinds of juice, soda, and an array of protein shakes in addition to coffee and tea.

Noticing me standing near the door, Doc jumped out of her seat and rushed over. "So I presume it all worked out?"

"Yeah."

"Congratulations!"

Someone coming inside the tent bumped into Doc. That someone was Luke in his Yellow Yeti jacket. He did a double take at seeing me.

"Give us a minute, bud," Doc said, shooing him past us. My eyes followed him to the lunch line where he dished up a plate of food.

"Dad thinks it's a bad idea," I told her.

"He would. Like I said, he's a helicopter parent. But you'll be okay. There'll be a lot of new faces for you to learn, but you'll get to know everyone with time. I think the plan was to put the new guide with A-Team. Some of the A-Teamers are a little obnoxious, but they're all good men. And you're really going to like your fellow A-Team guides."

Luke, now seated at the far table with that behemoth, linebacker-sized guide who had come to Winslowe Expeditions the other night, eyed Doc and me curiously and then made a goofy face. I laughed. Perhaps it would be okay with both of us working for Global. That is, if I could manage to keep my feelings in check.

Jim walked in. "Hey there, Emily. You're here already. Good. Come with me."

He escorted me over to the food, introducing me to Randall, the professional chef from San Francisco, as well as his Sherpa assistant, whom everyone called Cook-Phurba.

Jim and I sat down at the large table next to Norbu, Global's head Sherpa. Luke was at the table, too, but on the opposite end. Looking around at the dozens of people in this tent, the enormity of what I was embarking upon hit me like a wrecking ball. I couldn't get my head around an expedition this size. Dad was right about it not being a good idea to jump in last-minute like this with a completely unfamiliar company. I didn't know anything about any of these clients, other than that to be able to afford a full-service guided trip like this, most of them were wealthy beyond my wildest imagination.

At Winslowe Expeditions, I was just the tagalong daughter—I always exceeded expectations because there were no expectations. But here, I needed to be a leader and, with this many people around all the time, if I showed any cracks, I would be found out right away.

Luke caught my eye and raised an inquisitive eyebrow. I needed to go tell him why I was here. But just as I was standing up, Jim stood, too. He clinked his metal coffee mug with a fork to get everyone's attention.

My heart sank, realizing Jim was about to introduce me to the whole company.

"Everyone, this is Miss Emily Winslowe," Jim said. "She's joining our team as a guide. She's the daughter of Greg Winslowe—you might recognize that name for his first American ascent of Annapurna without oxygen and for being the expedition leader over at our frenemy, Winslowe Expeditions."

Luke's expression went from shock to accusation to hurt to anger. My heart thudded in nightmare slow motion.

"Emily has summited Everest six times, twice without oxygen," Jim continued. "Please make the time to introduce yourself over the next few days. She's one you want to be nice to because I hear she makes a mean high-altitude peanut butter fudge cookie."

I waved to everyone, then quickly sat in the chair next to Jim, my cheeks hot. I purposely avoided looking in the direction of where Luke was sitting, even though I could feel his eyes boring into me. The fleeting hurt that had crossed his face made my heart ache, but the anger that followed crushed me.

He was mad that I hadn't told him the news personally, and I didn't blame him. My mind churned, trying to figure out what I should do. Walk straight over and talk to him? Wait for him to leave, and then catch him alone later? Or—

Luke stood, stopping my thoughts in their tracks. Before I could act, he put his dish in the wash tub and stalked out of the tent without a word.

Chapter Twelve

I needn't have worried about being in close quarters with Luke: Global's large size and the separation of the four different teams into sub-camps made it so Luke and I wouldn't cross paths that much. In fact, in the past twenty-four hours we hadn't crossed paths at all. I was content to let this be, but at the same time, I couldn't stop replaying the expressions on his face at lunch yesterday. No matter how well everything else was going, I would not be at ease working for Global Adventurers until I patched things up between us.

I'd spent the rest of yesterday moving into my Global tent and filling out new-hire paperwork with the base camp manager. Today, I'd been stuck in the command center tent all morning, going through a mandatory company training, followed by a live-chat session with the human resources department to set up my accounts and finish the hiring process.

It was midafternoon by the time I caught up with the rest of the expedition out at the Nuptse ice field. All forty clients and a few of the yellow-jacketed guides were fanned out across the slope practicing self-arrests with their ice axes. Some of the Walkabout crew were out on the slope with cameras, and their big drone was flying overhead.

I walked toward the circle of guides gathered at the edge of the slope. Even though I now wore a handsome new Yellow Yeti jacket like the rest of them, it was going to take a long time to kick this feeling of joining a circus on opening day instead of traveling and training with the crew. Luke, I noticed, was not in the circle.

"Welcome to Global, Emily," said a man with a blond beard who was standing next to Norbu, the sirdar. "I'm Thom, the lead on-mountain guide." Unlike Winslowe Expeditions, where Dad was a part of the summit team, at Global, Jim stayed down in Base Camp to keep command and control of all four teams, hence the on-mountain lead guide position.

Thom introduced me to the rest of the guides and Sherpas in the huddle. It was one big blur of men in yellow jackets. By the time he finished, I was seeing double.

Literally.

Tyler, the last guy introduced, could be Thom's twin.

The man next to me laughed. He was the one I *would* be able to remember—Luke's behemoth friend who Thom had introduced as Hulk. Like me, he was one of the A-Team guides.

"Yes, they're twins," Hulk whispered as I looked back and forth between Thom and Tyler. "Tyler guides A-Team with us."

Of the Sherpas who were standing in the group, there were two Phurbas, plus a Dawa Lama and Ang Dawa. I'd have to ask the base camp manager for a roster to help me memorize names and faces.

"Phurba Sherpa is with A-Team, too," Hulk said, indicating the younger of the Phurbas, the one with the megawatt grin and the NASCAR bandana around his neck.

"Phurba Lama is with the UW team."

I nodded to the Phurbas, then listened to the guys' conversation for a while as I scanned across the hill to figure out which of the guides up there was Luke. He was the one farthest from us, going over the avalanche probing steps with a bunch of purple-hatted clients.

"Are all four groups going to be together on the mountain like this when we start rotations?" I asked Hulk.

"Kind of. The Cuban team will always be first because their climbers are fast and that keeps everyone else out of the way so the Walkabout crew can get their shots. The fourth team is the low-support group. They paid less, have fewer guides, and operate independently, though still under Jim's watch. A-Team and the UW team are the ones that have the most overlap on the mountain."

Out of the corner of my eye, I caught one of the clients sprinting down the slope and then jumping onto his bottom to go flying the rest of the way down the hill. I panicked for a second because he didn't have an ice ax in his hands, but then I realized his yells were more like whoops, and he was doing it on purpose. He was glissading, which is basically sledding without a sled. He wasn't gaining speed this way, so he tried rolling over to his stomach, looking like a penguin on a Slip 'N Slide.

If he had been trying to show off for the drone that had been overhead, it didn't work, because the minute he started messing around, the drone flew in the opposite direction.

"Meet Glen," Hulk said, nodding toward the client. "He's on A-Team."

"Glissading Glen," I said.

"Yep, that pretty much says it."

Hulk pointed out a few of the other A-Team clients, starting with the group of four businessmen who were all on second or third attempts to climb Everest. And then there was John Smith, which Hulk pronounced Johnsmith, who was "somehow related" to Global Adventurers's chief financial officer. Old Man Phil was the only client up on the hill who seemed to be taking the exercise seriously. "Cancer survivor," Hulk said. "He's a little off, but a nice guy, and he's worked hard to get here."

Jim arrived then from Base Camp and gathered everyone in. After a break to reapply sunscreen, he talked the clients through what to do if they fell into a crevasse while on the fixed line. Each of us guides took three clients and spread out along a practice crevasse that, unlike most real crevasses, had an actual bottom. While the clients put on their harnesses, I twisted some ice screws into the glacier and set up an anchor.

Luke's group was one away from mine, and I stealthily watched him for a minute as he finished building his group's anchor.

I guess I wasn't as stealthy as I thought because he looked directly at me. And even though his dark, side-paneled glacier sunglasses blocked his eyes completely, there was no mistaking that the anger was still there. My stomach churned.

I tried to catch Luke after we finished crevasse rescue practice, but he jetted out ahead with Hulk and Thom. I then tried to approach him after he filled his plate for dinner, but he pointedly walked in the opposite direction and went to sit with Glissading Glen at a two-person table.

Now I was back in my tent, sick with the knowledge that not crossing paths with Luke yesterday had not been coincidence but purposeful on his part. It made perfect sense for him to be mad. He shouldn't have had to find out about me working for Global from Jim's public announcement; he was my friend, and I should have made an effort to tell him as soon as I got the job despite being embarrassed about how I'd acted in his tent. Tomorrow at daybreak we'd both be at Global's puja ceremony. I'd catch him afterward, even if it meant doing something extreme to get him to talk to me.

I turned off my headlamp, but I was too restless to sleep, so I flipped over onto my back and stared up into the dark of the tent. The inside of this tent was exactly the same as my tent with Winslowe Expeditions, down to the clothesline of pictures across the ceiling and the waxed lettuce-box shelves. I should feel as much at home here as I did there. But I didn't. Not with unfamiliar clients in the tents surrounding me and my peers being guides I'd never been on a mountain with before. Not with that huge and intimidating main tent being the place where I'd be eating all meals when we were in Base Camp. And especially not while Luke was angry with me.

Tonight, I was as alone as after Amy's arrest, when the police had delivered me to that cold cement building with the metal bunk beds.

I felt around for my jacket and the front pocket where I kept my knife. On the end of the knife, looped through the eyehole at the bottom, was the very bracelet Luke had made me the day of the earthquake. I'd tied it there when it had fallen off.

I pulled the knife into my sleeping bag with me, twisting my fingers around and around the familiar cord. And that night, like so many others, I fell asleep thinking about what might have happened between the two of us if not for the earthquake.

Chapter Thirteen

At sunrise, we all gathered at the northern edge of Global City, around the chorten, which was a tower of glacier rock the Sherpas had built. The purpose of the puja ceremony was to ask Mother Chomolungma—Mount Everest—for safe passage this season and to apologize for the pricks of our ice axes, crampons, and ice screws upon her as we climbed.

Among the Sherpas, guides, clients, and support staff, we numbered nearly eighty, with each of us laying an ice ax next to the chorten to be blessed during the ceremony. I was superstitious and, like the Sherpas, had also added my crampons, climbing harness, mountaineering boots, and helmet to the piles of gear.

The Sherpas sat on air mattresses in concentric half circles around the chorten, with the clients in rows behind them, followed by the Western guides and support staff in the last rows. I hung back, trying to get a spot next to Luke, but he somehow ended up on the opposite side of the group from me.

The Walkabout film crew was already in place with

shoulder-borne cameras as Lama Rinpoche from the Tengboche Monastery started the thousand-year-old Tibetan Buddhist songs, prayers, and rituals.

I'm not sure how much Norbu had explained to the clients about the puja, but from my limited observation of him, it might not have been much. The Jim-Norbu dynamic was opposite of the Dad-Tshering dynamic; Norbu was a quiet, behind-the-scenes leader, whereas Jim was the gregarious, blunt one. Some of Global's clients had been to Everest before and would know what to expect, but I couldn't help feeling a little sorry for the ones who hadn't. It was very cold this morning, and these ceremonies could sometimes last more than two hours.

I closed my eyes and listened to the low, syncopated chanting. The sound was comforting and familiar, but it was also disconcerting because I was surrounded by strangers instead of people I knew well.

A pair of hands briefly squeezed my shoulders. I turned, hopeful Luke had decided to be friendly on the occasion of this important ceremony, but it was just Dad. Silently he took a seat behind me. It was considerate of him to come to Global's puja. My loneliness lessened. I was proud to have him see me here, sitting in the guides' row.

I closed my eyes again, feeling the cold wind on my face and hearing the caws of the crows floating above. As Dad had taught me long ago, I visualized our safe passage on the mountain. I envisioned an early start on summit day under a crisp and cloudless sky, stars lighting our way through the dark. Our clients would be out of their tents on time, ready to go. All would have found a way to drift to sleep for two or three hours beforehand. No one would be plagued by coughs or other symptoms of altitude sickness. There wouldn't be any traffic jams on the fixed line, and in the invigorating cold, we'd make steady progress upward.

On this day, Luke would be ahead of my A-Team with his UW climbers. Our teams would pass each other on the UW team's way down. His clients would be exhausted but on a high from their minutes at the top of the world. The sun would have just risen. It would be Luke's third summit, and I'd be about to break through to my seventh.

Between his glacier sunglasses and oxygen mask, I wouldn't be able to see much of his face, but I'd know from his raised cheeks that he was smiling. I'd be smiling, too—beaming—because he'd done it and my clients were so close and all of them were going to make it free and clear.

He'd hold up his hand for a high five, and I'd grab it and pull him in for a squishy hug across our marshmallow suits. Another hug that would last longer than it should and be oh so delirious because of the lack of oxygen.

I popped my eyes open.

Puja was for meditating, praying, and visualizing. Not… fantasizing.

I refocused my thoughts, but now only bad things were coming into my head.

I saw those four mountaineering boots, two of them green, at the cave below the summit on the Tibet side. I saw swatches of fabric in the middle of a snowy plain—swatches so small, the clients might miss them, but I'd know from previous trips which corpse lay below. I saw grotesque frostbite injuries. I heard the scream and thud of that poor Portuguese climber who slipped off the rope on Lhotse Face last year. I heard the crash of the avalanche in the icefall three years ago that instantly claimed the lives of sixteen Sherpas.

In an attempt to distract myself from the images, I watched the people in front of me. April, Walkabout's short, blond camerawoman, was filming Lama Rinpoche. Hulk told me yesterday that she was a pilot and was the one who operated the drone. Doc sat near the front with Claudia, the only other female client with Global this year. In the first row, Phurba was fiddling with his NASCAR bandana, and Glissading Glen and some of the other A-Team clients behind him were having a hard time sitting still, too. My eyes naturally tracked over to the other side of the group, where Luke sat with his eyes closed as he listened to Lama Rinpoche. Despite his closed eyes, he was not relaxed. His jaw was too hard, his back too straight.

As the puja progressed, the tone took a turn for the festive. I felt anything but. The music picked up, and Lama Rinpoche gave the signal to unfurl the eight spokes of prayer flags that flew from the top of the chorten to anchor points on the ground behind us. Jim and Norbu passed around bowls, and we all scooped handfuls of dry rice from them. Lama Rinpoche sprinkled oil over our equipment, with April and her camera scrambling to keep up with him. The music grew louder. Some of the Sherpas cheered.

On Lama Rinpoche's cue, everyone threw rice into the air, and for a split second it was like time was suspended before the rice hailed back down on us. Then the chang came out, along with cans of Nepal's national beer, Everest. It didn't matter that it was still early in the morning, everyone was in full party mode.

Like a robot, I went forward for my dip of tsampa barley flour. Doc smeared flour across my jaw to symbolize a white beard of old age. I faked a smile and did the same for her. I plopped some on Dad's face, then ducked out of the way as he pretended to dump a handful on top of my braided pigtails.

Then, we were all smearing tsampa on each other: Sherpas to clients, guides to Sherpas, Sherpas to everyone. Now, it was abundantly clear who the veteran Everest clients were. They were the ones escalating the tsampa tradition into an all-out food fight. The first-timers caught on quickly and joined in. Today, I didn't want any part of it.

I scanned the crowd for Luke, but he'd managed to slip away already. *Damn it.*

I drifted toward the edge of the melee so I could sneak back to my tent. Without warning, Luke stepped in front of me. I was taken aback, but I also knew this was my chance to put things right. I swallowed, getting ready to speak.

"Don't tell me Greg arranged this job for you," he said.

He was mad because he thought I'd gotten a handout? Never mind about putting things right. I turned on my heel and walked away, burning with an anger I wasn't accustomed to. *You mean, arranged this job for me like he arranged your fancy Kathmandu boarding school? Like he helped get your full-ride scholarship to University of Washington?*

"Sorry, Emily, wait. I shouldn't have said that," he said, practically yelling to be heard above the blaring music.

"If you must know, no, my dad did not arrange this for me. In fact, he didn't want me to do it."

"Please, let me take those words back," Luke begged. I bet he was worried about his karma. And he should be. I'd been about to apologize, and he'd attacked me.

"I was hurt you didn't tell me," he said.

"Like how you didn't tell me you were coming to Everest this year until I was *at your house*."

His shoulders slumped in defeat, which was satisfying. I crossed my arms on my chest and waited for a response.

"I wanted it to be a surprise," he said.

"We've covered that already. It was a surprise, all right."

"As was hearing Jim say you were guiding with us. Completely out of the blue. We were together the entire evening before that, and you never said anything. You let me go on and on about the pitfalls of guiding, and the whole time you knew you were going to be working for Global."

Oh god. He wasn't mad that I didn't tell him before Jim announced it; he thought I'd been *lying* to him.

"No, no, no. I *didn't* know that night. It wasn't until the next morning that I got the job."

Luke frowned, like he didn't quite believe me.

"You were actually the one who made me think of asking Jim in the first place," I said in a rush. "Because of what you said during checkers about the permit snafu. I guessed that you guys might need an extra guide to keep your guide-to-client ratios, and I needed a job right away. So I came up here and asked about it."

"Oh," he said, still a little taken aback. "I'm surprised you did that."

"Me, too. But I told you, I'm not in a very good place right now. Necessity makes things easier."

"True." He shifted his weight.

"I'm sorry, Luke. I should have found a way to tell you before Jim announced it. If I had, you would have known how it all went down."

"It's okay. I shouldn't have jumped to conclusions. And I'm really sorry about what I said about Greg. You know I think the world of him."

"I know."

"Are you mad?"

"No."

"You're sure?"

"Yes. And what about you? Are you going to stop with the vicious looks and avoiding me?"

He winced, but then his mischievous left dimple appeared. "No one would guess this, but you can be pretty feisty when you put your mind to it."

"Sorry," I said, returning his smile.

We looked at each other. Behind him, the juniper smoke from the chorten curled up in a helix. He might not still be angry, but he was still *something*. Despite having known him forever, I couldn't decipher what that something was. I bit my lip.

"Stay right here, okay?" he said.

He walked into the heart of the celebration and came back with a small mound of tsampa in his hand.

"Oh no you don't," I cried, blocking his hands so he couldn't throw it on me.

"I would never."

I relaxed and squared myself in front of him.

He dipped his fingertips in the flour and stepped closer. At five ten, he was only two inches taller than me, which put our faces quite near.

Slowly, he drew a line with the flour from my ear to my chin. My blood rushed at his touch. "For safety, summit success, and long life," he said in Sherpa as he spread the cool, silken flour along the other side of my jaw.

I scooped flour from his palm, repeating the benediction before tracing careful lines down each side of his jaw. His skin was warm and smooth, coated in the flour that others had layered there before me. Flecks of golden amber shone in his eyes. I took it one step further. I dipped my fingers back in the tsampa and drew a line across his forehead. A line that I traced as slowly as I could so it would make the contact last longer.

I knew I shouldn't be doing this. Allowing myself to dream. Or maybe it was just that I was still searching for closure from two years ago. But in this moment, this gravity-like connection between us was in control, and it felt right to be touching him.

I ran out of forehead, so I lowered my hand. We were just a foot apart.

What if I'd gone to Townsend College last year like I was supposed to? We would have been in Washington together after being apart only one year instead of two. Would that have changed things, made us keep closer in touch, like the distance was temporary, not permanent?

But, then, that *had* been our exact scenario at the point we'd said good-bye after the earthquake, and Luke had never used the email address I'd given him.

"Why did you never email?" I asked.

His eyes searched my face, as if what he found on it would determine how he answered.

"I did email," he said finally. "But you never wrote back."

My heartbeats thudded in my eardrums.

The sounds of the puja party returned, along with my awareness of the people around us. Which included the men of the A-Team descending on Luke and me, holding handfuls of tsampa like snowballs they were about to launch at us. I squealed and made a break for it.

Chapter Fourteen

Instead of going to the big top for breakfast after the puja, I went right to my tent, practically drunk from Luke's words. His email to me must have been after my old account was hacked, which was months after we said good-bye, but he had written nonetheless.

The signals that had passed between us at the puja were too powerful to have solely been my imagination. But it didn't make sense that I could be feeling that from him when he had a girlfriend. I mean, if I were his girlfriend, I would not have been okay with several of the things we'd done so far this season. Moonlight hike? Squishing together under his sleeping bag? A practically sensual application of tsampa flour? I guarantee that was *not* how he would put tsampa on Doc's face or Claudia's face.

Luke may be flirty and charismatic, but if he were in a relationship, surely he would keep a greater distance from me, despite us having been platonic friends for ten years. Either that, or he'd changed.

I got out my phone and went right to ^Olivia200x^'s Circ

account. There she was in all of her curly, honey-blond glory and a model-perfect outfit.

Olivia was a girl who liked to put herself in the pivot point of her Circs—self-Circing. Trekkers did this all the time. It required the use of a three-foot self-Circ stick, and the person taking the Circ had to spin in a circle holding the pole while grinning up at themselves on the phone. In her latest, she was in a courtyard at UW, turning slowly and pointing behind herself as a poster for an upcoming baseball game passed in the background.

Was she or wasn't she Luke's girlfriend?

If I really wanted to figure this out, I had to come at it methodically, like a private investigator. I scrolled Olivia's feed all the way back to the month Luke had arrived in Washington.

The first time I found him in one of her Circs was eighteen months back. They had gone hiking a few times. Little nature walks on wide, flat, sometimes paved paths. Paths that really shouldn't be tagged, as she had, with #hiking or #trail.

Then, twelve months back, there was a #hiking Circ with a glimpse of the two of them holding hands. My heart sank, but I kept scrolling. I figured out that the Circ Luke had sent me once from a ferry boat in the Puget Sound with the snow-covered Olympics in the background had been a trip she'd been on, too. I watched several more that also lined up with #YCCM Circs. Olivia had captioned most of these with #boyfriend.

Ten months back, there was a kissing Circ. It wasn't tagged with his name, but it was definitely him. A full-blown co-self-Circ of the two of them kissing. I stopped watching as soon as I realized what it was, but oh man, if only I could admit how I'd come to see this one, I would give him hell that he'd allowed it to happen.

There was another hand-holding picture, then a Circ

that Olivia had taken from shore of a paddleboarder out on the water. This lined up with the #YCCM Circ he'd posted once from atop a paddleboard. I switched over to his feed and found that Circ. I played it, paying attention to when the camera flowed past the shoreline, and, sure enough, in the background there was a lone blonde in a heavy winter jacket, sitting on a blanket spread across the rocks.

I wanted that to be me.

Except I wouldn't have sat on the shore and skipped out on the paddleboarding. We'd have plenty of time to sit on the blanket together afterward.

I stayed on Luke's feed, reexamining it. His Circs were almost exclusively #YCCM Circs, or work-related ones for the UW outdoor recreation center or his job on Mount Rainier. He'd never once used the hashtag *girlfriend* or tagged her—or anyone—in his Circs.

I returned to Olivia's much juicier profile and scrolled on. At around five months ago, I wasn't seeing him in the background of her Circs as much. When he was there, she wasn't using the boyfriend hashtag. And her Circs no longer lined up with #YCCM Circs.

I gave a silent fist pump. The information wasn't solid proof, but it was enough to give me hope.

Chapter Fifteen

It was a gorgeous day in the mountains with crystal clear views as we shepherded our clients on an acclimatization hike up a foothill near Base Camp. Jim had given the Sherpas a day off, so each of the guides had three clients. Mine were Old Man Phil, Glissading Glen, and Johnsmith.

The lack of wind and the bright sun today made it warm enough that I was hiking in nothing but a light fleece jacket, stretch pants, and a pair of gaiters around my calves and boots. In the distance, the sharp profile of Makalu was practically glistening in the sunlight. *This is what I love*, I thought.

Looking back, I noticed Phil, the nicest of the Global clients I'd met so far, had stopped to rest again.

I backtracked to reach him. His breathing had a distinct gurgle, but that was not uncommon here. Most of us would have chronic coughs by the time we left the mountain. Living on the side of Mount Everest slowly deteriorates your body. Even the Sherpas aren't fully immune to being as high as Base Camp for such an extended period of time.

"How's it going?" I asked.

Phil leaned on his ice ax like a cane. "I don't think I've ever…breathed…this hard…"

"That's what eighteen-thousand feet of elevation will do for you."

He nodded, looking at the distance remaining between us and the top of the snowy ridge. The fastest clients had already reached the top and were descending. "If you can manage it, it's better to adjust your pace slower so you can keep moving rather than trying to go faster and having to stop for breaks. When we're up on Everest, this will help you stay warmer."

He got moving again. Very slowly but steadily. I went to check on my other two charges.

Glissading Glen had started out in the lead of A-Team climbers but quickly burned out and was now steadily tied for second-to-last place with Phil. Johnsmith was moving slowly, too, and favoring a leg. I had already recommended that he talk to Hulk about it when we returned to Base Camp, since Hulk had majored in exercise science in college.

When I returned to the end of the line again, Phil was moving, but so slowly I could probably crawl on my hands and knees faster. He stuttered something I couldn't understand.

"What?" I asked.

"Just having a bad day. Not good sleep," he tried again after a breath. It wasn't a good sign if he was struggling at this elevation. Even the lowest of the four camps on Mount Everest was several thousand feet higher than where we were right now.

"Is Jim tracking stats today?" Phil asked.

I winced at the distress in his voice, and I felt for him. We weren't officially recording the clients' performances today, but unofficially we were always watching. If Jim didn't think one of the clients was performing well enough during acclimatization, he wouldn't allow them on the summit attempt, and their $82,000 fee would not be refunded.

"I wouldn't worry about your stats right now," I told him. "Today is casual. You're right that bad sleep can really have an impact. And it's the altitude affecting you. That's the whole reason we do hikes like this. Keep paying attention to the basics this week. Drink more water, rest whenever you can, eat even when you don't feel like it. The better you take care of your body, the stronger it will be as you acclimatize."

He nodded. "Thanks, Emily."

The Cuban team passed us then, heading down. Doc was right on their heels, the fastest of the UW team today.

"Hey there, MiniBoss," she called. It clearly wasn't easy for her to hike at this pace, but I was proud of her for doing so well.

Up ahead, Johnsmith was sitting down in the snow. To reach him, I had to pass behind Glissading Glen, who was unabashedly taking a leak in the middle of the boot-packed path.

"How are you doing?" I asked when I got to Johnsmith.

"My leg's tight, but I'm okay otherwise."

He finished stretching, and I gave him a hand up and walked with him for a while.

The next grouping that passed us on the way down was the rest of the UW team. Luke and Hulk were at the rear, between the fastest A-Team clients and slowest UW clients. I high-fived both of them. Instead of continuing down with Hulk, Luke stopped to talk to me.

"What's the deal with Phil?" he asked.

"He said he had a bad night's sleep."

"That's all he could come up with? He'd better hope Thom doesn't say anything to Jim about how far back he is."

"He better not!"

Luke groaned. "Don't tell me you have a favorite client already."

"No, but I like him. He seems different."

"He's a lawyer, so he's pretty much the same as the rest of them."

Same as the rest of them meaning rich, and sometimes rich *and* entitled *and* inexperienced in the mountains. Almost all our past clients were doctors, lawyers, or successful businessmen.

"Yeah, but he's really nice, like a grandpa." Not *my* grandpa, per se, but *a* grandpa.

When Glissading Glen caught up to us, Luke and I walked along with him, though off to the side. Luke pulled out his radio and asked Thom if it was okay if he finished out with A-Team.

"Sure, no problem. Your Huskies are on fire today," Thom replied.

After a while, Luke was starting to nudge ahead of me.

"Just so we're clear, this is not a race," I hissed. "I have to stick with these guys."

He stopped and raised his gloved hands innocently. I shook my head at him with a smile that continued to warm my face as we walked.

Ever since Luke told me he'd emailed, I'd been looking for a chance to re-open the topic. I needed to explain why I hadn't responded, and I wanted to press him for details. It wasn't as easy as that, though, seeing as we hadn't been alone since the puja. We weren't alone now, but we were out of earshot of anyone else, and that was as good as we'd ever get on Mount Everest, so I decided to go for it.

"That email you sent," I said. "I never got it. My account was hacked."

"Oh?"

"I think it was from an internet café in Thailand. I had to get a new email account."

"What'd you change it to? MiniBoss at WinsloweExpeditons dot com?"

I snorted.

"So you have an excuse why you never wrote me back," he said, "but how come *you* never contacted *me*?"

"I didn't have your email address."

"And it would have been impossible to get your hands on it, right?"

Touché.

There were many ways I could have gotten hold of him if I'd applied myself. But I never had. Circs were safe. Circs were centered in the world we shared—the world of big mountains and pipe dreams. Circs were like a secret language. To communicate by email or chat or Skype was real life. And in real life, with him surrounded by real Americans, it would be clear to him that we belonged to different worlds, and our relationship wouldn't be the same.

We walked in thoughtful quietness, our steps perfectly matched in the tattoo of our creaking mountaineering boots and the slush of the sun-warmed snow beneath the points of our crampons. Sometimes when I walked in the mountains, my mind became so still that it was like I was meditating. Other times, I daydreamed of climbing *World's 19ers* mountains, of Luke, and quite frequently of that little white bungalow that existed only in my mind. That was where my mind drifted now as I walked next to Luke.

Though the house was imaginary, I knew it as well as if I had been there dozens of times. It was slightly disheveled inside and out, with vegetables growing in the front yard among gladiolas and sunflowers. There was a rope hammock and rocker on the porch and a pull-up bar across one of the bedroom doorframes. In my daydreams, I'd pictured bonfires in the yard with good friends, drinking hot chocolate on the porch in the earliest hours of the morning, and pulling weeds in the garden while throwing a ball for a dog—my dog.

I saw packing for an expedition while a loaf of honey

wheat bread baked in the oven. I would actually enjoy the process because it wouldn't involve packing up the entire contents of a hostel room or campsite. I would be taking only the things I needed for the one trip because I'd be returning to this same place at the end. It was home. A real home.

Luke and I continued silently on autopilot until I realized we were almost on the heels of Hulk's group.

"We're going too fast," I said. We stopped and looked downslope to make sure my clients were doing okay. Johnsmith was limping along steadily, and to my surprise, Phil was pretty much keeping pace about twenty feet behind Glissading Glen.

"I had him eat two gel packs," I explained.

"Jeez, did you lace them with something?"

"What, like dexamethasone gel?"

"Yeah, good idea. Dex-gel. We should start a business."

I looked at him standing there against the backdrop of the stunning south-facing slopes. His clothes were new and bright, and the way he stood was so confident and at ease. Standing just like this, he could be in a catalog, one of the fancy, magazine-like Esplanade Equipment catalogs.

"What?" he asked.

Was my research right? Do you really not have a girlfriend anymore?

"Nothing. I was thinking about Doc. Did you see her practically up with the Cubans today?"

"Yeah. She's on fire, but I still think she's out of her mind for doing this."

"You're kind of a jerk, you know."

"I don't see why *anyone* would pay that kind of money to climb this mountain when the experience is way better on pretty much any other mountain in the Himalayas. Especially Doc. She knows better!"

"True. I mean, why not climb Pumori instead?"

"Oh, you and your sweetheart Pumori."

I cocked my head. "Is it the altitude, or is that jealousy I hear?"

"Absolutely not."

"You *should* be jealous. Look at that ridgeline!" I said, gesturing toward it. "Twenty-five-thousand feet of uncrowded yet perfectly accessible Himalayan bluebird vertical."

He grinned and gave me a playful shove. I wanted to fall into the flirtation and shove him right back.

But first, I needed to be certain about Olivia. Asking him directly was the only way to know for sure, and that was out of the question. I'd have to be more creative, and I had an idea.

"I don't think I've ever taken a Circ of my sweetheart Pumori before," I said. "Let me grab my self-Circ stick."

His eyebrows popped above his glacier glasses. "*You* have a self-Circ stick?"

"Yeah. It's an extra-long one."

"You don't do self-Circs."

"Not *yet*. I just got the stick."

"Did you eat some of that dex-gel you gave Phil?"

"What are you talking about?"

"You're off your rocker."

"Come on, you can be in it, too."

"Um. No. No self-Circs for me, thank you."

"I've seen you in self-Circs."

"Not by choice."

"Someone held a gun to your head?"

"It was a girlfriend. And yes, pretty much."

Was a girlfriend? This was promising, but I needed the 100 percent answer.

"Somebody who used to be your girlfriend?" I asked. "Or a girlfriend who you persuaded to stop taking self-Circs with you?"

"Now look who's jealous."

"Don't you wish."

His dimples were out. *Just slay me now.*

"It was somebody who used to be my girlfriend."

To hide my triumphant smile, I squatted down and pretended to dig through my day pack for the made-up self-Circ stick.

"Well, shoot," I said, zipping up my pack. "I must have left it in my tent."

When Luke looked down at me, there was a woman reflected in his sunglasses. A woman with an incredible smile and beautiful hair that fanned across her shoulders and glinted red in the sunlight. A woman who didn't look anything like the boyish teenage girl from *Vertical View* magazine and who matched the confidence and ease in the mountains that I'd admired in him just moments ago.

Was that really me? Was this what I looked like to Luke?

It was like a capsule of golden happiness had been snapped open inside me. I still struggled with how accomplished he was compared to me, but from this perspective, I could see something different. What if he didn't view me as a failure to launch who had balked at getting a higher education, but as a strong and driven woman who might someday be the first to climb the Top Five without oxygen.

Chapter Sixteen

Luke was already waiting at the Everest Base Camp signs when I arrived for the workout we'd planned over dinner last night.

"You ready for this?" he asked.

Bold with yesterday's confirmation that he did not have a girlfriend, I met his eyes and held them. "Am *I* ready for this? The question is, are you?"

We lined up on the trail. He pressed some buttons on his watch and then looked at me over his shoulder, his eyes flirtatious and taunting: *catch me if you can.*

My heart fluttered. *You Can't Catch Me.*

His watch beeped, and we were off in a sprint up the Base Camp trail. I loved the feeling of the freezing morning air searing my lungs.

Sprinting at this elevation was closer to trotting than running, but we pressed on as fast as we could until we reached the place where the glacier dead-ended into the fearsome Khumbu Icefall. Luke won by a few steps.

"You had a head start," I said.

"Uh-huh."

We jogged slowly back down the trail to the Base Camp signs where we stretched before the next round. This time, when Luke clicked his watch, I was ready. I elbowed him out of my way so I could stride ahead. I reached the end first and looked back at him with a smirk.

"Don't even think that you won that one," he said as soon as we'd caught our breath. "You were disqualified the second you brought those elbows out."

"Whatever. One more?"

He groaned, but I knew he wouldn't say no.

We took the final lap much slower. There was a fine line between keeping in shape to counteract the languid Base Camp life and not exerting ourselves too much, which would cause further muscle degradation from two months of living at this altitude.

Grabbing our packs, we went back up-glacier to find a good spot for pull-ups and abs. Since there was no pull-up bar in camp, we made our own using our ice-climbing axes and a tall block of ice.

"Fifteen?" I asked.

"You can't do fifteen."

"Watch me."

We pulled off our gloves, gripped the ends our ice axes, hung by our arms, and started the pull-ups. We both did fifteen.

"Jeez, Emily," he said with a whistle.

I was starting to get an altitude headache, but I couldn't have kept the smile off my face if I tried.

Over on a flat section, we spread out two backpacking air mattresses and rotated through crunches, lunges, and planks.

On the next set of pull-ups I did an extra.

"You didn't tell me we were going to sixteen," he protested.

"Seventeen next time," I said boldly. "If you can hack it."

"Of course I can." He eyed me. A tingle ran through my body. "I don't think *you* can."

I scoffed.

"Let's make it more interesting," he said. "If one of us makes it and the other one doesn't, then that person owes a favor."

I wasn't sure I could do seventeen ice-ax pull-ups with arms that were already tired from the previous two sets, but with how much he had slowed down on the last round, I figured that I had a better chance than he did.

"Okay, deal."

He reached out so we could shake on it. His hand was strong, hot, and callused. Another tingle ran through my body.

We did our next round of exercises and then went back to the ice axes.

"We're going one at a time," I said. "So I can make sure you don't cheat."

"Me?" He flashed both of his dimples, and my mouth went dry.

He faced the ice, gripped the handles of his axes, and began lifting himself easily and steadily. The form-fitting, long-sleeved performance top he wore did nothing to hide the definition and stretch of his lats, shoulders, and back muscles. His shirt gradually rode up, giving me a peek of his tan, taut waist, beneath which his workout pants cupped the tight, perfect bubble of his rear end.

I swallowed. The power of his body was incredible, and watching him this way, I saw there were nuances about him that I did not know in my role as just a friend. I wanted to know those nuances, too. And I wanted to be free to study him at all times, not just at times when I thought he wouldn't notice.

Luke hit ten and was still pulling steadily. He slowed at thirteen, and by sixteen, he couldn't pull higher than a forty-five degree angle. Just as I was imagining what sort of reward I might demand of him, he rallied and pulled the rest of the way up.

He hopped off the axes like it had been easy as pie. I shook my head. Without thinking, I reached for his bicep to give him a painful pinch. His eyes flew down to my hand on his arm.

It was like Luke and I were two halves of a strip of Velcro. Each time even a single of the tiny hooks caught, I was incapacitated. Imagine what it would be like if we were closer, if even more hooks caught…

To distract myself from that line of thinking, I did some arm stretches and made a show of getting ready for my turn.

"Whenever you're ready, MiniBoss."

I wiped my mind blank and stepped up to the axes, intending to soar through the burn by going as fast as I could. That got me to twelve. I suffered through thirteen and fourteen. Had it not been for the contest, I would have given in to my quaking arms right there. Crookedly, I pulled up to fifteen. I went for sixteen, but nothing happened. I exhaled and tried again.

Oh no. I couldn't fail at *two* short of the goal! I wiggled, giving each bicep a fraction of a second of rest, then pulled again. Ever so slowly, I raised up through the angles, the exertion making me exhale in ugly puffs. I dropped down hard and fast, which left me in a dead hang. I didn't even have enough strength to keep my grip on the handles. I was slipping…

I put my feet down and stood up. *Damn it.*

I turned around. He was grinning like the Cheshire Cat.

"Congratulations, Skywalker," I said. "You're the champion. What are you going to make me do?"

Still grinning, he shrugged.

"I don't want this hanging over my head, so you better decide."

"But I don't know yet."

I scowled.

"Hey, if you don't like the terms, then maybe you shouldn't go around claiming you can do seventeen pull-ups."

That accent of his! I'd gladly do anything he pleased so long as he kept talking.

"You have to decide," I said, still trying to play it tough on the outside. "Before we go back."

"Well then, we can't go back yet."

Good call.

He dragged the air mattresses up to the top of the pull-up ice block. I followed.

We put on down jackets, hats, and mittens to avoid getting chilled, since we were both sweaty. From where we were sitting, we had a primo view of the entire glacier and Base Camp.

"The Everest Base Camp signs should go here instead of down there," I said. "This would be a much better money-shot for the trekkers, don't you think?"

"Yeah," was all he said. No quip about them not being able to make it the extra half mile to this spot or speculating about what would happen if Pokémon Go hid a character at the bottom of the icefall or anything like that.

He had pushed his sunglasses onto his head. There were lines of tension around his eyes, and I wondered why. I had the urge to reach for his hand. An urge so strong that I had to tuck my hands inside my sleeves to keep myself from doing it.

We both took sips from his water bottle and split the four gel packets I'd brought. I assumed we'd head back down to Global City after we finished with the gel, but he didn't make a move to stand up.

"Global's pretty different than Winslowe Expeditions," he said. "It's gotta be kind of weird for you."

"It is. But not in a bad way. I'm just happy to have the job. It would be nice if I could find another job with Global Adventurers after the season is over."

"That's not a bad idea. They're a huge company, so they probably have lots of openings. And their headquarters is in Seattle, which is convenient."

"I'm sure it was weird for you working for them, too. I mean, you're used to Winslowe Expeditions style."

"Yes, but Global owns the company I guide for on Rainier, and I already knew their policies and some of the people."

"Hulk?"

"Yeah. We guided on Rainier together last summer. And Theo—he's the redhead with Walkabout—is a friend of one of my roommates. I also know most of the UW clients because I helped them train this winter."

I sighed. "All the faces—that part's hard. But I know I'll recognize everyone eventually, and the clients and staff have been so nice. I just hope I fit in okay."

He gave a little laugh.

"What?"

"Of course you fit in. Everyone loves you."

Not Americans. I had never fit in among my peers as a child, and even though I got along well with fellow mountain people, I suspected that regular city dwellers would still see me as an odd duck. Further, I was quiet around people I didn't know. Luke, on the other hand, was gregarious. Everyone always took an instant liking to him.

"*You're* the one everyone loves," I said.

"No, not everyone. The Global Sherpas don't love me at all. Haven't you noticed?"

I shook my head.

"It's nothing overt. They're Buddhists. They would never say anything. But I can tell."

"That doesn't make any sense."

"It does, though." He fiddled with his water bottle. "Think about it. I went off to the U.S., and I'm back in Nepal within two years, earning U.S. wages and hanging out with the *sahibs* while they haul my shit—literally—off the mountain. You just don't do that if you were raised here. You don't come back to Everest on the *sahib* side with a Western expedition."

Oh my god, I hadn't even considered this. If anything, I assumed he'd get along better with the Sherpas since he could speak their language. This explained the worry lines around his eyes.

"Would it have been the same if you were with Winslowe Expeditions this year?"

"I don't know. It was kind of pushing it there at the end because of my schooling in Kathmandu and how I wasn't doing the same level of manual labor once I was old enough. I don't even consider myself a Buddhist anymore. But I'm related to a lot of the Winslowe Expeditions Sherpas, and that makes it different. The Global Sherpas are not from Tengboche. They're not my clan."

He was playing it off casually, but I knew him better than that.

Luke nudged me with his leg. "Hey, don't worry, they're good guys. And they'll be nothing but great to you."

"I don't care about me. I just feel bad that—"

"No. I don't blame them. All they know of me is I'm the jerk who left the Khumbu only to come back to rape the mountain along with the other Westerners. I was pretty sure it would be like this, and it is."

And to think he'd put himself in this position just so he'd be able to come back here and check on Mingma and Pasang.

He watched me closely. "I knew what I was getting into,"

he repeated.

I nodded, and then something clicked. The worry lines weren't because of the Sherpas. They were because today was April nineteenth. The day Luke's Dad had died on Cho Oyu.

"Today's the day, isn't it?" I asked.

He looked into the distance. Toward the west, where Cho Oyu resided in China, at the far reach of the Mahalangur Range. He nodded.

It was as much as had ever passed between us about his dad.

"I'm sorry," I said.

"It shouldn't matter to me. I have hardly any memories of him. Not like you. You were twice as old."

He was talking about Amy. After all these years, he still assumed that I'd come to the Himalayas because my mother had died. So did everyone else. But Amy hadn't died in a tragic accident. She hadn't died at all.

I had no desire to hash over the details of what had happened ten years ago, but now that Luke and I were older, I also knew it wasn't okay to let this go on. Sometime—not on the anniversary of his father's death—I would tell him the truth about Amy.

Luke pulled his cell phone and earbuds out of his pack, offering me the left side. Without looking at the screen, I knew for certain that he would play Jackal Legs. And I was right. My heart skipped a beat.

I kept thinking about what he said about Global's Sherpas. Despite being a very direct person—which, by Khumbu standards, was practically the same as being aggressive—Luke was considerate and sincere, and he'd always been popular in Tengboche and at our Winslowe Expeditions camp.

I didn't know if I would have had the nerve to put myself in a similar situation. In fact, I *hadn't* had the nerve. It had been one of the reasons I'd always dreaded college. I would have been so out of place among the American college students and a randomly assigned roommate who would probably be a lot like Olivia. Someone who would see me as a weird outsider, just like my classmates in elementary school had. I may like crafts and baking, but I had no interest in or was clueless about everything else: fashion, makeup, guys, trends, partying, having female friends, dieting. I'd spent my life in remote locations and almost exclusively surrounded by men; all I knew about being a woman—an American woman—was from watching movies and reading *Going on Eighteen*.

Luke and I had been listening to Jackal Legs for almost twenty minutes when he paused the music in the middle of a song.

"I know what I want for my pull-up favor," he said. His eyes flicked over to me.

"What?"

"Peanut butter fudge cookies."

"Seriously?"

"Yes."

"You could demand anything in the world and all you want is a batch of cookies?"

"Yeah," he said. His dimples showed faintly. I wanted to skim the back of my hand across them. "I haven't had one of your peanut butter fudge cookies in two years."

"Okay, but you'll have to wait until I can go down to Dad's camp. I'm pretty sure Randall wouldn't let a guide bake cookies in his gourmet kitchen."

"Deal."

We shook hands for the second time this morning, this time through mittens. His eyes were slightly narrowed, much like they'd been at Mingma's house when I first turned around and saw him in the doorway. It was like he was testing me somehow. I challenged myself to hold his gaze, and as I did so, my pulse reverberated through my body like the beats of a drum. Did he like what he saw? Was I passing the test?

I reminded myself that he did not have a girlfriend, and I pushed further. "What did you say in the email you sent me?"

"Which email?"

"There was more than one?"

He hesitated before answering, as if choosing his words carefully. "Two. But one I never sent."

"Let's start with the one you sent."

"It pretty much just said *hi*."

Well, that was anticlimactic. His eyes bent into half-moons, knowing that he'd gotten to me.

"*Okay.* And what about the other one?"

"Wouldn't you just love to know? And I'm not going to tell you."

"Oh come on!"

"You never answered my question."

"About what?"

"About why you never emailed me, not even to tell me you were taking a gap year. Greg has my UW email address. So does Doc."

I couldn't just point-blank tell him that I'd been afraid I wouldn't keep his interest in real life. That I'd stuck to the safety of Circs rather than attempt more and risk losing a connection that was solid. To tell him this was too deep. Too revealing. And too dangerous, considering we had another six weeks of working closely together.

I couldn't take the risk of being wrong about the attraction I sensed between us, of revealing things that I could not take back. Instead, I dodged answering him by giving a shrug of feigned bafflement and a wide-eyed, innocent smile.

He shook his head and played along, but I could tell he was disappointed.

Chapter Seventeen

"Miss Winslowe," a man hissed. The tent shook.

"Miss Winslowe Emily," he repeated. I flipped over and popped my head out of the door. It was Cook-Phurba.

"Doc Teresa's in the kitchen," he said. "Eggplants. Red sauce."

I groaned. Doc used to do an eggplant parmesan extravaganza once a season for us at Winslowe Expeditions. And by *extravaganza*, I mean a kitchen disaster of epic proportions.

"Please, come," Cook-Phurba begged.

"Okay, I'll be there in a few minutes."

I reluctantly crawled out of my sleeping bag and put on my camp boots. I was tired from the workout this morning and could have used about three more hours of napping in the nirvana of my sun-warmed tent.

If I was going to be sucked into the latest reiteration of eggplant parmesan extravaganza, there's no reason Luke shouldn't be, too. After all, Doc was one of *his* clients.

I retied my ponytail and marched over to the UW section.

I shook Luke's tent with a one-two rhythm, which had always been like a secret doorbell between us. Groggily, he poked his head out.

"Surprise! It's eggplant parmesan night, and Doc needs help."

"No," he groaned.

Doc's beloved eggplant parmesan recipe had been a thank-you gift from a knee restoration patient who claimed his family owned an Italian restaurant in Seattle. Although it was the world's most complicated recipe, it never tasted very good, and Luke and I had a theory that the "secret recipe" had come straight off one of those chintzy cooking websites where they don't even test their own recipes.

"Come on. Get up," I said.

Doc spotted us the second we stepped into the big top, waving us over to where she was grating a monstrous pile of parmesan. Luke and I exchanged a knowing look.

"Where's Randall?" I asked.

"I told him to take the night off. He went down to Lobuche for a hit of oxygen and civilization."

Good thing. Eggplant parmesan for the number of people at Global was quite an undertaking. Already, the kitchen was destroyed. Cook-Phurba looked on, wringing his hands.

"It's okay. She does this every year," I assured him in Sherpa.

I eyed the two boxes of eggplants that still hadn't been cut. There were probably forty of them. "I can't believe Jim let you order all this stuff."

"This is nothing compared to what Randall orders daily."

"Randall's a professional, Doc."

The parmesan rind flew out of Doc's hand. She lunged to grab it, almost knocking the entire pile of grated cheese to the floor. "Are you going to get in here and help or not?"

Luke and I each carried a box of eggplants to one of the

largest tables. He mangled his first eggplant, so I slid closer and walked him through the steps of slicing them properly. We had a lot of eggplants to get through and quickly settled into a rhythm. Other than being outside in the mountains, cooking was my happy place. Being alongside Luke made it even better.

It took the entire afternoon for Cook-Phurba, Doc, Luke, and me to work through the cursed recipe, which included from-scratch marinara sauce and handmade breadcrumbs. The tent heaters had been going full blast in preparation for dinner, and with all the heat from the stove and ovens, I had to strip down to my short-sleeved undershirt.

"Please tell me you made the dessert ahead of time," I said to Doc as I set a pan of finished eggplant into a steam tray.

She glared at me, some parmesan still stuck in her sweat-dampened hair.

"We'll make no-bake cookies," I said. "If we put them outside to set, they'll be ready to cut in thirty minutes."

She nodded her approval. And gratitude.

"Come on," I said to Luke as I headed to the adjoining walk-in pantry. "Let's make sure Randall has all the ingredients."

He squeezed inside with me. Thankfully, the pantry was arranged with the same basic logic as Mingma's, and I easily located the rolled oats and vanilla.

"Do you see any chocolate?" I asked, trying not to be distracted by his proximity, by his smell, which made my body buzz with the desire to step even closer.

"Powdered or solid?"

"Randall has vegetable oil, so either will work."

"There's chocolate chips on the top shelf," Luke said.

"Perfect."

He stretched tall to grab them, and that's when I noticed something.

Like me, Luke had stripped down to a T-shirt, an extreme

rarity on this mountain, even while inside a heated tent. And there, on the bare wrist of the hand reaching over the top of my head for the chocolate chips, was the cord bracelet I'd tied there two years ago.

All the noises out in the big top ground to a halt and blew away. It couldn't possibly be the same bracelet. Mine had fallen off such a long time ago. But there was no denying that it was Dad's vintage cord, lavender with turquoise flecks. It was faded appropriately with age, and the bumps of the singed knots were dark and slick like beads.

I told myself it didn't mean anything—that it simply hadn't fallen off yet and he'd never bothered to cut it off. But when I looked from the bracelet to his face, it was clear that he had been watching me stare at it. He held my eyes, locking them into place with a depth of intention.

I couldn't speak. I couldn't breathe. Did this mean what I thought it did?

That constant sensation this season of being separated halves of Velcro, always reaching back for each other—what if no part of that had been wishful thinking?

Then, somebody was talking to us. Doc. "Hey, you two, can you grab me another package of napkins?"

I grabbed the napkins, my face burning.

Luke and I hurried back out to the kitchen, where we rushed to melt the chocolate chips on the stove, then measure and mix the rest of the ingredients. Even though we were completely wrapped up in the task at hand, there were so many questions hanging in the air between us.

Jim found Luke at the stove, needing to talk to him about one of the UW clients. Luke's face was a question mark as his eyes met mine.

"I can finish the rest. Go ahead," I assured him.

His expression didn't change. He hadn't been looking for permission to leave; he needed to know what my reaction was to what had just happened in the pantry. My mind was still spinning, but I managed a small smile. What did all this mean, and what should I do?

By the time I'd finished the cookies and put them outside to cool, most people were almost done eating. I slipped into the empty chair Luke had saved for me at the table with the UW team and the Walkabout crew. Red-haired Theo was in the middle of some story about a past film shoot, and everyone was dying with laughter.

"If you think that was bad, I should tell you about the time April—"

"No, Theo, really, they don't need to hear this one," April protested.

But Theo had already started, and he kept talking right over the top of her protests. By the time he finished, the whole table was roaring, April included, and even I was dying of laughter.

This was nice. Laughing took the edge off my nerves about Luke.

The atmosphere in the tent was as celebratory as it was the night before the eve of our first acclimatization rotation. This was the night to cut loose because tomorrow at this time, all of us would be in bed so we'd be ready to start through the icefall at three a.m.

Over at the other table, the A-Team was even rowdier than usual, and Claudia and her brother, Juan, had hijacked Doc's grunge music and replaced it with Latin music on the karaoke machine. A few of their Cuban teammates had gotten up to sing and dance.

Out of the corner of my eye, I saw Dad walk into the big top.

"Touch of empty-nest syndrome, Greg?" Doc yelled from the kitchen.

"Hi, Dad," I said, giving him a hug.

"How's everything going?"

"Great."

"I don't want to interrupt. I'll catch you in a bit, okay?" He shook hands with Luke before going over to the kitchen where Doc dished him up a plate of eggplant.

Most of A-Team and some of the UW clients were up dancing with the Cubans now. Ernesto, another of the Walkabout crew, dragged a protesting April up to dance.

As I sat back down, I scooted my chair closer to Luke, trying to get him to turn toward me. I was testing the waters, looking for an extra smidge of confirmation to make me braver. I scooted even closer. Our pants brushed. That got his attention.

"What did your other email say?" I asked. "The one you didn't send."

Once again, he held my eyes. Heat spread through me like an Etch A Sketch wand.

"You really want to know?" His voice wobbled, like he was nervous.

"Yes."

He leaned in to whisper in my ear, but we both retracted immediately. Whispering would attract too much attention in a tent full of gossip-starved clients.

Instead, he grabbed an adult coloring sheet and a blue marker from the caddy in the middle of the table. He flipped it over to the blank side and wrote something. He folded the sheet twice, hesitating briefly before slipping it under the table to me.

The paper was crisp in my fingers as I unfolded it.

My stomach did a free fall as I read his words.

My heart still belongs to you.

Chapter Eighteen

Before I could respond, there was an arm lifting me out of my chair and pulling me onto the makeshift dance floor. It was Juan. I quickly shoved Luke's message into my pocket.

I'd never Latin danced in my life, but it didn't seem to matter, with Juan directing me like a life-sized doll.

"You're a natural!" Juan yelled over the music.

My mind remained with Luke.

My heart still belongs to you.

I could have broken free of Juan and gone back to Luke, but I didn't. Not yet.

Ever since our exchange at the puja ceremony, I'd been looking for certainty. I wanted to be certain that he was available, certain he was interested. And now I had it. But that next step! That's what I wasn't certain about now. What to do or how to go about it. Before this had been testing. Flirtations. But to take action? No matter what, it would change things, and it would put Luke and me in a dangerous position, given that any sort of relationship between two guides was forbidden.

"Loosen up!" Juan said, giving me a playful shake.

I thought about Luke and how he'd been giving me small clues all along, but even that moment in the pantry with the bracelet hadn't been enough to truly make me believe it. Luke had always been the bolder and braver of the two of us, and tonight he'd had to literally spell out what his feelings were for me.

He'd *written* it out and…I hadn't responded.

I shot a glance in his direction, but he wasn't there anymore. He wasn't anywhere in the tent.

"Excuse me," I said to Juan, wiggling from his grip.

I went straight for the door. Luke wasn't outside, either.

I didn't have my headlamp, but the big top's skylights were bright enough to dimly light the way to the UW section. God it was cold out here in short sleeves!

I shook his tent with our signature one-two shake.

No response.

"Luke," I whispered.

Still nothing. My chest grew tight with panic. Did he think I'd blown him off?

After waiting a minute, I repeated his name, this time louder in case he had his earbuds on.

The UW Huskies pennant flapping from the top of his tent was my only response. Where could he possibly be?

Not knowing what else to do, I dejectedly started back to the warmth of the big top. I couldn't think about it. I couldn't analyze it. I just had to go with it.

"Emily," Luke said. He was standing in the door of the UW team tent where I hadn't even thought of looking.

All doubt was gone. My heart pounded out of my chest.

He stepped outside as I walked over to him. I was so caught by the longing in his eyes that I misjudged the distance and wound up practically on top of him, and then his hands were on my face pulling me the rest of the way in.

There wasn't time to think about what I was doing, about how all the mechanics of kissing your best friend would work. As soon as our bodies connected, our lips were together, and it was just him and me, kissing with the exhilaration of climbing through a crux even as your mind is telling you that you won't be able to do it.

We pulled away from each other slightly. My breaths were short and fast. I just kissed Luke. *My* Luke.

He nudged me around the corner to the dark side of the tent, and I didn't have a chance to have any other thoughts because he was kissing me again, and I was kissing back like I needed him to live. Like it hadn't ever been any other way between us. His mouth opened, and our tongues slid together. He tasted like the British wintergreen gum he always chewed.

He slid his hands down my shoulders until his warm palms were directly against the bare skin of my upper arms. Startled, he squeezed them and stopped kissing me.

"You're not wearing a coat."

I shook my head.

He unzipped his down jacket and pulled me in tight. I wrapped my arms around his waist as he zipped the jacket up my back. He pulled the knit hat off his head and put it on my head instead.

"Better?" he asked.

"Yeah."

I had stupidly been outside in sub-zero temperatures in nothing but a T-shirt, and he hadn't chided me about it. Further, he was sharing his jacket and hat, which was ultra-chivalrous. These things somehow struck me as more odd than us kissing, and it made me shy.

As if sensing this, he tightened his arms around me and twisted us so we both had a view of the sky. In the Himalayas, you're ten-thousand feet closer to the stars than anywhere else in the world, and tonight I felt that more than I ever had before. The netting of stars was a canopy just for us, exactly as described in one of my favorite poems.

...heaven's embroidered cloths,
Enwrought with golden and silver light,
The blue and the dim and the dark cloths
Of night and light and the half-light...

The poem had been part of a sophomore-year English assignment, and Luke and I had been hanging out in my tent when I read it for the first time. I'd made him put down his book and listen to me read the whole thing aloud.

Luke exhaled softly, and his face pressed a little harder against mine as we looked up at the stars. This was *Luke's* cheek, with the tiniest bit of stubble, warming mine.

We kissed again, this time more slowly and tenderly. Our first two kisses had made my body come alive, but this one touched my soul. The stars, they were more beautiful tonight because we were together. Everything was always more beautiful with him.

"Your dad," he whispered, breaking the trance. "He's at Global tonight."

"I know, and I haven't talked to him yet. I don't want him to come looking for me." Besides, there were eyes everywhere at Base Camp, and we both knew it.

Neither of us moved to go inside. I tipped my head up, letting my lips drift across his. His fingers slid through the base of my ponytail, pushing our lips together harder.

Slowly—carefully—he lowered his jacket zipper down my spine, and I stepped back, my hands not yet willing to release. He let his hands linger on my waist, his eyes solemn with the night.

Without the protection of his jacket, I shivered in the cold. Reluctantly, I slid his hat off my head and handed it to him. "Coming with me?"

He shook his head.

Just as we turned to go our separate ways, he yanked me back, grabbed my face in both hands, and kissed me one more time.

Chapter Nineteen

What do you do after you've kissed your best friend?

What do you do after you've kissed your coworker whom you're not allowed to date?

How do you react when you see the guy from last night during the day in front of the entire company?

What you do is eat a protein bar for breakfast and hide in your tent with your phone, typing question after question into *Going on Eighteen*'s advice column search bar. But this was Mount Everest—where normal relationship advice was not applicable.

I didn't have much longer to hide out, though, with our all-staff meeting for Rotation One starting in fifteen minutes. I killed the remaining time doing a fancy Katniss braid from a *Going on Eighteen* tutorial. I'd just have to play it cool the best I could. The most important thing was not doing anything weird or awkward that would give myself away, like turning beet-red as soon as I saw Luke.

Though I was right on time, I was the last one to the meeting. All the seats at the table were gone, but there were a few chairs open around the perimeter, with one of them being between Luke and Theo. Luke glanced at me, a smile playing on his handsome face from something Theo had said.

I froze in the tent door like an idiot. So much for not doing anything weird.

Thom gestured for me to hurry up and take a seat.

Play it cool.

The normal thing to do was to sit in the chair next to Luke, so that's what I did. I didn't dare look at him in these close quarters, but his proximity buzzed through me stronger than it ever had before.

Jim launched right into the plan for tomorrow and the rest of Rotation One, which would begin with the clients' two a.m. wake-up calls with tea and hot towels. He read through the client-guide assignments, which put me, Phurba, and the very experienced Dorje, together to work with Phil, Glissading Glen, and Johnsmith. He went on to cover the logistics of everything from radio check-in points to trouble spots in this year's route through the icefall. We even went over the meal plans so that all of us could help manage client expectations in case any of them mistakenly thought Randall and his gourmet food were going to be accompanying us higher than Base Camp. Not that they'd starve; they'd still have Cook-Phurba up there with them.

In all, we were there for two hours, which didn't leave much time for all we needed to do before tonight's early dinner and bedtime. I didn't see Luke after the meeting as guides were pretty much sticking to their teams' sub-camps today, and then I had gone down to Winslowe Expeditions to hang out with Dad and eat dinner.

After finishing a few last-minute things in my tent back in Global City, I settled into my sleeping bag. My thoughts went straight to Luke. Why did it suddenly seem more improbable that we would kiss a second time than to have kissed the first time?

My spirits sank as I considered it. Really, when *would* we have another chance to be alone together? Base Camp was so crowded, and everyone was always on the lookout for juicy gossip. And to repeat what had happened last night would be reckless. We'd be *deliberately* doing something that could get us fired. I needed this job badly, not only for the money but for my résumé and to help get a job after the season was over. Though Luke was reluctant about being an Everest guide, he needed the money, too. So did Mingma, for the rest of the earthquake repairs.

I reached for the pair of folded jeans next to me on the floor of the tent, fishing through the pockets to find the coloring sheet from yesterday. I unfolded it, smoothed it out carefully, and read the words over and over for reassurance.

My heart still belongs to you.

Eventually, I put the paper away and turned off my headlamp. Not long after, there were footsteps outside my tent, and then it shook all around me in a one-two rhythm.

My insides leaped.

"Come in," I whispered.

Tonight, clouds covered the moon and stars, and when Luke clicked off his headlamp inside my tent, it was pitch black. He sat on my bed cross-legged. I could tell because I was doing the same thing and our knees were touching.

Neither of us moved. I was all but holding my breath. Even though we were in physical contact, it felt as if there was a crevasse between us.

"So, what was Greg doing at Global last night?" Luke asked. "Because I know he didn't come for the eggplant."

I laughed. Okay, this was good. Joking was better than awkward silence. "I think he actually likes it."

"No."

"Yes. Doc invited him up, and he said he wanted to see

how I was doing. She thinks he has empty-nest syndrome."

"Good thing you moved only a third of a mile away."

"Yeah, good thing," I said, briefly wondering if Amy had any symptoms like that after they took her away. Doubtful. She hadn't wanted me in the first place, so why would she have had remorse when we were separated?

The silence slipped back between us. I swallowed and then reached bravely across the invisible crevasse. Luke did, too, our palms meeting in the middle. We matched our hands, then he twisted his ever so slightly so that when he closed his fingers, they were threaded through mine. My pulse jumped from sixty to a hundred.

He brought his arm back to his body, which pulled me in to him. Our hands were still locked together, pinned between our chests with our faces close enough that I could smell his wintergreen breath. Inch by inch, we leaned closer together until our lips brushed, then pressed. The kiss was gentle, and our tongues intertwined naturally. All my senses melted into him. His headlamp slid off his head, thumping as it hit the tent floor.

I unzipped my sleeping bag and spread it across us like a blanket. As we burrowed beneath it, I was sadly aware that he wouldn't be able to stay for long. We would be starting up the icefall in less than seven hours. I already dreaded the moment when he'd have to go back to his own tent.

Outside, a yak lowed, and the neck bells of its herd played a short melody on the wind.

"So where's that selfie stick of yours?" he asked in a peppy voice all wrong for the moment.

"What?"

"You heard me. Let's do a tent self-Circ."

He propped himself up on his elbow to feel around for his headlamp. I pushed him back down. "You said you're not into that."

"For you, I'll do it. And willingly."

"Not right now. It's late."

"What better time than the present? Come on, let's get that self-Circ stick."

He felt around for his headlamp again. I knew right where it had fallen. I snatched it up and held it tight against my chest. "No. I don't want to."

"Okay, then, show it to me."

He attempted to swipe the headlamp from me. "Show me your self-Circ stick, Emily Winslowe."

"No way."

He gripped the headlamp, trying to pry my fingers loose. I locked my arms tight to my sides like chicken wings. I fought valiantly, but also silently, since there were client tents five feet from mine, but in the end, Luke was able to wrench his headlamp from my grip. He shined it around the full perimeter of my tent.

"Where is it?"

I shrugged.

"Unless you produce a self-Circ stick in the next five seconds, you're going to owe me big time. Five, four—"

"Hey, wait—"

"Three, two, one." He shined the headlamp directly in my face. "Gotcha!" he said, clearly thrilled he'd sleuthed out my caper. "So now you have to do something for me."

"What?" I growled.

"You have to answer a question."

"What?"

"How'd you know that I'd been in a co-self-Circ?"

I scowled.

"You weren't Circ-snooping, were you?" he taunted.

I scowled harder and crossed my arms.

"Adorable. I would have never thought you had it in you."

I should have been ashamed about being caught, but how

could I be when he was so pleased about it all? I reached over and clicked his headlamp off, and we cuddled back down beneath my sleeping bag. His body shook with muffled laughter.

"What?" I asked.

"I was thinking about you on the client hike, how you pretended to look through your backpack and everything."

I elbowed him hard. In response, he grabbed my arm, yanked me on top of him, and kissed me with an intensity that made me completely forget why I'd elbowed him in the first place. Then he pulled back slightly, leaving me breathless and yearning for more.

"So," he said. "Who would you say wins YCCM?"

"We already settled that. I did."

"No," he said. "For *this* YCCM." His hand went to my face, tracing my jawline exactly as he had with the tsampa.

The air between us transformed. Now, it was charged with electricity like a summer evening thunderstorm was approaching.

"I was the one who came to find you at the UW camp last night," I said.

I reached up to his hand on my face, covering it with mine. It was his left hand, the one with the bracelet. I touched the smooth circle of aged cord and then slid my fingers beneath it.

"Well," he said, with a deep exhale, "I told you before that I came back here to check on Mom and Pasang, but that wasn't the only reason. So I win because I was the one who traveled all the way from Seattle to Everest Base Camp with the hope that I would catch you. And I mean *really* catch you."

My stomach dropped, then rose again. His hands slid down my back, constricting around me until I was tight against his chest, and he didn't relax his grip once I was there.

Chapter Twenty

Doc stood at the edge of the precipice. Her headlamp hardly made a dent in the gaping blackness, but it reflected brightly off the makeshift bridge of four aluminum ladders lashed together end-to-end. It was the only way across the chasm facing us.

"You've got to be fucking kidding me," she said.

Admittedly, this was an intimidating first Khumbu Icefall ladder crossing because it was so long. The fact that it was still black outside was a blessing, though. At least she wouldn't know this crevasse was probably one of the ones so deep you couldn't see the bottom.

"Congratulations, you're not in Base Camp anymore," I joked, trying to help her relax.

Doc unclipped from the rope with a resolute *snap*, stepping back to clip in behind two of the A-Team clients. "I need a minute."

I could empathize with her hesitation. Crossing the ladder bridges—which occur on the Nepal side of Mount Everest and nowhere else in the world—is terrifying the first few times.

Two clients later and Doc was next in line again.

"Come on, Doc, no sense stalling," I said. "There are about ten more of these you're going to have to cross before Camp One."

"That isn't very encouraging."

"Most of them aren't this wide."

There was a groan from deep within the bowels of the perpetually unstable icefall. That got her moving.

Her crampons clunked dully as she placed her first foot on the rungs of the frost-covered ladder. Taking another step, she shook her head. One more step, and she'd be standing above the open air of the chasm, feeling the full wobble and vibration of the ladder. "This is insane," she said, but she kept going.

Doc exhaled loudly as soon as her feet were off the ladder and back on snow. I tipped forward to the fronts of my crampons and bounced my heels a few times to stave off the shivers in the five-degree air as I waited for the rest of A-Team to cross. Five degrees wouldn't be bad at all if I were moving, but standing around in it was torture.

By the time the sky was lightening, I was so frozen that I eagerly anticipated the warmth of the coming sun, even though with the warming came added risk in the already unstable icefall. Because of their enormous size, the ice blocks all around us gave the illusion of stability, but in reality, the blocks were like sandcastles at the ocean's edge. The daylight increase in temperature gradually melted their foundations and each block could potentially be just a breath away from tipping.

Ideally, we would have been out of the icefall by this time, but there had been some traffic jams on the ladder bridges with the Go Big expedition coming down from a rotation. I'd heard reports over my radio that the Cuban team had already reached Camp One, but the tail end of A-Team had at least another hour to go.

I let my ascender hang on the fixed line so I could wiggle some feeling back into my freezing fingers and toes, and then I caught back up to the last client: Phil. His progress had been steady but tediously slow.

The sky grew lighter until we no longer needed our headlamps. I followed Phil through a maze of ice into a foreboding slot canyon, then up out of it using a vertical ladder. Even through the thick layers of my mittens, the cold from the metal zapped away any warmth I'd gained from wiggling my fingers.

On this plateau there was a clear view of the top of the icefall, after which would be the tents of Camp One. But first, we had to get through the rest of the icefall. Phurba, Glissading Glenn, Dorje, and Johnsmith were far ahead of us now. There was a block of ice as big as an office building to our right, and it was leaning at such a threatening angle that I longed to sprint away from Phil and up the plateau to get out of its way.

"You've got this," I said. "Just keep it steady."

He nodded, but instead of starting to walk again, he coughed. "I'm fine," he said through a few more coughs. "I just need a minute."

"Take one minute if you must, but it's really best to keep moving," I said.

Halfway through Phil's minute, there was a crash louder than thunder.

It took a few seconds to register that the crash was near but thankfully not on top of us. Thinking immediately of the men just ahead, I ripped off my backpack to grab the avalanche shovel and probes.

After several frantic radio calls, Jim had it all sorted out. All Global clients and guides were accounted for. It was a serac collapse somewhere between the rest of A-Team and us.

Tashi.

Now I was thankful for Phil's slow progress. Elated, actually. And I wanted out of this icefall. Right now.

Jim was on the radio from Base Camp, echoing that exact sentiment, urging the remaining A-Team laggards to hurry up and get out.

Five minutes of walking later, we reached the site of the serac collapse, where the fixed line dove eerily into a field of slushy snow. The outline of where the block had pulled away from the wall wasn't large by Khumbu Icefall standards, but large enough to have been deadly for anyone beneath it. We had indeed been lucky.

"We're going to have to come off the line," I told Phil. "We'll be able to pick it back up as soon as we're through this."

Phil was clearly shaken, but he was able to mimic my steps as I pulled my ascender off the line and clipped it to my harness. Honestly, I was shaken up, too. A serac collapse like that is exactly why you don't want to be in the icefall when the day starts heating it up.

The slope was barely angled more than a beginner ski run, but to be safe I got the spare rope out of my pack and tied us together with a pair of figure eights through our harnesses. I sent Phil out in front of me, and when he was about ten feet ahead, I began walking, too.

This was the normal way to travel on a mountain. A mountain that did not have a collective pool of money to string twelve miles of fixed rope up the mountain like a handrail straight to the summit. I'd never traveled on a two-person rope team with just me and a client, and it was not a good feeling. Phil was skinny, but he was tall, and if he fell, the force would easily take me down, too. Thankfully, the slope was so gentle that a fall was unlikely.

So, then, why was I nervous about this? My crampons crunched unsteadily through the mix of packed snow and ice. That unsteady sound was my answer. I hadn't been through the icefall this year, and I didn't know what this rubble was covering. What if we were on top of a crevasse?

"Phil!" I yelled. I motioned urgently for him to follow me back to the side we'd come from.

We had to get back to solid snow immediately. Sweat broke out across my forehead. I waved him on faster. As much as we needed to get out of the icefall, we had to do it the right way, even if it meant backtracking so we could belay each other across the rubble.

Even through the panic, I worried that I was being paranoid. That method of crossing would take a half hour, at least. A half hour that we didn't have.

I desperately wished Dad or another Global guide were here to weigh in on what the best option was. But there was no one; just me and my client. *This* was being a high-altitude mountaineering guide. There *is* no one else.

Just as my feet hit solid snow, there was an explosion, followed by a distinct *whoosh* and drop.

The rope hissed and cracked as loud as a bullwhip.

I didn't even have time to scream.

Chapter Twenty-One

I fell face-first to the ice, my shoulder slamming into the anvil end of my ice ax. I gasped and then frantically kicked my toe points into the snow to lock myself in place. Not a second later, the screaming rope caught up to me. Despite bracing myself, the force yanked me back a few feet and jerked the harness around my waist as if I'd been bungee jumping.

Even without looking backward, I knew what had happened. The danger I'd sensed had come true: the rubble from the collapsed serac had formed a snowbridge that was hiding a crevasse. And then the crevasse had gobbled up the bridge as we stood atop it.

Ever so slowly, I peered around, afraid to see what—or what wasn't—behind me. I had about ten feet between me and the newly opened void. It was a relief to have some distance, but Phil's full weight and life dangled from my waist. I strengthened my grip on the ice ax, hardly daring to breathe.

"Phil," I yelled.

"Down here," he called.

Thank god. He could speak. This was a good sign.

The problem was that with Phil's weight on my harness and having only one hand free, there was no way for me to build the anchor I needed to save us both. Especially since all the tools I needed to build that anchor were zipped in my backpack.

"Hold tight," I yelled. "Don't move."

I wanted to scream in frustration. My tools were right there against my back, but they might as well have been on the moon right now.

"Emily, come in, Emily," Jim said on the radio.

My radio had unclipped during the fall and was lying on the snow near my thigh. I strained for it, but the pain in my shoulder from falling on the ice ax made me curse.

Jim was on the radio again. "Emily, check in for us, please."

I didn't know how much longer I'd be able to hold this position, and with an unbridged crevasse opened between me and the rest of the Global crew, it was fully up to me to somehow get stabilized so Phil could ascend out of the crevasse.

"You okay?" I yelled down to Phil.

"I think so. I'm not that far from the top. I can just—"

"No! Don't move. Just wait."

I reached around to try to unzip my backpack, but the pain was too great. Instead, I threaded my left arm between the pack and my lower back, attempting to unzip it from the bottom. That didn't work, but I was able to nudge it enough that I might be able to reach the zipper pull with my teeth.

My radio crackled. "We're looking from both ends with binoculars," Jim said. "We don't see you. Thom's sending someone down from Camp One."

They wouldn't be able to get to us without a ladder. I prayed there was an extra in Camp One and that they would know to bring it.

Phil's weight dug into my bruised waist. My wrecked shoulder throbbed from my grip on the ice ax. Ironically, Phil and I were currently positioned in the ultimate mountaineering dilemma: cut your partner off the rope and save yourself, or both die together? But this was a commercial expedition where Phil was a paying client, not a partner.

Don't think about that. Keep your head. Gravity and friction are in your favor. There are other guides just a quarter mile away. Do whatever it takes to hang on.

I pushed my face into the small opening in my pack I'd managed to unzip, grabbing one of the avalanche pickets with my teeth. That's when I saw someone rappelling down the wall of ice from which the serac had broken off. *Luke.*

I yelled for him to stop and not come any farther because the wall was unstable, but he ignored me.

Luke landed safely on our side of the crevasse. Wordlessly, he twisted three ice screws into the solid snow, put himself on a flat rappel back to me, tied a figure eight on a bight to the other end of the rope, and clipped it to the daisy chain on my harness. He pulled the slack out of the rope, bent it through the ATC on his harness, and just like that, I was on an anchor, and Phil's weight was off me and onto Luke's belay.

He called directions down to Phil as I eased off the ice ax. I twisted around to sit and scooted farther back from the lip of the chasm. I kept a close eye on Phil as he pulled himself over the edge and crawled up to us.

When all three of us were at the anchors, I called Jim on the radio to give an update.

"What's Luke doing down there?" he replied.

Luke hadn't been the one Thom sent down? He must have come on his own while they were still trying to reach me on the radio.

"Yes, it's Luke with us," I said, trying to keep my voice

steady. "We're going to need a ladder to get across the crevasse, otherwise we'll have to descend to Base Camp."

Thom confirmed there was an extra ladder at Camp One and told us Hulk and Phurba were on their way down with it. Thank god, because I wasn't sure I had it in me to go all the way back down the gauntlet of the icefall right now.

"Well, that was a scare," Phil said when the radio calls were done.

You have no idea.

"Are you hurt?" I asked him.

"I don't think so. But I owe you a big thank-you."

"Luke's the one who should get the thanks."

Phil thanked him, but it was me who he hugged afterward.

In all this, Luke hadn't said a single word, and he continued to say nothing during the never-ending wait for Phurba and Hulk to arrive, set up the ladder, and redo the fixed line.

I snuck a glance at him. He was frowning, and his index finger tapped anxiously on his knee.

I couldn't even imagine what he must be thinking about me. I had made a terrible mistake in going across the rubble in a rope team instead of belaying Phil from a fixed anchor. Not only had I nearly gotten a client killed, it was *Luke* who had seen me in a position that could have only been caused by me backtracking out of a mistake, and *Luke* who'd had to put himself in a suicidal position to save my neck.

My head sagged with humiliation. I didn't have any idea how I was going to cope with what had happened, let alone the repercussions it would have on my relationship with Luke. Last night, everything had seemed so sure between us. Now, nothing was.

Chapter Twenty-Two

I yanked off my crampons, closed the tent door, and pulled my sleeping bag out of its stuff sack. I lay down immediately, burying my face in the chilly down.

The sleeping bag next to me was Luke's. As the two junior guides on teams with an odd number of guides, we shared a tent at Camp One and at Camp Two. I was glad he'd continued on to the main tent to check in with Thom, because I needed some time to pull myself together.

My radio crackled. "Emily, this is Greg. You there?"

I didn't have the energy to reach for my radio, but if I didn't, someone from Global would come get me.

"Yeah, hi D—Greg."

"Switch over to ninety-nine, will you?"

I sat up and spun the channel knob. "I'm here, Dad."

"You okay? I heard about what happened."

Dad would know about the serac falling and the snowbridge collapse, but none of the specifics of my actions. Only Luke knew that.

"Yes, I'm fine," I said. "Everyone's fine. I'm just warming

up in my tent."

He keyed the mic but didn't speak right away, as if deciding what to say. "All right, I'll let you go. Dinner when you get down?"

"Okay, Dad. Yeah, sounds good."

"Love you."

"Love you, too."

When we got off this rotation, I wondered if I would confess the details of what had gone down. What would he think?

I dialed back to Global's main channel and laid the radio on the ground. I was still shivering with a bone-deep freeze, so I hurried to take some ibuprofen for my shoulder and then crawled inside my sleeping bag.

Outside the tent, there were crampon-crunch footsteps coming my way. I pulled the sleeping bag over my face and pretended to sleep.

The tent unzipped, and Luke crawled in. He probably wouldn't disturb me. The thinner air in the on-mountain camps made it difficult to sleep, and all of us were careful not to wake a person who had managed to doze off.

From the dark bag where I was now trapped, I listened to him settling into his sleeping bag, then digging through his backpack. There was a *click*, followed by the snap of earbuds into a jack and the faint trace of music beats.

I was lying on the shoulder that had taken the brunt of my ice ax, and after a while I couldn't bear it anymore. I rolled over, sighing and smacking my lips a couple of times to make it seem like it was all in my sleep. Now I was facing Luke.

Sensing a bit of light, I cracked one eye open. I was still concealed by the sleeping bag hood, but there was enough of a gap that I could see Luke. I nudged the hood up a tiny bit more. His eyes were closed, but he wasn't asleep.

What would happen with us next? He had the easiest

excuse in the world to put the brakes on us. There's a reason guides in relationships are not allowed to work on the same expedition: in an emergency, there is preferential treatment. Today had proven that. Luke had acted outside of Jim's direction, leaving his own clients to come back for me, and in order to reach Phil and me across the crevasse, he'd taken a risk that Jim would have never allowed.

I wanted the relief of a good cry, but after endangering other people's lives as I had today, I didn't deserve relief. In defeat, I let the sleeping bag fall back across my face. The blessing about sleeping at elevation is that even though it is a struggle, when you add enough cold, terror, and exhaustion—like today—it's impossible not to.

The sun was on the other side of the tent when I woke. I sat up with a start, my head crashing into a pole. I swore loudly, which made Luke jerk awake. He rubbed his eyes.

Then, everything came flooding back. The weight of Phil's body hanging from my harness. Unzipping my backpack with my teeth. The relief at seeing Luke and how he hadn't been able to look at me afterward.

I might have a long list of impressive summits under my belt, but I had not been a guide or the expedition leader on any of them. All I'd done was walk up mountains behind Dad. I was a sham, and Luke knew that now.

"I brought you some hot chocolate," he said, reaching for a thermos in the corner. "It's probably not warm anymore, but it might not be frozen yet."

A lump of guilt lodged in my throat. He'd risked his own life to save mine and Phil's.

"Thanks for the hot chocolate," I said. "And for saving my life. You shouldn't have. But you did, and I'm beyond grateful."

"Of course I should have."

"No. It was too dangerous."

He looked at me oddly.

The shame. I pressed my fingers to my throbbing temple.

"Maybe we should talk about it," he said.

He waited for me to look at him, but I couldn't. Instead, I gently stretched my aching shoulder. "There's nothing to talk about. Other than to apologize. I made a huge mistake today, and I'm sorry I put you in that position."

"What are you talking about? What mistake?"

"You saw. I didn't have Phil on belay."

"That wasn't a mistake. That was a judgment call."

I shook my head in denial. He was making excuses for me, just like he had when I told him I'd canceled my admission to Townsend College.

"Really," he said. "I might not have even gotten a rope out at all in that spot, and I know for a fact Thom and Tyler wouldn't have. It's practically flat. And with a serac having just fallen, there's a lot of reason to get through there as fast as you can."

"But I hadn't been through the icefall yet this year. I didn't know what was underneath the rubble and, as it turned out, it was a crevasse. If I had made a mistake like that on the Lhotse Face, Phil would be dead."

"It *didn't* happen on the Lhotse Face."

"Yes, but there's no room for error on a mountain like this. You know that as well as I."

"You're shaken up," he said. "I am, too. But you're blowing this out of proportion. None of this was your fault."

His continued excuses made me even more ashamed. I had the sudden, irresistible urge to get out of the tent and away from this conversation. I reached for my boots.

"Emily! What are you doing?"

I pulled the tongue back on my right boot and forced my still-cold foot inside. I was too choked up to answer.

"Why are you acting like this?" he pressed.

"I'm having a hard time accepting how much danger I put everyone in, okay? I appreciate how you're trying to make me feel better. And just so you know, I don't blame you for not wanting to continue our—"

Relationship.

God! I couldn't even say it aloud. I stared at the tent wall, trying to find words. "We're friends, but you're not obligated—"

He dropped his hand from my arm. "What do you mean, not obligated?"

The sharpness in his tone made me turn to him. His face was slowly reddening as he waited for me to respond. Suddenly, he understood what I had meant. He sucked in a breath.

"Friends. Right," he said. "So I guess we're going to pretend like the last two nights never happened?"

My pulse and thoughts were all over the place. Yeah, pretend like it never happened. That would be easiest. And for the best. Just forget about it all. We never should have broken the rules to begin with, and we'd have to stop at some point, anyway, since we were going different places when the season ended. I hastily laced up my boots and reached for my outer jacket.

He touched my arm. I froze. "Don't leave. Don't pull away. Please. Talk to me."

I didn't really want to leave. I just didn't know what else to do. But he'd saved my life, and I owed him, so I let my jacket fall into my lap instead of putting it on.

"Listen," he said. "I know you don't want anyone to see that there's anything besides peanut butter fudge cookies and niceties inside the incredible, Swiss-tuned mountain machine that you are. You'll play, but when it comes down to it, you're going to show only the polite. The helpful. The considerate. I just wish you'd allow me to see everything that's there, even if it's messy. I wish I rated that with you."

"You do."

"Then tell me what's going on."

I fiddled with a zipper pull. "I don't know if I can explain it."

"Try."

He was silent as I considered what to say.

"I feel like you shouldn't have had to rescue me," I said, finally. "I feel like it proves something."

"What?"

"Well, climbing is the one thing I'm supposed to be good at—the only thing that puts me even remotely shoulder to shoulder with you—yet I had to be rescued within four hours of my first day guiding on-mountain."

"You *are* good at climbing. I know you feel like you made a mistake today, but once your nerves settle down, you'll see that's not how it is. And there's no way I'm equal to you in climbing. You're on par with some of the best out there, and you're just getting started."

"I wasn't talking about being equal in climbing. I meant life."

His face fell. I'd said too much.

"You're the daughter of the most respected climbing outfitter in the Himalayas, and I'm the son of his cook and one of his former porters."

"No Luke. It's completely the opposite. Look at all the places you've been and how successful you are with school and work and friends and life. You want to be a doctor, and I'm not even going to college."

"It's not like you think," he said quickly. "I don't want to be a doctor."

"You just switched your major for that."

"I know. I don't *want* to be a doctor. But I am going to try my best to become one. There's a big difference there."

"Why would you—"

"It's because of all the people who donated money for my scholarships. And everyone who helped me apply and compete, like your dad. All those good people who assumed they weren't just providing a privileged education to one individual, but that they were contributing to something that will help the people of this region. I've been selfish these past two years, majoring in atmospheric sciences for no reason other than it's what I like. But my guilty conscience eventually grew so loud that I had to listen to it."

I hated the heaviness in his voice. He looked at the tent ceiling briefly. "Being in the medical or dental field is the most direct way to give back, and of the two, being a doctor is slightly more palatable."

No. This didn't seem right at all. "Luke..."

He shook his head. "It is what it is."

I reached for his hand and intertwined my fingers with his. When he finally looked at me, his eyebrows were pulled in with worry.

"I was terrified today when I came around the corner and saw you on the edge of that crevasse. I just kept thinking, 'This *can't* be it.' After how long I've felt this way about you. And we'd just broken through. Or so I thought. You can be so hard to read, and now I'm getting the impression that you don't feel the same way about me as I do about you. I guess it makes me feel like *we* are on the edge of that crevasse."

I tightened my grip on his hand. "I *do* feel that way about you."

"But you called us friends. That must be how you think of us."

"No. I thought that what happened in the icefall had

changed how you saw me. And us. I was just trying to give you an out. That's the only reason I said that."

He wasn't meeting my eyes, and his hand was limp in mine. He wasn't convinced. My breathing tightened. What could I tell him that would prove how I felt?

"It's been years since you've been just a friend to me," I started. "Since way before the earthquake and all through our Circs. You want to know the reason I never emailed you? You were too important. I was afraid that if I emailed, it wouldn't be the same, and you'd stop Circ-ing with me, too."

His expression eased from doubt to hope. My breathing got a little easier.

He tugged gently on my hand. I followed, letting him twist me so that my back was against his chest. His head dipped to my ear. "Thank you for telling me that," he said.

He dipped his head farther, kissing my neck softly, just below my earlobe. Beneath his warm lips, my nerves hummed in response.

"Saying good-bye the way we did was really hard for me," I said.

"You mean the earthquake?"

"Yeah. The aftermath. With so many people dead and hurt. How everything was destroyed. It's not like we could pick up where we left off and pretend everything was okay."

My voice trailed as I realized I was telling Luke things I'd never said aloud. I didn't have a group of girlfriends. And Dad and I certainly never talked about stuff like this. I didn't keep a diary, either. I'd never talked about this with anyone—the earthquake or my feelings for Luke, and especially not how the two things were tied together.

"It was almost like everything between us had all been in my imagination," I finished.

"I know exactly what you mean." He wrapped his arms around me.

"Sometimes I think that if not for that earthquake, everything might have been different."

"It would have been. I mean, if it were up to me." He nudged the collar of my down jacket aside to kiss the crook of my neck. The humming spread through my body.

"But then you were gone."

"So were you," he said. "And now we're back."

My stomach did a little somersault. I twisted within his arms so that I was facing him. The tips of our noses brushed as I let myself get lost in all the shades of brown in his eyes.

"Yes, we're back," I said.

He drew a hand down the side of my face to cup my jaw. Any trace of doubt in his expression was gone. The bold, confident Luke I knew so well had returned, as evidenced by the slight dip of his dimples, which quickly faded as he studied my eyes, then my lips.

My heart jumped to overdrive. I wanted his mouth on mine more than anything I'd ever wanted in life and, finally, he gave it to me.

Chapter Twenty-Three

The next day, all four Global teams took a leisurely high-altitude walk between Camp One and Camp Two, where we spent the night. The following day, we climbed the grueling Lhotse Face to Camp Three, then returned to Camp Two to sleep. We were spending one more night at Camp Two before going back down to Base Camp tomorrow.

Doc had grabbed me right after breakfast this morning for a chick-flick marathon in the tent she shared with Claudia. Now it was almost dinnertime, and I was sitting between Theo and Dorje, out on the snow field behind the dining tent. Dorje was whittling a snow leopard from a chunk of wood for his granddaughter, and Theo was reading a comic book. The temperatures were mild, and the sky was deepening with the first hints of sunset. The clients were mostly still in their tents from their afternoon naps, and the few who were near us were quiet as they typed on tablets or read. It was nice. Cush.

April's drone flew overhead like a nosy bee. I looked up and waved.

Theo glanced up from his comic book. "Uh. No. Let's

not wave at the camera."

His Walkabout walkie talkie beeped, and he put it to his ear to hear better. "I'll tell her, April," he replied and then turned to me. "Don't worry. She said it was cute. But only that once, mind you."

April wasn't at Camp Two with us; she flew the drone from Global's command center in Base Camp. She'd do the same for the next rotation and the summit bid, too. Theo and Ernesto helped her on-mountain as needed with launch, recovery, and maintenance.

Theo handed me his open bag of nacho cheese chips. I took a handful.

"So, has it always been your dream to climb Everest?" I asked between munching.

He snickered. A few pieces of orange chips went flying onto the snow. "Sorry. Didn't mean to laugh. No offense. Climbing Mount Everest is great, but, no, it's never been on the top of my list. It's a little…much."

"Oh, is that so? I can arrange for you to pitch your own tent and stop having the Sherpas deliver hot towels and tea to you in the mornings," I threatened.

"You do and I'll have that drone stalking you 24/7."

I laughed and took more chips.

"Rock climbing's always been more my thing," he said. "But given this opportunity with Walkabout paying my way, hell yes, I'll climb Mount Everest."

I hung out on the sun deck for a while longer, then on a whim went to help Cook-Phurba and the other Sherpas finish up with dinner, which is what I would have been doing if this were Winslowe Expeditions. Phil was passing through the kitchen tent to get a cup of tea, and seeing me there, he offered to help. To my utter surprise, he asked this in Sherpa. Jerky travel-guide phrases, but Sherpa nonetheless. The Sherpas were so shocked that they actually allowed him to help.

Outside of the A-Team Sherpas, whom I got along with really well, I'd had little opportunity to get to know the rest of the Global Sherpas. I was having a good time cooking with this group, but I couldn't help feeling a little disloyal to Luke, seeing as they might not have been this lively and relaxed if it were Luke in here with me instead of Phil.

After dinner, Luke and I went straight back to our tent. The sun had already dipped behind Lhotse, but the sky was still bursting with color, making the inside of the tent glow. I crawled over to him, and when his lips touched mine, it awakened places deep inside me.

We kissed and kissed, and it was just like those first breaths of bottled oxygen when climbing higher up on the mountain. Replenishing, energizing, and making me feel like I could do anything.

He tugged off my hat, freed my hair from its ponytail holder, and ran his hands through it. I tried not to think about how long it had been since I'd washed it. The shadows from his eyelashes fluttered beneath his eyes as he scanned my face. From this close, he was surely seeing the light freckles across my nose and cheeks that he may not have noticed before.

I stared into his eyes. The same eyes I'd seen so many times facing me across the checkers table—triumphant after a move or in contemplation after one of my moves. They were the same eyes that urged me faster when we were in the mountains or made me laugh just when I needed it most. Now they were simply steady, like his arm that was holding me tight.

My breath stilled, but the rest of my body surged with desire. I kissed him with hunger.

The light was fading fast now, necessitating us to turn on my headlamp and hang it from the ceiling. We made final trips outside to brush teeth and go to the pee area.

"How's your shoulder doing?" he asked as we settled in our sleeping bags.

"Better. The ibuprofen helps."

"Good. No more ice ax pull-ups this season, eh?"

"Probably not a good idea."

As long as I took it easy, Doc said my shoulder would be healed by the next rotation. My waist was tender where my skin had blackened into a girdle of bruises from the force of Phil's fall, but that would soon ease up.

Luke pulled *World's 19ers* out of his pack.

"I can't believe you hauled that all the way up here," I said.

"This, coming from the person who backpacks across Southeast Asia carrying glitter and craft supplies?"

I sat up and scooted closer so I could read the book along with him. It opened naturally across our laps to our most sacred page: a map of the routes on Cerro Torre.

"Think a paraglide descent would work there?" I asked.

"Maybe," Luke said, "but you'd have to be really good at paragliding."

"Ever tried it?"

"No, but I've thought about it. You?"

"Dad's a purist. He would never. But I want to."

"My roommate does it a lot. There's a place up on Snoqualmie Pass. He'll do parasurfing out in the Sound, too. He's even experimented with paragliding in combination with backcountry skiing."

I laughed.

"What?"

"You have roommates."

"Seattle's expensive. Everyone has roommates."

I laughed again. "I know. It's just funny to think about."

"Two rooms, four guys. What could be more fun than that?"

"Yeesh."

"Really, it's not that bad. We have this awesome covered courtyard in our building where we hang out with our neighbors when it's not raining."

"Sounds fun." It was odd thinking of Luke having friends who were not me.

"I'm sure you could find a similar setup. The UW outdoor rec center has a roommate board for Seattle. Or if you're going to stick closer to Port Townsend, you could probably find a board like that at a climbing gym or gear shop over there."

"Yeah, that's a good idea," I said dismissively, turning to the next page of *World's 19ers.*

What he'd said the other night about not wanting to be a doctor had made me feel better about my own uncertain future and more on equal footing with him, but how could I account for all these other things that I couldn't relate to? How he had a job, paid bills every month, and probably had a driver's license, too. And the trips he did with his friends… it was total freedom in a way I'd never known and might not ever know considering that I had no money. All of this was intimidating in an entirely different way.

"Tell me more about your life in Washington," I said.

"Like what?"

"Anything." *Everything.*

"It's nothing exciting. Classes and trying to work as many hours as I can during the week so I can be in the mountains on the weekends."

"It's exciting to me. More detail, please."

"Like what?"

"Which classes you've taken, where you study, what kind of bike you ride, what you think of McDonald's—"

He burst out laughing. "Okay, here goes. I mostly study at my apartment, sometimes at work if it's slow. I bought my roommate's old mountain bike, and I put slick tires on it for better riding in the city. I detest American fast food—they pretty much have nothing on the menu for people who were raised Buddhist and still don't eat meat. And as for classes, I don't want to think about school right now."

"Why not?"

He groaned. "Somebody's persistent today. I don't want to think about it, because I register for classes in a few days, and next term is going to suck."

"Because of changing your major?"

"Yeah. Instead of thermodynamics and climate science next term, I'll have to take genetics and human anatomy."

"You're really going to go through with the medical school plan even though you don't want to?"

"It's not about me. That's the whole point." His voice was a touch rough.

The shadows from the headlamp seemed to deepen the turmoil on his face.

"What if you were paying your own way for college?" I asked. "What would you study then?"

"I would have stuck with atmospheric sciences. So I could forecast my own weather for climbing. Self-centered and frivolous, I know."

"You weren't majoring in that just for climbing."

"Well, I truly love that field, but climbing was the whole reason I got interested in it in the first place."

He turned his attention back to *World's 19ers*, flipping toward the back to the Alaska Range section. My throat was thick, knowing that if he became a doctor, he wouldn't have a chance to explore any of the mountains in this book.

"So if you weren't beholden to anyone, you'd get your degree in atmospheric sciences, and then what?"

He ran his hand across the page in thought.

"I'd climb. Cerro Torre. All the Top Five. And hopefully

I'd be good enough at it that a company like Esplanade Equipment would fund the trips. Then, when I'm old and I've climbed my heart out all over the world, I'd turn into a weekender and settle into a nice desk job forecasting for all the climbers and backcountry skiers who are still out there in it."

Goose bumps pricked my forearms. "I think that sounds like a great plan."

The sharp look on his face doused my enthusiasm.

"It's not," he said. "It's like a dysfunctional, ironic circle. My dad was killed on a Western mountaineering expedition, and his death was the only reason I've had such privilege in my life. Had he not died, I would have never gotten a pity scholarship to boarding school in Kathmandu and then college in the U.S. I'd be here, hauling loads up the mountain for Greg. And yet, if I had my way, I'd throw myself into the very sport my father died supporting, which I have the privilege of participating in only *because* he died."

I sucked in a breath.

"That's not all. If I had my way, I wouldn't come back to Tengboche when I finish college, other than to climb Himalayan peaks and visit Mom and Pasang. I've been away from here too long. It doesn't feel like home anymore. In an abstract way, the Khumbu Valley ceased to be my home the day my dad died. The Global Sherpas have been a tangible reminder of that this season. But to take my education and go elsewhere with it would be selfish. Counter to the reason scholarships like mine exist in the first place."

He closed the book and put it to the side. His head hung low like the dilemma was physically weighing him down.

I wanted to say something that would erase the feeling that he owed a hundred faceless donors a life that was wrong for him. But that was the American in me. I'd spent enough time in this part of the world to understand the other side and how deeply that affected Luke.

Instead of saying anything, I pushed his sleeve up a little to find his bracelet. He leaned in to me as I traced the bracelet's ridges, thinking of how it had been with him for every Circ high point and for the atmospheric science classes he liked so much. Perhaps he'd even fiddled with it in class just as I was doing now. This very bracelet had been with him every night as he slept, whether in his warm bed in Seattle or in a sleeping bag somewhere in the crisp mountain air of the Cascades. In a way, it was like *I'd* been with him.

I don't think he knew that I had kept the bracelet he made, and that it had been with me through everything, just like mine had been with him. I reached back for my Yellow Yeti jacket and pulled out my knife.

With it tightly closed in my palm, I paused to look at him. His eyes were still burdened, but now there was curiosity in them, too.

Wordlessly, I placed the knife in his palm, folding the bracelet-lanyard on top of it for him to see. It was in much worse condition than the one on his wrist, but it had been with me continuously all the same.

In response, he pushed me onto my back, pinning me beneath his arms. The burden was gone. Now it was lust, pure and unbridled. His hand fumbled for my headlamp, snapping it off so no one would see the shadow-profile of us as his lips crashed into mine.

Chapter Twenty-Four

Stepping into Winslowe Expeditions's main tent after we got down from the rotation was like coming home. Though it was small and lacked all the niceties of Global's big top, I liked it much better. Dinner wasn't ready yet, but the smells coming from the kitchen tent next door were delicious. Pertemba's food wouldn't be as good as Mingma's—nobody's could be better than hers—but it would be miles tastier and more satisfying than Randall's fancy but poorly adapted high-altitude cuisine. After dinner, I planned to make the batch of peanut butter fudge cookies I owed Luke.

There were three clients playing Monopoly in the tent. One was a repeat client from about five years ago. We exchanged a wave. Dad was at the other end of the table, reading something on his laptop. Weather, probably. I couldn't resist going over and taking a peek, since I hadn't checked any weather websites since before Rotation One started.

Dad gave me a hug. "I hardly recognized you it's been so long."

He was joking, but I felt that way about him for real. His clothes looked tired and dated, and though he was slightly younger than Jim, he looked much older.

"The weather patterns have been unusual this year," he said. "It's going to be a real gamble with the summit windows."

"Seems like it," I said. I'd overheard Jim and Norbu discussing the same thing.

Not wanting the Monopoly crew to listen in on our conversation, we shifted over to the communications tent.

"That was quite a scare you had in the icefall," he said when we sat down.

"Yeah." I quietly adjusted the waistband of my pants so that it didn't put as much force on my bruised waist.

"I'm surprised you all were still in the icefall that late."

"It wasn't *that* late. I was with the last client, and he was lagging."

"They have you with the slowest client?"

Slowest, in Dad's eyes, meant most dangerous.

"I'm the newest."

"Why didn't Jim have you turn him around if he was going that slow?"

The question surprised me. Dad wasn't one to criticize other expedition leaders, even to me. I decided then to not give him the full details of the snowbridge collapse.

"Jim doesn't use cutoffs on the first rotation," I said. "And he likes to time it so the clients have some daylight when they hit the upper reaches."

Dad gave a disinterested *hmm*. Years ago, he had switched up the Winslowe Expeditions acclimatization plan to include a week of climbing over on Pumori. It was safer this way because the clients would have one less rotation through Everest's unstable icefall. He and his clients were leaving for Pumori tomorrow.

"When's your second rotation?" he asked.

"Five days."

He clucked his tongue and shook his head. "That could put you up there right in the middle of the storm that's coming. It doesn't sound like Jim has been keeping a close eye on it."

I wouldn't know. Being the most junior guide of a dozen, you don't exactly have access to the expedition leader in the same way as when the expedition leader is your dad.

"They have Zebra Weather with the personalized forecast option."

"It doesn't matter what they have. Even the top models have never been fully accurate, and none of them account for the unpredictability this spring and more extreme weather we've been getting in the past few years."

Jeez!

"Tell me Jim's not having you guys overnight at Camp Three on the next rotation."

"It's how it's done at Global."

"It's not necessary. I don't like the avalanche risk up there. Plus the storm." He reached for his radio.

"What are you doing?"

"Global, this is Winslowe Expeditions."

"Hi, Greg, what's up?" Jim replied.

"Meet me on nine-nine."

"Dad, don't, please!" I lunged for the radio. He held it out so I couldn't reach. "You have your philosophy, he has his."

"Hi, Jim," Dad said into the radio. "Did you see the storm warning? What are your thoughts?"

"It looks like it's coming right for us at the moment, but my hunch is that it's not going to hit here. The one last week passed to the east, so I'm willing to bet this does the same."

"I'm not so sure. I'll be keeping a close eye on it."

"Right-o, Greg. I'll be doing the same."

"Okay, good. Later man."

Dad adjusted the volume on the radio and clipped it into

its holster.

"You shouldn't have done that," I said.

"Perhaps, but to be honest, Emily, I wish you weren't working for them."

"It's kind of too late for that now."

"Yes, but I wanted to say it. See, I'm trying to be better about talking about things that are unpleasant."

"Good job, Dad. *A* for effort."

"Let me ask you something—and don't answer aloud. Now that you've been through one rotation as a guide, how do you like climbing with partners who couldn't get themselves off the mountain if they needed to? How do you like the speed you're going? Is it the same experience being on the mountain with clients as it is when just you and I climb? Do you find the fixed line convenient and nice, or would you rather be on a rope team climbing with your ax instead?"

"I know where you're going. No, climbing with the clients is not nearly as great as climbing without them, but I don't see why you're so down on it. Guiding is competitive. This is so many people's dream job!"

"But is it *your* dream job? You did all of middle school and high school online and in a homeschool workbook. You didn't go on field trips. Or have career day. At a regular high school, you would have had a group of friends all setting out on different career paths, and you would have discussed that sort of thing. You've seen so little of what is out there, and I worry that you've given up on college too soon."

Not this again.

He reached over to the table for a stack of printouts. "These are some career worksheets I found online for you. To help you think about some of your options. They're for millennials. I read that your generation has trouble with making decisions."

I groaned.

"Really, Emily, I think the bottom line is—with climbing and everything else—don't you have to know what's out there before you can know what you want?"

His words hit a nerve, and I was touched he had put so much thought into helping me, so I took the worksheets. I'd probably fill them out, too, just out of curiosity. We stood up to head over to the main tent for dinner.

"Your grandparents have been emailing me about you staying with them this summer."

Yeah, stay with them *and* Amy. *Great idea, Dad.*

"Just tell them thank you but no thanks."

He frowned. "It's your choice, but I will say this. Your grandparents want to help you. Let them. Take them up on the offer and stay with them until you decide what to do."

There was nothing new about them wanting to help me. They'd been trying to "help" since their guilt kicked in a year after they made it clear they were done mopping up Amy's messes.

Grandpa's exact words had been *I don't care if he's on the top of Mount Everest, he's coming back here to get his daughter.*

Dad hadn't been on Everest, but he had been about to start his third attempt at K2 and, still to this day, he'd never had a chance to attempt it again.

It was late when I got back to Global City. I had the cookies for Luke, but he was stuck doing a video game tournament with the UW team, and I didn't feel like hanging out with a bunch of people right now. I brushed my teeth on the outskirts of the A-Team sub-camp and then hunkered down in my tent.

The talk with Dad tonight about careers made me anxious to get a follow-on job locked in for June. I couldn't assume I'd get another job with Global, especially after this last rotation. If nothing else, the accident in the icefall was a reminder that as much of a blessing as this job had been, it also had the potential to backfire if I didn't perform well as a guide this season.

Since I wasn't sleepy yet, I repeated some of my searches of U.S.-based guiding companies. That led me to a seasonal jobs website, where there was a staffing call for Esplanade Equipment's new CentralPoint project, a nonprofit venture that would establish eco-friendly community lodges in the major adventure hotspots around the world.

The sample list of jobs were mostly the kind that didn't require a college degree, and though the pay would be low, room and board was included. The list of proposed locations was amazing, as almost all of them were places with great mountain climbing, including the city of El Chaltén in Patagonia.

What better way to train for Cerro Torre than living right there in the nearest city, where I could have an actual job and get to know lots of other mountaineers? It would be so cool!

I clicked over to the application portal. All you had to do was fill out an online application, include a résumé, and write a statement about why you would be a good fit for the CentralPoint project. The hardest part would be the résumé, seeing as mine was nothing but a few scribbles on a piece of paper at the moment.

Briefly, I wondered if it was disloyal for me to pursue something that might line me up for the great peaks of the Patagonia without my fellow dreamer, but he was on track to become a doctor, not a climber. This was the most excited I'd felt about my future since having that awful conversation with Dad. I knew it was unlikely I would get one of these jobs, but I'd at least try. Tomorrow would be résumé-writing day.

Chapter Twenty-Five

I walked over to the command center right after breakfast to work on my résumé. When I arrived, April was the only one in the tent, Skyping with—

I did a double take. Was that Josh Knox, as in Josh Knox who was pretty much the best rock climber in the whole world?

"Sorry!" I yelped. "I'll come back."

"Don't worry about it. We were just getting off."

I went over to the long table of Global laptops, trying hard not to eavesdrop as they said their good-byes.

"That was Josh Knox, wasn't it?" I asked when she hung up.

"Yeah. He's my boyfriend."

"Oh. Wow."

She laughed. "So I'm guessing you rock climb."

"Not like that! But I love it."

"I'm just starting out," she said. "It's pretty fun."

I bet, with Josh Freaking Knox as the person teaching you.

April turned on the second screen at Walkabout's editing station to catalog the rest of her drone footage from Rotation One. I typed up my résumé and then dropped it off with Doc at the UW sub-camp for her to look over.

I still had some time to kill before lunch so I settled in at one of the small tables in the big top with a cup of coffee and Dad's career worksheets. As I did, my phone pinged with a #YCCM Circ. It was the tub of peanut butter fudge cookies I'd given Luke this morning at breakfast. The cookies sat high atop a boulder, and he'd shot the rest of the video like the cookies themselves were doing a self-Circ. I smiled and shook my head. For the first time ever, there was something written after #YCCM: #*Heaven*.

I replied in our usual way: identifying the location the Circ had been taken. In this case: #*DawgsOnEverest* camp. I added an eye-wink emoticon.

The first worksheet in front of me was massively thick—almost too thick for its staple. I did the first two pages before skipping ahead to the back, skimming over the long lists of professions that were grouped in a seemingly illogical way.

The second was a fun multiple choice quiz that quickly determined that I should become a baker. I could see that.

The third worksheet required free-form sentence answers that I didn't see how would result in magically telling me what my career destiny should be. At the table in front of me, Phil, who had been playing solitaire, stood up to get another cup of tea.

"What are you working on there?" he asked when he returned.

"Oh, just some quizzes from my dad. He wants me to explore other career options before I commit to full-time guiding."

"Sounds like a good idea."

"You're a lawyer, right?"

He chuckled. "No. But close. I work in a courtroom. I'm a stenographer."

I knew it! Phil wasn't some rich lawyer or doctor or businessman. I couldn't wait to boast to Luke that I was right about Phil being different.

"How'd you pick that as a job?"

"The town I was raised in was tiny, but it was the county seat. Working for the government was what people there did if they weren't in logging or manufacturing. I can tell you more about stenography, if you're interested. Though I should mention that we're losing a lot of jobs to automatic transcription these days."

An indoor career? Hopefully never. "I guess I should see what these worksheets suggest first."

Phil returned to his table and laid his cards out into a new game. I looked at the papers in front of me and sighed. I didn't need to do the worksheets. I knew what I wanted. I just didn't know how to get there from here. Or if it was even possible. Could a sponsored climber have a life of adventure in mountains all over the world *and* a steady home base to come back to? Maybe having a flexible job in addition to being a sponsored climber was the key. Like being some sort of seasonal specialty baker or something. *Hmmm...*

Regardless of how everything came together, it was my current job with Global that would afford me the opportunity to get that record-breaking seventh summit, and that was key to the sponsorship side of the equation.

Luke came in then with a group of the UW clients. His hair was wet and spiky from a recent shower. He walked right by me with a little wink, leaving the good, fresh scent of soap floating in his wake.

This, of course, made me ultra-conscious of the fact that I hadn't showered since before we left on Rotation One. It took a big effort for the Sherpas to make the water for showers, and a long time for it to heat up in the solar shower bags, so the guides usually waited until a day or two after each rotation for the clients to have their turn before we took our one-a-week shower allotment. As soon as we were through with lunch, I was going to beeline for the A-Team shower.

After dinner, the Sherpas converted the inside of the big top to a movie theater so we could watch the Yosemite rock climbing film April, Theo, and Ernesto had worked on last spring. It wouldn't release until this summer, but their boss at Walkabout had given them permission to show it here. Our Global clients were beyond excited for this privilege.

Doc handed back my heavily marked-up résumé as we stood in line for popcorn.

"That bad?"

"It's your first one. Make those changes, and you'll be all set."

"Thanks, Doc."

"Anytime. Still on for some primping and nail painting tomorrow?"

"Yeah."

"Great. I'll tell the guys to find a different tent for their morning video games."

Luke and I found each other when it was time to take seats, picking two chairs in the last row, up against the tent wall. The chairs were close together, close enough that nobody would be able to tell our legs were pressed together on purpose.

The movie was breathtaking. Yosemite was beautiful, and the climbs were of a scale beyond anything I'd ever seen. If I could climb walls like that, the doors would be open to a whole new arena of alpine climbing. Mountains like the sheer-faced Meru in Pakistan, or even the notorious Compressor route on Cerro Torre. I exhaled wistfully.

"What?" Luke whispered.

"I want to go there."

"Me, too."

"Gotta learn to aid climb first."

"He could teach us."

At the moment, the *he* on the screen was Josh Knox.

I elbowed Luke for being ridiculous.

"He's a good guy. He would, I bet."

"You know Josh Knox?"

"Yeah."

"*No.*"

"Yes."

Wow. I guess it made sense, considering Luke knew Theo, who was the coworker of Josh Knox's girlfriend.

We settled back into the movie, watching a scene shot at this gorgeous storybook lake on top of a cliff with trees, grass, and flowers, and a waterfall in the distance. It was beautiful here in the Himalayas but in such a different way than the scenery on the screen. Here, there was no plant life higher than the village of Dingboche. It was just rock, ice, and snow on a scale unlike anywhere else on earth. Yosemite, on the other hand, was *alive.*

Ever so slowly, Luke snuck his hand into my pocket and threaded his fingers through mine. He traced the inside ridge of my thumb, making tingles run through my body. I pressed my thigh tighter against his, and he hooked his toe around my ankle. It was torture being this close to him yet being able to touch in only this limited way.

We unhooked ourselves as the credits rolled. The Walkabout crew held a question and answer session afterward. Once it became clear the clients' questions were never going to stop, Luke nudged me and then slunk out the side door. I followed a couple of minutes later.

As soon as I stepped outside into the black night, Luke grabbed my hand. This took me by surprise and knocked me off-balance, but he caught me mid-stumble and pulled me into his body. I was sure he was going to blow it for both of us by kissing me right there in the open, but he moved his head to the side at the last moment. "I'll come to your tent as soon as it's clear," he whispered.

Then he let go and walked away.

Chapter Twenty-Six

Luke shook my tent with a one-two rhythm and then crawled inside. In an instant, his hands were in my hair and our mouths were together like it had been years since we'd seen each other.

He was leaning in to me so hard that I fell back onto my sleeping bag, knocking a little of the air out of my lungs and sending a jolt of pain through my right shoulder. All of which was of no significance compared to the effect of him, planked over me with his intoxicating, freshly showered scent and his lips matching my yearning for him.

I ran my hands down the rippled muscles of his back to the sliver of warm skin where his shirt had ridden up. I let my palm slip around to his stomach, where the band of bare skin was wider. I wiggled my hand until it was fully in contact with his stomach, warm and soft, taut and firm.

What would it be like to have his hands on my stomach like this? Or his bare skin pressed against mine?

I had a fleeting out-of-body memory of Luke and I as kids, licking lollipops on the stone wall behind Mingma's.

Sometimes it was as if my mind hadn't caught up with all that had changed between us, like the two versions of Luke couldn't be happening at once. He was the kid with the lollipop, but he was also this: the sexy, incredibly fit man with the warm skin that I uniquely had the privilege of touching in this most intimate way.

I put my other hand on his stomach, sliding both hands up his shirt and around to his shoulder blades. He followed when I directed his body down fully on top of me, his tongue reaching deeper into my mouth.

He didn't stay this way for long, shifting to his side as if not wanting to squish me. I immediately missed his warmth.

"Want to try something?" he asked, his voice low and husky.

"Yeah." I had no idea what was about to happen, but I trusted him.

"Okay. Shine your phone over here."

I picked it up from where it had slipped to the side, facedown and still open to the book I had been reading. I aimed it at him. He was pulling a sleeping bag out of a stuff sack. I'd been so preoccupied that I hadn't realized he'd brought anything with him.

He examined the zipper on my sleeping bag, and then the one on his.

"It should work," he said. "It's a good thing Winslowe Expeditions and Global both use Esplanade gear."

He unzipped both our bags, then connected one side of his to the corresponding side of mine. He took off his down jacket and crawled inside. I turned off my phone light and followed suit.

We lay on our sides facing each other. We weren't touching, but the heat radiating from his body was as strong as a caress. I scooted closer. Tentatively, he reached out and pulled me against him. We both had clothes on, but in a world where we were perpetually in puffy jackets, windproof pants, Gore-Tex, crampons, and helmets, we might as well have been skin-to-skin.

Without the usual bulk of our layers, Luke was physically smaller than he always seemed, but he was strong. I mean, of course he was strong. Look at the pace he could keep on the mountain. It's just that with us being practically the same height, I tended to think of us as the same in everything, but here in the conjoined sleeping bags, there was no denying that with the solidness of his torso and the mass of his shoulders and back, physiologically, he was man to my woman. No wonder he'd beaten me at ice ax pull-ups: his body was as dense as a boxing bag.

It occurred to me that I had never seen Luke in less than a T-shirt and shorts. Oh, but to be in Railay Beach together someday, wearing practically nothing as we swam and body surfed after a day of rock climbing. To stand chest-high in that warm aqua water with my legs wrapped around his waist as we kissed, our mouths and bodies an indecipherable swirl of skin and heat and wet.

I rested my head on his lower arm, intoxicated by that thought, his proximity, and the true form of his body. He put his arm around me, and we lay like that for a long time, simply holding each other as our body heat blended and surrounded us inside the sleeping bag.

Again it hit me that this was *Luke* lying with me in this perfect paradise high in the Himalayas. This was the same Luke who liked to tease me about babying Tinkerbell and using English measurements instead of metric, and who attempted to pull sneaky moves in cards and checkers whenever I was distracted.

As he absentmindedly twisted a lock of my hair, my heart swelled with such happiness that it was deliciously tight against my breastbone. Everything between us still baffled me, but I loved it. I tucked closer into him.

"How did this happen?" I whispered.

"This as in *us*?"

I nodded.

"It's hard to say." His voice was slightly husky and unfamiliar again—a voice I wanted more of, a voice I wanted to know intimately. "There have been so many times over the years, where we were together in the Khumbu, then apart for a long time. But for me, anyway, every time and all the times in between, I guess it was the fact that my feelings didn't disappear just because you did."

I smiled.

As if he could sense this, he ran his thumb across my lower lip, tracing my smile lines first on the left, then on the right, which made me smile even wider. When he kissed me, his lips were pulled tight, and I knew he was smiling, too.

It took me a second to get oriented. The sun was starting to light the tent—my Base Camp tent with all the pictures and decorations—but Luke was here with me, in the same sleeping bag, with his body curled around mine and our heads sharing my pillow.

The double-wide opening at the top of the sleeping bag let in too much cold air, and sometime during the night, we'd put our down jackets and fleece hats back on, but our legs were still nothing but long underwear.

"Morning, MiniBoss," Luke said. "Just so you know, you have drool all over your cheek."

Oh god. I slunk down in our double sleeping bag so that my head was hidden inside.

"Ems!"

I didn't move.

"Oh, come on." He pulled back the sleeping bag.

My hair flew everywhere from the static when I sat up. I patted my face, checking for drool but didn't feel anything. I shot him a scowl. "Maybe you should get out of here before everyone wakes up and catches us."

"It's five a.m. We have some time."

I lay back down in our cozy cocoon. Finally I could look at him. Really look at him, for once, in daylight. One side of his face was crosshatched with pillow wrinkles, and his bangs stuck out oddly from beneath his hat. His smile was light and playful.

He glanced at something on the ceiling. I followed his eyes to the photo of the snowy rhododendron. I wondered if he recognized it as the same flower he'd held steady for me. "How come you never post any of this kind of stuff on Circ?"

I shrugged.

"And you've never posted a single Circ with you in it."

I groaned. "Let's not go into the self-Circ thing again."

"No, not a self-Circ but one where you're in it for a second. You don't even have a picture of yourself on your profile."

"Not my thing."

"It's probably good."

"Why?"

"Well, you know my ex-girlfriend? If she had seen a picture of you, she wouldn't have been cool with #YCCM."

"Luke!" My face was on fire.

"It's true. I had to tell her you were like a sister to me."

"Eeew." I started to scoot away, but he wouldn't let me.

"So…I was walking by the Swedish camp yesterday, and they have a bunch of skis here. What do you say we borrow some and go ski Milam Peak today?"

"Nope. Sorry, I can't. We'll have to wait until tomorrow."

"Why?"

"Doc and I have plans," I said.

He scoffed. "For what?"

"Hanging out. And painting our fingernails."

"Seriously? You're going to skip Milam Peak for nail polish?"

"Not *skip*. Delay. And, yes."

He grabbed my hand and held it up for examination.

"What?"

"I don't think I've ever seen you with nail polish."

"That's probably true."

I don't think I'd had nail polish on since...the day of the arrest, actually. Being right-handed, Amy had trouble painting that hand with her left, so she always had me do it. When I was done, she would paint my nails and toes despite my silent wishes that she wouldn't. I was in Nepal with Dad before the last of the flakes from that final application had chipped off.

My stomach grew restless at the memories, and I hated that it did. As a child, Amy's arrest and my role in it had been traumatic, but in the bigger picture, it had been a godsend. So many years had passed between then and now. Why, then, did thoughts about my past life in Washington have a strong enough effect on me that I now wanted to go sprint hills until I'd sweated all the icky feelings away?

Chapter Twenty-Seven

Doc had successfully commandeered the UW team tent for the morning, and when I arrived, she already had her cache of beauty supplies spread out on the table along with a lit lilac-scented candle.

"Don't give me that look," she said. "I carried all this to Everest Base Camp with my own two legs."

I'd only ever known Doc here at Base Camp, on those Alps trips with Dad, and that one time she'd joined us in Railay Beach. Seeing her with all these products made me wonder what kind of primping she did when she was at home in Seattle. I guess I'd assumed that, being a surgeon, she didn't fuss with all that stuff, but perhaps she wore makeup and dyed her hair and spent an hour each morning in front of the mirror like Amy had.

"Don't you feel bad about not inviting Claudia?" I asked.

"Not at all. She's a great woman, but we won't see her again after this season. You and I, we go way back."

We took our camp boots and socks off and washed our feet with medical wet wipes before coating them with a travel-sized bottle of nail conditioner and filing the tops of our toenails.

"Emily, what are you doing?"

"What?"

"You're going to shred your nails doing that."

I watched her for a minute, then mimicked how she was working the file. Doc laughed and shook her head.

She had brought foam toe-spreaders, and we put these on before applying two coats of a ridiculously bright red-orange called My Chihuahua Bites. Just as we were switching to our hands, my phone chimed with a #YCCM Circ.

I was dying to see it but resisted so as not to be rude.

"Aren't you going to get that?" Doc asked.

I glanced down, quickly recognizing the location as the start of the Kala Pattar trail. There were clients in the background, which meant Luke must have gotten suckered into leading a hike today. At first, I was confused because this Circ wasn't a high point, real or contrived. But then, I realized it was a job-related #DawgsOnEverest post in which he'd snuck #YCCM into the hashtag list. I couldn't help smiling.

"Oh, a guy! You didn't tell me there's a guy. You're just like Greg. Unless you ask point-blank, you'll never get an answer. So, where did you meet him? Let me guess, a super sexy Aussie climber from your last trip to Thailand?"

My cheeks heated. I shook my head.

"Oh, wait a minute. This is all making sense."

Shit. What if she suspected Luke? We'd both be fired.

"What's making sense?" I said to stall while I tried to think of a diversion.

"Luke."

"No."

She gave me a look. "I was noticing how well you two were getting along as you cut those eggplants the other day."

"No! It's nothing. We're just—"

"This is adorable." She put down her nail file. "*So* adorable. Don't worry. Your secret's safe with me. You guys are perfect. He used to ask about you every time he came over to my house for dinner."

She hopped out of her chair and was soon digging through the first aid box in the corner of the tent. "This calls for extra primping. We'll do your hair, too. How long has it been since you got it cut?" She found a pair of surgical scissors and raised them victoriously in the air.

"A long time," I said, self-consciously stroking my hair. At least I'd showered yesterday, otherwise she'd probably recommend I shave it all off.

"It's not your fault. Greg treats you like a guy. But I'm serious about the trim. You could use it. Not that you need to do something other than be yourself for a guy. There's a happy medium. Let's find that."

"All right, *Mom*."

"I'm not old enough to be your mom."

"You could be, if you were a teen mom."

"Emily, I was one hundred percent focused on grades in high school. I didn't sleep with anyone until…well…your dad. I was never going to be a teen mom."

I almost dropped the bottle of top coat. "Did you just say you and Dad—"

"You know this."

"No, I don't know this."

"Does that man tell you *anything?* No, actually, I'm not surprised. The president should give you two the nuclear release codes. You're harder to crack than a safe."

I didn't know what to ask first. It made perfect sense, but how could I have never picked up on it, even if Dad hadn't said anything?

"He always said you were his friend," I offered. Actually,

he'd always said that she was *our* friend.

"That Greg!"

"I can't believe Dad has a girlfriend."

"Had. It's been over for a while now." She put my hands on the table and brushed the polish across my fingernails.

My head was still playing catch-up. When had it started? When had it stopped? Those trips to the Alps, where we'd stayed in an actual hotel? She had probably been paying for everything! This was horrifying. My dad was such a kind spirit—how had he let her do that?

"Don't feel bad for me, I'm the one who broke it off," she said, misjudging my expression.

"When did it stop?"

"It was the winter before the icefall avalanche."

I frowned. That's when the Alps trips had stopped, and Doc hadn't come to Railay that year as planned.

"The long distance was too much, and there was never going to be an end to it," she said.

No wonder Dad was adamant about me exploring careers other than guiding. He'd started Winslowe Expeditions as a way to support me, and in doing that, it had cost him a relationship with a beautiful, accomplished woman whom we both adored. I covered my face with my hands.

"Oh, no, no, you're going to mess up your nail polish," she said, pulling my hands back.

"So, basically, you guys broke up because of me," I said.

"Partly."

"You're actually admitting that?"

"You're the one who said it."

"Yeah, but I thought you're never supposed to say that kind of thing to the kid."

"Don't get me wrong, I love how dedicated he's been to you since you came to live with him, but the cost of living in the U.S. is so high, and Greg wasn't going to explore moving back until he no longer needed to support you. Really, it's my fault. I was the one with the flexibility, but I wasn't going to leave my practice in Seattle for a year-round volunteer medical job somewhere here in the Himalayas."

I frowned.

"You know, it's all okay," she said. "Greg and I are friends now."

Yeah. A friend who borrowed money for his daughter's plane ticket.

"How did we end up talking about this?" she asked. "This is all old news. And you have hot, new news. You couldn't have picked a better guy than Luke. He is the best."

She motioned for me to move to one of the chairs closer to the light for my haircut. "I don't know what I'm doing, so I'm just going to trim straight across the back above your split ends, okay?"

I nodded.

"I think it's safe to assume Greg has no clue about this new romance of yours?"

"Romance?" I scrunched my nose. That word was so medieval.

"We have only a few more weeks here—what's going to happen then? I'd be pissed if you broke his heart. Or if he broke yours."

"We haven't talked about that yet. Seriously, it *just* happened."

Behind me, Doc snipped away with the scissors. I hoped she was at least a little better at trimming hair than she was at making eggplant parmesan.

"So, you and Luke would have had the perfect scenario if you hadn't gone nutso and rejected Townsend College. Now I'm sad I helped you with your résumé for that CentralPoint thing."

"But CentralPoint would be such an amazing opportunity,

and you said it: he could break my heart just as easily as the other way around."

"You know, Luke isn't in a position to leave Washington for a while. He has two years left of college and then medical school after that."

"Doc, it's only been a week since we first kissed."

She brushed through my trimmed hair. "You can stay with me, you know. My place is small, but you're welcome as long as you want."

"And continue the Winslowe family charity case?"

She grabbed a chunk of my hair. "I'll cut this right off," she threatened.

"Okay, okay! I'll think about it."

"You're getting sassy this year, MiniBoss. You better think about it, for real. It would be fun. I work long hours during the week, but I have most weekends off. We could do nails in a real spa, with some of my girlfriends. We could climb Rainier. You'd be like my live-in mountain guide."

She handed me a tiny mirror so I could look at my hair.

"Looks great, thanks," I said.

I held the mirror for her so she could trim her bangs.

"Luke aside, you really shouldn't give up on college just yet," she said. "I know Greg's talked to you about it being okay to change majors. Maybe just come home to Washington for a while and explore some options."

"Washington's not my home."

"Well, then, where is?"

"Here, probably."

She set the scissors down and stared at me. "Here, as in Everest Base Camp?"

"Yeah. Why not? I've spent more time here than any single place."

"This is no one's home, not even the Sherpas," she said as she finished her bangs. "This is a temporary village on the shoulder of a wrathful deity."

We didn't finish the discussion because Cook-Phurba walked in with a plate of sandwiches, which Doc must have arranged ahead of time with Randall.

"Much appreciated, Phurba," she said.

After we finished eating, Doc mixed up a bright yellow face mask from some mystery ingredients and a bowl of salt from the kitchen. I declined when she passed the bowl to me.

When she was all done applying it, she asked me to drop off the sandwich plates over in the scullery.

"I'm leaving this on until after my siesta, and I would prefer if the men didn't get a look at this."

"No problem."

We loaded the beauty supplies into her backpack. "Well, this has been a highly successful girls' day," she said. "We both have fresh hair and perfect nails, were able to skip the tiresome politics talk at lunch, and uncovered two secret relationships."

I hugged her cautiously, not wanting any of that mask to end up on my jacket, even though, technically, it would blend in perfectly.

"I gave you a hard time about calling me mom, but you *are* like a daughter to me. I think you know that. But how about we just call it 'little sister?'"

"The math doesn't work out on that, either, you know."

"It could."

I gave her a smile, but I was still unsettled from all that we'd talked about.

We have only a few more weeks here—what's going to happen then?

I had no idea. About Luke, what I'd be doing for work, or where I'd be going when the season was over.

Instead of returning to my tent for a nap, I went to the command center to submit my CentralPoint materials and continue looking for a job.

The command center was bustling this afternoon with the twins on two of the laptops, Norbu and a few of the Sherpas checking weather, and April and Theo over in the corner fixing something on the drone.

I talked with everyone for a while, then logged in on a laptop on the backside of the table so no one would see what I was doing. After I'd finished submitting all the materials to Esplanade's CentralPoint portal, I filled out the catchall application for U.S. national parks summer jobs, clicking the toggle buttons next to waitress, hostess, food service worker, hotel clerk, rental clerk, and housekeeper jobs in any location near mountains. Jackson Hole, Glacier, Denali, Yosemite, Estes Park, and Sawtooth National Parks.

Next, I started checking for ski resorts that were open in the summer and had on-site staff lodging. This was a tedious process, and before long I was sidetracked, browsing recent trip reports for the peaks in Patagonia.

But even as I daydreamed about Cerro Torre, Fitz Roy, and all the others, I was still being pulled by the image of a very different place: my tiny white bungalow.

Now that Doc knew about Luke and me, I was extra self-conscious about hanging out with him in the big top, so I kept to the A-Team during dinner. After dinner, the clients sucked me into a three-hour A-Team Trivial Pursuit tournament. Phil, Phurba, and I were a team—and we won. Which was a big surprise, considering our educational levels in comparison to everyone else. Afterward, the men were still jazzed up on too much after-dinner soda, milling about outside, so I went to my tent instead of attempting to sneak over to Luke's.

Doc's reminder today about the limited time Luke and

I had left at Base Camp together was weighing on me. But it shouldn't be. It was too soon to be overanalyzing Luke's intentions and making plans for a joint future. *Going on Eighteen* articles were forever warning about putting the cart before the horse like this. I shouldn't let the uncertainty of my future and what would happen with Luke and me after the summit bid cloud the joy of finally being together with him.

It was late by the time it finally got quiet outside, but I was dying for the burn of Luke's kiss. Since I wasn't sure if he was still awake, I brightened my tent with my headlamp and then lay down on my sleeping bag to beckon him using a Circ of my decorated tent ceiling. Just before I finished, I remembered what he said about me never putting myself in Circs, so I dipped the screen across my face before it hit three hundred and sixty degrees and snapped off. I added #YCCM to the Circ and hit send.

I awoke to the muffled, high-pitched beeps of my watch alarm beneath my pillow. I realized Luke had not responded to my Circ last night, but that was understandable. To save battery, all of us generally turn off our phones at night. I sat up and dressed quickly, excited to get outside and meet him for our ski day. Even more exciting than skiing, it was the first time we'd be alone together out of the prying eyes of the Base Camp gossipmongers since crossing the *friends* line, and we had the entire, glorious day ahead of us.

Chapter Twenty-Eight

Luke was waiting for me at the Everest Base Camp signs with a pair of skis already strapped to his pack and the skis for me leaning against a rock next to him. He must have grabbed them from the Swedish camp on his way back from Kala Pattar yesterday.

"See, one day to wait wasn't so bad," I teased when I got to him.

I longed for his familiar voice and accent to wrap around me like the embrace he couldn't give me out here in the open, but he hardly reacted, which was weird.

I shrugged it off as I bent down to lash my skis to my backpack. "So, I found out something interesting yesterday."

"What?"

"Doc and Dad were a thing."

"Yeah."

"What do you mean, *yeah*? This is a big deal!"

"They aren't anymore," he said.

"Yes, as I found out yesterday. You knew they were a couple?"

"Well, not for sure, but I'd always assumed."

"And you never said anything to me?"

"I assumed you knew."

"Yes, but—"

"It's not that big of a deal."

My internal alarm went off, and I bit my nails anxiously. It was unlike Luke not to play along with me, but he started coughing, so I didn't push it. Once we began walking, I handed him one of the toasted bagels with cream cheese I'd made at the big top. As soon as we finished them, he picked up the pace. Quite a lot actually. Which was good because we had a long distance to cover today, and it would be best if we could get back before nightfall.

At Gorak Shep, we turned north, uphill and deeper into the Himalayas. Milam Peak was four miles ahead in the distance, barely a molehill compared to the jagged goddesses around it. It was a good five-thousand feet of vertical, though, a rival for any ski resort in terms of longest run. As we continued, Luke's pace didn't relent. I was feeling it today, especially in my injured shoulder, because the skis added an extra fifteen pounds to my pack.

After three miles, we veered off the trail, crossed a small stream, and ventured into unbroken snow. I was sweaty and winded, and we hadn't even started on the steep part yet. Luke and I put on gaiters and screwed the plastic baskets onto the ends of our trekking poles to turn them into ski poles. Then, we unrolled skins along the bottoms of our skis that would enable us to walk up the slope on top of the snow.

Luke was still on turbocharge as we skinned up the slope, and I struggled to keep pace. When we paused for water about halfway up, he still wasn't joking around or teasing or anything like that. The hairs on my arms pricked up nervously. Something was wrong.

We continued upward, step after step, with the typical

uphill view of white, white, and more white, with the vastness of the panorama open to our backs. We reached the top of Milam Peak, which was windblown and had exposed rock in places. Mount Everest loomed in the distance, its jet stream plume flying in full force today. I briefly wondered if I would make it to the top this year and actually get that seventh summit.

Silently, we unclipped from our skis and switched our layers around for the descent. Luke broke a granola bar in two and tossed half to me. He smiled, but it came out more like a wince. Adrenaline shot through me, not in a good way. There was definitely something wrong.

"It's beautiful today," I started, testing him out.

He surveyed Milam's south slope. "Yeah. It's perfect. But it's a long way back, so we should be probably start down soon."

The volume on my internal alarm doubled.

My comment to Doc yesterday came echoing back at me: *maybe he's going to be the one to break my heart.*

I told myself not to jump to conclusions. Just because he was acting oddly did not mean it had anything to do with me. Maybe there had been a confrontation with one of the Sherpas.

Sometimes, it was normal for us not to talk, I reminded myself as I choked down the granola bar. But it was not normal for us to be two feet apart like this with him barely managing to make eye contact with me.

We peeled the skins off our skis and walked over to the lip of the bowl on the south side to switch the rest of our gear for skiing down. I snuck a glance at him. His face was somber as he used one of his poles to knock the caked snow off his boot. *Say something, Emily!*

"So, uh, is something wrong?" I asked.

"You could say that."

My stomach hit the floor. I knew instantly: the problem *was* related to me.

"What is it?"

He shook his head, saying nothing. He stepped over his skis and got ready to click in.

What in the heck? He wasn't going to answer?

Before I could figure out a different way to come about this, he jammed a pole into the snow and looked right at me. "Doc was joking with me last night—about us."

Oh.

"I'm sorry. I didn't mean to tell her," I said. "She was right there yesterday when you Circ-ed me from Kala Pattar—"

"I don't care that Doc knows. She likes to gossip, but she wouldn't about us. The thing that's bothering me is something else she said. She mentioned your mom. And the way she said it, it was like…she wasn't dead."

My body froze while my mind went into a tailspin. *Form some words, Emily, form some words.*

"I've never told you that she's dead."

"So it's true? Your mom is alive?"

I didn't move for a minute, then I nodded my head.

He turned away from me faster than I could blink. "I almost called off skiing today, but I thought I'd give you the benefit of the doubt. Because surely there is no way you've been lying to me about this for ten years."

"She was in prison! That's why I came here to be with Dad. She might as well have been dead. It's a technicality, really. I haven't spoken to her since the day she was arrested."

"A technicality? No. It's a big deal. A *really* big deal." I couldn't see his eyes because he had on glacier glasses, but I didn't need to, not with that icy tear in his voice.

He jammed his boots in the bindings and grabbed his ski poles.

"Hold on!" I begged.

"Nope, sorry, I can't." He wiggled his heels to test the bindings and then pushed over the slope without me.

Chapter Twenty-Nine

"Wait, Luke. Wait!" I yelled, though it was clear he wasn't going to stop.

He flew down the slope, angled straight to the fall line, not even putting in any turns.

Oh god, what had I done?

I scrambled to get my boots clipped in, then I pushed off with my poles as hard as I could. There was no pleasure in the five minutes of downhill that had taken four hours to climb. It was nothing but bad adrenaline. I wanted to gun the fall line, like him, but the skis were too long for me, so I was forced to keep my speed in check.

I'd known that I needed to tell him the truth about Amy, yet I hadn't bothered to follow through on it.

As the slope leveled off, my speed dropped away quickly. I poled with all my might to keep my momentum going. When I reached him, he was in the final steps of reattaching his skis to his backpack.

"Luke," I blurted. "I'm really, really sorry that I never told you about my mom. It wasn't intentional. It's just something people assume, and Dad and I never correct them."

His jaw was set, and he didn't bother turning in my direction. "It blows my mind that you lied to me for that long about something of this magnitude."

"It was out of practicality. An American single dad raising his daughter in the middle of the Himalayas…our situation made more sense to people if they thought Amy had died. And the result is nearly the same. Even though she's living, she's still dead to me."

Now he turned. "That's *exactly* it. The result is *not* the same. Yesterday, Doc told me she offered for you to stay at her condo because she didn't think you wanted to go back to Port Townsend, where your mom was. Where a person you've been pretending is *dead* happens to live. It all makes perfect sense. You didn't decide not to go to *college*, you decided not to go back to *Washington*."

"No, that's not true," I said immediately.

"Then tell me you're still planning to come home to Washington after the season's over."

"I never said I was! You know what kind of position I'm in financially. I have to take whatever job I can get after this."

"You said it the other night, when I was talking about roommate boards near Port Townsend."

"I said it was a good idea, not that I was going to do that."

His face went hard.

"You have to understand," I said. "Washington is not my home. It wasn't even my home when I was living there." The rising panic choked me. I couldn't go on. My whole world was imploding.

"You know, I'm not just some guy at a frat party, and you're not some girl I happened to sit next to in class," he said. "We've known each other for a decade. We were going to climb the Top Five. I lived for your Circs, always waiting, hoping to get one from you. Going a few days without was torture. But it's clear that you entered this knowing we had only a few weeks together, max. Knowing you had no intention…"

His head drooped. I wanted to reach out for him. Or to say something, only I couldn't figure out what would make this better.

"Honestly, Emily, I just feel so stupid for ever thinking it was a possibility. My mistake. Even the choice to go to UW in the first place. Yes, it was the best of the scholarship options for being close to good mountains to climb, but it was also the closest university to Townsend College."

He'd picked UW because he knew I'd be going to Townsend College? This fact would have normally given me happy butterflies, but now it just made my panic worse. He'd picked a college based on me, and I hadn't even mustered the nerve to find his email address so I could tell him I was taking a gap year instead of coming to Washington last year as planned.

He reached down for his backpack and put it on. "I should have known all along that a girl like you would never see me seriously."

Still stunned, I watched him take off down the trail.

"Luke!" I yelled.

I knew he could hear me, but he kept walking. I hurried to lash my skis to my backpack.

He had gotten quite a head start, so I pushed into a jog, my poorly attached skis slashing at my calves like giant knives.

"Stop!" I screamed when I got closer.

This time, he obeyed, turning back to me.

"It's okay," he said in a voice so hard it could have scraped ice off a windshield. "It will be fine. We'll just get through the rest of this season. We can be amicable. I know *you* can. That's kind of your specialty, right? You'll go on to do more of this, I presume." He swept his arm toward Everest. "It's the most lucrative mountain out there. I promise you this: I will not. I won't go further than Tengboche. This is the last time. You can have it all to yourself from now on."

My blood boiled. These were some vicious things he was throwing at me. "So you're just going to write me off? Without even giving me a chance to explain? Didn't it occur to you that my future has been a huge question ever since that bomb Dad dropped on me? And I want to know what you meant by *a girl like me?* And how is it any less of a lie that you show up out of the blue this season even though you had known months in advance that you would be coming here?"

"I hardly think the two things are comparable."

His tone was haughty. I was going to explode with anger. This time when he walked away, I didn't stop him.

So much had happened this season, I couldn't keep up. So many changes, so many possibilities dashed before they had a chance to ignite.

It took only about five minutes for my anger to die down. With Luke's head start, I had no chance of catching up with him, but I did my best not to fall farther behind.

Dad and I might both be guilty of a lie by omission, but it's not like he and I had planned it out or anything. We'd never discussed this fact between us. In fact, Dad and I didn't talk about Amy at all, ever. To him, she was just some woman from the past who'd gotten herself knocked up on purpose. A woman to whom he had paid child support. Before I came to live with him, he'd seen her only two times a year: pickup and drop-off for his designated three-week yearly visit. They hadn't even been boyfriend-girlfriend.

I didn't know about Amy's caper with the pregnancy until much later, but I'd always sensed what a burden I was to her and how fundamentally different we were. How different I was than all the other girls my age. My childhood in Washington had been unhappy. I didn't start loving life and being excited for the future until I got to the mountains with Dad. And once I was here, what reason did I have to ever reflect on and relive my unhappy past?

Luke had so easily jumped to the conclusion that it was Amy who had kept me from Townsend College, just like Doc had that day in the medical tent. He knew nothing about the situation, but in all the turmoil inside me right now, the clarity and confidence of his observation had me second-guessing myself.

I really, truly didn't think college was the right path for me, but considering it would have been mostly paid for, would I have at least given it a try had Amy settled somewhere different than Port Townsend when she got out of prison?

As I hiked the rest of the way, staring at Luke's back ahead of me made my stomach raw with turmoil. I told myself things could not be over this fast. He was just angry. And hurt. He'd simmer down, and we could talk through this.

Finally, as we passed Gorak Shep, Luke's pace slackened enough that I was slowly closing the gap between us. As if he knew I was right on his heels now, he stopped at the *Y* in the trail before Base Camp.

It was close to sunset now, and we both had our glacier glasses off, so when he looked at me, I could tell he was as torn up as I was. It stung to know I was the reason, but seeing him hurting gave me hope. Indifference would have been impossible to bear.

He gave me a weak half smile. "You were right to call me out about how I didn't tell you I was coming here this season. It was purposeful, so I suppose it's fair to call it a lie. The reason I did it was because I had to know what your first reaction to seeing me would be. Your reaction when you hadn't had a chance to steel up and hide what you truly thought. And, yes, I understood that your future is unstable right now, but I didn't know the whole story, and because of that, I thought there was hope of *us* continuing after the season. I was *sure* there was hope. I mean, didn't you feel it? How can that *not* be hope?"

I swallowed. There were tears in my eyes.

"When I said 'a girl like you,' I meant a girl whom I would never be good enough for. A girl who is so talented in the mountains that she could be sponsored by any company if she ever thought of asking. One who is incredibly smart and funny and so perfectly unspoiled that she doesn't even know it. A girl who is so beautiful that I sometimes think she can't possibly be real. The girl who all the guys here dream about, the one whose name is on the wind across all expeditions, ever since that year she turned sixteen and climbed Manaslu without oxygen."

There were tears in his eyes, too. I stepped in to him, dropping my head against his shoulder. Very tentatively, he put his hand around my upper back.

"So there you have it, Emily," he whispered. Then he stepped back so that we were no longer touching. "But in the end," he continued, his voice turning savage, "none of this means anything anymore...because I have no idea who you really are."

Chapter Thirty

Dinner at Global that night was excruciating. The effort of keeping my eyes away from Luke while I pretended to pay attention to conversations was escalating my headache into a raging migraine. One glance at him and I'd be completely and utterly ruined. Just the thought of what had happened made it hard to breathe. This was full-on panic.

Also, I was doing my best to avoid Doc. She'd see that I wasn't okay, and I wouldn't be able to tell her why. If I told her what had happened, she would think it was her fault, which it wasn't. Regardless of how Luke found out, I was the one responsible for this. I was the one who let everyone believe Amy was dead for no reason other than that it was easier for me that way.

At my first chance, I bolted back to my tent, taking painkillers to dull my headache. What was wrong with me for being so averse to returning to Washington? It's not like Port Townsend was the only city in the state. The Seattle metro area had several million people. Chances were miniscule that I would ever run into Amy if I lived somewhere else.

So what if I'd had an unhappy childhood? People went through so much worse than I had. A mother arrested for dealing methamphetamine, a single night in a holding facility for children, then getting shuffled to a dad I hardly knew. A dad who happened to have the coolest job in the world and ended up loving me and introducing me to the life I was made for.

I put on music, not for the enjoyment of it but to block out my mind. But every song I owned, it seemed, had a memory of Luke attached. I tore my earbuds out and threw them over onto my lettuce-box shelf.

Now I was left with the soundtrack of the groaning icefall, hissing generator, footsteps on gravel, and passing conversations. My ears strained for his voice. My mind willed my tent to shake in the one-two rhythm.

It couldn't be over. It couldn't.

I hid out for most of the next day in the Winslowe Expeditions camp, which was vacant except for the base camp manager, since everyone else was on Pumori. I went into Dad's tent and lay down on his foam mattress. Even though he hadn't been there for several days, his tent still smelled familiar and homey in the same way Winslowe Expeditions's main tent did. I wondered if my tent had a scent, too, and what it smelled like to Luke.

I took a look around Dad's tent. It was practically empty, since most of his things were with him on Pumori, but I was surprised to see a tiny, book-style picture frame on the ground near the sleeping pad. I picked it up to look at it closer. It was plastic and lightweight. One side was a several-years-old picture of me that I hadn't seen before. There was ocean in the background, so it had to be Railay Beach. The picture on the facing frame was of Doc and Dad in front of a palm tree, both wet from swimming. The pictures and frame must have been a gift from her.

With the gaping hole in my heart that was Luke, I felt intensely bad for Dad. After all, if he still had a picture in his tent, he must still have feelings for her. It would be the same way for me, years from now, about Luke.

No.

I refused to believe it, not yet.

All those amazing things he had said about me before he walked away—that's where the hope was. I was going to fight for this. If he could just hear the whole story, he would understand. My lie hadn't been intentional but one of self-preservation. One that I didn't think would hurt anyone—but it had. Though I'd considered our losses equal, in reality, they were not. Someday, Amy and I might reconcile. Even the thought of it made me nauseous with disgust. But that possibility was there, and that was the difference. Luke's dad was *dead*. Gone forever. Luke would never have a chance to see him again no matter how hard he wished for it.

It's no wonder he'd reacted so strongly yesterday. I had been cruel to allow the lie to go on as long as it had. Luke, of all people, deserved nothing but truth from me. I owed that to him.

The smell of Dad in his tent was taking me back to a memory. All the way back to when I was ten years old and the first nights at Mingma's when Dad had left me so he could do a previously planned Annapurna expedition for Esplanade Equipment. He'd given me one of his fleece jackets to use as a pillow. That jacket had smelled of him like this tent did. I used it like a security blanket. Those nights had been ugly. I had a concept of the danger involved in that particular climb, and in the darkness of the night, I cried. Big, choking cries that I tried to silence into his jacket so as not to worry Mingma or wake Baby Pasang.

Looking back now, I knew that Luke had heard me those nights. It had been the reason he'd been extra nice to me, showing me how to play Nepali games, helping me learn my chores, and teaching me soccer moves.

In all our time, Luke and I had never spoken of those first nights and my not-so-silent weeping. He had to have assumed that I was crying because my mom had died, when in reality it was because I was terrified of what would happen to me if my second of two parents didn't return to get me.

I swallowed a guilty lump. All along he'd thought we had something major in common—a deep understanding of each other because we'd both had a parent die. But that had never been true for me.

Luke was right about me ruling out Washington when I thought about where I would go after this, though it hadn't been done consciously. Even when I'd filled out the application for national parks summer jobs, I hadn't checked the toggle boxes next to North Cascades, Mount Rainier, or Olympic—the three national parks in Washington. Washington was tainted for me in the same way Cho Oyu was for Dad. He'd told me once in a rare moment of talking about feelings that he couldn't see the profile of that mountain without also seeing Gyalzen's body. Luke's father. My dad would never climb that mountain again, even though it was becoming a popular and lucrative destination for guided clients.

The heavy wetness of western Washington's forests would always take me to that day my happy, fancy-free exploring morphed into a terrifying taste of a battle for survival that landed my mother in prison. Even thinking about it was making the hairs on my arms stand up.

But couldn't I train myself out of this kind of reaction? Certainly I wouldn't let something as trivial as a bad memory keep me from Luke.

That is, if he ever spoke to me again.

My radio squawked. "Hey, Emily," Thom said. "We need to post a pre-departure blog for Rotation Two. Can you get that done today?"

I forced myself to get up and return to Global City. Mustering excitement to write this post would be impossible. On top of everything else, it was a reminder that this time tomorrow, on Rotation Two, I'd be sharing a tent with someone who loathed me. I had an enormous task ahead in bridging all that had happened yesterday, but I had to find a way.

Thankfully, I had the command center to myself when I arrived. I scraped together a blog post, essentially writing the same thing Tyler posted before Rotation One, except with a different itinerary. I opened the shared photo file and picked a few candids of the clients hanging out in camp.

Norbu came in for a fresh radio battery and then left, leaving me again with the command center to myself. I checked my email for a response from CentralPoint or any of the other jobs I'd applied for. Nothing.

That's when Luke stepped in, stopping short as soon as he saw me. For a brief moment, daggers of hostility flew from his eyes, then he turned on his heel and stepped right back out. The tent door flapped dully behind him.

So much for pretending everything was normal. My pulse shot through the roof, and my chest was too tight to catch a complete breath. *It couldn't be over.*

With renewed fervor, I applied for more jobs, anything and everything that was in a mountain town and didn't require a college degree. Because now, unless I could pull a miracle and turn this situation around, I had two reasons to never go back to Washington state.

Chapter Thirty-One

It was snowing as we started toward the icefall in the thick blackness of a cloud-covered, starless morning. Today we were going all the way from Base Camp to Camp Two. The storm Dad had warned about was still on its way. We'd gone over this in detail at our guides' meeting last night, but Jim was certain it wouldn't hit until the afternoon, and we were planning to kill two days at Camp Two anyway for acclimatization before our overnight at Camp Three.

As always, Phurba and I were in the rear with the slowest clients, and we had to wait for the others to start before we could get going. The gaggle of us was nothing but faint black profiles of people with headlamps floating through the air, but even so, I knew exactly which silhouette was Luke.

"Ready?" Phurba asked in Sherpa when it was our turn. Today, he was wearing his NASCAR bandana as a buff around his nose and mouth to protect from the cold. I nodded, and we stepped off after our clients. It was unbearably cold with the low pressure system in front of the storm, and it was even colder inside the icefall.

From the start, everything seemed off. My crampons didn't seem like they were on tight enough, my harness was twisted uncomfortably, and my pack was heavy with all the extra gear I was carrying for the clients, since I was too proud to pass any of it along to the Sherpas. Even the drone wasn't feeling it this morning. April had it flying up ahead with the Cubans when we started, but the winds had picked up too much, and she'd had to fly it back to Base Camp.

I'd had a terrible night of sleep, since I had not been able to put the brakes on thinking about Luke. Also, I dreaded crossing through the section of the icefall where the serac had fallen last time. Just being in the icefall again had my pulse at an anxious clip. I kept my eyes straight ahead so that my headlamp beam didn't light up any of the terrifying ice blocks surrounding us. If I couldn't see them, they weren't there.

I was with Phil again today. He was coughing a lot, but at least he was keeping pace.

"You're doing great," I told him.

"Sometimes you need a reminder of what it's like to be alive," he replied. "That's the whole reason I came here in the first place."

I think he was referring to what happened in the icefall. Chills ran through my body because today the icefall's normal creaks and groans sounded more like ominous cracks and gasps.

We continued on in the morning's gripping cold. I was wiggling my toes and fingers constantly and breathing through my balaclava in an attempt to warm the air before it hit my lungs. Oddly, it was getting colder instead of warmer as sunrise neared, but there was nothing to do other than to keep moving forward.

"Cold," Phurba said as we waited for the clients to cross the ladder over one of the precipices. He seemed antsy at the clients' slow progress, and this unsettled me further.

"No kidding," I replied, trying to keep my tone light.

It was six thirty, and we should have been able to turn off headlamps by now, but it was still too dark because of the cloud cover.

By the time all of A-Team was through the last ladder bridge of the icefall, it was snowing heavily and winds were picking up. Sensing the degrading conditions, the clients naturally went faster. When there was finally enough daylight to turn off the headlamps, the visibility was so low I couldn't even see the side of Nuptse.

Dad would be pissed if he knew Jim had us heading up in this. He would never have left Base Camp with a storm sure to hit, even if it wasn't forecasted until later in the day. That was one of the big differences between a small outfit like Winslowe Expeditions and a huge company like Global. The cost of a long weather delay when multiplied by the number of staff and clients on our expedition would have a catastrophic impact on the profit-loss margin, and with Jim reporting directly to a corporate oversight panel, these things mattered a lot.

Though the clients were moving faster than normal, it wasn't fast enough.

"These guys need to pick it up," Phurba said.

I nodded in agreement.

The full force of the wind hit us once we exited the icefall. Here, I should have been able to see up the Western Cwm to Camp Two, but all that was visible was Camp One and the slope of the cwm that seamlessly blended into the clouds ahead and to the sides. Hulk and Tyler and the others at the front of the group were already hidden by those clouds.

Camp One was vacant when we arrived. Having pushed our clients through the last half of the icefall, I wasn't sure they had enough power left to make fast enough progress up the cwm before we were trapped in the storm. I halted Phurba and Dorje to discuss it. "Think we should hold off here?" I asked.

Phurba glanced around and nodded. "Yeah, maybe."

I swallowed. It was such an easy slope, but the storm… You don't risk getting caught in any storm outside of camp on Mount Everest. Or anywhere in the Himalayas, period.

"Jim, this is Emily," I said into the radio. "We're in Camp One. I've got Phil, Glen, Johnsmith, Phurba, and Dorje. We might need to call it here."

"Okay, Emily, hold on." The wind howled so loudly I could barely hear him. Even though my back was to the wind, ice flakes lashed the exposed slivers of skin between my glacier glasses and balaclava.

"Emily, this is Jim. We have some supplies at Camp One, but the sleeping bags are up at Camp Two. It's just a straight shot from where you're at. How long do you think your clients will take?"

If it was just me, I could do it in forty-five minutes. I looked over to Phil, our weakest link. He was coughing but otherwise holding up okay.

"If your guys can manage it, I'd rather not have the group separated when this storm hits," Jim said.

It could take *two hours* for Phil to cover the distance.

"Yeah, yeah, Mr. Jim." It took me a second to realize that this was Dorje responding to him in the radio. "We keep going."

Before I could question Dorje, he was signaling for our clients to get moving. My body bristled. This was not the right decision.

But, then, what did I know? Look what happened in the icefall last time. And in the mountains, it wasn't a question of risk or safety, it was choosing your risk. Getting stranded at an unequipped camp wasn't a good option, either.

We kept going, and it seemed visibility was worsening by the minute. After a half hour of walking, I insisted everyone rope up so no one could accidentally wander out of sight.

After an hour—the point that Jim would have likely expected we would arrive at Camp Two—he called me on the radio.

"Total whiteout here," I yelled over the wind. "Can't see the camp."

"You lost line of sight?"

"Never had it."

He spouted off a list of instructions straight from Mountaineering 101, including roping up, planting pickets as we progressed, and turning on headlamps. Already done, done, and done.

"Just keep going. Be sure to stay on the boot-packed trail so no one ends up nose diving into a crevasse."

Great.

Phurba was at the head of the rope. I was at the back with Dorje. Johnsmith was slowing down. Why hadn't I noticed how bad his limp was getting? I clapped his shoulder. "Keep moving," I told him. "We're almost there, and we'll bring you to Doc Teresa so she can look at your leg."

We kept on in faith. Yes, it was a low angle and there was no skyscraper-tall cliff to walk off, but it was damned scary to be in a whiteout with three grown men all depending on me and the Sherpas. The lack of visibility made me claustrophobic, and I yearned to pick up the pace and get the heck to Camp Two. Instead, I did the only thing I could: wiggled my fingers and toes and rubbed my arms and thighs in an attempt to stay warm.

Up ahead, at the max point of my visibility, Phurba waved his arms in excitement. "I see the tents," he told me over the radio.

I couldn't see anything but whiteness beyond him, but by the time my trailing end of the rope arrived at where he had been standing, I saw the tents through the shifting snow. Phurba was helping Glissading Glen off the rope and into his tent.

Thank god.

Phurba and Dorje took care of Phil and the rest of our group while I walked Johnsmith into the cook tent, where Tyler volunteered to get Doc.

I tried to conceal my chattering teeth from Thom and the Sherpas while I looked anxiously at Johnsmith, praying it was just his leg that had slowed him down. What if I'd missed signs of altitude sickness? It was hard to tell, not knowing him very well and being delirious with cold myself.

Doc entered noiselessly and checked Johnsmith's vitals.

"He's just chilled, and his knee is swollen. We'll give him some heat packs and ibuprofen."

Doc made sure he took the right amount of medicine, then stood back with me. "Get to your tent and warm up, Em."

My tent, where Luke would surely be. Doc broke open two packets of hand warmers for me and nudged me toward the door.

When I reached our tent, I struggled to unzip it with my stiff fingers, then practically fell inside as a gust of wind trucked by and pushed me down. Luke was lying in his sleeping bag, listening to music on his phone. It wasn't as big of a deal to see him as I'd thought. That's the blessing of being hypothermic. You don't care about anything.

As soon as I managed to get my boots off, I slipped deep inside my sleeping bag, cinching the cord around the top of my head. I pulled the hand warmers out of my pockets, rubbing them across my body—feet, knees, sides, hands.

Dorje had made the right call today about continuing to Camp Two. We'd have been in grave trouble if we'd been stuck in Camp One without sleeping bags. At the moment, I was thankful to be right where I was, even if the other person in the tent hated me.

Chapter Thirty-Two

Everything was all messed up. There were seracs the size of semitrucks falling toward me like dominoes, but they disappeared before they hit. There were huge pine trees and rain. Headlights that flashed from side to side as cars drove a wet, windy road. The cars morphed into people with headlamps, and the road became a trail. The rain turned into snow that was being sucked down a gorge toward the raging river at the bottom. I was being pulled, slowly, by my waist, into this gorge. There was nothing to hold on to. Nothing to stop me.

I knew, logically, I was having a nightmare, but my brain was curious what was going to happen next, and it took me a long time to wake up. When I finally succeeded, I sat up and calmed myself by stretching my aching shoulder.

Luke's back was to me, his itchy, dry cough repeatedly interrupting whatever he was listening to on his phone. With the storm howling all around us, the tent was in constant motion as the wind pulled it one way, then pushed it hard in a different direction.

I was dying of thirst. I pulled my water bottle out of my pack, but it was frozen solid. I would have to boil some water if I wanted anything to drink, but that would involve melting snow on my stove, and that meant going outside to get the snow, which was the last thing I wanted to do.

Luke flipped over to his back, pausing abruptly when he noticed I wasn't asleep anymore. His neutral expression was forced. He was not happy to see me.

"You were shaking," he said.

"Yeah. It was damn cold out there, and it's supposed to get even colder."

His only response was a single nod before facing away again and turning up the volume on his phone. This was going to be a long day.

No. Not a long *day.* A long *couple of days* in the tent. Great.

I grabbed my frozen water bottle and put it between my legs with the hope of melting enough for a swallow or two. Mr. Music over there, with his much faster clients, and therefore extra time in the tent, had probably already brewed a ton of water for himself, but I would rather die of thirst than ask him for any.

I checked my water bottle. Still frozen solid. I tore open a pouch of energy gel and sucked it down, hoping it would make my dry mouth feel better. It made it worse. Now I was even more thirsty, and I had nothing to wash away the super-sweet aftertaste.

Irritable from my thirst and the icy chill from the bottle leaching through my pants, I glared at Mr. Music. It took some nerve for him to be acting like an asshole, especially when he had promised he'd be civil.

I tapped him on the shoulder. He looked over. I motioned for him to sit up and was a little surprised when he actually did.

"You said you'd be normal," I said.

His eyes were dead, and this gave me a pang of guilt. But I had to ignore it in order to keep going. "We have at least ten more nights sharing a tent before we tag that summit, and we have to be able to work together like civil people."

Still, he wasn't reacting, and I struggled to keep hold of my anger. At the moment, it was the only thing protecting me from panic and grief.

"Fake it?" he asked. "That's what you want me to do? So, what, should we get the checkers board out and pretend we're thirteen again?"

"Yes!" Having to speak loudly to be heard over the wind gave me more conviction. For once, there was no worry about being overheard. "You promised you'd be civil."

"Well, Emily, guess what? It doesn't work like that."

"It has to."

"Oh yeah?" His eyes were fiery.

"Yes, definitely, yeah. You have to stop acting so...so angry."

"You're so used to everyone walking around on eggshells. Your dad, you, the Sherpas—you guys are afraid to death of anything unpleasant. Well, I'm not *acting* angry, I *am* angry."

He put his earbuds back in.

Blood burned beneath my wind-raw cheeks. He'd basically just slammed a door in my face. I got control of myself, then dressed to go out in the storm to get some snow to brew.

Outside, the winds had to be at least fifty miles an hour, sustained. They pushed me so hard, I could barely zip the door. Keeping a careful hand on the tent frame, I went around to the back and packed snow into my three wide-mouthed bottles.

I was covered in blowing snow from just a few minutes outside, so I zipped myself in the vestibule to shake it all off before going the rest of the way inside. The wind and cold had zapped my anger, though I still wished I was anywhere else in the world besides a five by seven tent with Luke.

Now I perfectly understood why all those *Going on Eighteen* articles advised readers to not get tangled up with coworkers. It wasn't the getting together part that was the problem; it was the falling out. They liked to warn about crossing the friendship line as well. Once things went bad romantically, the friendship would be gone, too.

I had *both* cases on my hands, and in an isolated and high-stakes situation the *Going on Eighteen* writers could never have envisioned.

My mind jabbed me with the words, *fight for it*, but at the moment, I couldn't muster the strength. All I wanted was a drink of water.

Back inside the tent, Luke continued ignoring me. I tried to not let it hurt.

I set up my stove and dumped a bottle of snow in the pot to melt, but the push-button igniter wasn't working. I lit one of the backup matches and held it next to the flow of gas. Nothing. Great.

I turned off the gas and vented the tent door a little so there wouldn't be a buildup of propane. I shook the canister. It was nearly full. I reassembled it and tried again. The stove would still not light. My nerves were tight with frustration. All I wanted was a drink of water, for god's sake. I was thirsty enough to consider putting my face in the pot and taking a bite of snow despite the risk of contamination. I tried one more time to get the stove lit. It didn't work. Damn. My whole body was shaking, and I was seconds from losing control and throwing the stove across the tent.

It was like my inability to produce a sip of water was representative of all that was wrong in my life. I didn't seem to be in control of anything, including the ability to reach the one person my soul needed as much as my body needed water.

Just like that, my built-up frustration morphed into sorrow. Tears sprung to my eyes and ran down my cheeks, too big and too fast to stop.

Chapter Thirty-Three

My tears were sorrow, but they were also relief. My back was to Luke, whose back was to me, and I knew the roaring wind would easily cover my sniffles, so I didn't bother trying to stop.

There was nothing left for me anywhere on earth. No home. No future. There was no one in my court, on my team. This was my truth. And it would be okay. It would somehow, sometime become okay.

Something hard and heavy nudged my hip. It was one of Luke's water bottles. I picked it up and drank gratefully but was careful to take only just enough to quench my immediate thirst.

"Talk to me, Emily," he said.

He was saying this only because he felt sorry for me because of my crying. Out of pride, I was tempted to thank him for the water and crawl into my sleeping bag. To remain alone rather than risk further heartache.

But I didn't want to be alone. I wanted him. And even though it was from pity right now, I had his attention.

Fight for it.

This was my chance, possibly my only chance, to make things right. I pivoted on my sleeping bag and lifted my soggy face to him. If he wanted true and unprotected, this was what it looked like.

"My very first reaction when you showed up in Tengboche was that I had a big problem on my hands," I said. "Because my feelings for you were every bit as strong as they were two years ago. Stronger, even. They overpowered me, and I didn't know how I was going to function around you and keep that fact hidden."

Luke's water bottle was still sitting on my sleeping bag. I twisted the lid back and forth. "No matter what I've ever said or didn't say, I hope you understand that none of it was intentional, and none of it was an indicator of my true feelings."

I stilled my fingers on the bottle, closed my eyes briefly, then lifted them to Luke. His face was emotionless, but at least he was holding my gaze.

I reminded myself of the tears on his face at the *Y* in the trail. I *loved* him. *Keep going. Fight for him.*

"You knew you'd be seeing me for *months* before you got here, but I had no idea I'd *ever* see you again. When you came back, you were so accomplished, and I felt like a straight-up failure-to-launch, a troll living in my dad's basement. You were out experiencing the real world—a world I'm intimidated of going back to—and leading expeditions of your own. And even if I thought there was the remotest hope of my feelings for you being mutual, until recently, I thought you had a girlfriend."

I paused to take a breath. "You are the biggest happiness I've ever had. The biggest heartbreak, too. I just want to see that somewhere in your eyes there is still hope. That you don't hate me. That there's at least still a friend in there somewhere."

When I stopped to search his eyes, instead of hope, his face was even more statue-like than before. I looked down, ashamed.

I almost didn't catch it when he started to speak, because his voice was so quiet. I had to scoot closer to hear him over the wind. The familiar, woodsy smell of his deodorant overwhelmed me.

"I'm sorry I'm angry and that I've been awful. You mean the world to me, but I feel like it's all been an illusion. I'm going to lose you again in a few weeks, and I don't know what to do."

The finality and raw emotion in his voice renewed my tears. This time, he put his arms around me gently. It was too loose, but I'd take it.

"Tell me about your mom," he said.

I took a few breaths.

"Dad and I didn't set out to deceive people about her. It's what people assumed, and we let them. It was just easier that way."

"No, tell me *about* her. As in, what she was like."

My chest clenched. "She was a lot different than me. She hated being outside. She liked perfume and makeup and dressing up." *And methamphetamine,* I thought silently. "I was always getting in trouble. I was a hassle for her."

"You? Getting in trouble?"

"Yeah, all the time. I was kind of sassy, and I would always get bored with the normal stuff."

"Like what?"

"Oh, you know. Dolls and cartoons. Tea sets. Dress-up. So I wandered off a lot and would get messy and muddy and ruin my clothes and lose my jacket and mittens. I was always climbing things I shouldn't, and then I'd get hurt. There were lots of trips to urgent care."

"I can't picture it."

"I changed." My voice cracked.

Luke tightened his grip around me.

"There was a child protective services investigation against Amy once because I kept getting hurt. And because of that investigation, she almost got caught. See, she did meth. And she sold it. To minors, too."

"And that's when you changed."

"No. It was only later, after she *did* get caught."

"Emily..." He lifted his arms so that they were surrounding my shoulders protectively. "It blows my mind that we've been friends for ten years and I didn't know any of this."

"I've never talked about it to anyone. Not even to Dad."

Even now, I didn't like thinking about it, let alone talking about it or rehashing any of the details. It contained such ugly truths.

"You never talk about your dad, either," I said.

"None of us talk about the dead."

"But still."

"Mom told me not to. Before you even got to Tengboche the first time."

"Because you thought my mom was dead?"

"No. Because it was Greg's expedition he died on."

Oh, Luke. Internally, I wept for him.

"Mom didn't want you to feel bad about it."

I slid my hand beneath his, and we threaded our fingers together.

"It's okay. I was only five. Pasang wasn't even born yet. I have very few memories of him."

"But you have your name, and you hear that a hundred times a day."

He nodded slowly. "My dad loved working in the mountains, or so Mom tells me. There were a few years when he had the international record for most Everest summits. Because of his paid work with the Western expeditions. From what Mom has said, I'm sure he would have loved to have been a sponsored climber like your dad, but this was almost twenty years ago. The possibility probably never even crossed his mind."

An extra strong gust of wind pushed the tent low enough to tap Luke's head before it sprang back. I was still not back in my sleeping bag after gathering snow, and I hadn't realized that I was shivering. I slid out of his embrace to crawl in for warmth.

We sat side by side, sleeping bags up to our shoulders. Was it okay to scoot closer to him? I did, and he didn't move away. This was an improvement. I put my head on his shoulder, and he still didn't move away. Instead he rested his yellow-hatted head on top of mine.

"How did your mom get caught?" he asked.

I exhaled. I'd never, ever told the story. I didn't need to; the people directly affected by what happened already knew what had gone down.

"You don't have to tell me," he said, sensing my tension. I exhaled again, my heart racing like when I was on the edge of the collapsed snowbridge.

He unzipped the sides of our sleeping bags so we could hold hands.

"We were at my grandparents' house," I said. "Amy's parents. In Port Townsend. They have a nice place, and we used to house-sit when they traveled. I loved it there because they lived out of town, in the woods. Amy always went on benders when we were there. She didn't know what I was doing, and she didn't care. I was free to roam.

"One day, I wandered too far, and it started to drizzle. And it was foggy, too. I had a rain jacket on but not rain boots. My pants and shoes were soaked almost immediately.

"And then it started to get dark. I was lost. And cold. Just when I was getting really scared, I somehow stumbled through the trees and onto a road."

Tashi for me, but not for Amy.

"A driver stopped. I tried to figure out where I was so I could tell them how to get back to my grandparents' house, but they took me to a fire station instead. Then the police came and drove me to my grandparents' house. All the lights were off. They knocked, and no one answered. I told them the house was dark because my mom was sleeping and that I'd be fine, but their suspicion was already raised, and in America you don't leave ten-year-olds home alone like that. I was scared because I thought I'd have to go back to the station with them, so I kept insisting Amy was home."

Luke's eyebrows bent inward with concern. He rubbed the back of my hand with his thumb.

"The door was unlocked, so they went in with me so I could show them my school picture on the wall to prove that I belonged there. But once they were inside, they searched the house. They found her in the guest bedroom. And her boyfriend. Or maybe he was one of her suppliers. She was passed out. He was, too. They woke them up. There were handcuffs. And they took both of them away."

"Oh, Emily," Luke said. He hugged me tightly.

"They took me to stay at a strange place. It was like an office building but with bunk beds. They gave me some other girl's old pajamas to wear. They got ahold of my grandparents the next day, and I went back to their house. Then Dad got called off his K2 expedition to come get me, and you know the rest of the story."

Luke didn't say anything, and I was afraid to look at him. It was unnaturally dark in the tent for it being only three p.m., which made everything seem ominous.

"I'm a jerk," he said. "I never even gave you a chance to

explain."

"I wouldn't have told you back on Milam Peak. Not everything. I was too stunned."

I thought about the day after Amy was arrested, how I stood in the shadows of the hallway, listening to my grandparents argue about what to do with me. They had been so angry. It was Amy they were mad at, but it felt like it was me who was in trouble.

"She was a terrible mother, and she was in the wrong that day and a thousand other days, but it will always be because of my wildness that she was caught and went to prison. I'm as much dead to her as she is to me."

Luke cupped my jaw and turned me to look at him. His eyes were pleading. "I don't even know what to say."

"You don't have to say anything."

"I'm sorry. I wish I could take back so many things I said earlier."

With his hand still cupping my face, he leaned in, brushing my lips with the most tender of kisses.

It was just one kiss, but it was a kiss that meant the world to me. There was still so much between us that was complicated and tangled, but even more than his words, this kiss showed me that things between us could be repaired. There was hope.

Our radios crackled with Thom's voice, then squealed with interference. I clicked mine off.

"…all guides report to the cook tent," Thom finished on Luke's radio.

We bundled up, and then helped the Sherpas check on the clients, put more stakes in the tents, and deliver hot tea, water, and dinner before the storm got worse. The temperature had dropped even more by the time Luke and I returned to our tent. We lay in our sleeping bags, pressed together for the illusion of warmth and to steady each other's shivering as we attempted to sleep.

It was hard to tell when morning arrived because it took dawn a long time to make a dent in the thick clouds. Just as Luke and I were getting ready to check on clients again, Jim came on the radio, telling us the strongest part of the storm was about to hit and forbidding any of us from leaving our tents.

Luke and I ate granola bars and packages of dried fruit for breakfast as the wind battered the tent like football players in a game of tug-of-war. I don't think anyone except Dad expected the storm to be this strong. Dad, who was surely biting his nails as he watched the grim progression of this storm.

We were in the best expedition tents money could buy, but in winds like this, there was no guarantee that we wouldn't simply be snatched up and blown off the mountain.

There was nothing to do but lie and wait. It was so, so cold, and each gust of wind was stronger and louder. It was possibly the highest winds that I'd ever been in, and if *I* was nervous, I could only imagine how terrified the clients were. Of them all, Doc would be the most aware of the potential for devastation this storm had. From her many years at Everest ER, she knew intimately that climbing with a guided company was no guarantee of getting off this mountain alive.

At some point, Luke unzipped the top part of our sleeping bags so we could lie with our arms around each other.

I tucked tightly in to him, forcing myself to stop anticipating the lift and slide of the tent being torn loose. Luke wrapped himself farther around me, his head dipping down to press a firm, deliberate kiss on my cheek.

Our foreheads were touching now, my eyes closed to the warmth of his contact. Just for that moment, it was like the storm went silent and the tent was still and solid.

"I love you, Emily," he said.

My heart surged. "I love you, too."

We clung to each other as the winds picked up even more, punching the tent so flat that it bounced off our bodies. We lay and waited, praying that the clients would be okay.

The force of the wind yanked out one of the stakes. The corner of our tent came alive in the wind, lashing out against the storm like a half-rigid bullwhip. Then all we could do was pray that *we'd* be okay.

Chapter Thirty-Four

Except for the two feet of snow left behind, it was as if the storm had never happened. The sky was bright blue, and with the parabola effect from the walls of snow and rock surrounding us, it was so hot that it seemed like the sun had mistaken Mount Everest for Thailand today.

After the winds had peaked during yesterday's storm, they stayed sustained at that level for an hour before gradually backing down to a reasonable force. They died down altogether sometime in the middle of the night, but we stayed an extra day at Camp Two for avalanche reasons. Now our group was rallying for our climb up Lhotse Face to spend the night at Camp Three.

Lhotse Face is as steep as a double black diamond ski run, only instead of it being a narrow chute, it spans the full distance from Everest's west flank to Lhotse's east flank, like a drive-in movie screen for giants. The fixed line runs right up its middle, and when there are several teams on the line at once, it looks like an escalator straight to the sky.

The Cubans were already up on the line as the rest of

us waited in Camp Two. I purposely brushed against Luke as the UW team positioned to get started. He glanced over and nudged me back, the intensity in his eyes reigniting our kisses in the tent this morning. Even though we were in broad daylight with clients all around, he grabbed my elbow for a split second and gave it a quick but firm squeeze.

Things were different with us now. Like the storm, we'd blown into Camp Two with anger, uncertainty, and pain, but we were leaving Camp Two with everything sure, beautiful, and new. There was still the huge question of what would happen at the end of the season, but for the world we were living in right now, he was mine and I was his.

Luke continued checking the harnesses of his UW clients while I headed over to the cook tent. He looked back at me, and seeing that I had been watching him, a smug smile crept across his lips.

I shook my head at him across the distance. His smile grew bigger.

My crew got on the line once the last UW client had clipped in. It didn't take very long under the blinding sun before all members of A-Team had our down suits peeled halfway off with the sleeves tied around our waists like a belt.

For once, I was happy to be stuck in the back, since going fast in this heat would be even more miserable. The sun's rays sizzled through my hair like they were searching for a chunk of scalp to fry. I insisted that Phil, Glissading Glen, and Johnsmith stop frequently for water breaks.

Camp Three was two thirds of the way up Lhotse Face. The Sherpas had built it weeks ago by cutting tent platforms straight into the snow and ice of the face. Here, the tents were three-person, which meant I'd be sharing with Doc and Claudia instead of Luke. By the time Tyler, Hulk, and I finished getting all the A-Team clients situated with enough water for the night and oxygen flowing properly, Doc and

Claudia were already laid out in our tent like they'd been there for hours. I had a nagging altitude headache, so I wasted no time arranging my sleeping bag in the open spot between them. Woozy and lethargic in the sauna-like heat of the tent, I drifted easily to sleep.

After a brief guides' meeting later that afternoon, Luke caught my eye, then traversed over to the side of the slope and around the corner to a big pile of boulders. A few minutes later, I followed.

There, the storm had swept the rock clean, and it gave us a place to sit that was hidden from camp but with a wide view of the incredible panorama. It was like we were seated on thrones at the top of the world.

"It's been a while since you've been this high. You holding up?" I teased.

In response, he grabbed my face with his mittened hands and kissed me thirstily. His hands traveled down to my waist. I leaned in for more, and we kissed until we were both panting from the altitude.

I'd like to see a *Going on Eighteen* article talk me through this one: how to literally not run out of air when kissing at twenty-three-thousand feet.

"So…you think we'll kiss at the summit?" I asked.

The question was hypothetical, of course, as we'd be with different teams, likely hours apart. But it was fun to pretend that it was just us climbing this mountain. Simply walking up to the top, untethered to the fixed lines and with no one to watch over. If not for the jet stream blowing on the top, we could do it right this moment, he and I. We could head to Camp Four tomorrow, then set our alarms for ten p.m. to make our summit bid, and be back at Base Camp right on the heels of the clients finishing this rotation.

"Hmmm," he said. "If you make A-Team step it up, and I get the Dawgs tangled behind a different team, it's possible we could summit at the same time."

"You'd kiss me right on top of Chomolungma, in front of everybody?" The thought made me laugh. The summit of Everest was all about jockeying into position for the quintessential victory photo while battling cameras that refused to function properly in the cold. It was all oxygen masks and clients digging summit trinkets out of their pockets as we guides made sure no one dropped a mitten or fell off the side.

"How about this?" he said. "I will wrap my arms around you wherever our teams pass and keep you like that for way too long."

"Deal," I said, leaning in to his body and using his shoulder as a pillow. I closed my eyes and relished the feeling of him solidly beneath my ear, thankful for the rare stillness on the mountain from the boulders blocking the wind.

"So that storm made me think about something," I said.

"What?"

"How unpredictable the weather has been here in recent years. And how you changed your major. You know, weather modeling and avalanche forecasting don't just help climbers and athletes. They help Sherpas, too."

"True. But it doesn't help in the same way as medical care."

"I think it's equal. Climbing Sherpas have the highest job mortality rate on Earth. And how many of those deaths are weather- or avalanche-related?"

"Most."

Including his own father's. "So as a forecaster, you'd be in the business of preempting. You're keeping the doctor out of work. You're saving lives before they are at risk of being lost."

"Hmm."

"Seriously, Luke. Don't you think you'd be more effective in something you're passionate about? And having grown up here and loving mountains like you do, don't you think you could do a better job of it than someone in, say, New Orleans, who has never stepped foot in the Himalayas? You're like a textbook in mountaineering history. You know the past storms. You know what went wrong on expeditions, and you know what the weather view looks like from the ground, not just from the satellites."

"It's something to chew on."

"Yes, it is something to chew on!"

I noticed then that his mouth was rippled in his trademark *W. Amused and content.* He was trying to get a rise out of me. I smacked him. He grabbed my hand and kissed it.

Afterward, his mouth remained in a *W*, so I knew he was actually considering the idea. It wasn't the answer to everything, but perhaps it could satisfy his sense of duty in a way that better suited him. Also, if he didn't go to medical school after he graduated, then maybe there was hope of us doing the Top Five together someday. I gave an internal fist pump of victory.

We stayed there on our perch for a little while longer, watching the cloudless sky start its transformation into an airbrushed canvas of neon pinks and purples. Luke's arm was warm around me. Together, we were part of the circle of the great Himalayas that stretched out to the left and right of us and joined on the other side of the horizon.

Dad was at Global City within an hour of us returning to Base Camp. Luke and I had finished putting gear away and were starting a game of cribbage at one of the side tables in the big top.

Dad was glaring—*glowering*—at Luke. He *knew*.

"Dad! Stop it!" I hissed.

He cleared his throat. Luke quietly excused himself on a bogus chore.

"How was Pumori?" I asked.

"Fine. You have some explaining to do, MiniBoss."

I groaned. "Doc told you, didn't she? Speaking of, *you* have some explaining to do. I had no idea—"

"So there *is* something going on. And, no, Teresa didn't say anything to me. Your cook, Phurba, told Pertemba that one of the Global Sherpas saw—I'm not sure I can say this aloud…"

"Maybe you shouldn't, then."

"He saw…that guy"—Dad pointed to the door Luke had exited from—"coming out of your tent so early in the morning it was still dark."

Oh god. People were gossiping about us? We'd been so careful, but I guess we hadn't been careful enough.

"Don't you know I was caught in a whiteout?" I said, trying for a diversion.

"Spending the night, Emily? With *Luke*?"

"What's new about that? We share a tent up on the mountain all the time."

"This was in Base Camp."

"We used to sleep over sometimes in Base Camp."

"But you were kids then. Now—" He cleared his throat. "Now, neither of you are children."

Oh, this was awkward. "You love Luke," I pointed out.

"Yes, I do. He's like a son."

Annnd, it was getting worse.

Dad snapped his arms around me with a *whomp*, like a human mousetrap. "First you're going off to college, and then you're going off to who knows where—Tanzania, maybe—and now *this*!"

I was tempted to bring up Dad's secret history with Doc again, but if I wanted to divert, it would be best to stay off the topic of relationships. "You're going off to who knows where, too."

"You know the location of every expedition I have planned for the next twelve months. Back to what we were talking about. Luke—*our Luke*—is your boyfriend. Okay, let's see, how do I put this? I hope you and he are being careful—"

"Dad, stop!"

This was unbelievable. I'd never even seen Luke shirtless. I looked around, making sure no one was overhearing this conversation. The only other clients in the tent with us were watching a movie over in the far corner. The traitorous Cook-Phurba was not here at the moment. He better not be eavesdropping on the other side of the tent fabric. Perhaps I would suggest that Doc do a replay of eggplant parmesan night and then *not* help Cook-Phurba when he came begging.

"I'm a guide now, Dad. I think you can trust me to handle things"—I cleared my throat—"domestically."

"You're only twenty," he said.

"Yeah, I'm *twenty*." The sad part was that at the old-maid age of twenty, I actually could use some help, *ahem*, domestically.

Dad steepled his hands. "He treats you well?"

"Well, sometimes." I laughed. "Just kidding, Dad. You know Luke. Of course he does."

"I'm still not happy about this, but I guess Luke is better than someone I don't know. But you two need to be more discreet. You do not want Jim to find out about it. In fact, this is serious enough that if you were not my daughter, I'd tell him myself. But because you are, and because I know Luke—even though I'd like to wring his neck right now—I know you two will be responsible and not let a personal relationship get in the way of what you need to do to protect your clients."

"Of course," I said, though I didn't see the difference between Luke and me guiding together and Dad guiding with his own daughter along on the trip. But then, that probably should never have happened, either.

Dad plucked a cookie from the basket on the table. I took this as a good sign that he was going to stop talking about Luke. He took a bite, frowning as he chewed.

"I didn't make them," I said.

He set the cookie down and didn't eat the rest of it. *Take that, Randall.*

"So how come you thought I was thinking about going to Tanzania?" I asked. "That's kind of random."

"You applied for a CentralPoint job, didn't you?"

I looked at him oddly. "Yes, but what does Tanzania have to do with that?"

"You probably haven't checked your email since you got down."

"No."

"Barrett Browning called me on the satellite phone about it yesterday."

"Barrett Browning as in the CEO of Esplanade Equipment?"

"Yes. You've met him. On that Island Peak trip."

I barely remembered. I was only fourteen that year.

"CentralPoint's a pet project of his, and when the human resources department saw your application and recognized your name, they forwarded it to him."

"Oh, wow. And he called you?"

"I think he just wanted an excuse to catch up, but he also wanted to make sure it was you because he's going to email and offer you a job."

I was speechless. I'd have somewhere to go after this! Somewhere to *be.* A job that didn't involve French fries in a national park cafeteria. A job with my favorite outdoor equipment company in the world. "That's great news!"

"Okay, so this is good? He wasn't sure you'd be okay with Tanzania. Frankly, *I* wasn't sure you'd be okay with Tanzania, but I guess you are?"

"Why do you keep saying Tanzania?"

"That's where the pilot location is. Barrett said it's opening midsummer."

There was one major mountain in Tanzania: Mount Kilimanjaro. The highest mountain on the continent of Africa, and therefore one of the highly commercial Seven Summits mountains. It occasionally gets some snow on top, but it was much closer to hiking than alpine climbing.

Dad analyzed my frown. "So are you *not* feeling Tanzania?"

I tried to look less shocked. It was an amazing opportunity, but *one* mountain?

Further, Tanzania was remote and a place that had absolutely no connection to Luke.

"It's okay if Tanzania isn't right," Dad said. "I would never do it. It's beautiful but…"

But there was just *one* mountain.

"You know, you still have your plane ticket to Washington and, uh, with you and Luke, you might be more interested in using it now."

"Dad!"

"I'll be the first to admit, I'm still rooting for Washington, especially since you'd have a free place to stay with your grandparents. Or with Teresa, I hear."

"Speaking of, do you think there might be something about Doc that you may have conveniently forgotten to tell me, for like ten years?"

His face grew red. "Like what?"

"I should make you say it after what you just put me

through with Luke."

"She's doing her own thing now."

"Right. *Now* she is. But I know it's not that simple. You still talk all the time, and I saw her picture in your tent."

He started nibbling on Randall's bad-tasting cookie for distraction.

"Don't worry," I said. "I'm not going to press you. Because, really, I don't want to know. But know that I know. I am on to you guys."

"Okay, yeah, so, uh, Tshering's waiting for me back at camp. I want you down for dinner again before you guys leave. Don't forget."

"I won't."

"And we will be discussing Jim's decision to send eighty people up the mountain with a storm that was all but a sure bet, and what you will be doing if he tries a stunt like that during the summit bid."

My temporary upper hand was gone. I nodded obediently.

I walked him to the door so he wouldn't be tempted to look around for Jim and grill him personally about the storm.

We hugged good-bye.

"Your face is getting chafed, MiniBoss. You need to use more moisturizer."

I touched my face. Yes indeed, my cheeks were rough. Thank god Dad was not hip enough to put together the low winds on Everest yesterday with Luke's five days of stubble as the cause of the chafing.

He walked down the rock to the trail, a bit of humor in his shoulders. Shoot, maybe he *was* hip enough. Now it was my face turning red.

Chapter Thirty-Five

I went straight to the UW team camp to tell Luke that we'd been found out. But right as I was giving his tent a one-two shake I realized being at his tent in broad daylight like this could fuel more rumors.

Luke popped his head out of his tent, nodding for me to join him inside.

I tipped my head the other way, for him to join me outside.

He shook his head and again motioned for me to come into his tent. This was way more obvious than if I had just disappeared inside. There was no one nearby, so that's what I did, if just for long enough to explain that we had to stop hanging out in each other's tents. But as soon as the zipper was up, we were kissing like we hadn't seen each other in months. His touch lit up my body, and my breathing was all over the place.

When we finally broke, I took off my jacket. It was practically subtropical in his tent with the comparatively thick air at Base Camp and the sun that had been heating it all morning.

I touched my face, which was now even more chafed.

"You need to shave, buddy," I said, grabbing his chin playfully.

He snatched me in for another kiss.

"Okay, seriously. Mercy. Do you have any lotion?"

He tossed me a tube, and I slathered it gratefully on my face.

"So what's the deal with Greg?"

"Shhhh. Don't talk so loud."

"What's going on?" he whispered.

"The Sherpas have been talking. Dad knows about us."

Luke's eyes went dark. "Do you know who it was?"

"It was Cook-Phurba—talking to the Winslowe cook, Pertemba."

He relaxed a little at this.

"Do you think the rest of the Sherpas know?" I asked.

"They *think* they know, and they are watching, but I'm pretty sure they don't have any evidence, because if they did they would tell Norbu, and he would have to bring it up to Jim."

It was Cook-Phurba's first year on the mountain, and Randall and Jim had hired him because he'd been to a culinary trade school in Kathmandu, not because of his Mount Everest climbing connections, so perhaps our secret was safe for now.

"I'm sorry, Emily," Luke said. "I should have been more aware. Even if we aren't doing anything obvious, it still might seem that way to others because we're always hanging out. People here don't know our history like everyone at Winslowe Expeditions."

"It's not your fault. We'll just have to be more careful from now on."

He shook his head, looking so sad that I scooted in front of him and put my hands on his knees.

"We get so little time together as it is," he said, shifting so that we were even closer and he could speak more quietly.

I nodded somberly.

He sighed. "This is exactly why I was upset when I found out you were guiding with Global."

"Not because I didn't tell you?"

"Oh, it was that. For sure. But the bigger deal was that if we were guiding for the same company, we'd have to hide anything that developed between us because it's not allowed."

His lips drew up into a teasing smile. "I couldn't tell you that part when we were at the puja, could I?"

His smile fell away as quickly as it came.

"It will be really bad if more people figure out what's going on," he said. "I'd lose my summer job on Rainier, and it would make it much harder for you to find work."

I nodded my head in agreement. "I tried to not come in your tent, but you were making a huge scene. Now I don't know how to get out without being seen."

"Then you'll have to stay until the coast is clear. Like when everyone has left for dinner." His words were joking, but his face was anything but.

We lay down on his sleeping bag, and I snuggled in to him. We were heavy with the knowledge that this bubble of safety we were in right now could be our last time alone together in the privacy of a tent before our night in Camp Two during the summit bid.

The next night after dinner, I snuck out to meet Luke at the place we'd done ice ax pull-ups. There were enough rocks there to partially hide us, and the closest tents were from a different expedition and too far away for people to recognize us in the dark.

He had gotten there ahead of me and was sitting on a large rock. He pulled me onto his lap as I clicked off my headlamp, burying his face in my neck and inhaling deeply. The kiss that followed blazed with yearning, making me think of not just him but of everything that I wanted. My white bungalow. Cerro Torre. Freedom in the mountains. People whom I knew long-term instead of a revolving door of fellow travelers.

"I missed you today," he said. "I'm always wanting more of you than I can have."

He wrapped his arms around me and rested his chin on my shoulder as we looked out over the Khumbu Glacier. It was late for Base Camp, and most climbers were in their headlamp-lit tents. Of all the glowing colors in front of us, the Swedish expedition's tents were the prettiest of all, with their deep shade of violet fading gently into the black places on the horizon where mountains blocked the stars.

I tried to shift so that all my weight wasn't on Luke, but he held me firmly in place. In the end, I was glad for it. The skies were clear tonight, and without the insulation of the clouds, the air was icy cold.

Satellites shuffled through the faint nebulas overhead, some moving imperceptibly slow, with others as fast as an airplane. I named the constellations silently in my head, stars that were steady like cairns in the sky no matter where in the northern hemisphere Dad and I went and no matter how remote our climb.

Luke's lips grazed my neck as he raised his head to whisper in my ear.

"Had I the heavens' embroidered cloths, enwrought with golden and silver light, the blue and the dim and the dark cloths, of night and light and the half-light…"

It was the Yeats poem. I'd read it to him just that one time, so long ago. I held my breath to see if he would continue.

"I would spread the cloths under your feet…"

His warm jaw brushed against the chilly bottoms of my earlobes, sending tingles down my arms and legs. I didn't want to move. I didn't want a single breath to take from the words that were coming next.

"But I, being poor, have only my dreams; I have spread my dreams under your feet: tread softly because you tread on my dreams."

Chapter Thirty-Six

This morning, most of the UW team and some of the A-Team clients were departing for two nights in Dingboche. The higher levels of oxygen in the air at the lower elevation could be restorative, and it was some time away from the drudgery of waiting in Base Camp for the weather window to open that would kick off the summit bid. I stood behind the big top, holding a cup of coffee and watching the group disappear down the trail. The twins and Hulk were with them.

So was Luke.

We'd been able to overcome the blowup on Milam Peak, and everything about Amy was out in the open now, but neither of us had brought up the other part yet: what would happen with our relationship when the season was over. There was hardly any time left together as it was, and now we had two days fewer.

I went to the command center to check email. Barrett Browning had, indeed, emailed with a job offer as promised. I replied, thanking him and asking for time to think over his offer.

I didn't want to go to Tanzania, but with CentralPoint being a new venture, there weren't any other locations right now. Another problem was that out of the dozens of applications I submitted over the past weeks, Tanzania was the only job offer I had. In my inbox were lots of "application received" notices and auto-responses saying the positions were no longer open. I checked my junk folder just in case and found an email offering an in-person group interview. In Montana next week. Right.

I would apply for more jobs before our summit attempt, but it was unlikely I'd hear back from them before I needed to be on my way to a paying job. So my choice was a great job with a great company in an absolutely wrong location or… nothing?

What about Luke?

I ate lunch with Doc, who had opted to not go down to Dingboche, saying she'd get caught up on her oxygen during the trek back to the Lukla air strip after the summit bid. The next day, she and I hiked Kala Pattar together. She was a fast walker, but she was purposely trying to keep the hike low-exertion, which translated to no exertion for me, and thus my mind had all the energy in the world to wander.

I could have asked her what she thought about CentralPoint Tanzania, but I already knew what she'd say. She'd see Tanzania as something temporary—a Band-Aid that solved what I would be doing after the summit but offered nothing toward a long-term plan. Life as a series of Band-Aids was not Doc's style.

The thing is, Tanzania was not actually a Band-Aid or temporary fix. I couldn't just go work there for a few months until something better came along, not with Dad's connection to Barrett Browning and how Barrett had been personally involved in hiring me. No, this was a program Esplanade was launching for the long run, and I'd need to be there two or three years before it would be okay to cut and run. Two or three years in a place without mountains.

If you don't climb for yourself in the beginning, you might never get the chance.

Right. And I would be paying my bills how?

Sponsorship.

To get a sponsorship, I needed that seventh summit. But even then, it's not like I'd get to the top of Mount Everest and find a magical sponsorship offer tied onto one of the prayer flags. There would still be a lot of time, work, and luck involved in this dream, and how would I pay for dinner in the meantime? How did Luke play into all this? It seemed impossible, but could he? Was there a way? And what about that white bungalow? That was a dream, too: having the permanence of a place of my own and people to come home to.

I pictured the house, this time with music playing outside on the porch for a group of people rather than me listening to it alone on my earbuds as I was accustomed. I wasn't sure who all the people were in this vision. Roommates, perhaps? Neighbors? Friends? And, of course, my dog would be there. And a few hens. Maybe a goat?

Now I was getting carried away.

I pictured the house again, this time in the quiet, when I was the only one home. There were wet-with-dew gladiolas crowding the fence. I was fresh from a short hike in one of the state parks and, while I cooked lunch, I had the front door wide open to the fresh, chilly air.

I sighed. It would be a wonderful life.

When we got back to camp, I insisted Doc go get her nail polish remover for me. We met in the UW tent where she handed me the original bottle of polish. "You sure you don't want to reapply?"

"Nah. I just want it off."

She gave in and exchanged the polish for the bottle of remover.

"I've got something else for you," Doc said.

She dug through her backpack. "I'm assuming you're on birth control, since periods and climbing harnesses are such a bad combo. But birth control doesn't protect against STDs."

It took a second for it to register that the handful of colorful, individually wrapped items she was holding out were not some sort of candy but *condoms*.

"Oh. Doc. No." I wanted to die. "Not on Chomolungma!"

"You don't believe all that, do you? You're not even Buddhist."

"Well—no, but it *is* a holy mountain." The Winslowe Expeditions Sherpas were always linking hanky-panky on the mountain to ill-fated expeditions of years past. "Luke and I *just barely* started being more than friends. It's not like—"

She rolled her eyes.

"Are you encouraging this?"

"No. Not at all. But I'm not *not* encouraging this. Actually, I should officially go on the record here as saying you should *not* do this. Since I'm old enough to be your mom and all."

Was I supposed to be doing this, Chomolungma or not? Regardless of the minuscule length of time Luke and I had been more than friends or how little time there was left until the season was over? If this had been anyone but Doc having this conversation with me, they would assume I was playing dumb, but Doc knew me and what my life was like. Surely she knew I *was* dumb in this area. Was this talk a hint? Is that what Luke expected? He was twenty-two, after all. Had he had sex with Olivia?

She shoved the condoms into my jacket pocket. I was still too stunned to resist.

"I can't even… I'm going to leave now."

She patted me on the shoulder. "Don't worry. I won't tell

Greg."

I went back to my tent. It should have been funny. I should have been able to chuckle about this.

But instead, the whole exchange had left me ungrounded. I was all too aware of my inexperience in not just that but everything. My remaining time with Luke was slipping through my fingers. All I wanted was him, back here, in my tent under the concealment of a black and starless sky.

There were a thousand people squished onto this island in the Himalayas that was Everest Base Camp, but remove just one—one certain one—and I might as well be a castaway.

A Circ arrived from Luke as I was lying down to sleep the following night. It showed a dimly lit teahouse and a whole line of recognizable faces from Global, a few of whom were holding cans of Everest beer. Luke would have to be standing on a chair to get that angle, and this made me smile—it was a high point.

At the end of the Circ, he swiped the camera across his own face, giving me a quick nod before the Circ ended. He'd tagged it #YCCM #ICYS.

I'll catch you soon, I guessed.

In return, I sent him the Circ I'd taken of the highest point Doc and I had reached on Kala Pattar yesterday, which he would appreciate because it had not been taken from the top. Both of us are a little superstitious about turning around before standing atop the highest point of any hike we are on. I added a secretive code of my own after #YCCM: #MYL for *miss you lots.* Then, I replaced my profile picture of Tinkerbell as a calf with an actual picture of me. A picture Dad had taken in Kathmandu before we started our hike to Base Camp. I'd showered at the hotel the night before, and my hair was down and nice, my smile large and natural. Which was because, if I recall correctly, I'd just received a Circ from Luke.

The next afternoon, Luke wasn't with the group as they trickled into the big top. I went outside to see if there were people still on the trail. There weren't, but as I looked around, I noticed a speck down by the Everest Base Camp signs that could be a person. With a pair of binoculars, I could make out this person's yellow jacket and guessed that it was Luke.

I grabbed my own Yellow Yeti jacket from the tent and walked toward the signs. He was sitting on a rock with his back toward Base Camp, but as I approached, the angle was just so that I had a peek of his profile beneath the bill of his Huskies cap. I was dying to see him but also a smidge intimidated. Two days apart and it was like seeing him again for the first time. It reminded me of when he was standing in the doorframe of his house and I could barely speak because he was so handsome and worldly. Except now, he was more handsome because I knew him even better.

I knew more about him than I ever had before, yet there was so much still to discover, and with everything about our future up in the air, I might never have the chance to discover.

Sensing someone behind him, he twisted around.

"Hi. How was it?" I asked.

He raised his elbow and coughed into it before answering. "The trip was good."

I walked the rest of the distance until I was as close to him as I dared, being that it was daylight and we were in plain sight of anyone on the trail or in possession of binoculars. Even from here, I could smell fresh shampoo and soap on him. Being this near but unable to touch—my body screamed in protest.

"Lucky, you got a real shower," I said with a pout as I planted myself in front of him.

I could tell something was grating on his mind because he didn't even crack a smile. My adrenaline kicked up a couple of notches. Why had he stayed down here instead of coming all the way up with the group?

"You're quiet today," I said eventually.

"I'm just thinking," he said.

"What about?"

"Olivia. My ex-girlfriend."

I stiffened.

"I was thinking about when we broke up." He shifted, adjusting his cap, then pulling it back down low. "Remember when we were talking about Townsend College and you said that sometimes you have to get something out of the way to see what it was blocking?"

I nodded.

He reached for my hands. "I know exactly what you meant by that because that's how it was with Olivia. I wasn't thinking about it like that at the time, but looking back it's clear she and I broke up because of you. Things were fine with her. But I was so aware that I'd be seeing you this spring, and at the time, I thought you'd be starting at Townsend College a few months after that. Subconsciously, I knew if there was any chance of *this* happening, I wanted to be free. She was that thing I had to get out of the way so I could *see* you."

My blood rushed inward to my core, making my limbs tingle.

"It made me realize that even if I *wasn't* leaving for Nepal soon, that it wasn't right to stay with her any longer," he continued. "Not once I truly admitted to myself that I was still dreaming about you."

He used his thumbs to trace the lines on my palms. "Deep

down, this was what I was hoping for all along."

My face cracked in a smile that freed my spirit from all it had been weighed down with: worry about why he was being so quiet and the decision I needed to make about Tanzania and my immediate future. I wanted him to say those words again and again. Why could we not be somewhere private right now? I needed his arms, his body, his lips.

"It's an odd thing to be in love with your best friend," he said. "It's like you're operating on different planes. It's like a dream. Like it's happening only in your imagination. You need this person so much, even if they are halfway around the world and probably not thinking about you at all. You're just so happy to hear from them, to be around them, and whatever they give you, it's enough."

My heart was happy-crying. I knew exactly what he was talking about. I nudged the toes of my camp boots against the toes of his hiking boots, the best I could do while in the public eye.

"Now, all the planes are together in one," I said.

"Yes." He looked off to the east with an expression that was unbearably sad.

He was sad because all this—the crossing of planes—was only temporary.

"Thom thinks Jim's going to send us out on Friday," Luke said.

It was the earliest possible day of our estimated weather window, just two days from now.

"No," I whispered.

"Yes, unfortunately."

He stood, stepping directly in front of me so that his back mostly blocked me from Base Camp. I stood, too, slipping my arms beneath his open Yellow Yeti jacket and wrapping them tightly around his waist.

"I'll come by tonight," he said quietly.

"But we can't risk someone seeing."

"I'll come late, and I'll leave well before dawn. Is that okay?"

I answered his question with a single nod as he ran the side of his thumb along my cheek. Then, we had to step apart in case anyone was looking our way. He coughed some more as we started back to Global City. It was a cough that had gotten much deeper than when he'd left, and I made a mental note to keep tabs on it to see if it got worse.

"I brought something for you," he said as we walked. He handed me a small bouquet of greenery, the stems tied at the bottom with a bit of white cord.

It had been five weeks since I'd seen anything alive other than humans, yaks, an occasional stray dog, and crows. This small touch filled my heart to the brim.

"You're the best," I said.

He didn't respond, but when he glanced over at me, his eyes were crinkled and happy, and it felt like a kiss.

As we finished the walk to Global City, I fingered the leaves and stems of the bouquet and the cord holding them all together. I thought about what Luke had said about the crossing of the planes that were all the different ways we knew each other. Now, we knew the bliss that was their combining, but what would happen when we had to pull them back apart?

Chapter Thirty-Seven

I waited up for Luke a long time, our brief embrace from this afternoon living on in my body. At last, my tent shook in a one-two rhythm, and he crawled in quietly.

"Everyone wanted to socialize tonight," he said. "Right in front of your tent."

Before I could reply, his lips were on mine, taking my breath and my heart along with it. We made quick and quiet work of zipping our sleeping bags together and crawling inside. Our jackets came off right away, and then our shirts. *All* of our layers of shirts. I wasn't wearing a bra, so it was nothing but hot bare skin on hot bare skin. My breasts pushed into his chest as his mouth found mine again in the dark. He tasted like the lemony menthol of his cough drops.

All the new sensations swirling through my body made me dizzy. The headiness of his kisses demanded my full attention, yet I was also aware of the exact location of his slightly chilly fingers as they traveled across my belly and along the line of ribs where my bra band would have been. As those fingertips grazed the bottoms of my breasts, my nipples hardened, then electrified. I wanted his hands—maybe even his mouth—to continue on to my breasts.

Instead, he moved his hands around to my back as we twisted onto our sides. I leaned in to find his mouth, but he pulled back so I couldn't reach. "Hold on a minute," he said.

His hands were still on my back. He slid them slowly down my shoulder blades to the taper of my waist and across the small of my back. Then he did it again, his hands following the exact path as before.

"I've always wondered how this would feel," he whispered.

"What?"

"Your body. You're a powerhouse. A mountain-climbing machine."

"Luke!" Now I was self-conscious. And it wasn't true. After this long at high altitude, I'd lost a lot of muscle, and almost all of my bust.

His hands drifted up to my triceps, squeezing them before rounding across my shoulders and cupping them.

"Not all bodies can do what you do. And *this* is what it feels like."

His hands studied the muscles of my back again, as if they were a map written in Braille. I had to admit, it was sexy.

"Now can I kiss you?" I asked.

He let me, and as we kissed, he slipped his hand over my breast like it was the cup of the kind of lacy underwire bra I'd never owned. He circled my nipple with his thumb, bringing heat and pressure to the junction of my legs. I sighed, which was as much in reaction to the sensation as it was with the surprise of his touch so strongly affecting a place that he wasn't even touching.

I wrapped my arms around him. His kisses paused as my hands explored the soft skin above the tight and defined muscles of his back. Then his mouth was back on mine, more insistent than before. My panties grew slick, and my mind drifted to the condoms in my jacket pocket.

But if we kept going, Luke would realize I had no clue what I was doing. That I'd never been even remotely close to where we were headed. Should I say something?

He pulled back with alarm. "Emily. I'm sorry. I shouldn't have—"

I didn't realize I had stiffened. "No, it's not that. It's just…I've never done this before."

He rolled back against me. I couldn't see his face in the perfect blackness of my tent, but a smile was pressing his cheek into mine. His lips slid down to the pulse point at the base of my jaw, and he kissed me there before feeling for my hand and lacing our fingers together.

"I guess we could start with this," he said, moving our joined hands down his stomach to his jeans button.

Oh my god. This was really going to happen.

I followed his lead, popping the button free. The zipper teeth clicked in the quiet of the tent as I slowly lowered his fly. He pulled his jeans the rest of the way off, leaving nothing but long underwear bottoms. Then he untied the drawstring on my thick fleece pajama pants and helped me slide them off. As we moved, the sleeping bag kicked frigid mountain air across our bodies, and in the stark contrast between hot and cold, goose bumps pricked along my arms.

We found each other again, our newly freed legs intertwining eagerly. My body relaxed as I followed his lead. A lead that I wasn't sure I even needed, as it seemed like my body instinctually knew what to do. We kissed exactly as we had before, his hand cupping my breast and his thumb playing with my nipple, except this time there was no denying his hardness pressing against me. The yearning ache in my body wound tighter.

My hungry hands were all over his back, chest, and shoulders, trying to feel what I'd never seen with my eyes.

He exhaled loudly in response as he pulled my leg up his hip and squeezed my bottom. His hardness pressed directly across the damp part of my panties, releasing a rush of need so strong that I did something I could never fathom under normal circumstances: I nudged his head lower, toward my breasts.

He cupped them with both hands and then, one at a time, took a nipple into his mouth, drawing a spiral around it with his tongue. It was so mesmerizing that I hardly noticed the footsteps on the rock just outside the tent. Until the footsteps stopped. We froze. Thankfully, the steps continued into the distance.

I wrapped my leg tighter around him, and we continued kissing. His hand explored the length of my bare leg, making my skin prickle deliciously. Our kisses deepened, perhaps as deep and overtly sexually as we had ever kissed, our tongues wet and hot.

"Okay, hang on, Emily," he said, pulling away slightly. He was breathing as heavily as me. "We should think about this."

"You don't want to?"

"It's not that, believe me. It's just, for your first time... For *our* first time... With people walking by... And it's so dark in here, and it'll be messy, and then I'm going to have to sneak back off to my tent." He framed my face with his warm hand. "It doesn't match how I feel about you."

My body reverberated with protest. If not now, there might not ever be another chance, first or otherwise.

As if emphasizing Luke's point, more footsteps passed by the tent.

"But this could be all we have," I whispered.

He ran his hand slowly through my hair. His careful, caring touch was a gentle salve for the parts of me that still burned for him.

"That's just the thing," he said. Something about his voice reached deep inside me, connecting with a place that made me feel more alive than any of the ways he'd touched me tonight. He twisted a piece of my hair and laid it along my bare shoulder. "It doesn't have to be."

I knew exactly what he was implying. He was quiet for a long time, letting his words sink in.

"I can't leave Washington for another two years," he said. "For all the people who have contributed to my scholarships and worked to get me where I am today—Greg included—I will finish my degree. You said you still don't have anything lined up next, so why not figure it out in Washington? April was telling me her roommate is going to Antarctica for six months, and I bet you could sublet that room."

Washington.

Luke was trembling a little, and I realized it was because he was nervous.

"I know you have bad associations in Washington and your mom lives there," he said. "I completely understand why you wouldn't want to go. But your mom is one person. I'm another. For all that she's not, *we* are a lot." He slipped a hand back to my face. "Aren't we?"

I put my hand on top of his. I couldn't imagine this being it for Luke and me. "We are," I said.

As more cold air snuck in the wide opening at the top of our sleeping bags, we shivered. After putting some of our layers back on, we re-wrapped ourselves in each other.

He swallowed. "What if you came back…for me?"

Time went into slow motion, into a zone where elation and fear could exist at the same time. Luke tilted his forehead onto mine. "I know you're going to need to think this over, and I don't need an answer right now, but I'm really asking you. Officially. Will you come with me to Washington?"

Chapter Thirty-Eight

It was more than a touch scary imagining Luke in his real life and me there with him. It haunted my thoughts as I drifted to sleep last night. And when the sunrise woke me too early this morning, I scooted down in my sleeping bag and thought about it some more.

I had wanted to be able to say yes to him immediately, that it was a great idea and of course I'd do it. But Luke was right; I needed to fully consider it. There were implications in this decision that ran deeper than simply crossing my fingers that it would all work out. I would make a decision, and I would do it with intention, not on a whim.

What would it be like to be in a modern Western city with Luke? To be out in the open with him, not having to hide away in a tent or behind rocks? To not be constantly at the mercy of the hourglass of our dwindling time left together?

I launched Circ and scrolled through Luke's account, studying the world that was his. And could be ours. I wanted him with all my heart, but everything in the background of the Circs he'd taken at UW and in the Seattle metropolitan area overwhelmed me. Was there really a place in all that for me?

I left my tent with plenty of time before our pre-breakfast guides' meeting in the Cubans' team tent. It was our final review of the details for the summit attempt, and even though no one had yet had coffee, the group was stirring with excitement. Almost everyone in the tent had summited before, and to most of us, the excitement wasn't the prospect of standing on top again. It was that we knew how excited the clients would be in a few minutes when Jim gave the official announcement that we were leaving tomorrow.

When we broke to go into the big top, I wound up next to Luke. He snuck me a smile. Despite not being thrilled to be working on Everest this season, he was excited to get cracking tomorrow, same as everyone else.

Jim's news was followed by cheers, confetti poppers, and some bottles of champagne Glissading Glen had kept stowed away in secret.

The big top cleared out quickly after breakfast. After five days of purposeful lethargy, we were all suddenly on fire with repacking gear, mending holes in clothing, deciding which trinkets to bring to the summit, calling home, and doing final posts for blogs and video diaries. I hurried through my own preparations so I could spend some time down at Winslowe Expeditions.

When I arrived, Dad was busy with Tshering and a grumpy client, so I went to the kitchen tent to make a batch of peanut butter fudge cookies for the Winslowe clients. Pertemba, the gossiping traitor, was in there, too, but at least he was polite enough not to bring up Luke. As I worked, I relished the smell of the fudge mixture heating on the stove and the feeling of Mingma's favorite wooden spoon in my hand as I mixed the dough. I had been away from a kitchen for far too long.

I continued to think about Luke. About whether or not I could take the leap to follow him to Washington. And I was pretty sure I could.

It would be scary to go to the United States without a job already lined up, but I could stay with Doc for a few weeks, and once I found a job, I could move into that vacant room in April's house. I'd ask her for more details later tonight. I wanted to talk to Dad about it first, to make sure that turning down Barrett Browning's personal Tanzania offer wasn't the stupidest thing in the world. Especially considering that my time in Tanzania could lead to an actual career with Esplanade Equipment, where I could help start up future CentralPoint sites. Like Patagonia.

As I rolled the cookies into balls and set them in neat rows on the cookie sheets, a vision came to me. I was sitting on the porch of that little white bungalow, a blanket over my lap. Luke came out of the front door, two mugs of hot chocolate in his hands, smiling as he handed me one and sat down.

I had wondered what it would be like to be with him in his world.

Amazing.

That's what it would be like.

I challenged myself to picture the white bungalow again, but this time in Washington. I added drizzle to the vision and put the house on a hill with a view of the Puget Sound and the forested islands beyond. The sky would be gray with low clouds in the direction of the water, yet to the east, where the clouds were higher and thinner, the sun would be a breath away from breaking through into a misty rainbow.

I remembered Puget Sound views like this from when I was a child, especially along the drive from the South Sound, where Amy and I lived, to my grandparents' house. It reminded me that not all memories of Washington made me anxious.

I could do this. I could continue my life back where it started.

Now, I envisioned the bungalow having a campfire ring out in the front where a big, warm fire was going with friends gathered all around it. These friends were fun, outdoorsy people, and we'd all be talking about the different things each of us had done that day. Paddleboarding, paragliding, hiking, rock climbing. Maybe some of the friends would be getting in from a big expedition, which was the reason we were gathering in the first place. Maybe Luke and I would have been among them. A mountaineering trip to Bugaboos in British Columbia, perhaps?

Dad found me as I was pulling the first sheet of cookies out of the oven. In a peace offering of sorts, Tattletale Pertemba said he'd bake the second sheet for me, and I followed Dad over to Winslowe Expeditions's tiny communications tent.

"Let's talk about tomorrow," he said after somehow managing to swallow down a red-hot cookie. "I'm going to be blunt here. Your clients are under no illusions about the danger of this mountain. They know there is no guarantee that they'll be coming back down. By this point, they've signed three or four waivers acknowledging this. You are a *guide*, not an emergency responder. It is not your job to put yourself in unnecessary risk to get someone to the top, or to get them down if you would be clearly risking your own life to do so. It is not the Sherpas' job, either."

Sheesh. "Okay, Dad—"

"This is serious. I'm not worried about your technical skill, judgment, or performing at altitude. But I know you, and I worry about the people part."

His voice trembled, and I realized that me working for Global had been a bigger deal to him than he'd let on. It wasn't just that I was guiding for my first season with somebody else's company, it was the first mountain I was climbing without him. From here on, he could no longer personally look out for my safety.

I put my arm around him. Heck. I also wished it was him and Winslowe Expeditions I was about to launch this summit attempt with.

"You need to be prepared that if you find yourself in a situation that is risking your own life or others' lives, you will need to leave your client behind," Dad said, his voice still rough. "It will feel wrong, and it will be the hardest thing you'll ever have to do, but never forget: it's a commercial game up here. We offer a product that lots of people want: a chance to stand on top of the highest mountain on the planet. We don't do it because we are bighearted. We do this to make a profit. Do not sacrifice yourself for that."

I grimaced. He was right, but it was too terrible to think about. Especially as I pictured the trusting faces of Johnsmith, Phil, and Glissading Glen.

"Okay, Dad." I exhaled, trying to force the inauspicious thoughts out of my head. "I need to get back to Global soon, but I wanted to see what you think about Tanzania first. I have to email Barrett before we leave. Like tonight."

"Tanzania? You're still considering that?"

"Well, kind of, but I'm actually thinking of—"

I stopped because Dad had pulled his soft-sided briefcase out of one of the big electronics boxes. My curiosity had me sitting up straighter as he lined up the numbers on the lock. It was the one lock that even I didn't know the combo to. He popped the lock but didn't unzip the case.

"If you go to Tanzania, just know that you'd be giving up climbing for a long time," he said. "With your skill and passion for mountaineering, it doesn't make sense to me why you'd be willing to do that. Let's talk more about your idea of trying for a sponsorship."

"That was part of my original plan for what I was going to do instead of college. Another reason I'm hoping to summit this year but, still, it's such a long shot."

"Not as much as you think. I'm positive you would already have sponsorships from some of the smaller companies if we hadn't been keeping your name off Miss Eleanor's register. If you work on your rock and ice climbing so that you're climbing a few grades harder, and if you get a couple more peaks under your belt, with peers instead of me, I bet Esplanade Equipment would sponsor you. Do you understand what a big deal an Esplanade sponsorship would be?"

I nodded. Esplanade was the best-of-the-best in terms of mountaineering products and the caliber of their athletes.

"Mountaineering is, and has always been, such a core of their entire brand that I wouldn't put it past them to consider sponsoring a long-term project like the Top Five. *If* they had the right athlete. I may be biased, but I think they could see that in you."

My chest swelled. It was one thing to imagine an inroad to something impossible, but quite another to have someone else independently confirm it. Dad was an internationally respected alpinist, and to have his endorsement of my skill meant more to me personally than some company making the same determination.

"Do you think there'd be a chance they'd sponsor two people for the Top Five?" I asked.

"Well, you couldn't do it alone. You'd need partners."

"What about Luke? Do you think he'd have a chance at a sponsorship with them, too?"

Dad thought about this. "He doesn't have nearly the experience you do on peaks above fifteen-thousand feet, but he's been tearing up the Cascades ever since he started college. And if he's anything like Gyalzen…"

He looked away, but not before I saw the sheen in his eyes.

Going back to Tengboche to tell Mingma that her husband—Luke's father—was dead was the hardest thing Dad had ever done.

I stood up and hugged him.

"Gyalzen could have done it," he said, composing himself. "Luke needs more experience on the really high stuff, but I think he could do it, too. Is that what he wants? I thought he was going to medical school."

"Maybe. I don't think he's fully committed to that yet."

"You guys and those *World's 19ers* books you are always lugging around."

"Yeah."

"Well, you wouldn't have a better partner than Luke."

"I know."

"Be careful with him."

For a split second, I thought he was about to give me another protective-Dad warning. But what he actually meant was for *me* not to hurt *him*.

Dad opened the briefcase that was still on his lap. "Listen, Emily," he said. "Something's been bothering me, and I know you're not going to want to talk about it, but it's my job to say it even though you're twenty. Even if you were forty. I'll still be your dad even when you're in…Tanzania. *If* it comes to that."

He paused to look directly at me, to make sure I was paying full attention.

"I worry that one of the reasons you decided not to go to college is because of what happened with Amy. We never talk about it, and that's my fault. I knew you didn't want to, and I left it at that. I should have insisted."

I shifted in the chair and crossed my arms. "You're right about me not wanting to talk about her. I still don't. And that's okay. I'm okay with the fact that I do not have a relationship with my mother."

"I understand that, because I didn't have much of a relationship with my own parents. Teresa has always voiced something different, though. And you know what? With how things have come together this season, my opinion has changed. I don't think it was a coincidence that you first considered taking a gap year shortly after Amy was released and started living in Port Townsend. I have a bad feeling that all this is wrapped up in your decision about Tanzania."

I wanted to scratch at my skin, which was crawling with invisible pinpricks. I didn't know where this was going, but I didn't like it.

"Amy has been wanting to contact you," he said. "Since she got out."

I gave him a sharp frown I hoped would discourage him from going any further. He ignored me, riffling through the briefcase. "She wrote you a letter. It got here last week."

Sheer panic grabbed me, panic equal to the moment the snowbridge had collapsed in the icefall.

"I don't blame you if you have no interest in reading it," Dad said. "You can tear it up and throw it away if you want. But for something—someone—in the past to completely halt everything you have been moving toward, that's when we have to turn around and look back down the trail. If you don't, you'll never get higher than where you are right now."

He pulled an envelope out of the case. Chills ran through my body even before the paper hit my hand.

It was my own stationery from when I was a little girl. Childhood stationery I had never used. Inside the bubble-gum pink envelope would be scallop-edged paper decorated with unicorns. I could taste the pasta from lunch in the back of my throat. It was like the night of the arrest was happening all over again.

"Emily?"

I snatched the envelope from his hand and shoved it deep

into the interior pocket of my jacket. I stood.

"You okay?"

I nodded vigorously. "We've got an early morning. I have to get back."

It took 100 percent effort to fake nonchalance as I gave him a good-bye hug, hoping he didn't notice how much I was sweating. I left right away, before I lost it completely.

Chapter Thirty-Nine

I waited outside the communications tent until my eyes had adjusted to the dark. With the sky clear and star-filled, there would be just enough light for me to walk without my headlamp. Tonight, I wanted to be invisible.

Instead of taking the Base Camp trail, I went the direct route between Winslowe Expeditions and Global City, struggling over the rocks and ice. Despite the exertion, I was shivering, just like I'd been that night in Port Townsend. My mind traveled back to my previous life, back to the ballet class Grandma paid for, suffering through the minutes until I could change out of the itchy pink leotard and get away from the girls who always made sure there was no space for me at the bar.

I was back to our unkempt apartment, eating raisins and saltines for dinner again because it was almost bedtime and Amy wasn't home from wherever she went during the day.

Back to those woods behind my grandparents' house, where I ran free and wild, dodging around trees and powering up hills, eager to see what was on the other side. Tired but happy. Until the raindrops started to fall.

Reaching my tent, I crawled right into my sleeping bag and set my alarm for two a.m., just five hours from now.

I needed to get to sleep immediately, but of course I couldn't.

I didn't read the letter. I wanted nothing to do with it or her. Ever.

Instead, it was Luke's words from a couple of days ago that were in my head. The same phrase, over and over.

I'm always wanting more of you than I can have.

Always?

No, *not* always. I was only twenty. He was my first love. My only love. These things didn't last.

And yet I had spent the whole day telling myself it was okay to go all the way back to the United States for him. I would end up stranded. Stranded in a place I'd never wanted to be in the first place.

Even if Luke could somehow promise me permanence, it wouldn't be right this early in the game. What did I expect? A marriage proposal? We'd been together a month. I wouldn't even recognize him in street clothes, surrounded by a bunch of other people our age. He'd never seen me in anything other than trail clothes or mountaineering gear. In fact, I didn't even own any real clothes. I had no idea what American college students wore. My surgical-scissors hair trim would never hold up against girls like Olivia with those perfect, blond spirals.

Cold sweat pricked out across my temples. This was not what happy felt like. The happy I wanted was steady and reliable. A boyfriend could never provide that. Nor should he. It was up to me to build my own complete and solid happiness. The boyfriend should be icing on top, not the cake itself. If you put your whole world in one person, and that person leaves, they take *everything.*

The letter was just the reminder I needed.

This was what it felt like to be abandoned.

It had happened with all four of the people in my life who were supposed to be there forever: my mother, my grandparents, and my father. Luke would leave me behind someday. He didn't think it now, but he would.

It's why going to Washington for Luke wasn't viable.

My thoughts were coming faster now, jumbled and out of order.

Luke was my whole world, past and present.

But he might not be my future.

With all my heart, I wanted to be able to follow him to Washington, but I would just be setting myself up to be abandoned again. And considering that, I couldn't risk losing the opportunity in Tanzania. It was the only option I had, and it was a good one, seeing as it could lead to a career with Esplanade Equipment. A career wasn't the same thing as the sponsorship I dreamed of, but it would be even better from a long-term perspective.

Coworkers could be like family. I knew this from Winslowe Expeditions. So could neighbors. And animals. The first stray puppy I met in Tanzania would be mine.

The CentralPoint facility Barrett was building would certainly not be small and painted white, but it could be my white bungalow in all the most important ways. It would be full of people. Travelers. Tanzanians. Fun Esplanade staff members. And in Tanzania, a goat won't be a problem. A nice milking goat for making fresh chèvre.

The facility would be sparse but clean. I could braid a rug out of old climbing rope and make some decorations to spruce it up. There I'd have photos in frames instead of dangling from the ceiling of a tent, curling from the cold and condensation.

There might not be mountains to explore in Tanzania, but there were other types of adventures in Africa, like wildlife preserves and sleeping in the bush. And I'd be helping the local people through the facility's community projects. Helping people was right up my alley.

But Luke.

I thought of him again at the rock, how there had been stars reflected in his eyes when he looked at me. Even in memory, the beauty of it caught my breath. And then wrenched me with guilt.

Tread softly, because you tread on my dreams.

I shut my eyes tight to the feeling of his lips, soft as down against my forehead.

Be careful with him.

How could I do this to Luke? *My* Luke?

But I would. I had to.

As much as I was in love with him, I had to build a life where I was the center instead of the satellite in someone else's life. I'd never find permanence if I was waiting to be cut loose at any moment. The mountains, and any prospect of earning a sponsorship, would have to go on hold for now. Before I lost the nerve, I sat up, turned on my phone, and accepted the job in Tanzania.

Chapter Forty

We set out into the icefall under the best of conditions: there were no expeditions ahead of us, the sky was clear with the moon lighting our way, and the brutal cold of the night was keeping all the mousetrap seracs glued in place as best as they ever would. Despite this, the group's celebratory spirit from yesterday was gone. Everyone knew we had a long road ahead to the summit and to getting safely back down.

Tonight we'd be at Camp Two. Tomorrow night, Camp Three. We'd spend half a night at Camp Four, then we had about twenty hours of pushing through the topmost—and hardest—section of the climb to the summit and back down to Camp Four. We'd sleep there that night and then take another day and night to descend into Base Camp, where everyone would celebrate, and then disperse out of the Khumbu region and back to their regular lives.

I had one thing on my mind: a prayer that we'd get through this without any of us ending up in an ominous situation like Dad warned about last night.

Just one more time up, and one more time down.

And just one more night alone in a tent with Luke. Tonight. At Camp Two. Because tomorrow night, at Camp Three, I'd be sharing with Doc and Claudia again.

Instead of looking forward to having the excuse to be alone with him, I dreaded it. It put the pressure on about giving him an answer about Washington, but I also believed the middle of a summit attempt of the world's tallest mountain was not the right place to tell him I would be going to Tanzania, not Washington.

Luke was already inside our tent when I reached Camp Two; I could tell from his coughs. I took a deep breath and unzipped the door.

"That's not sounding good," I said as I crawled in.

"It would be better to not have a cough right now, but I'll be fine."

He didn't look fine. He was pale, his eyes were dilated, and he appeared a lot more tired than he should be.

I gave him a dubious look.

"I'm fine, really."

He started to say something else but lost it to his cough.

Was this a standard Khumbu cough or a sign of something worse? If it progressed into altitude sickness, pulmonary edema, or cerebral edema, he likely wouldn't be in a frame of mind to figure out what was happening to him, especially not once we got higher. I silently checked him against the list of symptoms: rattling breath, extreme fatigue, cough, blue finger beds, drowsiness, shallow breathing. Basically the exact symptoms all of us had while climbing here.

"I did something big last night," he said after taking some sips of water and getting control of his cough.

"And what was that?"

"I canceled my entire class schedule for fall and registered for the ones in the atmospheric sciences sequence."

I gave him a high five. "That's fantastic!"

"Some classes I wasn't able to get because it's not my major anymore, so I emailed my old advisor to help me straighten everything out."

"I'm so happy you took that step."

"It's thanks to you. Because of what you suggested when we were at Camp Three."

"It was nothing you didn't know already."

"Yeah, but to hear someone else have the same observation made me more confident. Before that, it had seemed like a lame excuse I'd made up to try to rationalize it for myself."

I was dying to tell him what Dad had said about Gyalzen's love of mountain climbing and how Dad thought Luke had potential for a sponsorship, too. That would make him even happier. I'd tell him before we left this season, but how could I broach that topic now without also delving into my decision about Washington? And the fact that I was giving up my own climbing dreams for the foreseeable future?

We lay down in our sleeping bags to nap, but neither of us could sleep. Him because of his cough, and me because I felt like a traitor for not telling him I'd accepted a job in Tanzania.

When we crawled back into the tent after dinner, Luke was noticeably quiet, aside from his cough, which had gotten even worse. We both settled into our sleeping bags. The tension in the air was thick enough to touch.

"We're four days from leaving Everest," he said. "You haven't answered my question about Washington. That means no."

I shook my head to deny it.

"Then look at me and tell me otherwise."

So I looked at him. His eyes were determined. And also really tired. "Not here," I said. "Not right now."

"Yes. Here. Now."

I pleaded with my eyes.

He shook his head. "Say it."

I looked down. "I really wish it were different, but I'm not going to come to Washington."

He said nothing. Behind him, the tent vibrated with a random gust of wind.

"I was going to say yes, but yesterday Dad gave me a letter from Amy, and it made everything clear. You have to understand, I've spent my whole life being left behind by other people. People who didn't want me in the first place."

"That's not true."

"It *is* true. My mom never wanted me. I overheard her on the phone once. She purposely lied about being on birth control. She thought if she got pregnant, my dad would stay around and marry her. He didn't."

Luke slid next to me and lifted my drooping head.

"Dad lost his sponsorship and entire way of life when he had to take custody of me. He is my whole world, but I'm just a small piece of his. I know he wishes it wasn't this way, but he's had to cut me loose, and now I have nothing."

"But you have me."

The light from my headlamp was low, and it threw odd shadows around the tent, obscuring Luke's expression.

"For now, I have you. And when you leave it will kill me. I need to stand on my own."

"I'm not going to leave—"

"It's way too early to say that. Besides, nothing is certain. I can't go from following my dad to following you. I need to find a place where I can build a world where I'm its center. If not for you, I'd never consider Washington to be that place. So to go there just for you…it would be a repeat of what happened with Amy, then Dad. You have to understand, I can't put myself in that position again."

"But you said you were going to say yes before you got the letter."

"Yes, but—"

He picked up my hand and rubbed it between his. "Long distance, Emily. You wouldn't mind *visiting* Washington, right? You could visit me, and I could visit you, wherever you end up living. Montana or Wyoming, maybe? I can drive to Montana in seven hours from Seattle. I'm going to be there for only two more years, then I can go anywhere. We don't have to be at good-bye yet."

The icy weight of dread slowly filled my core, then spread in burning dots all the way into my fingers and toes. *Tanzania.* A long-distance relationship *wasn't* possible. Not in the way he was thinking.

I swallowed. "There's something else I have to tell you."

A coughing fit racked his body, one that made him wheeze as he struggled for air. He unwrapped a medicated cough drop and slipped it in his mouth. The coughing settled down.

"Luke, that cough—it's only going to get—"

"Don't. You said there was something else."

"I do know where I'm going after this. And it's not Montana or Wyoming." I fiddled with my zipper pull. "It's not anywhere in the U.S."

"Tell me." The jaggedness of his voice sent chills down my spine.

"Barrett Browning, he's the founder of Esplanade Equip—"

"I know who he is."

"He offered me a job. In Tanzania." I forced myself to look him in the eyes. "I accepted the job last night, after I got the letter from Amy."

In slow motion, his face went hard. The ferocious depth in his eyes terrified me.

"Please understand, I didn't want to, but I had to," I pleaded. "I don't have any job offers anywhere else."

"I don't even know what to say." He dropped my hand and scooted back. "But I think I understand. Of course it's easier not to face it. It's easier to bump up against the unpleasant and then go the other way. And when a convenient situation is handed to you on a silver platter, even though it has nothing to do with anything you'd actually want, you take it."

My chest constricted as if I was having a heart attack. My whole universe had cracked open, and everything was running everywhere.

"I would do anything for you. Don't you know that, Emily? I would leave my scholarship, if that's what needed to happen. But I can't do that knowing you wouldn't do the same for me."

A tear chilled my cheek as it rolled down. I reached for his hand. He moved it away.

"We still have a few days left," I said. "Can't we be together for the rest of it? I love you, Luke. I don't want things to end; it's our circumstances. I don't start in Tanzania until July, and I still have my Seattle ticket. Maybe I can come to Washington with you for a while before I leave."

There was empathy in his eyes, but his eyebrows were scrunched in resistance. "I wish I could play pretend with you, but I'm just not built that way. It would be a miracle to have even one day with you where we didn't have to hide in a tent or meet somewhere out in the dark. To introduce you, just once, as my girlfriend. Or for us to have a whole night together, somewhere indoors where it was warm and comfortable, where we could wear normal clothes, or nothing at all. Of course I want that more than anything else. But it would be a lie because, really, I'd be dying inside."

His voice was quieter now, the edge that had been there had faded off. I had to strain to hear him. "Getting closer to you this last month has been a dream. I let myself believe that it was real. But it has always been too good to be true. And now, here in this godforsaken place, so far above life but even farther from heaven, I'm going to have to try to find a way to start breathing again."

What had I done? How could I walk away from my best friend? A person I'd fantasized about for more than two years and loved ferociously. He was right. I'd taken the easy path. Out of all the universities that had offered him scholarships, he'd picked Washington because that's where I had been planning to go. Yet I wasn't willing to face my demons in order to do the same. I wasn't worthy of him.

"Luke, please," I begged, reaching for him again.

This time he let me put my arms around him. "I wanted to believe it could be different for us," he said. "That's what I wished for when you tied the bracelet on me two years ago. But you've told me otherwise in one way or another all along. It's been me who couldn't see the truth for what it was." He ran his hand down the side of my face, his thumb reaching across my cheek to the tear line there. With his tear-damp thumb, he traced my top lip, then the bottom.

We lay down to try to get some sleep because tomorrow we had the Lhotse Face to climb. I started crying again when he slid over and spooned his body around mine. I refused to budge, even though his cough rattled my sore shoulder. Because this was the last time he would ever hold me like this.

Sunrise came. Both of us were subdued as we pulled out of the fog of the subzero night and feverish, oxygen-deprived dreams.

I was dressed and ready to get out of the tent before Luke, but I wasn't going to be the first to leave. He didn't seem to have the same qualms, but then, before unzipping the door, he turned back to me.

I wasn't sure what was more alarming, his bloodshot eyes from coughing all night or the depth of the sadness in them.

"Maybe I just need more time to process everything," I blurted. It's what had been running through my head all night on a loop. "Amy's letter last night was out of the blue. It was such a shock. And I *just* emailed Barrett. I could write him back and change my mind."

Luke examined me with eyes that glistened with sorrow. "I want to believe that could be true, but it's like you said yesterday about not repeatedly putting yourself in a bad position. I can't put myself in that position with you again. I can't let myself hope."

He leaned in, presumably to kiss my cheek, but I wouldn't accept just that. I rose up on my knees and turned my head in to him. When our lips touched, my legs wavered. He put his hand on my waist to steady me.

I poured my whole heart into the kiss, my entire soul, but it didn't change the distinct feeling that he was kissing me good-bye.

Chapter Forty-One

Somehow, the Go Big expedition, which had been behind us all day yesterday, managed to weasel their way in among the Global teams right before A-Team started up the Lhotse Face. Jim was pissed, swearing over the radio, but no individual or expedition owned Everest, and there wasn't anything that could be done except A-Team waiting an extra hour in our tents while the Sherpas guarded the route in case the Swedish expedition, also with us at Camp Two, got any ideas.

In the tent, I tried to close my eyes and get a little rest to make up for being virtually unable to sleep last night, but I couldn't stop thinking about Luke. He had a pullover stashed here for the way back down, and I hugged it to my body, the smell of him in the fabric making me more heartsick.

What had I done? I was all set to go to Tanzania, but at the cost of losing the person who was the most important to me next to Dad.

It didn't make sense, logically, how a single pink envelope could have that kind of sway over me. I'd kept Amy and all that had happened out of my mind for ten years, so how was it possible for her claws to be in me so deep that they'd overpowered all other factors and moved me to choose Tanzania?

But I also wasn't wrong in putting a priority on independence.

You can't be cut loose when you're the center of your own world.

From outside the tent, Phurba called to me. It was our turn on the Lhotse Face.

By the time all of A-Team was clipped to the line, it was late morning and even hotter than our last trip up. Between my lack of sleep and not drinking enough water yesterday, I was struggling as much as the clients. Claudia's brother, Juan, who had terrible blisters and could no longer keep pace with the Cubans, was climbing with A-Team today, and because of that, April was occasionally flying the drone over us. The heat made me so irritable that I wanted to swat at it as it hovered close above our heads.

Directly ahead of me, Phil somehow managed to get his ascender stuck on the line. It took me several minutes to untangle him. Then, out of the pure silence of the windless morning came a panicked yell, followed by the hiss of something big and heavy flying through the air. I ducked and screamed to Phil and Juan to do the same. It was an ice ax. The most deadly thing to drop. It had to be from the Go Big team; we made all our Global clients keep their axes on lanyards.

Tashi that no one had been hit. There's no question the ax would have killed someone, even with helmets on. It made me think about regrets. Because I had one—a big one—that was very presently on my mind. *Luke.*

If nothing else, I should have tried harder last night to avoid telling him about Tanzania. He wasn't faring well as it was, and I'd torn him up further. To not tell him would have been to lie, but maybe it would have been safer, and that was more important right now.

We forged on ahead. Foot down, slide hand, step, pull. Foot down, slide hand, step, pull. As if my mind and heartbeats weren't already a mess, the dropped ice ax further exacerbated my tangled mess of anxiety, franticness, unrest, and regret. What was the worst thing that could have happened if I had decided to go to Washington? That it wouldn't work out? Ironic, because every mountain I'd climbed in the Himalayas had higher stakes than that.

If I could get my head together, maybe I could talk things through more with Luke. Maybe he could help me see my errors. That is, if he was even willing to talk. He'd clearly said this morning that he wasn't going to put himself in that position with me again.

Either way, thinking straight was not going to happen until I was on bottled oxygen. As it was, my blood pressure was high enough for me to feel my pulse in weird and painful places, like my temples. Why did people do this? I mean, look at us here, this huge gravy train of people. This morning, we'd all walked right by a corpse from last season and it didn't faze anyone. All of it was totally irrational. But if Everest was proof of anything, it was proof of the power of irrationality.

By the time we made it to Camp Three, it was eighty-six degrees. I battled through deliriousness to help Phil, Glissading Glen, and Johnsmith with their oxygen. I meant to just rest in the sun break of the ladies' tent for a few minutes before going to find Luke, but I collapsed to sleep practically upon impact and didn't awake until Doc was shaking me.

"Emily, Thom has been calling you," she said. "He wants you to meet with them over at the twins' tent."

I sat up groggily. My boots were still on, and I hadn't changed out of my sweaty layers. *Stupid.* Even though it was warm in the tent, the sun would soon be setting, and I had a chill from being in damp clothes. In a majorly delayed reaction, I realized that the reason I was so groggy was because I'd gotten everyone else's oxygen set up except my own.

I put on my oxygen mask and cranked the valve to max, taking some long, full breaths. In less than a minute, I was back to full force. Whew, ecstasy! I dialed the valve back to the minimum setting and quickly changed my clothes, hanging the damp ones over the tent poles to dry alongside Doc's and Claudia's.

Over in the twins' tent it was Thom, Tyler, Hulk, and Norbu. Before I could even wonder where Luke was, I realized I'd walked into the middle of a conversation about how to rearrange the teams now that we didn't have Luke anymore.

What?

Tyler filled me in: Luke had been in such bad shape by noon that he didn't even argue when Doc point-blank ordered him to descend.

"How long ago did he leave?" I asked. If it was just a few minutes, I was going after him to make sure he was okay.

"Almost an hour."

And where had I been through all of this? Sleeping!

"He's with Phurba," Tyler said. "Phurba will catch up with us in the morning before we leave for Camp Four."

Jim came on the radio then, apparently not finished being angry at us for having let Go Big get ahead of us earlier. He ordered us to wake up early enough to not let that happen again, which was a legitimate possibility since Go Big's tents were higher than Global's and it would be easy for them to cut us off.

After Jim was done, I learned that Luke wasn't the only one having serious medical problems. Two of the UW geologists were still recovering from the food-borne illness they'd picked up in Dingboche. Johnsmith's knee was too stiff to bend, and some of Juan's blisters were so bad Jim was considering not letting him continue on the summit bid.

Back in the ladies' tent, Doc was eating a Toblerone candy bar. It was her favorite, but with the way she was biting each small triangle in half to chew and swallow, it might as well have been spoiled cheese or something.

"What's going on with Luke?" I asked. "Is it pulmonary edema?"

"I honestly don't know, and I didn't get to properly examine him. He's been coughing for a while now, so that points to a run-of-the-mill high-altitude cough, and I suspect he has a cracked rib from all the coughing. But I didn't like how gray his lips were and how he was practically incoherent. It's likely a combination of things, but he had to go down. He'll be at Camp Two tonight, and if he doesn't improve, the Sherpas will put him in the hyperbaric chamber."

My stomach churned, thinking about Luke down there with only the people who might have secretly wished something like this would happen. My eyes welled up.

"I know," she said, rubbing my shoulder.

"Greg to Emily," came a call on the radio.

I switched over to nine-nine.

"Hi, Dad," I said. It took an effort to keep my voice from wavering.

"How's it going, MiniBoss?"

"Oh, you know. Tell me again, why is it we do this?"

He laughed. "Things are looking good with the winds for tomorrow night, but always keep an eye behind. Jim's not up there with you. He's not seeing what you're seeing."

"Okay, Dad, got it."

"All right. You take care and stay safe. Would you mind passing along the same to Teresa?"

I raised my eyebrow at Doc. "Tell her yourself. We're

sharing a tent. She's right here."

"Hey, Teresa. You watch out for that weather, too." He cleared his throat as he did only when extremely uncomfortable. "Okay. Both of you. Stay safe."

I switched back to Global's primary channel and gave Doc a pointed look. "Has there been a development in your love life that you haven't mentioned?"

She blushed crimson.

Claudia, who had awoken from her oxygenated nap, was as eager for an explanation as I was.

"I've been dating this guy on-again, off-again," Doc said to Claudia. Then, to both of us, "And as of three nights ago, it's back on-again."

I smiled smugly. "By *guy,* she means my dad."

Claudia howled and slapped both of us on the back.

"Emily's dad is Greg Winslowe, the owner of Winslowe Expeditions," Doc explained.

I thought of the condoms she had shoved in my pocket. Were those really from the medical tent, or were they from her—or Dad's—personal collection? *No.* I didn't even want to know. Five gazillion times *yuck*.

"Just for the record, now that we're out in the open, it would have worked out better for Greg and me if you'd gone to Townsend College like you were supposed to."

Doc was joking, but her words were distressing.

"You know, if you had gone back, there's a good chance he would have returned to the States next year. He's got that land out by Mount Rainier."

Yes, there was a small piece of land that had belonged to his grandparents. It was remote, especially by today's standards. Once every couple of years Dad would bring up the idea of building a cabin there, and when we were last in Kathmandu, I'd seen him looking through a tiny-house magazine at the English-language bookstore.

"He can still go back even though I'm not," I pointed out.

"That's right. You have Tanzania. When in doubt, take a job in Tanzania."

"It's for Esplanade Equipment," I said defensively. "It's a great job."

"What's this about Tanzania?" Claudia asked.

"Emily is going to work in Tanzania after this."

"I can't tell…are congratulations in order?" Claudia said.

I said, "Yes," at the same time Doc said, "Depends."

After that, the three of us sat around in a weird high-altitude game of taking sips of electrolyte water. Physically, I felt much better than when I'd first arrived at Camp Three, but I was far from relaxed. How could I be, with what Luke was going through right now?

Just after nightfall, I went outside to pee and to gather more snow to make water for Doc, Claudia, and me. The partial, translucent cloud cover gave the fabric of the stars an ethereal quality. There were no clouds over the ridge of Lhotse, where the moon hung in a perfect sphere. I gazed down the twenty-five-hundred vertical feet to the glowing tents of Camp Two, where Luke could be lying in a hyperbaric chamber right now.

I have spread my dreams under your feet: tread softly because you tread on my dreams.

Against all protocol, I called Luke on the radio. I wanted to hear his voice. To hear that he'd be okay. To tell him I was thinking about him and that I'd do anything for him so long as he took care of himself and pulled through this.

I waited on the station for ten minutes. Then ten minutes longer. There was no response.

Chapter Forty-Two

The two times I'd climbed Everest without oxygen had been no less than excruciating. For seventy-two hours straight, my lungs had been on fire. Even resting in my sleeping bag was no relief once we were higher than twenty-five-thousand feet. With every step—every single one—it was a fight not to give up. Not to collapse into the cusp of suffocation.

Though I had plenty of oxygen flowing through my mask as A-Team baby-stepped from Camp Three to Camp Four, I was suffocating just as I had on my climbs without oxygen. A mental suffocation as I worried about Luke and second-guessed my Tanzania decision.

I walked in a trance, my mind locked on Luke. With one step it was doubt. The next, doom. Then grief, denial, love. Then back to doubt.

There was no talk about Luke's condition over the radio. Jim would be working directly with the Everest ER doctors at this point and communicating on a different channel. I hadn't been able to figure out which one, and it wasn't for lack of effort.

All I knew was that, as of this morning, Luke was sleeping and was not in the hyperbaric chamber. But had he been in one last night? Which camp was he in now? Was he going all the way down to Base Camp today? Was he truly strong enough to walk out on his own?

I kept a careful eye on Johnsmith and Phil as we reached the Yellow Band, a steep limestone section that was bare rock even in high-snow years. As we ascended, our crampons screeched against the rock and ice like fingernails on a chalkboard.

We moved out of the band and went off the fixed lines to slowly crunch across the long, wide plateau toward Camp Four. Phil was steady today, and for once he wasn't the last one in the whole company: Juan was, because of his blisters.

Ahead of me, Phil, Glissading Glen, and Johnsmith were stopped, looking up. Without looking myself, I knew we'd reached the Geneva Spur, which is a large stretch of patchy black rock that looks a lot more intimidating than it actually is.

It wasn't long after reaching the top of the Geneva Spur that my altimeter beeped, marking our arrival at twenty-five-thousand feet. We'd officially crossed into the Death Zone. Without supplemental oxygen in the Death Zone, most of us would be dead in twenty-four hours, assuming we didn't succumb to hypothermia first. By thirty-six hours, all of us would be.

As we reached the slight downslope that led to the South Col—and location of Camp Four—the guys stopped again. This time in awe. It was the first view of the summit of Everest they'd had since the trek in, unless they'd hiked Kala Pattar. I didn't spoil the moment by telling them that it wasn't the true summit they were seeing but rather the South Summit, which, at these guys' pace, was two hours of climbing away from the true summit.

As soon as we entered Camp Four, I sat with Phil while he waited for the Sherpas to finish pitching the A-Team tents. Because of the high winds, the Camp Four tents aren't pitched until we arrive.

"I know the hardest is yet to come, but I can feel it," Phil said, his eyes fixed on the South Summit. "We are so close. I know I have it in me."

"You've just got to keep it steady. As long as you stay ahead of that cutoff you'll be fine."

Phil took off a glove and pulled a tiny action figure out of his pocket. He handed it to me.

"Is this Sir Edmund Hillary?"

"Yes. It was my brother's. We've been armchair mountaineers since we were boys. Read every book out there on Mount Everest. My brother's not alive anymore, but I'm going to leave this on the summit for him."

I examined the toy. "That's a really nice gesture," I said. "We'll make sure to get a picture of that for your family."

He shook his head. "There is no family. I'm the last one left."

I had no idea. "I'm sorry."

"It was cancer. From a closed-down aluminum plant near the house where I grew up. My parents and two sisters went first. When my brother and I were diagnosed, we said that if we got through it, we'd climb Mount Everest."

Phil paused to catch his breath.

"Don't exert yourself," I said.

"My brother didn't make it, but I pulled through somehow. Took me fifteen years to be strong enough to come on this trip, and I could have never paid for it if not for the victims' compensation monies from the aluminum company."

What he must have gone through! I held the well-loved antique toy in my mitten for another minute before handing it back.

"That plant took everything away," he said. "But I have this."

Phil had always been our weak link. Even on his best day, it was a question of whether he'd be going fast enough to make the cutoff time on the final day. He'd worked so hard, and now I understood why. It wasn't just his profession and quietness that had set him apart from the others. It was his focus and determination. He needed this badly. I would help him however I could tomorrow.

The Sherpas called up to us; Phil's tent was done. He tried to stand but was too tired and fell back to his bottom. I gave him a hand.

Once Phil was in his tent, I went to the twins' tent for our final guides' meeting before the summit push. "Turnaround time is noon," Jim reminded us on the radio. "No matter the circumstance, even if you're two hundred yards short of the summit, you're going to turn your client around."

We reviewed the conditions at each of the trouble spots between here and the summit, as well as the latest weather report, which looked good. Tyler assigned me to be with Glissading Glen and Phurba to be with Phil.

"Do you mind if I pair with Phil?" I asked Tyler.

Phurba looked relieved when Tyler said yes. Despite working on Everest for three previous seasons, he'd yet to have the opportunity to summit, and not being paired with the weak link meant his chances were much better. I was happy for him. I no longer cared about my own personal chances of summiting. It wouldn't matter in Tanzania.

After the meeting, I went to the ladies' tent where I found Doc and Claudia haggard, to put it nicely. No one was interested in talking. They were barely functioning, even with the oxygen flowing. The three of us forced down energy gels and split the last two Loftycakes Luke had brought me in Tengboche that I'd saved especially for this day. Sadly, at this altitude, the cakes tasted no different than eating a piece of crumpled notebook paper. I got the stove going to make us some warm broth and tea. That was more palatable.

It was still light outside, but it was time to attempt to get a few hours of sleep before nine p.m., when my watch alarm would go off for our ten p.m. departure. I took some painkiller for my shoulder that throbbed from the extra weight of the oxygen tanks in my pack. I called Dad on the radio, and over channel ninety-nine asked him to track down Luke and make sure he was getting the medical care he needed.

Falling asleep was going to be next to impossible with all the adrenaline in my body. I tried breathing exercises. I tried mantras. I tried meditation. But nothing was stopping the twenty-minute time blocks that were slipping through my fingers each time I gave in to the urge to check my watch. Giving up, I fished my knife out of my pack. I ran my thumb over the ridges of the bracelet like a rosary, saying a silent prayer for Luke.

It was such a cruel twist of fate, me being up here without him. We'd been able to break through so much to find our way to each other, only to have me let it disintegrate right in front of us.

"I love you, Luke," I whispered aloud.

Chapter Forty-Three

It was drizzling, the sky low and gray. Waves came to the shore near my feet, turning the smaller boulders as the water filled in. I picked up a wet rock and threw it into the water, and then another. Drops of accumulated drizzle fell from the rim of my hood onto my nose and cheeks.

A dog ran up. A big, yellow dog that seemed to know me. It dropped a stick at my feet, and I threw it into the sea. The dog splashed into the water, but on the way back out, ran past me.

I turned and there was Dad, and suddenly we were indoors at somebody's apartment. It was modern, with big windows, tall ceilings, and white couches. Doc was in the kitchen, pulling something out of the oven. The dog was circling frantically, the stick still in its mouth, mud from its paws layering on the carpet with each circle until the whole floor was brown.

Out in the living room, there were other people. I knew all of them, but the only faces I recognized were Theo, April, and Hulk.

The yellow dog was still circling. Something was beeping. A fire alarm? No one else seemed to hear it. The dog barked. I looked back to the kitchen, but there was no smoke. The dog barked and barked. Someone whispered my name.

I looked the other way, down the hall. Luke was leaning against the wall, watching everyone in the living room. Watching me. The dog ran to him, then back into the kitchen. Luke's mouth lifted playfully, then it went serious. He turned away from me and walked toward the stairs. He stopped when his foot hit the first step, looking back to make sure I was coming. And I was, I was coming.

The fire alarm was still going off, but he didn't hear it, and it didn't bother me anymore. I reached him, and he put his hands on my waist, drawing me in for a kiss. I was no longer wearing my wet jacket, and I didn't care who saw us. He slipped his hand up my shirt, running it across my stomach before sliding it down my arm and lacing his fingers with mine.

"You sure?" I asked.

He moved up to the next step, still holding my hand. Our arms stretched across the distance.

The beeping wasn't a fire alarm; it was my watch alarm.

I took a step closer to Luke.

The beeping.

I had to wake up. But I wanted to go up the stairs with Luke. Where was he going? He peeked back and his dimples were showing. I took a second step, then another.

It was cold. There was something on my mouth. I couldn't move my arms. I couldn't see.

I sat up, frantic to unzip my sleeping bag and free my arms. I tore off my oxygen mask.

Luke.

I leaned on my knees, trying to catch my breath.

Luke. Luke. Luke.

I didn't want to move. I didn't want to lose the dream. The feeling. It was just out of my grasp, and it was slipping further away. *No.*

I wanted to be anywhere but here on Mount Everest. I wanted to be back on those stairs, following Luke to a bedroom, where it would be nothing but us. Indoors, where it was warm and where we had all the time in the world.

Reluctantly, I felt for my headlamp and turned it on. Every surface inside our tent was covered with a crust of hoarfrost that glistened in the light. It wasn't pretty. It was ugly and very, very cold.

Where was Luke now? I wanted to assume that he was doing better, but altitude sickness was illogical. Just when you think someone's in the clear, they don't pull through.

I leaned over Doc, shaking her gently until she awoke. Claudia was awake already but not wanting to get moving. I helped her sit up.

With the severe cold and the lethargy of the altitude, it took us the rest of the hour I'd allotted for us to choke down a few bites of food, make tea, drink the tea, and finish getting ready.

When we finally left the tent, Theo was waiting next to the door with his handheld camera to get a shot of Claudia departing for the summit. He asked her a question, but his voice was so slurred that I didn't have the faintest idea what he said. Or what her response was.

The three of them walked in the direction of the lights of the hovering drone, where the first members of the Cuban team had already started climbing.

The best summit days are the ones where there is no wind, with no clouds blocking the light of the moon or the stars. On these days, it feels like you are walking on a trail right through the nebulas of the Milky Way.

This was not one of them. Thick clouds made the night

pitch-black and ghoulish. All any of us could see was what was directly in our headlamp beam, and up ahead, the line of pinprick dots of the team members' headlamps disappearing into the distance. This was the scary kind of outer space. The lonely kind, like the Apollo had gone back to Earth, leaving us alone on the dark side of the moon.

We trudged at our dreadfully slow but steady pace up the relentlessly steep, never-ending Triangle Face. I kept running through my dream, doing everything I could not to lose the feeling of it. As long as I could recall it, it was like Luke was happy and healthy and here with me.

The beach in the beginning of the dream looked a lot like Golden Gardens in Seattle. Amy used to take me there. It was a wealthy area, and in retrospect I knew our visits there had something to do with the meth. She'd go inside a house, and I'd go out on the beach by myself. But I was never sad to be left alone there. I'd simply felt free, which had been the same feeling in the dream.

The beach could also be the one from the Circ where Olivia had sat on the rocks while Luke was out paddleboarding.

What did the dream mean? That beautiful things didn't have to be spoiled because of Amy? That there was a place for me in Luke's world? To not be afraid of being alone? Because in that dream I *hadn't* been alone. There was that dog, and then my dad and Doc. April and Theo. All those people at the party. Luke.

We took a short break when we reached the relatively flat section at the top of the Triangle Face called the Balcony. The front portion of A-Team, led by Hulk and Tyler, were already well ahead of us, moving up the southeast ridgeline.

It was daylight by the time we reached the knife blade ridge of the Cornice Traverse, which provided clear views down the sheer faces on either side of us—eight-thousand feet below into Nepal on our left, and eleven-thousand feet below to Tibet on our right. I was too cold and my head too foggy to appreciate the beauty of it.

We hadn't gone much farther when there were reports of the Cuban team's summits. I checked my watch and did a quick calculation. With the distance remaining and the time taken thus far, we were ahead of the turnaround time, but only by a hair, and with the distance we still had to go, we were bound to slip behind it.

The prudent thing to do would be to call the inevitable now and turn back toward safety instead of making the call after another hour of exhaustion. But this was Phil's one and only chance on this mountain. After all that he'd been through, and all those years living for this, I didn't have the heart to call it yet.

I took a couple of steps so I was right next to Phil. "We've got to pick it up so we stay ahead of the cutoff."

He froze.

"Do you think you have it in you to move faster?" I asked.

"I'll find it. I have to."

I could give him thirty minutes more, but then I would have to reassess.

Chapter Forty-Four

Somehow, Phil mustered the strength to keep the gap between us, Phurba, and Johnsmith steady instead of opening.

My hopes raised as we neared the South Summit and that gap had not widened. The spread-out line of the Cuban team passed by us on the way down, exhausted but satisfied. I hugged both Claudia and Theo and gave high fives to everyone else.

The clouds broke then, allowing warming sunbeams through. As we stopped to change out our oxygen tanks, the radio call came that the first four of the UW team had summited, which included Doc. I joined the chorus of cheers on the radio back to them. These fastest UW climbers had been Luke's. Wherever he was right now, he'd be happy they'd made it.

I saw Luke-From-My-Dream again, leaning against that wall, and my blood rushed exactly as if it were happening for real. I realized it *had* happened for real. That stance in my dream was exactly how he'd stood in the doorframe of Mingma's house that day.

I felt the tingles from when his eyes turned serious in my dream. The floating bliss of him taking my hand on the stairs. I felt the utter and total faith I had in him, even though the words from my mouth had been, "Are you sure?"

What if you came back, for me?

Luke had no intention of leaving me behind, of stranding me in a world he owned. What had actually happened was that *I* had left *him* behind.

Tread softly, because you tread on my dreams.

All these years, my past had been as silent as death, but it had been there. And it was still there. I hadn't been able to give Luke a chance because I hadn't truly faced the villains within it.

There was a saying carved into a block of wood on the altar in Mingma's attic. I'd asked her once what it meant.

He who cannot forgive breaks the bridge over which he himself must pass.

I could forgive Amy and be free. I could forgive her for using a pregnancy to coerce Dad into marrying her. For treating me like what I'd been to her: unwanted. Difficult. An outcast. I could forgive her for the drugs and be thankful it wasn't until after the pregnancy that she turned to that life. I could forgive her for being arrested and not caring that she left me alone. Maybe someday I could even let go of my guilt for being the cause of the arrest in the first place.

Furthermore, just because Luke was the reason for moving somewhere, it didn't mean that I'd lose my whole world if our relationship went sour someday. I could make it my home, Luke or not. I could embrace western Washington for what it was: an alpinist's paradise. There was a reason so many of the major U.S. guiding companies were based there. And like the Himalayas, the north part of the Cascades was remote, rugged, and there were even bits of unexplored terrain left.

I saw myself back in my tent at Base Camp, typing an email to Barrett. *There's been a change of plans...*

If I did this, I could have both Luke and mountains. And if I tagged the summit today—which was looking promising—then I'd have my chance at a sponsorship back. I even had the hope of permanence in Washington, from a people perspective, anyway. Doc lived there, and after what she told me yesterday, I'm pretty sure Dad would relocate if I were living there, too. After working for Global, I also knew even more people who lived in Washington: Hulk and Phil, and the UW clients, and the Walkabout crew.

"Luke, I'm coming home with you!" I wanted to yell down the Nepal side of the mountain.

I wished there was some way to tell him this, short of declaring it over the radio. But I'd see him soon enough. I'd be in Base Camp two days from now. Maybe once everyone was safely returned to Camp Four, I'd call him and ask him to switch to a private channel.

Phil and I stopped at the South Summit to change out oxygen canisters. He was having trouble controlling his cough after the brief minute of breathing Mount Everest's actual air. "That's all there is left," I said, pointing to the summit, the actual summit. "You can do this."

I wanted that summit with a renewed vigor. I wanted my new home base in Washington and a sponsorship to go with it. I wanted Luke.

We reached the place where the Hillary Step used to be. Now, instead of having to climb up a two-story cliff—which always caused a dangerous bottleneck of waiting climbers—we simply continued up the snow on the fixed line. Not long after, we met a line of Global climbers. I picked out Doc among them. I was happy for her, but at the moment, all my attention was on Phil and getting him up to the summit. I gave her a quick hug and kept going.

Thom put his hand out to stop me as we passed him. "You have only forty-five minutes. That's not enough for Phil."

The summit was less than a half mile away. The length of two city blocks.

I pretended to be confused about what he meant as I slipped away to rejoin the blue marshmallow-covered zombie that was Phil, sludging and lurching along through invisible corn syrup toward the triangle of snow that met the gray sky. No wonder Thom had no faith. But the lurching and sludging were a sign of effort and purposefulness. A client who did not have this would look aimless and wandering, stopping frequently to sit down. Despite his turtle pace, Phil was giving it his all. Surely the high of reaching the summit would put him in good spirits, and that would help him greatly on the way back down.

The last of the UW climbers, most of the low-support team, and the lead A-Team climbers passed us on their way back down from the summit. All I managed was a nod. Tyler, bless his heart, did not make mention of the time. Up ahead, Phurba and Johnsmith were on the summit already. From behind, Go Big's climbers were passing us one by one.

I'd purposely not been looking at my watch, but when the sun disappeared behind the clouds, making it seem much later, I couldn't ignore the time anymore. We were five minutes past turnaround time, and we weren't even on the summit yet. My heart rate increased. I couldn't turn Phil around this close to the summit. I couldn't turn *me* around this close. But I had to.

"Phil, we have to go down," I yelled over the wind.

He ignored my order, even when I grabbed his shoulder to stop him.

I couldn't blame him. I wanted it, too, and we were *so* close.

Instead of trying again to turn Phil around, I caught up

to him and pushed myself under his arm like a crutch and helped him to walk a little faster. It took us fifteen minutes to finish the final, half city-block in the sky, but we made it. He practically fell onto the snow bench the Sherpas had carved at the top for photo ops.

"Two minutes," I yelled to him. "We're going down in two minutes."

There were about twelve people on the summit with us, all from the low-support Global team and Go Big.

I took a picture of Phil. The huge smile on his face made it all worth it. I was too nervous about the time to bother taking a Circ, but I gave him a hug, then took a selfie of the two of us together. It would serve as my proof of summit for Miss Eleanor.

After that, he turned a slow circle, looking at Cho Oyu to the west, Kanchenjunga to the east, Makalu toward the south. How many nights had he fallen asleep to the beeps of hospital machines while dreaming of standing right here?

He used his hands to pat the snow down and make a place for the Edmund Hillary action figure, which he set there carefully. Then, he opened his pocket and pulled out a tidy stack of thin strips of newspaper, yellowed with age. Only because the summit was so small could I see what they were as he unfolded them: the obituaries of five people who shared his last name. He held them out, and they flapped from his hand like a flag. Then, he released them to the wind.

I had almost forgotten my own summit item: the white silk kata scarf Mingma had given me in Tengboche. I silently recited a short Buddhist prayer of gratitude.

"Luke, this is for you," I whispered aloud as I knotted the scarf around a picket in the snow, just below a NASCAR bandana that must have been from Phurba. I was so happy that he'd finally gotten a summit.

As the white scarf whipped in the wind, I made one

request, directly to Chomolungma. For my bravery in life to be equal to the bravery I had in the mountains.

Phil protested not at all when I told him it was time to leave.

"Thank you," he said.

We started back. It was physically easier to move downhill but inherently more dangerous. Two-thirds of mountaineering accidents occur on the descent.

I was right about the high of the summit helping Phil. To my great relief, we were making good time now. If we kept this up, we'd be within sight of the rear of A-Team, and hopefully everybody would be too tired and oxygen-deprived to notice that we'd missed the turnaround time by twenty minutes.

The high of Phil and I both getting the summit had helped me, too. I was practically hallucinating that I was already back down to the relative safety of Camp Four, lying in my warm sleeping bag and calling Luke on the radio.

But then, ahead of me, Phil came to a stop.

His body moved a little from side to side, like he was looking around, or deciding what to do. Then he sat down, and he didn't get back up.

Chapter Forty-Five

"Phil, you have to stand up."

"Give me a minute."

"No, now! You have to keep moving."

I grabbed him by the armpits and yanked. My injured shoulder protested, and I let him go.

"We can't be wasting time right now," I said. "We have very little oxygen left to get back to the South Summit."

Not to mention very few hours before dark. Or before the jet stream assumed its usual position right across the top of Everest.

I gave another yank, and this time Phil stood. He wasn't being competent with his ascender on the fixed line. He stumbled on his crampons and fell face first into the snow.

Oh shit.

I yanked his pack open, quickly confirming my suspicion: he'd exerted himself so much getting to the summit that he'd blown through all of his oxygen. His tank was on empty.

I helped him sit and then called Jim on the radio. I prayed Dad wasn't eavesdropping on Global's channel, because if he was, he'd hear an edge to my voice that Jim and the rest of the guys wouldn't notice.

No one rogered up. My gut churned. Were they busy with something else going on? I realized I hadn't been paying any attention to radio calls in the last hour or two. At altitude, your mind sheds things without you even knowing it.

I waited, then repeated my call, practically yelling into the microphone to make sure I could be heard over the wind.

"Emily, did you just call?" Jim asked.

"Yeah. Phil's out of oxygen."

"Where are you?"

"Midway to the South Summit."

"Hello, Jim, it's Norbu. Ang Dawa is right at the cache. I'll have him walk a canister back."

"Okay, good," Jim said.

In the meantime, I had to get him moving. I administered a shot of dex, and then short-roped him.

I stood in front of Phil, pulling at his arms like they were the reins of a stubborn burro. Eventually, I coaxed him to his feet and let him walk ahead while I held onto the rope I'd tied to his harness. It was like walking a Great Dane straining against its leash, and I had to brace with my full body to help stabilize him. I eyed the sixty-degree slope to our left and the eleven-thousand foot drop-off at the end of it.

Oh shit. Oh shit. Oh shit.

Jim called me on the radio. "Norbu's sending Ang Dawa your way with oxygen for Phil."

"Okay, roger," I said.

"Emily, did you copy?" Jim asked.

Something was wrong with my radio. I clicked the button to see if it was sticking, which it was not.

"Yes, roger, copy," I repeated.

"Good. Thanks, Emily."

I tried not to be anxious with our slow and sloppy

progress, but every minute that ticked by was a minute colder, a minute closer to darkness, a minute more of oxygen deprivation. Further, there was a lot of chatter on the radio, and being oxygen deprived and exhausted, I couldn't make sense of any of it. Some sort of incident on the Yellow Band.

Ang Dawa appeared in front of us like an angel. With a fresh tank of oxygen, Phil came alive, like one of the windup dolls in the Nutcracker ballet my grandma had taken me to a couple of times. Now he was apologizing profusely, like Amy used to do when she was high.

"Never mind that," I said. "Let's get moving."

It was way too late to still be above the place where the Hillary Step used to be. Dad would be losing his mind about now, but I gave him kudos for not interfering and tying up the channels. In the middle of the Cornice Traverse, my vision darkened like a tunnel. My oxygen had run out. I insisted Phil and Ang Dawa go ahead because I wouldn't be able to keep their pace without oxygen.

By the time I got to the cache on the South Summit, I was so woozy that each step was like trying to stand up in a canoe. I dropped onto my hands and knees to swap out a fresh oxygen bottle and put my mask back on. The air was warm and moist, immediately easing my dry cough and spreading warmth through my veins. I let myself enjoy a few minutes of full flow, during which I was so high, I could have paraglided off the South Summit, no matter that I didn't have a rig.

I clipped back onto the line to catch up with the others. The light was starting to fade. I was haggard and practically hypothermic, but this was normal on Everest. My mind went right back to where it had been before the summit.

Luke. Luke. Luke.

I had to get to Camp Four to tell him I was coming to Washington.

As I walked, I let myself dream. Would we switch our

flights so we could fly out of Kathmandu together? Those long hours in the air together would be paradise. We'd play cards and watch movies and joke around and, since we wouldn't have to hide our relationship anymore, we could also be holding hands freely and kissing.

There was still a lot of chatter coming across the radio, some of it in high-speed Sherpa. Now that I was on oxygen, I channeled my focus into the broken conversations to figure out what was going on.

"...I'm really concerned at this point."

"...blood in the snow...frozen mincemeat..."

"Yes...bad situation."

I couldn't tell who was talking or who they were talking about. My body tensed. What if they were talking about Luke?

No, it wouldn't be Luke. They wouldn't be talking about him on this channel.

"...how long were they off?"

"At least thirty minutes. There was..."

How long was what off? It was Jim now, talking to Thom. There must be more than one situation going on down below us. I continued listening, trying to make sense of it. That's when I heard something that made me stop in my tracks. Thom used the word "she."

She's totally blind.

The Cuban Team, minus Juan, had gotten into Camp Four a long time ago. There was only one other *she* in the entire Global outfit.

One of the people in trouble down below was Doc.

Chapter Forty-Six

I picked up the pace to catch up with the others.

"What's going on down there?" I asked Ang Dawa. "Is it Doc? Is Luke okay?"

"Luke's not with us."

"I know, but where is he? Is he okay?"

"I don't know."

"What about Doc?"

"She's snow-blind."

I'd heard correctly. Guilt struck me. When I'd given her a hug on the summit slope, she hadn't been wearing her glacier goggles. I hadn't been thinking clearly, or else I would have said something.

"She's doing okay otherwise," Ang Dawa said. "Dawa Lama's walking with her."

I relaxed. Doc was strong, and the snow blindness would likely be gone by morning. "What else is going on down there?"

"Juan's feet," Ang Dawa said. "Can't walk."

The blood from his blisters had probably frozen his feet

solid inside his boots. Not being able to walk this high on the mountain was a really bad thing because he was still a long way above the highest altitude a helicopter could land, which is Camp Two.

The small group of us continued descending. The last of the light disappeared sometime before we reached the Balcony, and we turned on our headlamps. The winds were picking up, and the cloud bank that had been gradually rising from the valley all afternoon was upon us now, greatly reducing visibility. All we had left ahead of us was the steep descent of the Triangular Face, then the last bit of gentler slope before Camp Four. But at this pace, that was probably another three hours of walking on top of the eighteen hours we'd already been going today.

I kept thinking about the tent awaiting me at Camp Four. I could practically taste the warm tea on my dry lips and feel the cozy heat of my thick sleeping bag. Talking to Luke on the radio would be wonderful, too. I'd finally have relief from my gnawing unease about his health, and I'd find some way to secretly tell him I was coming to Washington so that he wouldn't have to suffer any longer from thinking everything was over between us.

At last we saw the lights of Camp Four through the snow that had started falling. I practically collapsed with relief. But as we got closer, it was clear that the camp was in chaos. Several of our guides were caught up in the critical first steps to save Juan's feet and more were responding to Johnsmith, who had passed out while drinking water. Furthermore, there had been conflicting reports of four people dead in a Camp Four tent from apparent carbon monoxide poisoning, and Thom and some of the Swedish guides were trying to locate them.

I asked Tyler what I could do to help, but seeing my unsteadiness on my feet, he told me to go back to my tent.

But when I got there, Doc was not in the tent. I shook Claudia awake, and she confirmed Doc hadn't returned yet.

I found Norbu first. "Where's Doc Teresa?"

"Tent."

"She's not there."

He spoke rapid-fire Sherpa into his radio.

"She's still up at the Bulge. They're going back up there with a splint and more oxygen."

"Why a splint? I thought it was snow blindness."

"Yes. Dawa Lama was helping her walk, but she tripped. She thinks her leg is broken."

Guilt hit me again. If only I'd said something about her glacier glasses being off! "Who's up there with her?"

"Phurba Lama."

"You mean Phurba Sherpa?"

"Phurba Lama. And Hulk."

No.

"Hulk is with Juan and Johnsmith, and I passed Phurba Lama a few minutes ago. He's over by Phil's tent." My mind raced. Was Doc alone up there?

"I'll go get Hulk," Norbu said.

I shook my head. Hulk was in emergency response mode right now. Of all of us, he was the one with the most medical experience.

"I'll wake some Sherpas," Norbu said.

It would be another twenty minutes to get them going, and who knew how long Doc had already been sitting up there in the snow, alone? We must have walked right by her, but the clouds made it impossible to see anything past the beams of our headlamps.

"I'll go now, and the Sherpas can follow with the splint," I said. "The oxygen will help her stay warm. How far back is she?"

"Twenty minutes. Just to the side at the top of the Bulge."

Norbu went to wake the Cubans' Sherpas, updating Jim on the radio as he walked away. After twenty-one hours of aerobic exertion in zero-degree temperatures, part of it without oxygen in the Death Zone, I was in no shape to be doing anything but collapsing in a tent.

Dad would be pissed if he knew. But this was Doc. I had to go.

With a fresh tank of oxygen and a spare in my pack for Doc, I headed back out.

Chapter Forty-Seven

I staggered uphill, carefully sticking to the boot-track trail. The winds were blustery, and the snow was coming down much harder now. Neither was a good thing.

After about fifteen minutes, I started sweeping my headlamp to the left and right of the boot tracks so I wouldn't walk right past Doc. Assuming she was huddled in a ball for warmth and had a layer of blown snow on her, she wouldn't look much different than a rock.

I found her at twenty-six minutes of walking. Indeed, she was curled in a ball, but only a partial ball, as one of her legs was extended on the snow.

"Doc, I'm here."

"Emily? Is that you? Thank god."

I helped her sit up so I could switch out her oxygen.

"Don't touch my leg."

I pawed the snow off her as I waited for the oxygen to kick in.

"What in the fuck…are you doing…here?" she asked once the oxygen had revived her.

"Long story. Norbu's sending guys up with a splint. You think you broke your leg?"

She snorted. "Think? I know."

"How's everything else? Are you warm?"

"Good, considering. I have hand warmers in my mittens. I have feeling in my left foot. My right, I have no idea. I'm not touching it until Hulk gets here with the morphine."

Norbu hadn't mentioned morphine. Did he know to send some? I pulled out my radio.

"Emily to Jim."

"I'm hearing a call, but it's garbled," Jim replied. "Say again, please."

"This is Emily. I'm here with Doc Teresa."

"Emily?" he asked. "Where you at?"

"With Doc. By the Bulge. Make sure whoever Norbu sends with the splint has morphine."

"It's very hard to hear you. I think what you said is you need more oxygen."

After all the hours climbing in the cold, dry air today, my voice was almost gone. I sheltered the mic from the wind and projected louder into the microphone. "No, *morphine*."

"I'm not hearing a response. I think something's wrong with your mic. Try blowing onto the button to warm it up."

I did what he said, then repeated myself. There was no response. I tried again.

"Emily, I'm not hearing you if you are trying to respond. Just hold tight right there. Norbu has guys on their way right now."

Doc and I hugged for warmth as we waited.

"You want to know something funny?" she asked.

"What?" We were both too cold and miserable for small talk, but we had to keep each other alert and functioning as we waited.

"I signed up to climb this year only because of Greg."

"Why? Everest isn't a big deal to him. You've climbed way harder stuff than this. Like in the Alps."

"I know he doesn't care about Everest, but I thought it would piss him off that I was going to do it after all these years and that I was going with Global Adventurers instead of him."

"Doc!"

"Yeah, I know. I'm real mature, right? Well, you know what they say about karma. Chomolungma got me back good."

"I thought you didn't believe in any of that."

"I don't. It's just kind of funny—high-altitude funny. It was such a stupid, drastic thing to do. And completely unnecessary. I was the one who had broken it off in the first place. Greg. He's such a nice guy through and through."

"*Too* nice sometimes."

"Yes, like not telling you bad news, or giving those refunds, but aside from that, there's nothing wrong with *too nice.*"

"What refunds?"

"The ones from the icefall avalanche year, when the Sherpas shut down the mountain."

"Dad gave the clients refunds for that?"

"Not a hundred percent, but all that he could. With the earthquake the following year, he couldn't recover."

That certainly *was* nice of him. The best Global had done for clients was to give a 10 percent discount on return bookings.

"Is that why he has no money?" I asked.

"Yeah."

The reason for Winslowe Expeditions's bad financial situation didn't change the fact that it existed, but it was a small weight off my shoulders. Even though Dad had assured me otherwise, I worried that my gap year and all the costs of having me tag along had been one of the reasons for his downfall. It also meant that Dad hadn't been an incompetent businessman, just one who had been too nice for his own good.

Doc and I shivered against each other. Where were the Sherpas? God, it was miserable to be a sitting duck outside in these temperatures with no break from the wind.

"So what did your mom's letter say?" Doc asked.

"I never read it." Ironically, it was here with me on Mount Everest, in the breast pocket of my jacket where I'd shoved it the night Dad gave it to me.

"You should."

"I will." And I would. Someday in the future, when I had truly achieved forgiveness, I'd actually read it.

"Ever thought about it from her perspective?"

"What? Doing drugs?" *Or getting pregnant to ensnare a guy and then abandoning the child?*

"Not that. Just…being in love with someone who doesn't love you back?"

Doc was getting crazy.

"People change," she said. "People grow."

"Yeah," I said.

The wind was really picking up now, making it hard to talk. If the Sherpas didn't get here soon, our boot path would be covered up by the blowing snow.

I called Norbu on the radio. There was no answer. I called again, to Jim, and then to Thom. I even switched channels and tried Dad. I wasn't hearing anyone else's radio calls, either, and surely there would be a ton of talk with all that was going on right now.

Shit. I reduced the flow on our oxygen tanks as a precaution.

Your clients are under no illusions about the danger of this mountain. They know there is no guarantee that they'll come back down.

No. We were not at that point yet.

Doc and I huddled together again. I was shivering like crazy. She wasn't shivering at all, now, and that was even more alarming.

We couldn't wait for them any longer. We needed to somehow start down.

With her broken, unsplinted leg, walking was not an option. We'd have to try scooting. I helped her turn so her back was downhill. She used her good leg to push and then screamed into her oxygen mask.

There was blood on the snow where she'd been sitting. I tried not to panic.

"It's not from the break," she assured me when she'd recovered enough to speak. "Just a gash from the crampon when I fell."

"Scoot more," I said.

She pushed again. And screamed again.

We'd never get all the way to Camp Four like this.

Just to our right was a bank of snow that might offer some protection from the wind.

"Has anyone left yet?" I asked into the radio. There was no response. Again, I tried not to panic. If only I knew for sure that the Sherpas were actually coming. But with these winds, and the badly drifting snow…it would be questionable for Jim or Norbu to allow someone out in these conditions.

"This is Emily. We are moving fifty feet to the northwest," I yelled into the radio.

"We have to get to that windbreak," I told Doc. "Five or six scoots. Let's do this."

Tediously, painfully, we made progress. Doc was halfway unconscious with pain by the time we got there. Sadly, the windbreak was so little it was hardly noticeable.

I tried the radio again, hoping that the bad reception would be miraculously gone in our new location. No such luck. But I seemed to have sound back.

"Emily, there is no visibility," someone was saying. Jim, I think. "The guys have gotten back down. All tracks are snowed over. They couldn't locate you."

"We're still right here; we had to move because of the wind!" I said.

Jim couldn't hear me. He kept on talking. "…it's a whiteout. Can't send them back out."

Just like that, we'd gone from waiting around to a dire, life-or-death situation.

Jim kept talking, but panic made me unable to listen. We could not spend the night exposed in the Death Zone with windchill at negative fifty and increasing. And we had only three hours left on our low-flow oxygen, if we were lucky. How much should I tell Doc about what Jim had just said on the radio? I looked back at her. She was lying down. "Doc?"

She didn't respond.

I shook her. Still no response.

I ripped off my mitten and felt for her pulse. Still there. Her oxygen was flowing okay. I could give her a shot of dex, but if she'd already given herself a shot—or two—within the last few hours, it could be lethal.

But being unconscious and breathing wasn't a completely bad combination. Hope overtook the panic. Being unconscious, she'd be able to bear the pain from her broken leg.

I struggled to stand and then hooked my arms beneath her armpits so I could pull her like a sled down to Camp Four. With seemingly superhuman power I lifted her up, then gave a yank to get her moving.

There was a searing in my shoulder like it was going to pull right out of the socket. In my oxygen-deprived, frozen, and exhausted state, I found it nice to have feeling in my ice-block limbs, even if it was pain. And then something popped, and I fell backward. Everything went black.

Chapter Forty-Eight

My eyes opened to a blinding white light. I was cheek-down in the snow, and the light was my headlamp beam shining onto it.

My first thought was Luke. I could not die on this mountain without him knowing that I had changed my mind about coming to Washington. I could not die without seeing him one more time.

I had no idea how long I'd been lying there, but I was terrified of that light running out. I tried to push up into a sitting position only to realize I couldn't feel or move my right arm. I tried again with the other side and was able to struggle upright.

Doc.

She was lying on her back in the snow like she was getting ready to make a snow angel. I looked away.

I couldn't do this. I couldn't bear to see her body. She was my mom. My mom-sister. Sister-friend. Mom-friend. Role model. Prospective stepmom. Friend. She'd been a better mom to me in the few months a year we'd see each other than my actual mother's ten years combined.

But if there was a chance she was still alive, I had to check.

I forced myself to look back, praying her face wasn't iced over. I would vomit.

Thankfully it wasn't, but the bits of skin on her face that were exposed were well on their way to black. The snowflakes that were falling on her cheeks were still melting. That was a good sign.

A familiar voice came on the radio. *Dad.* At first, I thought it was a hallucination, but he kept talking.

"Jim suspects your radio isn't functioning, or that you might be in a position where you can't make a call out. But that doesn't mean you can't hear, so I'm radioing at the top and bottom of each hour from here in Base Camp. This is the fifth call."

I fumbled for the button. "Dad! I hear you!" My mouth was so dry that hardly any sound came out.

He kept talking. If only I had a swallow of unfrozen water to drink, I might be able to bring my voice back. I tucked into a ball, shoving my hands in my armpits and stilling my shaking body the best I could so I could listen.

Dad was perfectly calm. This fact was unbelievably soothing.

"Hand warmers," he was saying.

Yes! I had unused hand warmers.

"Wiggle your toes. Rub your fingers."

I obeyed.

"Now for the unpleasant part. Last we all know, Teresa was snow-blind with a suspected fracture. Jim said you had two tanks of oxygen and that Teresa was approximately twenty minutes from Camp Four. We don't know that you reached her, so you could have plenty of oxygen. But if you did, and you each have only one tank, you're both nearly out by now. If you can get yourself down, you need to leave. Right now. If she's with you and she's conscious, I know she's telling you the same thing."

Thank god Doc wasn't hearing any of this.

"It's a whiteout up there. I know you can't see, but you've been across this stretch into Camp Four a dozen times. If anyone knows it, you do. Just go very slowly so you can catch your mistake if you get turned around and are heading for the Kanchenjunga Face."

I shook my head no. I wasn't leaving Doc.

"I'm going to repeat this. If you're in a place where you cannot help any more, you need to go down. You need to leave Teresa."

Dad! My heart twisted for him. It was a situation a thousand times worse than the one he'd warned me about, with two people he loved—the *only* two people he loved—being unaccounted for in the Death Zone. Never could he have imagined he'd be ordering his daughter to leave his girlfriend to die alone on the mountain.

What would I do if it were Luke unconscious next to me? I wouldn't leave him for anything. So I wouldn't leave Doc, either.

Luke.

"I'll be back on the radio in another thirty minutes, and I'll be listening in the meantime," Dad said. "Keep trying to communicate with us. If you absolutely cannot do anything else, don't let yourself fall asleep. Stay awake at all costs. As soon as it's light or the winds die down, there will be people looking for you. I love you, Emily."

After more than twenty-four hours of exposure in the Death Zone, you don't just pull yourself up by the bootstraps, stand, and walk out of there. Besides, I wasn't nearly as confident as Dad that I could find my way to Camp Four in these conditions. *If* I could even walk on my frozen feet. And I *hadn't* done all I could for Doc yet. I had one thing left: heat.

Jim was on the radio now. "Greg is right. With the windchill tonight, it is better to try to reach Camp Four than wait for light. Sunrise is still a long way off. If you can get yourself down, you need to do that. Then you can lead us right back to Teresa if you were with her."

It was a trap—he wouldn't let anyone back out in this, especially if he knew the frailty of Doc's condition. Her chances were not good considering that we'd have to get her all the way down the Lhotse Face before a helicopter rescue was possible. As Dad had bluntly said four nights ago, you don't risk staff for clients who don't have a chance.

I tried not to let my immobile right side terrify me as I used my other hand to dig for the hand warmers. I had three packages left. I tore them open with my teeth and slipped them into Doc's mittens the best I could and put two down her jacket. I distributed what was left along my own body. Dexamethasone would be okay now. I had three syringes with me. I stabbed one straight through my down suit into my thigh and did the same for her.

I lay down next to her. All that was left was time and body heat, and the hope that the friction of my shivering body against her down suit would provide a little bit of warmth for us both.

The freeze of the snow radiated up from the ground like an ice bath. The wind drove pellets of snow into me with the force of a lash. It hurt so badly. Part of me longed for it to be over—*really over*—as soon as possible.

I heard Luke's voice. I was truly losing it now, slipping out of reality, like the dream last night. Was this what it felt like to die of exposure?

"Emily, Greg just got ahold of me. We're in the Global command center now." He started coughing and let go of the mic button for a few seconds.

"I don't know if you can hear me, but I'm going to be

doing the same thing as Greg," Luke said. "I'll be calling every half hour."

"I'm here. I'm right here," I said, my voice as rough as Tinkerbell's tongue against my jacket. I didn't even know if I keyed my mic. Or if his voice was real in the first place.

A dog barked. The sound was so close that I startled and jolted against Doc. But then the sound morphed into the spine-tingling yell of a yeti. Not the happy Yellow Yeti on our jackets, but the real, horrible, dirty white yeti, baring its gorilla-like fangs and growling. Was I hallucinating? Unbearably humid air raged across me like I was lying on the beach in Thailand. A tsunami was coming, the waves growing taller and taller. I cowered into Doc.

"We just have to get through till morning," I whispered in my non-voice to the unresponsive Doc. "The guys will come get us, and you'll get that helicopter ride you've always wanted."

My headlamp beam was dimming, crowning shorter as the blackness crept in. With my left hand, I managed to click it off to preserve what little power was left, and then everything went black again.

I was so, so tired. And I was hot. Like sunburn hot. But all over my body. Inside my body, too.

Stay awake at all costs, Dad had said. But I'd let myself drift out of consciousness.

Water.

I was dying of thirst, and I couldn't feel my hands. *If* I survived the night, I'd have no hands left. They'd have to be amputated from the frostbite. I wouldn't have toes, either. I'd probably lose my nose. If I didn't survive, I hoped Dad would push my body off the side into Tibet as the Winslowe

Expedition team made their summit bid. If he didn't, I would end up as one of those corpses climbers used as a landmark, forever frozen in the exact body position they had died in.

My regret was singular. *Luke.*

For not being brave enough to take a chance on the person I loved until it was too late. For being so self-centered and careless with his heart. That he would never know that I had changed my mind about coming to Washington with him.

Stay awake at all costs.

My will was fading. Already faded. Was *this* dying?

I couldn't be dying yet because my clothing was suffocating me. I sat up. The wind was oddly still. No wonder I was so hot. I'd just ventilate a little bit.

As I pulled my parka zipper down, I was vaguely aware that the wind wasn't really still and that I shouldn't be hot right now.

My hand paused on my breastbone. Right next to my breast pocket, where the unread letter from my mother was.

Do whatever you have to do to stay awake.

Reading the letter. That would get my adrenalin going. My fingers were like frozen fish sticks, but I managed to get the envelope out of my pocket. I gripped it tightly, biting little pieces off the top until I had enough to pull the letter out.

This time, I had no reaction to the pink stationery. I realized I was looking at it without having clicked my headlamp on. Visibility had improved, and there was light bleeding through the clouds from the moon.

I couldn't see well enough to read the words without the light, so I clicked on my headlamp.

Emily,

First: I am sorry. For who I was and for who I was not. An apology will never be enough, but I owe it to you. I'd say it a hundred times more. A thousand.

I did a twelve-step program in prison. Making amends is one of the steps. That's how I'm able to have a relationship with my parents again. But apologies are not the same thing as amends, and I knew you wanted nothing to do with me. Once I got out, I did the only thing I thought could possibly help you. I moved in with Dad and Mom to save money, and I work two jobs so I can help cover the remainder of your Townsend College bills.

When I heard you'd changed your mind about coming back to Port Townsend, I knew I had to at least try to contact you. It's presuming a lot to think I might be the reason, but just in case, I figured now is the time to apologize to you directly.

I follow you as closely as I can through Greg's communications with Dad and your Circumference account. I'm incredibly proud of who you've become. You are all Greg. All of the things that I loved about him. You're even a mountain climber, too.

I know better than to hope you'd ever be willing to have a relationship with me now, but if you are, I'm here.

Amy

A letter like this should be a dream come true. A girl's long-lost mother apologizes and assures her she still wants her. Or you'd think it would make me angry, like when Dad had given it to me in the first place. Instead, I simply felt nothing, like the cold had numbed my emotions just like it had my body.

The wind wanted to grab the paper and carry it away, but I resisted its pull, crumpling it best I could into an outer pocket.

I wanted to reread it later.

I *would* reread it later.

This mountain wasn't going to be the last of me. I wasn't

going to die here. I wasn't going to give in that easily. I might fail, but at least I'd fight to the end. I had other mountains to climb. With Luke. And cookies to bake in a real kitchen in my little white bungalow.

I was still suffocating in the heat, but I knew it was an illusion from hypothermia. I gritted my teeth and zipped my parka back up.

I thought about Luke-From-My-Dream, beckoning me to the stairs.

I'm following. I'm coming, I said to him. *I will do anything for you.*

I continued to fight the urge to tear off my down jacket. Instead, I rubbed my legs with all my might. I blew hot air down the neck of my jacket and ratcheted down the cinch on my hood now that I wasn't wearing the oxygen mask anymore.

I noticed then that it wasn't delirium making me think the winds had died down; they really had. If they stayed this way and I could make it to camp, then Norbu would get a fresh team with oxygen and a splint up to Doc immediately.

I examined her chest, which was still rising and falling. Barely.

I knew definitively. Leaving her was her only hope.

Chapter Forty-Nine

I rolled over to my side, then planted an ice screw and tied one end of my spare line to it. It was a bad knot, but it wasn't meant to catch me. It was just a pointer back to Doc.

With a Herculean effort, I stood.

I didn't say good-bye to Doc because it wasn't good-bye. I refused to think otherwise.

Controlling my own body was like trying to move an Avatar by telepathy. Or walking on prosthetics for the first time.

I'd gotten only about five steps when I saw something ahead, sticking out of the snow. My heart lurched. A body. Luke's body.

My vision cleared a little, and I let out my breath with relief. It wasn't a body, it was an ice ax.

Luke is not here, I reminded myself.

The ice ax wasn't just any ice ax, it was *my* ice ax, which was a sign I was walking in the right direction.

Ahead, the cloud bank was thicker. I summoned the confidence from finding the ax and stepped into the cloud bank. The darkness enveloped me.

All I had was the feel of the slope beneath my feet. I took one careful step at a time, making sure each foot landed directly down the fall line. And with each step, I repeated a mantra: *save Doc, get to Luke.*

When I ran out of line, I planted pickets, one every ten steps. Then I ran out of pickets. I started blowing my whistle, once each step. *Save Doc, get to Luke, whistle.*

My whistles were weak because of my shallow, oxygen-deprived breathing, and they went unanswered. I tried not to panic. I tried not to think about the Kanchenjunga Face and the possibility of walking straight off it if I got turned around badly enough. Or how I might never see Luke again.

Then, like a dream, there was shouting. At the same time, on my radio, someone was calling to Jim that they were hearing whistles.

I stopped walking and kept whistling.

Then, there were lights. Three of them. And out of the murky cloud bank stepped Hulk, Norbu, and Phurba.

I wanted to collapse in relief, but I couldn't. Not yet.

My brain was numb and my body stiff as they guided me toward Camp Four where Thom, Tyler, Theo, Ang Dawa, and Dawa Lama were waiting.

I mumbled directions about the rope and the pickets. "She's breathing. Needs oxygen, now. And morphine. Hurry."

Norbu, Hulk, and Phurba left immediately.

"My radio's busted," I said hoarsely to the guys left in front of me.

"You don't say," Theo said.

"Can I have someone's?"

"What?" Theo asked.

"Radio."

Tyler handed me his to use.

"Dad, this is Emily."

"Emily! I'm here."

"Is Luke with you?"

"Yes. Right next to me."

"Okay," I breathed. "I'm at Camp Four. They're going for Doc right now. And Luke, I love you, and I'm coming to Washington."

I was aware of nothing more until I awoke inside a tent rich with afternoon sunlight. Doc's and Claudia's sleeping bags were gone, but someone had been taking care of me, because there was an unfrozen cup of tea in the corner where I wouldn't knock it over in my sleep.

Hulk popped his head in. "Good, you're up. Feeling okay?"

I nodded.

My shoulder radiated with pain, and my hands were laying in bowls of water. They hurt like an MF; so did my feet. But this was a good thing—a sign frostbite hadn't completely taken them.

"You, Phurba, and I are the last ones up here," he said. "Think you can make it down to Camp Three?"

I didn't want to get up and leave the warm tent and comfortable sleeping bag. Compared to being alone and exposed high on the shoulder of Everest, Camp Four felt like a plush, safe hotel in the middle of a city. In reality, though, it was in the Death Zone and a dangerous place to linger.

Then I remembered.

"Doc!"

"The guys in Camp Two got her on a medevac helicopter to Kathmandu about an hour ago."

"How's she doing?"

"Rough, but she has her spirits."

I relaxed. That was a good sign. "And the others? Where is Luke?"

"Ah, Luke," he said with a knowing smile. "He's safe at Base Camp. As for the others, Juan's doing okay. He's in Camp Three. Norbu and the guys were able to lower him down the Lhotse Face. He'll need a medevac tomorrow unless we're able to get his boots on. All the other clients made it to Camp Two today."

I'd get more details later, but for now, I had to get going so we could make it to Camp Three before nightfall. I pushed myself up and took survey of my hands. Hulk and the others had done an excellent job in treating them despite being thrashed and exhausted themselves. My fingers seemed to be okay except for some dark patches along my pinky fingers and the tops of my index fingers.

It was the same with my feet: there were some black patches that I would have to watch carefully for months to come, but nothing that would prevent me from moving right now. Last night had seemed to last an eternity, but in reality Doc and I had been without oxygen for only about four hours, and that was a saving grace.

Hulk helped me make an arm sling to take the weight off my dislocated shoulder, and I took a double dose of ibuprofen. We set out for Camp Three, where Phurba, Hulk, and I shared the last remaining tent in our camp. Poor Phurba's eyes were so puffy and dark that he looked like he'd been in a fight, and Hulk could barely keep his eyes open.

Guiltily, I realized neither of them had gotten more than an hour or two of sleep last night, perhaps none at all, so I volunteered to make the water for tonight. They passed out almost immediately after drinking it, and I was right behind them.

The next morning, Hulk, Phurba, and I made quick work of the Lhotse Face. The two of them lingered in Camp Two to help with the last of the clients but insisted I keep going because of my shoulder, so I continued down the Western Cwm for Camp One, where I'd wait until the wee hours of the next morning for the final trip through the icefall to Base Camp. If I had ten-thousand dollars to my name right now, I'd spend every penny of it to hire a helicopter to fly me down to Base Camp. I needed to know the details of how Doc was doing at the hospital in Kathmandu. And I was desperate to get back to Luke. I would not be at ease until I could see him with my own eyes and know for absolutely sure he was okay. That *we* were going to be okay.

Despite the torturous wait to see him, the beauty of the day was not lost on me. It was a flawless mountain morning with the sun sparkling on the snow and a light breeze keeping the temperature in check. The Western Cwm was a magnificent place, with its impossibly steep walls rising several thousand feet on three of four sides. It was like being an ant in the bowl of one of those old-fashioned metal snow shovels, held up high for the best view of the Himalayas in the world.

Directly ahead was the stately profile of my sweetheart Pumori, glistening in the sunlight. The crisp air filled my lungs, and the creaks of my boots were the quiet metronome of my brisk pace. God, I was hooked on this. Being here alone and free in this vast beauty. Feeling powerful. Loved. Safe. Lucky.

Yes, I was *tashi*, indeed.

Overcome with thankfulness, I lifted my face to the sun and gave a prayer of gratitude. Gratitude for both Doc and I having survived the night in the Death Zone. Gratitude for the conditions being a thousand times better than they could have been. Gratitude for Amy's letter and how reading it had given me the extra bit of *oomph* I needed to steel myself against the elements and start toward Camp Four. Gratitude for having been given another chance—infinite chances—to be in places like this again.

I decided then that I would write Amy back. Probably not right away, but eventually, after I was completely settled in Seattle. I didn't know that I'd ever reach a place where I could be around her in person, but I could give letters a try.

Feeling even lighter and happier than before, I continued toward Camp One. As I hiked down the cwm, there was a long and dispersed line of climbers from other expeditions following the boot-packed trail, heading up the mountain for their chance at the summit. That's how it would always be on Everest; no matter the cost or danger, there would always be more people waiting in line.

After a while, I noticed there was a yellow-jacketed Global staff member among the people in the line. Getting closer, I picked out a purple ball cap on the person's head.

Luke?

I stopped in my tracks. What was he doing up here? He was supposed to be recovering down in Base Camp.

But it *was* him. He unclipped from the line and walked toward me.

I fell to my knees. He was here. For me. Perhaps that was the luckiest thing of all. That he'd seen me through two years of silence other than #YCCM Circs, a ridiculously long time this season for me to believe that a relationship was possible, and my unintentional betrayals that amounted to *me* abandoning *him*, again and again.

I didn't deserve him, but he was *here.*

"My god, Emily," he said.

Then he was on his knees, too, reaching carefully around my sling to bury me in his arms. My whole body went into free fall.

I breathed deeply into his neck, reveling in his smell and the feel of us together again.

He tucked his head in to me, his moist breath flowing past my ear. "Were you serious?" he asked. "Are you really coming to Washington?"

"Yes," I replied without hesitation.

He shuffled back a little so he could see my face. His expression was soft but inquisitive, as if he were trying to assess my level of conviction.

"I'm coming to Washington," I said. "To be with you."

Any lingering traces of uncertainty on his face evaporated completely. We faced each other across the small gap, grinning. Then, I was back in his arms. My heart was going to burst. I loved him so much.

I could have stayed in his embrace forever, but he didn't give me that. He popped to his feet, a huge grin still on his face.

"What?" I asked as he gave me a hand up.

"We're going to climb Mount Rainier together this summer," he said.

"Yes. And climbing in the Bugaboos this fall, right?"

"Of course."

"Let's go paddleboarding in the Puget Sound right away."

"Okay," he said. "And there's a premiere coming up for Walkabout's Yosemite film. We won't want to miss that."

I groaned. "I don't have any clothes for a premiere. Or clothes for anything, for that matter."

"Don't worry. Doc will take you shopping. By the way, she's going to be your stepmom soon."

I froze. "How do you know?"

"Greg told me. Between our radio calls to you. He was planning to propose when she got down, but now he'll have to wait until Kathmandu or Seattle."

I smiled. Despite my previous prodding, Dad hadn't

breathed a word of his plans to me. Yes, America's nuclear codes would be safe with him.

Behind Luke, many of the climbers in the line had stopped to watch us.

I turned to start walking down the mountain.

"Not so fast," Luke said, pulling me back and digging something out of his pocket.

It was a bracelet for me, from what had to be the last of Dad's vintage lavender cord.

"You made that?"

"Two nights ago was kind of stressful. Gave me something to do with my hands."

I took the bracelet from him and examined it. "You did a good job. I'm impressed you remembered how." I unzipped my pocket to slip it inside.

"What? You're not going to put it on?"

"People are staring," I said.

"I bet."

It wasn't just people now. We'd caught the attention of a tiny drone from one of the other expeditions, and it was hovering over the climbers, facing us.

"I'll put it on in Camp One," I assured him.

Luke shook his head. He opened his hand to show me a book of wax-coated waterproof backpacking matches.

"Seriously, we're making a scene right now."

"Says the girl who blew our cover over the radio for everyone to hear."

I looked at him oddly.

"You did realize you were on the all-mountain emergency channel, not Global's channel."

Luke's left dimple cut deeply into his cheek, trying to hold in a laugh as I processed this.

Tyler. He might have thought of warning me that he was on that channel when I'd borrowed his radio. No wonder people were staring. Thanks to the scary-efficient Everest Base Camp rumor mill, probably every person, yak, and crow knew our entire story by now.

Luke nodded as if confirming this.

Defeated, I turned my wrist up and held it out for him to tie on the bracelet. When he was done, he struck a match. The flame blew around wildly as it neared my skin and then puffed out.

"This doesn't seem like a good idea," I protested.

We twisted so that my back was to Lhotse, which made a small windbreak for when Luke lit the second match. This time, it held steady. Very carefully, he touched the top of the flame to the knot. The coating turned to liquid. A drop of it fell to the snow.

"Make a wish," he said.

I obeyed, closing my eyes tight.

He blew out the flame, then blew gently on the knot for it to firm up faster.

I turned to start down to Camp One, but he stopped me by reaching for my hand and stepping across the last bit of distance between us.

The closeup view of his gold-flecked brown eyes completely transfixed me. He scanned my face as if memorizing it. A chunk of hair had come loose from my three-day-old ponytail. He reached for it, holding his breath as he tucked it behind my ear.

In a lot of ways, I felt like I had been holding my breath my whole life.

But I wasn't anymore.

Right there in front of everybody and the mountain herself, I let go and fell happily, deeply into his arms and into his kiss.

Chapter Fifty

That drone had filmed everything. Our initial hug, Luke tying the bracelet on my wrist, and then the kiss that had been so raw and passionate that I blush every time the meme version of it pops up online.

The drone hadn't been from one of the expeditions. The rumors that had been started by my all-mountain radio call hadn't stopped at the confines of Base Camp. The drone belonged to an Australian paparazzo who'd been doing a Base Camp trek and had caught wind of the story. After he sold his footage, it didn't take reporters long to discover my six secret Everest summits.

Reporters also went wild with Luke's story. Unknown to me, Luke hadn't simply been climbing the heck out of the North Cascades while at UW. He'd been tackling some of the hardest routes in them, including some remote big walls with none other than Josh Knox.

And my story and Luke's story combined, with our against-all-odds romance thrown in? International media sensation.

Thankfully, the hullaballoo lasted only a few days. We were surpassed by the pictures of the couple from America who trekked all the way to Base Camp to get married—backless, ballroom-style white wedding dress and all. Brrrrrr.

The parts of the story that mattered to the climbing community had lingered on in a way that was shaping up to be really good for Luke and me, such as being included in *Vertical View's* upcoming "Adventure Athletes to Watch" article. Good things were happening for Winslowe Expeditions and Global Adventurers, as well. What I loved most was that because of some new opportunities that had opened up for Dad in the United States, Tshering had fully taken over Winslowe Expeditions operations for the next year, and he and Dad were talking about him taking full ownership of the company eventually.

I'd been in Seattle now for almost two months. Tonight was April, Theo, and Ernesto's Yosemite film premiere. Luke was getting back from guiding a Rainier trip later this afternoon and would be meeting me at the house I shared with April. Dad and his fiancée—aka Doc Teresa—were coming. Phil was driving into town for it, too.

But first I had to finish my shift at REI Co-Op's flagship store in downtown Seattle. I'd gotten the job the good, old-fashioned way: a paper application I filled out in the customer service office the second day I'd arrived in thc United States. My final customers of the day were a cute couple who had no clue about the outdoors but were excited to be going on their first car-camping trip. I recommended a retro, two-burner, car-camping stove instead of one of the high-tech, expensive backpacking stoves they'd been looking at initially.

I pulled off my apron as I walked toward the staff room. The smell of all the brand-new equipment was heavenly, and I loved working at a place where there was an indoor rock-climbing tower on site. I spent all my breaks climbing it.

Hanging on the far wall, above the staff room door, was a collection of ultra-enlarged images of some of the American climbing greats: Jim Whittaker, Ed Viesteurs, Josh Knox, Scott Fischer. And Dad, in a picture taken on the Eiger when he was just a few years older than me.

After I'd clocked out, I grabbed my bag from one of the lockers and walked through the store toward the main doors.

"I would have recommended the more expensive stove," said someone with a touch of British accent.

It was Luke—my Luke—leaning against a hiking boot fixture. He wore a T-shirt, jeans, and his purple Huskies ball cap.

A teasing, satisfied grin broke out across his face.

"That's Grinchy," I said. I grabbed his hand, and we pushed out the front doors and down the stairs to the sidewalk.

I needn't have worried about my life here in Washington being dependent on and wrapped up in Luke's life. Guiding on Rainier kept him away a lot, and it would be the same when UW started in September. The campus wasn't far, but with neither of us having cars in a big city like this and having a jigsaw puzzle of school and work schedules, there were only certain times when we'd be able to see each other.

The true problem was not getting enough of each other.

The second we reached the corner of the building, he yanked me around the side, pushing me up against the wall like he was going to kiss me. But then he stopped, his face just inches away. His deep brown eyes bored into mine, making blood rush across my torso until at last, he let me have his lips.

In order to be free for the premiere tonight, he'd had to work back-to-back Rainier trips, and we hadn't seen each other for a week. Our kiss went from zero to obscene in seconds flat. My body tightened everywhere. It was responding like we were alone in my bedroom, not—

I pulled back. "Okay, so I work here."

He shook his head at me, his expression tortured but jovial. I flicked his hat off. He caught it midair and put it back on.

We took a minute to gather ourselves, then continued down the street hand in hand toward the house. I'm not sure I'd ever get used to seeing Luke in jeans and a T-shirt. Or jeans and flip-flops and a hipster flannel shirt, looking way more American than I'd ever feel. On most days, the U.S. still felt foreign to me.

I glanced over at him. Actually, I hoped I never got used to how good he looked in his regular clothes. Because every time it caught me off guard, I also got a little kick of pride knowing that this sexy stranger had chosen *me*.

He smiled as he caught me looking at him, his dimple popping out and making me melt. As friends, I thought I'd known all the variations of his smiles, but ever since that day on the Western Cwm, I'd gotten a different one: the soul-lifting smile he reserved only for his girlfriend.

"So, you're back a lot earlier than you thought," I said.

"Just a little. Hulk needed to pick up some supplies from REI, so I came right here with him."

"Hulk was at the store? Did he see us just now?"

"You're forgetting, MiniBoss. Everyone has already seen."

My face went hot, more in indignation of Luke's triumphant dimples than embarrassment of the Everest paparazzo footage he was alluding to.

It was a long walk from work to April's house. I'd get a bike eventually, but for now, with the gorgeous, warm summer we'd been having, every block was a pleasure. Especially with Luke's arm slung across my shoulders—both of which were pain-free and fully functional, thanks to the excellent in-network physical therapist here that Doc had recommended.

"There it is," Luke said as we reached the top of the hill. Mount Rainier floated in the sky like a solitary white ghost, keeping a wary eye on the endless gray blur of the suburbs below. I hadn't climbed it yet, but we had a trip planned in two weeks. Josh, April, Theo, Hulk, and a few others would be coming, too. I couldn't wait.

When we got to April's house, Josh's truck was not in the driveway for once. He must still be at the theater, helping April with the final preparations.

The funny thing about April's house is that it was my white bungalow, except that the house wasn't white. It was gray with yellow trim. There had even been gladiolas blooming when I walked up to the house for the first time. I'd almost had a heart attack.

I unlocked the front door to the delicious aroma of my *dal bhat* in the crockpot. We went right to my room to put our backpacks down and so I could change out of my REI work clothes.

I started to take off my green polo shirt, but Luke took over and finished for me, leaving me in just a camisole. He took a step closer and traced my collarbone with his thumb. Leaning in, he left a warm trail of kisses from my earlobe down my neck. My knees turned to jelly. With Luke, I was more at risk of fainting than when I'd climbed Nanga Parbat without oxygen.

"I missed you a lot this week," he whispered, his breath hot across my ear. I shivered.

He pulled me over to my bed. It was just a twin because even pushed against the wall that was all that would fit in this tiny room. But it was a bed with a mattress, box spring, and unbelievably soft flannel sheets. He sat back against the wall, and I crawled over to him, straddling his legs so that we were face-to-face. It was such a luxury to have him all to myself while not hidden away in a tent.

"I missed you, too," I said as I leaned in for a kiss. His mouth immediately opened for mine, and our tongues twisted together. One at a time, he lowered the straps of my camisole off my shoulders. When they were both down, the rest of the camisole slid to my waist.

I was still a little shy around him like this. Though we'd been off Everest for two months, it was rare that we ended up alone, indoors, during the daylight. I reached for the sheet. He laid his hand on mine, thwarting my attempt to cover up.

He traced the scalloped edges of the fancy strapless bra I'd bought to wear under the dress I was borrowing for the premiere and had been test-wearing while at work today. My nipples pinched, anticipating more. I helped him pull off his shirt, taking a minute to admire the defined solidness of his torso before sliding my hands down his chest and hard stomach. I'd never get used to *this*, either.

The *W* of his lips pulled up mischievously, making his left dimple appear.

"What?" I asked.

He just smirked. Rebelliously, I pushed him onto his back, which only made his smile bigger.

"So, uh, I'm assuming you haven't gotten your mail recently," he said.

"Oops. No." I wasn't used to having snail mail and was constantly forgetting to check the mailbox.

"Want me to grab it for you?" he asked.

"I'll get it later."

"How about I go grab it for you?"

I raised an eyebrow at him. "Seriously?"

He flicked my bare stomach just above my navel, then put his shirt back on. "Trust me."

I wrapped myself in the sheet and fell back on the bed, looking up at the ceiling where I'd hung the picture garland from my tent and a bunch of newly made tissue-paper flowers.

Luke came back in and handed me my portion of the mail.

There was some junk mail and a few envelopes from City Community College, where I'd registered for a cooking class this fall. And then, there was a letter from Esplanade Equipment.

"Open it," he said.

I did. It was an invitation to join the crew of an Esplanade-sponsored mountaineering film in Patagonia in December. All expenses would be paid.

I looked at Luke, not comprehending. This had to be some sort of practical joke.

"Congratulations," he said. His eyes were sparkling.

Was this real? And if so, how had he known that I'd be getting this letter?

He reached over to his backpack and pulled out an identical letter. On the second page was a list of the invitees, ten in all. Luke's name was on it, so was mine.

"I'll be able to be there only for the part that's during winter break, but I'm going. And did you see? It's Walkabout that is contracted to film it."

"Wow." That was all I could say.

I skimmed the letter again, this time noticing a second signature on the bottom. *Barrett Browning.* The ink was smudged, which meant he'd signed it personally. I guess this was proof he wasn't upset at me for un-accepting his CentralPoint Tanzania job offer.

I stared down at the Esplanade Equipment logo on the letterhead. It was the same logo on all our Winslowe Expeditions tents, and most of my jackets, backpacks, and climbing gear. A logo that represented the highest quality, safest, most dependable gear in the outdoor industry. A logo that represented the very essence of the freedom and adventure that people seek in the mountains. And now the logo was on a letter addressed to me.

This offer was *real*.

"Oh my god," I whispered.

He nodded and then studied me with eyes that still sparkled. We kissed long and slow, like we had all the time in the world. Because we did.

Then, I was the one studying him, getting lost in the eyes of the person I loved more than life itself. With whom I would soon be going to Patagonia.

I have spread my dreams under your feet, I thought. *I will always spread my dreams under your feet.*

Luke twisted my bracelet around my wrist thoughtfully. His thick eyelashes cast shadows down his face.

"Sometimes I think about how lucky you were," he said quietly. "How lucky we all are. How lucky I am to be with you, here in Seattle."

I nodded and threaded my fingers through his. *Tashi.*

I still had nightmares about that never-ending night in the Death Zone, and random things would sometimes catch me off guard if I wasn't prepared for them. Like how tonight Doc would be in a cast again after a second surgery to correct the damage from going down the Lhotse Face with a broken leg. That, and the fact that I'd never see her in sandals again, nor would we ever have a repeat pedicure session: she'd lost a total of five and a half toes.

That was small fries to all that could have happened. I'd heard of crazier survival feats on Everest than hers, but not by much.

Luke kissed me softly on the forehead. I slid next to him and lay on my side with my hand resting on his chest. He fingered the bracelet again.

"I want you to know something," I said.

"What?"

I hesitated. I was getting better at coming straight out

with my feelings, but sometimes I still got hung up on the threshold of releasing a thought. I shut my eyes briefly, thinking of the silent prayer I'd said on my seventh summit of Mount Everest. *For my bravery in life to be equal to the bravery I have in the mountains.* I thought of all Luke had bravely and faithfully done that had enabled us to finally take that step beyond friendship.

When I opened my eyes, they caught on the corner of the bulletin board next to my bed where I'd pinned a scrap of paper with Luke's handwriting.

My heart still belongs to you.

"I want to tell you what I wished for when you tied on my bracelet," I said.

He took my wrist in his hand, delicately closing his thumb and middle finger around it like a second bracelet. My pulse rushed.

"I wished that you would love me for as long as the bracelet held fast. And then I wished it would never ever fall off."

I swallowed and looked deep into his eyes as I waited for him to say something. His face was somber and full of emotion, yet it also seemed like he was biting back a smile.

"Well then," Luke said, his smile slowly breaking free. "You're in luck, because my heart will *always* belong to you."

Our kiss was tender and wistful, but then firm and definitive, alive with possibility. For the first time in my life I had everything I'd ever wanted all in the same place. I had mountains and a way to pay for them. I had a home where I had friends and family, acceptance and permanence. And most importantly, I had love and my best friend Luke.

Acknowledgments

In all kinds of writing, Mount Everest is used as a simile for something being the most difficult in the world. As it turns out, penning a novel set on Mount Everest was my own Mount Everest, and I have many people to thank for helping me on my way to the summit.

First, to my husband, the keel to the boat that is our family. Without him I'd never be able to stand on the top deck and stargaze. Thank you for being such a sport in listening to me rattle off Everest trivia for months on end and helping me puzzle out some of the technical mountaineering scenarios in this book.

Thank you to my editor, Karen Grove, for having faith in the concept of *Leaving Everest* and being patient with me through the many iterations it took for the words on the page to match the vision. I'm continually honored to be among the supportive and talented authors on your Embrace list. Thank you, also, to the full production team at Entangled Publishing, especially Embrace's creative and tireless publicist, Holly Bryant-Simpson.

Thanks to my agent, Melissa Edwards, for her continued support, career guidance, and responsiveness. For reading early drafts of this book, thank you to Karri, Rebecca, Lauren, Kelly, and Beth. An especially big thank you goes to fellow Navy veterans Jessica Riehl (for designing the Mount Everest map) and Amanda Matti (for all her teamwork in marketing)..

As an author with two young children, I'd like to acknowledge that I would not be able to write novels without the help of our trusted caregivers. This includes the kids' child development center teachers, YMCA child watch staff, adored babysitters, Gram-Mer, and friends and family who have taken a shift with the kids while I write and edit. Also, a nod of gratitude to the president and vice-president at my "day job," who have been incredibly generous and supportive of the book-writing process, enabling me to have a rare work-life-fiction balance.

A special thanks goes to Garrett Madison, eight-time Everest summiteer, and Kim Hess, 2016 Everest summiteer and Explorers Grand Slam hopeful, for taking the time to answer all my oddball author questions about the mountain. Steve Tickle, a longtime Everest Base Camp trekking leader with Namaste Trekking Expeditions, also tackled a slew of oddball questions for me. Dr. Diana Y. Paul, author and professor of Buddhist studies, was a huge help with religion questions. I'm also grateful to the authors and filmmakers of all the research materials I used in preparing to write this book, especially Alan Arnette and the wealth of information on his website and his real-time coverage during Everest climbing seasons. Mistakes and deviations from what I've learned from these sources are my own.

Thank you to my friends and family who read *Leaving Everest*'s predecessor, *Lessons in Gravity*, especially those who typically read in different genres or don't read for leisure at all. Finally, to readers of *Leaving Everest* and *Lessons in Gravity* whom I don't know in person: all of us have a finite amount of reading time (don't I wish this was otherwise!), and it means a lot to me that you picked up a book by a new-to-you author and devoted hours of your precious reading time to my characters and stories.

About the Author

Megan Westfield grew up in Washington State, attended college in Oregon, and lived in Virginia, California, and Rhode Island during her five years as a navy officer. She is now a permanent resident of San Diego, along with her husband and two young children. Aside from writing and her family, her great passions in life are reading, candy, and spending lots of time outside hiking, skiing, camping, climbing, running, and biking.

Connect with Megan Westfield and learn more about her upcoming books at www.meganwestfield.com.

Also by Megan Westfield…

LESSONS IN GRAVITY

Discover more New Adult titles from Entangled Embrace...

Cinderella and the Geek

a *British Bad Boys* novel by Christina Phillips

I'm not looking for love or a Happily-Ever-After because I know how that ends. I just need to concentrate on my degree and look after myself. But there's something about my boss, Harry, I can't resist. It's crazy since he's so hot and smart it should be illegal. But I'm off to pursue my dreams, and he's taking his business to the next level. There's no way this fairytale has a happy ending, but that doesn't keep me from wishing for it.

Straight Up Irish

a *Murphy Brothers* novel by Magan Vernon

I need a wife if I want to help save my family's billion-dollar pub empire. There's just one problem: I never plan on marrying. So, I need someone who understands that this is just another business deal. I don't do commitments. And my brother's beautiful executive assistant, Fallon Smith, fits that bill. A fake wedding and a whole lot of whiskey. What could go wrong?

NOVA

a *Renegades* novel by Rebecca Yarros

He's Landon Rhodes, four-time X Games medalist and full-time heartbreaker. This tatted-up adrenaline junkie has earned his nickname Casanova, going through girls in an attempt to forget the one who got away. But now she's back and determined not to let him destroy her again. The problem is, he will stop at nothing to prove to her that they are meant to be together.

CRAZY LOVE

a *Defying Gravity* novel by Kendra C. Highley

In typical living-on-the-edge fashion, Luke Madison dropped out of college to chase his dreams in Aspen, not realizing the dire consequences he's triggered. If Luke can't pull off a miracle, his family could lose everything, and there's *no way* he'll let that happen. Not even when he meets Charlotte, a pre-med student who distracts him like no other, even as she tries to resist his charm. But when Luke risks everything one last time, losing isn't an option. Even if it means losing Charlotte.

Made in the USA
Columbia, SC
21 February 2018